I0760602

Proving

SEVENTH IN THE IMMORTALS OF INDRIELL SERIES

MELISSA A. CRAVEN

Proving: Immortals of Indriell Book 7

By: Melissa A. Craven

Midnight Hour Studio INC

Atlanta, Georgia

For more information contact: Hello@Melissaacraven.com or visit the author's website at **Melissaacraven.com**

Cover design by: Daqri Combs (Covers by Combs)

Edited by: Rebecca Jaycox

Interior design by: @BooklyStyle

ISBN: 9798433587632

First edition for print March 14, 2022

Printed in the United States of America

This one is for the fans who love
Allie and Aidan as much as I do.

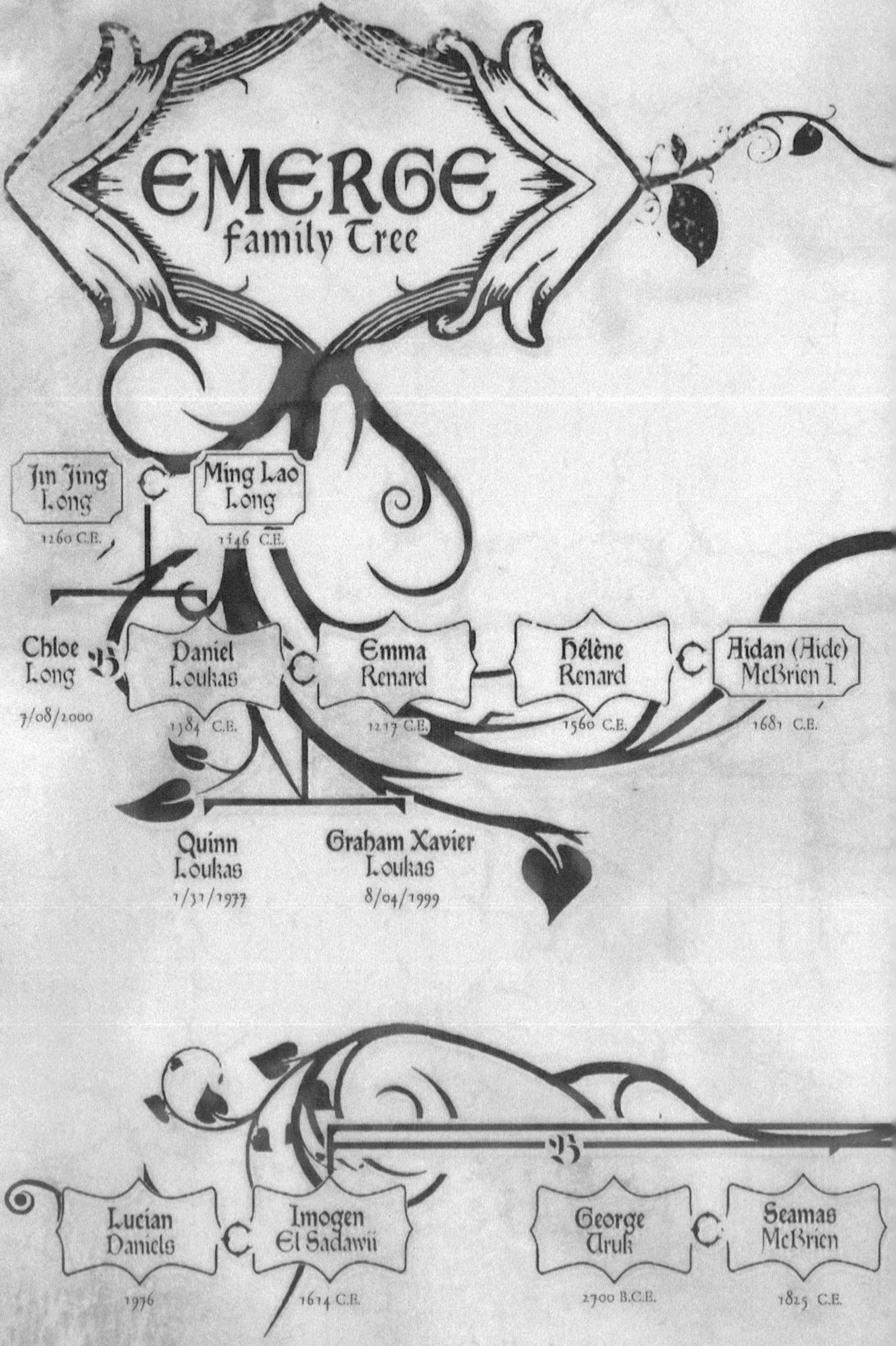

EMERGE
Family Tree

Jin Jing Long
1260 C.E.

C

Ming Lao Long
1146 C.E.

Chloe Long
7/08/2000

B

Daniel Loukas
1384 C.E.

C

Emma Renard
1217 C.E.

Hélène Renard
1560 C.E.

C

Aidan (Aide) McBrien I.
1681 C.E.

Quinn Loukas
1/31/1977

Graham Xavier Loukas
8/04/1999

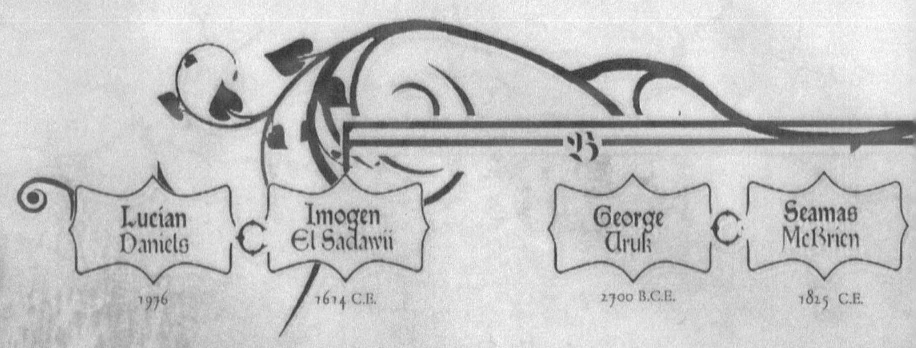

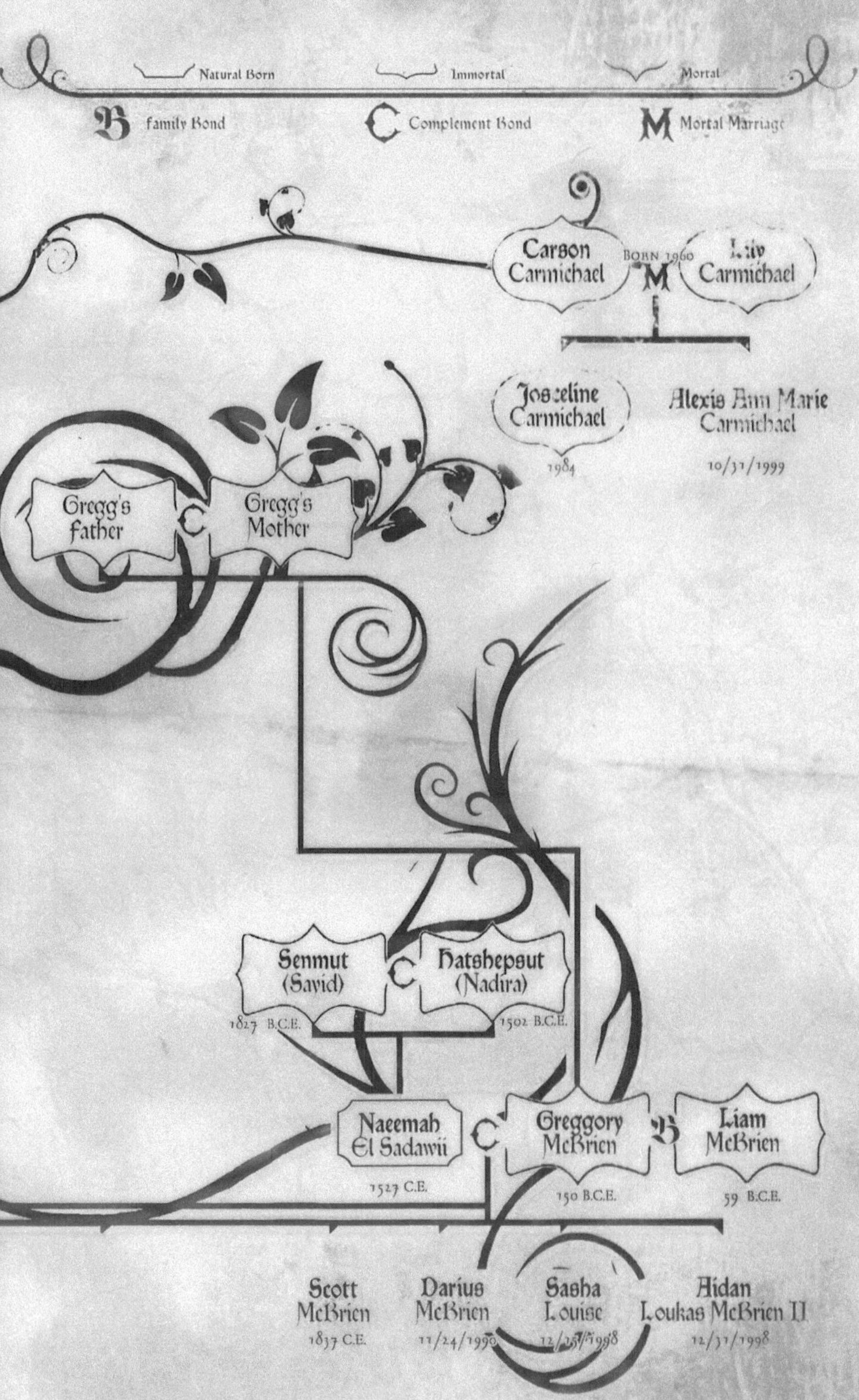

Natural Born
Immortal
Mortal
B Family Bond
C Complement Bond
M Mortal Marriage
Carson Carmichael
BORN 1960
M
Liv Carmichael
Josceline Carmichael
1984
Alexis Ann Marie Carmichael
10/31/1999
Gregg's Father
C
Gregg's Mother
Senmut (Savid)
1827 B.C.E.
C
Hatshepsut (Nadira)
1502 B.C.E.
Naeemah El Sadawii
1527 C.E.
C
Greggory McBrien
150 B.C.E.
B
Liam McBrien
59 B.C.E.
Scott McBrien
1837 C.E.
Darius McBrien
11/24/1990
Sasha Louise
12/25/1998
Aidan Loukas McBrien II
12/31/1998

Who Wants To Live Forever?

There's no time for us
There's no place for us
What is the thing
That builds our dreams
Yet slips away from us?

Who wants to live forever
Who wants to live forever?

There's no chance for us
It's all decided for us
This world has only
One sweet moment
Set aside for us

Who wants to live forever
Who wants to live forever?

Who dares to love forever
When love must die?

But touch my tears
With your lips
Touch my world
With your fingertips

And we can have forever
And we can love forever
Forever is our today

Prologue

Allie | Kelleys Island | December

Allie tossed and turned in her sleep. The sheets twisted around her body as her mind resisted the onslaught of dreams filled with shadows.

The Power is corrupted and will remain so until a new generation is born with the strength of their ancestors, led by one with an unsullied, natural connection with the Power. Her heart will guide her, giving her the restraint to wield her Power wisely. She will gather her equals, and together, they will stand against those who persist in the corruption of the natural order. She will be strong and fierce in her beliefs and steadfast in her love. Born the second child of the seventh daughter of her line, she alone will possess the skills and the knowledge to heal what has been broken. She alone will have the courage to judge unbiased and mete out the ultimate punishment. Until the time of her birth, may we prepare the way and hope for the future of all the races of men.

But how? Allie chased the shadowy figures through a maze of cracked and shattered mirrors, reflecting the stark fear on her pale face. Everywhere she turned, her own empty eyes stared back at her. She didn't have the answers.

After all this time, the prophecy still made little sense to her.

The elusive shadows laughed at her as she stumbled along the pathway littered with crumbling stones and the roots of giant trees towering over the unending maze.

Allie stumbled to her knees, exhaustion weighing her down as the enemy cackled and pulled farther ahead. Tilting her head to the sky, she could just make out the shining stars through the canopy of trees. "How am I supposed to do this impossible thing?"

Like always, Allie jolted awake at that moment. She blinked at the stars scattered across the ceiling of Aidan's bedroom in the underground, remnants of Naomi's special gift. The dream had plagued her for weeks. A sheen of sweat covered her body as she sat up, clutching at her heart as if she could still its racing with a mere touch.

Releasing a steady breath, Allie pulled her knees up to her chest, leaning her head forward. The dream wasn't a difficult one to decipher. She knew Marcus Servius was the enemy. She knew she would eventually have to use her Judgment gift on him. And she knew her friends would help her along the way. It was the *how* of it all that kept her up at night.

"You okay, babe?" Aidan rolled toward her, his voice rough with sleep.

"Just a dream." She pasted on a smile as she reached out to brush her fingertips along his arm. "Go back to sleep."

He gave her a sleepy smile and shook his head. "You've been flopping around like a dolphin at sea." He tugged on the sheet wrapped around her middle. "Clearly, it was not a good dream. You're wrapped up like a mummy."

"No it wasn't." She sighed, wriggling around to help him disentangle her from the sheets. "It was awful."

"Am I falling down on my one job?" He tossed the damp sheet to the floor and pulled her into the comfort of his arms. Immediately, she felt cooler as he called on his power to drive the heat from her body.

"Mmm, that's better." She snuggled closer. "Have I mentioned how wonderful it is to have a temperature-controlled boyfriend?"

Aidan chuckled, running his hand along her back. In an instant, she was covered in gooseflesh. "Don't do that with me, Lex."

"Do what?"

"Avoid the difficult questions with humor."

"I don't do that." She hid her smile against his chest.

"You're such a bad liar." He laughed again. "Did I fail you? I'm supposed to keep the dreams away."

"You could never fail me." Allie looked up at him. "It's not possible." She reached to smooth the hair away from his face. "It was just your run-of-the-mill, normal bad dream. No clairvoyance involved."

His arms tightened around her. "You would tell me if there's anything you're worrying about, right?"

She laid her head back against him. "Of course."

CHAPTER 1

Allie | Atlanta | January

"This feels a wee bit excessive." Allie tugged on her seatbelt. She wasn't a fan of flying in anything smaller than a skyscraper. "Do I really need my own helicopter?"

"Yes," a chorus of voices echoed through her headphones.

"It's important to get you back under the safety of Sterling Tower as soon as possible." Aidan shot her a look over his shoulder.

"Hey, there, Mr. I-Just-Got-My-Pilot's-License, keep your eyes on the road."

"There are literally no roads where we're going." He shot away from the airport where they'd just left Livia and Liam sitting on the tarmac in their private jet.

Allie clutched a hand over her heart. "Aww, you almost made a pop culture reference." She gave a mock sniff. "I'm so proud. But it's, 'where we're going, we don't *need* roads.'" She dropped her voice into her best Doc Brown imitation.

"Does anyone ever know what she's talking about?" Alísun cast a glance at Aidan from her perch in the co-pilot seat—she was only riding. Aidan had made her swear not to touch anything before he let her ride up front.

"I've learned to just roll with it, Grandma Alí. It's one of her most endearing qualities." Aidan's voice crackled over the radio as he exchanged a secret smile with Allie's grandma. The two were thick as thieves lately. It was super cute.

"All four of you are watching the *Back to the Future* movies with me this weekend."

"Oh no, is it another ridiculous mortal time-travel fantasy?" Darius rolled his eyes. "If it's like *Outlander*, I'm not watching it. People can't travel through stones—it's absurd."

"Whatever, you totally got teary when Jamie and Claire were separated."

"Which time?"

"All of them."

Aidan let the helicopter drop and Allie grabbed onto Darius and Grandpa Alex, seated on either side of her. "If you don't stop doing that, I'm going to kick you out and fly this thing myself."

"But it's so much fun." Aidan turned, giving her his heart-stopping grin, the sight of it so rare, she would let him crash the darn helicopter just to see it again.

With a laugh to rival his smile, he turned toward Sterling Tower in the distance. So much had changed in the short time since they'd last left. Too much. Sometimes, she wished she could go back to when they were just kids. When their biggest worry was how exhausting their training was. If past Allie had known what present Allie was dealing with, she'd have done a lot less complaining back then.

"Seriously, though, I could have ridden home with everyone else," Allie muttered, staring out the window at the gridlocked traffic below. "It's not like it's far."

"You're too important, darling," Grandma Alísun insisted, as per her usual. She sat in the cockpit beside Aidan, helping him monitor all the dials and systems on the flight panel. This from the woman who still couldn't operate a toaster oven.

I'm not made of glass. Allie sighed, thinking of everything that awaited her once she arrived. She had a million things to deal with. Not least of all were the newest arrivals at Soma. More than a hundred new students had showed up while they were away dealing with Marcus' threat to the Coalition—which had not worked out quite as well as she'd hoped. Lots of people were injured, killed, or missing in the aftermath of his attack. Allie wished she could have done more to warn them before it was too late. They still didn't know if anything they'd done had even helped.

"Like it or not, Allie-girl, you're a big deal." Grandpa Alex leaned in, his eyes twinkling with mischief. "And princesses who are big deals get to travel in style."

Allie shook her head, a smile tugging on her lips. "I can't take you seriously in that shirt, Gramps."

"What?" The Scholar rubbed a hand over his hot pink belly covered in his latest graphic tee, sporting the words, *WARNING! If zombies start chasing us, I'm tripping you.* "It's funny because it's true."

Allie gave him an indulgent smile. She secretly loved his cheesy t-shirts. "What about the Dreamworld barrier?" She ran a nervous hand through her hair. "How will we land this thing? And by we, I mean you?" She leaned over Aidan's shoulder. He was stupid-cute, sitting there in the cockpit, looking all handsome and sure of himself.

"Quinn's sending a few of his walkers up to meet us on the rooftop. They'll open up a rift for us."

"You have to fly this thing through an opening in the

Dreamworld? That does not sound like something a rookie pilot needs to be doing."

"I've got this, babe." Aidan patted her hand where it rested on his shoulder. Even from her vantage point in the backseat, she could see the smile on his face. Allie was a hundred percent on board with anything that made him smile these days. Aidan loved flying. It was a new skill. One he'd thrown himself into over the months since his return from the Milan Initiative.

He and Daniel spent every spare moment helping Aidan get his flight hours in, so he could fly on his own without supervision.

Aidan rarely used his trust fund for anything substantial, but he hadn't batted any eye over purchasing the top-of-the-line helicopter he'd then given to Allie just a few weeks ago. He'd claimed the First Princess of Indriell needed a fleet to go along with her handsome pilot, and the chopper was the first of many he hoped to acquire. She was happy just to have her handsome pilot back home and acting more like his old self again.

"Oh, look who it is." Aidan's voice took on a hard edge. "Mr. Cocky-Ex-boyfriend himself."

Allie peered out the window to the rooftop of Sterling Tower. She could just make out the arrogant stance of Quinn's right-hand dreamwalker. Briggs also happened to be Allie's sort of ex-boyfriend. Not that she'd ever been overly invested in their brief relationship. Briggs had been a distraction. A delicious one, but nothing serious.

"You expected Alexis to pine for you after you left her?" Grandpa Alex asked in a dry, humorless tone.

"Of course not," Aidan agreed. "But that doesn't mean she had good taste in boyfriends."

"Well, I like him," Darius added, just to needle his brother.

"Be nice. All three of you." Allie glared at her grandfather. "All of that is water under the bridge, and we've got a whole new bridge to navigate." She sucked in a breath as Aidan approached the widening breach in the Dreamworld that kept everyone inside Sterling Tower safe.

Grandpa Alex took his headphones off and leaned into Allie's side. "I can see the wheels turning in your head, dear one." He took her hand in his. "One thing at a time."

Allie nodded. "Focus on what's important for today. The rest is crap that can wait for tomorrow."

Aidan set the helicopter down gently on the helipad, just like a pro. She wished she had time to hang out with him. Girlfriend-Allie wanted to learn to help him with his pre and post-flight checks, but First-Princess-Allie had ten-thousand things waiting for her attention. Even now, her secretary, Mrs. Mitchel, stood ready to brief her the moment she stepped away from the chopper.

Allie blew Aidan a kiss over the noise, miming that she would see him later. He gave her one of his boyish smiles and reached out to catch her kiss like a dork.

My dork. With a sigh, she took Darius' hand and left Aidan to finish taking care of his baby—she hadn't believed for one second the helicopter was a present for her so much as she was an excuse to purchase himself something he never would have otherwise.

"Welcome home, Ms. Carmichael, Mr. McBrien," her secretary yelled over the wind. Allie fell in step between her and Darius, with her grandparents following behind. For a moment, she felt like POTUS returning to the White House. How ridiculous was that?

Stepping inside, the noise faded, and Allie could hear

herself think again. "Catch me up to speed, Mrs. Mitchel." They walked at a brisk pace along the hallway and down a flight of stairs to the elevator bank.

"How did it go with the Coalition?" Mrs. Mitchell asked hesitantly. "I'm still not sure why you've been so worried about protecting them. Though, I guess I'm not privy to such details."

Allie held up a hand to stall her secretary's chattering. "We're still waiting for more details from my contacts. We've done all we can to help them." It weighed heavily on her mind, but in the days since Quinn and her grandfather had returned from their meeting with the Cleveland Coalition, they hadn't received much intel beyond Vince's assessment that it was a disaster.

Allie's gut told her it was likely still a slaughter for those who hadn't heeded the warnings Vince and Kayla, along with Allie's mortal parents, had done their best to deliver. Only time would tell just how much of the Coalition had survived Marcus' attack.

"I suppose that's all you can do." Mrs. Mitchell sighed. "Though, if you ask me, it's far more than they deserve, but no one ever asks me," she added under her breath.

"What was that?" Allie struggled to hide her smile. She loved her assistant's muttering. It was highly entertaining. .

"Oh, nothing, dearie." Mrs. Mitchell stepped onto the elevator, holding the doors open for Allie and her entourage.

"The new students are the most pressing issue that needs your immediate attention." She glanced at her notes as they rode the elevator down to Allie's office. "We have one-hundred-and-seventy-three new students."

Allie's jaw dropped. "Shut your face! How many did

we turn away after screening?" She shared a panicked look with Darius.

"Only twelve potential students were found to be plants from the Senate, and four others were questionable. Ms. Livia reviewed their files while you were all away, and she believes those four might have connections with her father's people. The rest are legitimate students who want to train here at Sterling Tower."

"So many new mouths to feed." Allie sighed. They were already bursting at the seams.

"We will figure out how to make it work," her grandmother said. "That's not something you should worry about right now."

"We have to shelter and clothe them, too, ma'am," her secretary reminded her.

Allie scowled, racking her brain to figure out what they could do with so many kids. It would be miserable for everyone if they were sitting on top of each other for too much longer. Money wasn't even the issue, it was space.

Stepping off the elevator on the office floor, Allie turned to her assistant. "Can you track down a set of building plans? I need to see how we're using the space we have. In a building this big, there has to be more room somewhere." Allie hurried into her office, eager to get her hands on those plans. In all the time Allie had spent at Soma, she couldn't remember ever going below the tenth floor, except for trips to the basement level to access the Warehouse.

Ms. Mitchell nodded, tapping on her phone to send out instructions. "And how was Mr. Quinn's bonding ceremony?" she asked eagerly. "Was it beautiful? I bet it was beautiful." She turned starry eyes on Darius.

"It was. I'm sorry you missed it." Darius smiled, moving to his side of the desk where he spent a great deal of time helping Allie do her job. Grandma Alísun and Grandpa Alex took up their usual spots on the sofa, ready to help her make sense of whatever calamities needed their attention the most.

"How are the plans coming for their surprise?" Allie winced at the pile of paperwork on her desk. It was time to bring Soma into the modern world and go paperless.

"Oh, fine, fine. We'll be ready as soon as Mr. Quinn and Ms. Santi return. Are they on their honeymoon?" Mrs. Mitchell's eyes went all dreamy over the thought of the newly bonded couple.

Allie almost hated to burst her bubble. "I'm afraid we're living in dangerous times, Martha." She dropped into her desk chair with a weary sigh. "There will be time for things like honeymoons someday, but right now, Sasha and Quinn are needed in the field. I had to send them out right after the ceremony." Still, Allie wanted to surprise the newlyweds with a celebration of their union once Quinn returned with news of the escaped prisoners currently at large among the mortal population.

Allie cringed at the reminder. She needed an update on their activity. "Have my traveling companions returned?"

"They are en route from the airport." Mrs. Mitchell checked her text messages. "They should arrive soon. Shall I have them escorted to your offices?"

"No. Let them rest. I just want to know when they've arrived safely. I need to speak with the Elder council this afternoon. Are they in residence yet?"

"Several returned yesterday. I will call them to the conference room in an hour. Will that be soon enough?"

"Yes." Allie nodded. "Until then, why don't you update us on everything else."

Chapter 2

Chloe | Sterling Tower | January

Chloe took off for the Warehouse the moment she stepped into Sterling Tower. The trip back home to Ohio was weird, and if she didn't get away from all the happy couples, she was going to puke all over them. She slammed her finger down on the button for the basement, willing the elevator doors to close faster.

"See you tonight?" Graham grabbed the doors before they smashed into his face. "Dinner at our place, Chlo?"

"Sure, sure." Chloe would have agreed to anything at that moment. She adored Graham and Ezra. When Graham first realized they were Complements and found out Ezra had known for months, she'd worried how, or if, she would fit into her childhood best friend's life. But it was more like Ezra—and his Syntrophos—had fit into theirs.

She was sad she didn't live with Graham anymore. The building was bursting with young Immortals, more than Chloe ever dreamed existed. And that meant living alone was a luxury they couldn't afford. To make matters simple for the new couple, Wes and Graham had traded apartments, which meant Chloe now lived with Wes, a near stranger, in a one-room studio apartment.

Awkward.

Not that Wes wasn't wonderful. They just didn't know each other well, and that led to a lot of weird moments at home. Wes wasn't a talker. Not like Ezra. He was more of the strong, silent type in that Syntrophos relationship.

Chloe breathed a sigh of relief when the doors closed, and she punched the button for the basement again. The Warehouse was just like the Yard back home on Kelleys Island. Except it wasn't underground. The huge terrarium existed within a warehouse building that connected with the tower. It defied the physical boundaries of the building housing it. An old hermit Immortal named Harold lived there and created the gorgeous landscape, complete with lakes, rivers, mountains, and grassy hills. It was Chloe's favorite place to retreat when life at Soma got to be a little too intense.

Despite the chill of the Atlanta winter outside, Chloe was greeted with warm summer sunshine the moment she stepped through the doors into the Warehouse. Her sigh of relief only lasted a moment.

Before, whenever she came down here, there were always people present in little groups here and there. Now, the hillsides swarmed with people. Tents filled the lawn from the entrance all the way to the lake.

Allie had said a ton of new people showed up while they were gone. She'd seemed excited about it, but like almost every other time they spoke these days, Allie got pulled away mid-sentence before they could finish their conversation.

Just as Chloe was about to head back to her apartment for some awkward peace and quiet with Wes, something familiar caught her attention. The presence was fleeting, but unmistakable. "Dahlia?" Chloe scanned the sea of tents, searching for bouncing blond curls. She hadn't seen her best friend from Connecticut—the place she thought of as home now—since she'd left almost six months ago.

Chloe had her reasons for leaving, but she'd left careful instructions for Dahlia to follow her to Sterling Tower in one year—only after Chloe gave her the go ahead—which she had not done. She wanted to be certain it was safe for her Scholar friends before they made any major moves. With the Immortal world in utter chaos and Sterling Tower at the center of it all, now was not the time to bring her friends here.

Pain lanced through her head, and she reached for her airPods, stuffing them in her ears. Music was always a sweet relief from the noise. Chloe's gift bombarded her with information from her surroundings. Most of the time, it was more than she could decipher at once, but she was learning. Right now, the crowd of people on the lawn all demanded the attention of her gift. All their indecipherable thoughts and indecision came at her like a wave of white noise.

But Dahlia was definitely here. Chloe could feel the pull of her equal guiding her toward the lake and the rows of cabins there that had once served as a day camp for young Immortal children not quite ready for full time residence at Soma.

Soma was a school now. Mostly. A place where all those of their generation could live and train without fear of their gifts being exploited. It was a wonderful place. If a little overcrowded at the moment.

Chloe ignored the colorful threads connecting the people she passed. They used to be red threads. But with practice, and help from her new teachers, she'd learned to sort and label the information her gift sent her. Now, her threads were color-coordinated. With the right level of focus, she could follow those threads, observe how certain people were linked, and help them make their best decisions as they moved forward. It was exactly like playing the role of puppet master. Though Chloe approached the job with care and consideration for those she "manipulated," she could see how ... tempting it could be to use her power for personal gain. To allow herself to think, *I know what's best,* and force her will on others. It was faster and easier that way, but she had to be patient with those she helped; let them come to their best decisions on their own, with her guidance and advice.

Thoughts of the evil Chloe portrait her Complement had painted just a short time ago kept her from going down that road. She didn't want to become that version of herself. Justice and his prophetic painting would keep her honest. Just thinking about him had her pulse pounding. If she'd seen Dahlia here, would Justice be with her? Or was he with his *wife,* Scarlet?

She followed a few threads, slipping from one to the next, looking for her equal. If she tried to focus her gift here, she'd end up with a migraine faster than she could blink. Crowds were not Chloe's friend.

But Dahlia was. Chloe could feel her equal's presence strongest near the lake. Even with all the constant foot traffic, fresh grass still crunched under her feet, and the warm air smelled sweet with the scent of tulips. As she neared the cabins, Chloe caught sight of golden blond curls bouncing in the breeze.

"Dahlia!" she shouted, picking up her pace. The girl turned, and her eyes locked with Chloe's. A beautiful smile lit her face. "Chloe!" Dahlia, in all her tall, curvy glory, came running to meet her. Familiar arms wrapped around her, and all the tension Chloe had felt these last months just vanished.

"I missed you, bestie." Chloe hugged her tight.

"How freaking dare you leave in the middle of the night without a goodbye?" Dahlia nearly crushed her.

"I left notes." Chloe's eyes burned with happy tears.

"Ugh, your notes sucked, babe." Dahlia squeezed her again. "I know seeing him with her was hard, but I would have come with you if you needed space."

"I know." Chloe stepped back, searching her friend's face. "I just didn't know how to handle it. How to watch him marry her. I had to go." It was a lame excuse, but it was the only one she had.

"Well we're all here now and that's all that matters." Dahlia draped an arm around Chloe's shoulders and led her toward the cabins.

"We?" Chloe pulled away. She wasn't ready to see Justice. Not with *her.* Fear and anxiety shot right through her at the thought of the happy newlywed couple.

Dahlia gave an unladylike snort. "Did you think we wouldn't come after you?" She shook her head with a smile. "It took us a while to prepare and save up enough cash for traveling, but the minute we called a house meeting after reading your *notes,* the consensus was unanimous. Well... almost." Dahlia led her into one of the larger cabins.

"What do you mean, almost?" Chloe followed her inside, dreading the thought of not seeing Justice among her friends. She wasn't sure which thought was worse, seeing him here with Scarlet on his arm, or not seeing him at all.

"Chloe?" Noah and Jonah leapt from their computers, nearly stepping on them in their urgency to greet her. "Hudson, Chloe's here!" Dahlia shouted up to the loft. Footsteps thundered down the stairs and three pairs of arms wrapped around Chloe. It felt like coming home in a way returning to her family never had. Her family was here and, and she was happy to have them in her life again, but these people ... they were *her* people.

"Chloe?" Another familiar voice reached her ears, and the boys let her go. Chloe turned to see Justice at the door. He looked the same. The chin dimple she couldn't get enough of, and the ever-present stubble of a beard that just wouldn't grow. He was perfect with sunlight streaming through his dirty blond hair, looking as handsome—and as clueless—as ever. One look into his clear blue eyes and she knew he still didn't see her the way she saw him. Her heart shattered all over again, the way it did every single time she gazed into his eyes and saw nothing there. Nothing but deep abiding friendship.

She wouldn't wish her situation on her worst enemy. There was *nothing* worse than knowing and loving her Complement when he didn't have a clue what she was to him.

"You're here?" The stupid words fell out of her mouth. "You're all here?" She glanced around the room at the best people she knew.

"Not everyone." Justice crossed the room to hug her. "Scarlet left." He leaned on her. She could feel his own heartbreak, and if she could get her hands on Scarlet, she'd wring her neck for hurting Justice.

"We took a vote," Dahlia explained. "We all wanted to come here. Not only for you, but to be where it's all happening. We're young Immortals of this generation too. We might not be warriors, but this is where we belong. With you, doing whatever we can to help."

"Scarlet didn't agree." Justice stepped back, giving a weary shrug. "She didn't want to get involved in anything dangerous. But I couldn't leave you to face this place on your own." He smiled despite his sorrow. "I saw where her loyalties lay ... so here we are."

Chloe lunged for him again, wrapping her arms around him. "I'm so sorry she hurt you, but I'm so glad you guys didn't listen to my carefully worded instructions to wait a year before you came. I wanted to make sure it was safe for people like us before I brought any of you here."

"Well, that's a load of crap, Chlo, because there was no way we were waiting that long." Hudson laughed. "We're family. Like it or not, we belong together, and none of us are going to leave a member of our family to face such dangerous times all on her own. It just isn't happening."

"What he said." Dahlia and the boys pulled her into a group hug again.

Even though Justice still didn't realize Chloe was his Complement, having her family with her again made her feel whole in a way she hadn't in a long time.

Chapter 3

Graham | Sterling Tower | January

"I'm exhausted." Graham walked through the lobby with Ezra and Wes after Chloe ditched them for some quiet time. He knew it hurt her to see him so happy with Ezra. Not that she wasn't thrilled for them. She was just in a tough spot waiting for Justice to see her.

If he ever got his hands on that idiot, he ... wasn't going to say anything to ruin it for them, but he would have a few things to say to the guy once he finally figured it out

"I'm beat. Let's just go get some food at the dining hall and take it home." Ezra called for another elevator. "We can have second dinner when Chloe comes over."

"Second dinner?" Wes shook his head, leaning against the elevator wall. "What are you, a Hobbit?"

"Are you new? My appetite is legendary." Ezra rubbed his flat stomach.

"You hoard food like a dragon hoards gold." Wes rolled his eyes.

"Watch out, you two, your dork is showing." Graham loved watching Ezra and Wes bicker. They were adorable. Graham slipped his arm around his Complement. He still couldn't get over it. In just a few short months, his life had completely changed for the better. He had his family back, and now his world was complete with Ezra, and Chloe and Wes too.

The life he'd left behind in Salem seemed like another lifetime, though he still had work to do with the League of Ancients. His role there wasn't finished yet. He still had family and friends in the League, and he wouldn't leave them behind.

All the blood rushed from Graham's face as the elevator doors slid open and he stepped off.

"Brooks?" Graham reached for Ezra's hand, turning pleading eyes on him. It kind of felt like he just got caught cheating, but not really. Ezra was his Complement. Brooks was sort of an ex-boyfriend. One he kind of ended things with in a cowardly letter before he left Salem.

"Graham!" Brooks' smile lit his face. The same smile that used to take his breath away.

"Give me a minute?" He asked Ezra, his voice gentle.

"Of course. But just one." A smirk tugged at the corner of his mouth.

"You're enjoying this aren't you?"

"Immensely." Ezra gave him a push toward Brooks.

"Uh, when did you get here?" Graham stumbled forward. Part of him wanted to run away, but he owed Brooks an explanation.

"I came with your aunt and uncle. We've been laying low within the League since you left so we could slip away quietly." Brooks watched Ezra over Graham's shoulder. "The Alderman thinks I'm doing an internship abroad and Lou and Gabrielle have been so kind as to chaperone me."

"I'm glad you made it out of there safe." Graham gave him an awkward embrace.

"I see you have big news." Brooks nodded toward Ezra, where he waited with Wes.

Graham raked a hand through his hair. "I do." He nodded, not sure how to say it

"It's okay, Graham," Brooks whispered, a tortured look in his eyes that completely gutted him. "I get it." He shrugged, casting his eyes down at the carpet.

"I-it's not like that," Graham stuttered, his heart fracturing for Brooks. "It's ... complicated."

"He's your Complement." Brooks lifted his eyes to meet Graham's. "It's not complicated at all."

"How did you know?" Graham gaped at him in surprise.

"I saw you right when the elevator doors opened." He shoved his hands in his pockets. "I used to love the way you looked at me." His mouth turned up into a sad smile. "Even when things had cooled off between us, you still had a brilliant smile for me every time I saw you. But, man, you never looked at me the way you looked at him just now. I knew the second I saw your face you'd found your forever."

"I'm sorry." Graham's shoulders fell. "It wasn't the best timing."

"Don't apologize." Brooks took a step forward, clapping Graham on the back. "I can't be mad at you, Mr. Cutie-Cute. It's not like you didn't sort of break up with me first."

"I always thought I'd have a chance to explain myself and then Ezra happened."

"That would be me." Ezra waved. He was about two seconds away from grabbing a bag of popcorn.

"It's okay." Brooks forced a smile. "I know I will have that with someone someday. We were never forever. We both knew that."

"Do you think we could be friends?" Graham didn't

want to voice what he really wanted to say. He missed Brooks like crazy and was desperate for his friendship. Not to mention they needed to be able to work together within the League.

"Give me some time to get used to it first, but yeah. We're good, Graham. I'm happy for you. Truly."

"I'm glad you're here, Brooks. It's not safe for any of our generation to be out in the world these days."

Brooks nodded. "And who knows?" He adjusted his perfectly starched collar. "Maybe my Mr. Forever is somewhere in this enormous building right now." He winked, waved to Ezra and Wes, and disappeared into the crowd heading for the dining hall.

"Well, that was painful to watch." Ezra came up beside him.

"I'm sorry you had to see that." Graham sighed, turning back to his husband-to-be.

A smile played around Ezra's mouth. "I'm fine, but that was some kind of awkward, babe. You're kind of adorable when you're flustered." Ezra took his hand, and they melted into the crowd together.

CHAPTER 4

Allie | Sterling Tower | Late January

"There is never enough time in the day to get everything done." Allie poured over spreadsheets and cost analysis for housing, feeding, and clothing all the residents inside Sterling Tower. At the rate they were growing, they were going to spill out into Peidmont Park across the street. Something had to give.

"Hold still." Livia poked her with a sharp hairpin. "You aren't supposed to be working right now." She tugged on Allie's stubborn curls, sweeping them up into an elaborate updo Allie couldn't hope to accomplish on her own. It would be a miracle if her hair stayed put for the duration of Graham and Ezra's wedding ... bonding ceremony. Her mortal brain could *not* make that shift in thinking.

Allie shook her head, shoving the thought of yet another wedding out of her mind. She didn't like to think about how her friends were all coupling up around her. They were too young. Too young to be making lifelong commitments, much less fighting battles and rebelling against the system. And it was all her fault. She was the one pulling them all in like some mythical force they couldn't resist gathering around. No wonder they were finding their Complements left and right. It wasn't fair. They deserved to be young and reckless and uninhibited for years to come before they had to be so adulty.

"Go ahead, shake your head one more time and see what happens," Livia muttered around a mouthful of pins.

"Sorry." Allie shoved her laptop aside. She would have time for the mindless paperwork later. The building plans quickly caught her attention. She still couldn't make heads or tails of them. Sterling Tower was an enormous building with more than twenty floors, plus the vast grounds of the Warehouse. It just didn't seem possible that they were having such an issue with housing.

"How many residents do we have, Mrs. Mitchell?" Allie asked her assistant who was busy calculating how much they needed to increase their food budget in order to feed everyone. It took an astronomical amount to feed so many young Immortals when they each had an appetite to rival three mortal teenage boys.

"Nine-hundred-and-eighty-four at the last census," Mrs. Mitchell replied absently.

"That is nearly double our max capacity." Livia pulled her hair, braiding a crown of tiny flowers into her hair. "We'll have to send some of these kids back to their families. Maybe start with the locals and let them come just for training during alternate schedules."

"There has to be a way to keep them all. Something I'm not seeing yet. This building is huge; we should be able to handle a thousand kids and then some."

"Well, you could start by charging more to help cover the costs of their care," Livia muttered.

"I don't like charging them anything, much less an amount most can't afford. Besides, money isn't even the issue." Allie studied the layouts for the upper floors. Each defined space was desperately needed for training purposes. The dormitories were overflowing already. They simply had to find space for more dorm rooms.

She turned the page of construction documents, her eyes gliding over the familiar rooms. The upper floors were where everything happened. The middle floors were permanent residences for the older students who were all sharing already. Allie flipped the pages to examine the lower floors. She didn't go there often and wasn't as familiar with them.

"What are these spaces for?" Allie pointed to a series of enormous rooms on the eleventh floor.

"Those are the senior staff residences." Livia glanced at the plans. "I believe that's Mrs. Mitchell's apartment there." She tapped on the corner suite that housed several bedrooms, an office, and several other rooms Allie didn't recognize.

"Mrs. Mitchell, how many people live with you?" Allie scowled at the largest apartment on that floor at nearly three-thousand square feet.

"My husband and our French bulldog, Biscuit." She looked up from her paperwork. "Our youngest left home a few years ago, but all four of our boys visit often."

A tremor of anger shot through Allie, but she reined it in. She'd learned a long time ago when it came to older Immortals, getting them to change their way of thinking was like asking them to put toothpaste back in the tube.

"And when they aren't visiting, how many empty rooms do you have?" Allie made a monumental effort to keep her temper in check.

"The four bedrooms for the boys. We've kept them just how they had them when they were children." Martha's eyes sparkled with an indulgent smile for her *boys*, none of which were younger than forty.

Allie beckoned her forward. "Come show me what each of these other rooms are if you don't mind."

Mrs. Mitchell stood and smoothed a hand down over her perfectly wrinkle-free skirt and leaned over Allie's shoulder. "That's the living room, kitchen, formal dining room, and the study." She pointed to the small squares representing each. "And that's the music room. My husband loves to play his instruments. And that is the gym and the solarium for my plants."

Allie nodded. In her eyes, she didn't see the home Mrs. Mitchell had raised her children in. She saw a dormitory where at least twenty residents could live comfortably. They could put at least three bunk beds in Mrs. Mitchell's gymnasium alone. She leaned back in her desk chair, careful not to bother Livia's work on her hair.

"There are similar homes for other staff members on floors nine through fourteen." She studied the layouts and square footage of each. There were at least eight such apartments on each floor—that could mean comfortable housing for everyone.

"Mrs. Mitchell, given our current circumstances and that we have children living in tents on the Warehouse lawn, wouldn't it be a more efficient use of space to move you and your husband to a two-bedroom apartment and move twenty students into your three-thousand square foot home?"

"But we've lived there for nearly thirty years." A tremor entered her voice. "That is my home. It's where we raised our children and where they come home for the holidays. It's where they will bring their families someday."

"I know it's a huge ask, Martha." Allie stood and went

to her assistant's side, draping an arm around her. "But you have ten potential bedrooms that are going unused when we have kids who don't have access to a decent bathroom. The last I heard from Hal, the boys are using the forest so the girls can use the outhouses at the campgrounds. We can't keep them out there much longer."

"Of course, you're right, Allie." Mrs. Mitchell sniffed. "I will talk to my husband tonight. We will discuss a plan."

"I'll make you a deal." Allie just hoped her roommates wouldn't freak out on her. "You and Mr. Mitchell can move into the penthouse. It's not as large as your home, but it will be more comfortable for you and your family when they visit."

"Absolutely not." Mrs. Mitchell pulled back as if Allie had slapped her. "You are the First Princess of Indriell. You will be our queen one day. I wouldn't dream of it."

"It's okay. Aidan and I can take a smaller apartment with Darius and Pilar across the hall from us. Naomi can take a room near us so we're all together. It'll be fine."

"I will not separate you from your Syntrophos." Martha shook her head. "Henry and I can take a smaller apartment. We'll put some of our things in storage if we need to."

"I promise, I'll make sure you have everything you need, and whenever your family comes to visit, we will make them comfortable, too."

"Unless..." Mrs. Mitchel chewed on her bottom lip. "Perhaps we could stay in our home and convert each room to house the children who need the space." Her eyes brightened at the idea. "We could be like ... house parents."

"I love that idea!" Allie beamed at her assistant. "It's the perfect solution."

"We could use the Soma gymnasium after hours, so I don't suppose we'd need our own personal gym." Mrs.

Mitchell sniffed. "We can downsize and make room, though Mr. Mitchell will need to keep his music room as it is. It will be ... cozy."

God help me if I have to go through this conversation with all the staff members. "That's the spirit." Allie clapped her on the back. "We'll start making plans after the wedding and before you know it, we'll have the Warehouse back to normal and everyone will be comfortable."

She turned back to the construction documents to look at the lower floors that were mostly staff offices, conference rooms, and break rooms. The second and third floors were where most of the shops were for clothing and various other services the kids needed access to, but the tailor might not need five thousand square feet. And the school supply store probably didn't need all the space they had either.

Most of the lower floors weren't being used as they once were when Soma employed personal accountants, career advisors, and concierge services for their students as a means to keep them beholden to Soma financially. Most of those offices were empty or being used as classrooms. Which meant once they did some temporary housing reassignments, they might actually have room to expand for long-term solutions that would give Mrs. Mitchell her home back. Allie envisioned a new Sterling Tower with endless possibilities and a better use of space.

"Let's prep the fourth, fifth, and sixth floors for long-term housing. We can make them a step up from the dorms with fewer students per room—more like the studio apartments on the fifteenth floor. We will need several hundred new beds once we have everyone in their temporary spaces. Mrs. Mitchell, can you get with Brooke in supply management and get them ordered?"

"Yes, ma'am." Mrs. Mitchell turned back to her

computer to take notes. "Should we order cots or more permanent beds?"

"Permanent ones with comfortable mattresses and upholstered headboards. And bunk beds, too. Lots of them. We will move everyone from the Warehouse into the staff apartments while the other floors are being renovated. Once we have everyone settled, we'll move into the next phase."

Allie crossed her office to the bathroom where her dress hung in a garment bag. "Good work, ladies. I can't tell you how much better I feel about giving these kids proper housing where they're not piled on top of each other and peeing in the woods." It was an enormous weight off her mind. One of many such worries.

"All I did was your hair." Livia moved behind her to check her dress in the full-length mirror in the bathroom. "And remember once again how glad I am that you're in charge of this place and not me." Livia elbowed her playfully. "You're much better at it."

Allie checked her mascara and smirked at her sister in the mirror. "Who are you kidding? I'm flying this bus by the seat of my pants."

"That's a comforting thought." Livia took the garment bag from the hanger and unzipped the bag. "You've got to get dressed so you don't miss this bonding ceremony."

"Another one." Allie shook her head with a sigh, shedding the dressing robe she'd worn to work this morning. Just last week, Tessa and Dean McBrien had their bonding ceremony in the Warehouse where Hal, who had a soft spot for Tessa, had transformed the rolling green hills into a gorgeous garden.

Tess and Dean had always known they were equals, and over time, they each slowly realized that they were also Complements. For them, it wasn't a lightning and thunderbolt kind of moment, but a progressive transformation from two people who chose each other under dire circumstances, to two people who would go on choosing each other for the rest of their lives. Still, they were so young to be getting married.

Dean's sister, Erin McBrien and her new wife, Gemma—one of Aidan's Syntrophos soldiers—had completed their bond just a few months ago. It was all happening so fast for so many of the young Immortals around her. The mortal side of Allie's brain wanted to ask them what they were all rushing into, but she knew enough to keep that opinion to herself.

"I know what you're thinking." Livia removed her floor-length silver dress from the hanger. Yards of shimmery silk sparkled in the bathroom lights. "But try to be happy for Graham."

"He's just a baby!" Allie blurted, yanking the dress out of her sister's hands to step into it. "They both are. And don't tell me I'm being overprotective of Graham because I know that already. It's just ... he's barely twenty years old." She shook her head, her precarious curls bouncing on top of her head.

"He's nearly twenty-three, Allie. Doesn't that make him an adult by mortal standards?"

"By our standards, he's a child. We all are." Allie threw her hands up.

"But they are Complements." Livia gave her one of those stony looks that weren't so scary anymore. "They know their mind, and they're ready for their life together. You didn't give me nearly as much crap about rushing into marrying Liam once I finally realized he was mine."

Allie rolled her eyes. "You're both old. It worked for you two."

"I am not old. I just celebrated my two-hundred-and-twenty-fourth birthday. That is not old. *Liam* is old." She gave a playful smirk that just barely lifted the corner of her mouth.

"And you two had life experience. And time to make stupid mistakes and be yourselves before you came together."

"They may be young, but you cannot deny that Ezra and Graham both have had more life experience at their young ages than most adults my age. Trust in them to know they are ready for this. If they weren't, their bonding wouldn't be happening." Livia moved to zip up Allie's gown, placing her hands on her shoulders as they gazed into the mirror at each other.

Livia was beautiful in her pale gold gown that made her olive skin glow.

"Set your worries aside for the rest of the day and be happy for your friend. Graham has found the one thing we all seek, and he's found it at a tender age. It is something to celebrate. He will never know what it's like to feel the kind of soul-crushing loneliness so many of us have experienced. Be happy for them."

"I am. You're right." Allie shook her head again. "It's just my mortal brain having a hard time understanding something I've never experienced and hope I won't experience any time soon." She heaved a sigh, gathering her clutch purse from the vanity.

Allie forced a smile she didn't quite feel and grabbed her sister's hand. "Come on, we've got a wedding to get to."

"Bonding ceremony."

"Whatever."

Chapter 5

Aidan | Sterling Tower | Late January

"How do you handle this so well?" Chloe slammed the door to the penthouse behind her. Fei Long burst out of her in a cloud of golden mist. A sight Aidan would never get used to seeing.

Adjusting his tie, he turned, arching a brow as she dropped onto the too white leather sofa at the center of the room, her dragon pacing furiously behind her. Chloe's dark hair billowed around her bare shoulders, blue and teal streaks peeking out from underneath. Her black knee-length dress wasn't quite right for a bonding ceremony, but it suited her—and her current mood.

A mood Aidan understood all too well.

"Who says I'm handling it at all? Certainly not well." He returned to fussing with his tie, no matter what he tried, it was either too short or too long.

"You make it look easy." Chloe leaned her head back against the sofa cushions. "Meaning the whole living with your Complement under your nose thing. Not murdering your tie."

"I can't ever seem to get it right." Aidan tugged on the loose ends, wondering if he could go without. He was going with Allie after all, and she was sure to be wearing flip flops or sweatpants, or some other fashion faux pas not suitable for a formal ritual. He wouldn't put it past her to bring a snack in her pocket since the last bonding ceremony they attended lasted for several days.

"Don't these constant ceremonies make you want to go out and just ... blow things up?" Fei Long growled, a spiral of dark smoke curling up from her nostrils.

"Yes." Aidan frowned at himself in the mirror. "I think I'd prefer to go through my Awakening again than to attend another happy celebration with the most infuriating redhead I've ever met."

"Okay, hands off the tie." Chloe kicked off her shoes and stood on the couch. "Come over here." She snapped her fingers, and Aidan cracked a smile for his long-time friend. She'd changed in the years she was away, but now and then he caught a glimpse of the girl she used to be.

"If you can fix this, why did you let me keep fussing with it?" Aidan moved to stand in front of her. Even standing on the couch, she was just slightly above eye level with him.

"I don't know if I've ever seen you suck at something so bad." She adjusted the length of the tie, her gaze focused on her hands. "Pardon me if I enjoyed the anomaly."

"Allie usually does it for me. Or Naomi, but Allie went to the office this morning, and Naomi is with Pilar and Darius."

"And you needed some peace and quiet to prepare for yet another happy celebration that isn't yours?"

"Exactly." Aidan sighed. It wasn't that he wasn't thrilled for Graham and Ezra.

"It's so unfair." Chloe yanked on the wide end of the tie.

"You trying to strangle me?" Aidan coughed.

"Sorry." She pushed the perfect knot up to his collar.

"It's not fair, Chlo. But life isn't fair. You know that better than anyone."

"Don't you feel the urge to run every time you see her and she smiles at you the same as always?" She gripped his shoulders as she let out an angry snort, a puff of smoke leaving her nostrils.

"Every single time." Aidan helped her down from the couch. "But the other part of me can't stand the thought of actually leaving her."

"So we're doomed to this feeling of wanting to be with them every second of the day, but hating it at the same time?"

"I don't ... hate it." Aidan reached for his suit jacket draped over the back of the white leather chair. "But the urge to run is strong. I just know the second I give into it I'll want to come right back here."

"Justice has only been here a few weeks, but I don't know how much more of this I can take." Fei Long lashed her tail angrily, knocking over one of Livia's priceless white sculptures.

"Sorry!" Chloe reached out with lightning quick reflexes and snatched it before it could crash against the floor, setting it back on the narrow table behind the couch.

"It's fine. We really need to redecorate. Livia's things are far too fancy and breakable for a house where we have Fei Long and Allie knocking things over all the time."

"Be smaller, Fei," Chloe snarled at her dragon who snarled right back at her.

Aidan smiled. "I swear she just gave you a Ming Lao look I've seen a million times."

Chloe's face softened as she watched Fei Long shrink

down to a manageable size. "She has Mom's warrior spirit, that's for sure." She reached for Fei Long, scratching behind her ears.

"She soothes your spirit, doesn't she?" Aidan sat on the chair arm.

"She does." Chloe sighed. "She's like having a little piece of Mom here with me. You know, in clumsy dragon form."

Aidan laughed as Fei Long leaned into Chloe's scratches.

"She'll help you get through this. And someday, probably not any day soon, you and I will laugh about all of this."

Chloe snorted again. "Until that day comes, can you teach me your tricks? What do you do when you want to shake Allie until she sees what's right in front of her? I just can't fathom how you can be in a relationship with her and hold back the floodgates of your love until she's ready for it. I have a hard enough time maintaining my friendship with Justice."

Aidan's shoulders slumped. He knew that feeling too. "I think what helps me the most is reminding myself that she's my world." He shrugged. "It's my job to be whatever she needs me to be. If that means she needs me to be her boyfriend for a while until she's ready for me to be her husband, then I'm okay with that."

"And if all she wanted was your friendship?" Chloe's eyes grew bright with tears. "Would you be able to handle that?"

Aidan's throat clenched at the onslaught of her pain. "No, Chlo. I don't think I could handle that half as well as you do."

"Be careful you don't play the boyfriend role too well. Then she'll never want to let you go."

"I don't want her to let me go."

Chloe frowned as her eyes grew blank with the light of her gift for a brief moment. "Aidan, I think she's going to have to see beyond the idea of you before she's ever going to be ready for what's next."

Graham | Sterling Tower | February

"You ready for this, little man?" Quinn stepped toward the doors that would take Graham to his Complement. "You're sweating. You need a minute?" Quinn handed him a blue square of silk from his pocket. "Your something blue. I heard Allie telling Santi about it before our ceremony."

Graham took the pocket square and mopped his face with it. "I think that's a tradition for mortal brides, brother, but I'll take all the well wishes I can get." He stuffed the fabric in his pocket for later. "Is it hot today? It feels hot." He fanned his face, searching the hall for a convenient air-conditioning vent to stand under.

"You're about to bond with your Complement. I think it's a requirement to freak out."

"I'm not freaking out." Graham paced the length of the hall in front of the elevator bank. "I love Ezra. It's just moving really fast, you know? It feels like we just met, and now we're living together and bonding, and I'm only twenty-three. Ezra's even younger."

"Doesn't matter." Quinn shrugged, reaching to still Graham's pacing.

"It doesn't matter? You realize I don't have a real job. Yeah, I've got money from my work with the League, but I always planned to give that to charity. It feels like blood money."

"It doesn't matter." Quinn shrugged again. "You're both ready for this. You wouldn't be here about to fulfill your bond if you weren't ready to see each other. That's all that matters."

"You're right." Graham let out a soft sigh. "I'm just not sure how it's done?"

"What, the wedding night?" Quinn grinned, and Graham punched his shoulder.

"No, funny, guy. The part where I have to give my power over to my husband to complete the bond."

"That's to be expected." Quinn shoved his hands into his pockets. He normally wasn't a suit wearing kind of guy, but today he looked like someone on the cover of a magazine. "I felt the same way going into my bonding ceremony and Dad said—"

"Dad said what?" The elevators opened and Daniel stepped off with Emma and Parker, all dressed in their wedding finery. Quinn and Santi's ceremony had happened on the spur of the moment, so the family was going all out for Graham and Ezra's big day. He kind of felt bad about that, which was why he'd planned a surprise for his brother and new sister-in-law. But that would come after.

"You told me to let my instincts guide me." Quinn reached for Parker, slinging him up on his shoulders. The little boy squealed with delight, slapping his hands over Quinn's eyes.

"You'll be fine, son." Daniel took Graham's hands in his. "Just relax and let it happen. Handing your power over to someone isn't easy, even when you trust that person more than anyone else in the world. That's why our most sacred ritual takes time."

"I don't want to keep everyone waiting." Graham took another deep breath. He was hyper aware of the clock ticking forward.

"Don't even worry about that, darling." Emma came to stand with her husband. "We are all here to support you. To give you comfort during the most vulnerable moments of your life. You will take all the time you need and not worry about us." She fussed with his tie. "My babies grew up too fast."

"You still have Parker to fuss over." Graham took his mother's hands, letting his father step aside. "And if my husband to be has his way, you'll be a grandma before you can blink."

"Merci." Emma fanned her face. "Is it hot in here? I'm not ready to be a grandma. I'm far too young." She grinned, her gaze sparkling with a hint of tears in her diamond bright eyes. They always reminded Graham of starlight. She was a pillar of strength, his mother.

"But if you're to be a father soon, I want to be called grand-mère." She smoothed a cool hand across his cheek, patting his face like she did when he was a kid.

"It's time." Quinn stood at the doors leading to the rooftop of Sterling Tower. That was where Santi and Quinn were supposed to have had their ceremony before circumstances changed their plans. Ezra and Graham were utilizing most of their wedding plans like hand-me-downs. It didn't bother either of them. As Ezra often said, he was just looking forward to the marriage.

"I'm ready." Graham patted his pocket, searching for the ring he'd made for Ezra. It was one mortal custom his

Complement adored, and Graham wanted to surprise him with it after their bond was complete.

Graham knelt down beside his little brother. He hardly more than a toddler, but he was a smart kid. "Hey bubba." Graham smiled at Parker's toothy grin. "I need you to do me a big favor today."

"What dis?" He grabbed for the chain Graham looped around his neck. "Can you keep an eye on this?" He held up the simple platinum band etched with interlocking alpha and omega symbols with an inscription on the inside. *My First. My Last. My Constant.* "This is a gift for Uncle Ezra, and I need you to hold it for me for a little while."

"You got it, bubba." Parker gave him a thumbs up.

"Please don't let him lose it or swallow it." Graham ruffled Parker's dark curls.

"We'll keep it safe until you're ready." Emma took Parker's hand.

"All right, let's do this." Graham took up his place at Quinn's side. Ezra and Wes would be along shortly. Their closest friends were already waiting for them.

Quinn clapped him on the back and opened the double doors to the rooftop. Except it wasn't the rooftop of Sterling Tower.

"What is this?" Graham stepped over the threshold. He'd expected a windy day with flowers and a few seated guests around the decorated pergola Santi's grandfather had built for her ceremony. Green grass crunched under his feet, and the sky was a blaze of sunset colors, yet it was early afternoon.

"It's my gift to you and your husband." Quinn followed him along a path of rose petals, undisturbed by their footsteps.

"You did this?" Graham turned around in a circle. Gone

were the city noises and skyscrapers. Birds flew overhead, their song echoing all around. It was like stepping into a painting. "Is this ... the dreamworld?"

Quinn nodded. "I brought a little magic here for your special day. I wanted you guys to have something that was just yours. Not a hand-me-down from me and Santi."

Graham pulled his brother into a hug. He didn't have the words to thank him. "I don't know how you did this, but it's beautiful. I can't wait to see Ezra's face." Graham's eyes devoured everything. The trees swaying in the breeze. The quiet, peaceful setting was so perfect, it chased all his anxieties away in an instant.

"It's not exactly a dreamscape. I just pulled the barrier in a bit and created a safe little bubble of the dreamworld for your bonding ceremony. They're all waiting for you at the end of the path."

Graham's heart hitched in his chest. He was so ready for this. The brothers walked along the path under a canopy of dogwood trees that seemed to morph from nothing. Blossoms rained down on them, their perfume sweet and refreshing.

A small lake took shape at the end of the path. An island stood at the center with the pergola Graham had expected waiting for Ezra and Graham to come and complete their bond.

All of his favorite people were here to bear witness to their bonding. An Immortal's bonding ceremony was a private, intimate experience to be shared with only a few trusted family and friends. Graham's parents would sit with Parker and Gregg, Naeemah and Jin Jing. Allie and Aidan stood on the island with Chloe and Sasha. Quinn and Wes would join them to stand watch over Ezra and Graham until their bond was complete.

Later they would celebrate with all their friends and family. That was when Graham would share his gift for Quinn and Santi.

"You stopped sweating." Quinn stood with him at the edge of the water. "You good, little man?"

Graham nodded. "Thanks for the cool breeze." Now that he was here, waiting for Ezra, he was excited. Still nervous, but no longer afraid. They were young. They had next to nothing, and if it weren't for the free apartment thanks to Allie and Soma, they'd be penniless, but they had each other, and that was all that mattered.

The doors opened, revealing Ezra beaming with excitement between Wes and Santi, who he'd become fast friends with upon his arrival at Sterling Tower. They'd taken an instant liking for each other, like they were born to be brother and sister.

Santi linked her arm through Ezra's, but Graham only had eyes for his Complement.

"This is amazing," Ezra shouted, dancing down the pathway to the amusement of their guests. His pale gray, perfectly tailored suit the epitome of high fashion and the only thing he'd wanted for their special day.

"You can thank Quinn for this," Graham shouted back, turning around with his hands lifted, taking in the magical setting all over again.

As Ezra neared, Graham couldn't help himself. He walked back along the path to meet him. Their eyes locked, and nothing about what they faced felt intimidating any longer.

Sinking down to one knee, he knew he was getting all the mortal traditions backwards, but he didn't care. "I have a gift for you." Graham patted down his pockets before he remembered.

"Parker! I need you, bubba." He called over his shoulder, and the little boy came running, clutching the chain around his neck.

"Unca Ez." Parker slammed into Ezra's knees, nearly knocking him over.

"What's this?" Ezra scooped him up, glancing back at Graham still down on one knee.

"He's holding your gift." Graham stood up and lifted the chain from Parker's neck. "Let's try this again." He sank back down to his knee as Parker wiggled out of Ezra's arms.

Graham grinned up at his husband when his brother got down on one knee beside him. "I made this for you. Parker helped." He nodded at his little brother. Graham's hands shook as he removed the ring from the chain, tucking it into his pocket.

He placed the ring in Ezra's hand and the interlocking symbols began to turn.

"It's beautiful." Ezra studied the design, his face lighting up when he read the inscription before he slipped it on his ring finger. "What does it do?"

Of course, Ezra would know he would never give him something that wasn't imbued with power. Not something he made with his own two hands.

"It protects your identity." Graham stood, taking Ezra's hands into his. "No matter where we go. No matter what dangerous shenanigans we get up to, this ring will shield your identity from our enemies. They will never know you are my Complement. To anyone who holds ill will against us, we will be nothing to each other, so they can't use our love against us. And thanks to Imogen, they'll never even see the ring on your finger.

"Beautiful *and* useful." Ezra grinned, admiring his ring again. "I'm a lucky guy."

Graham wasn't sure if he meant the ring or Graham. Ezra took his hand again. "Let's do this."

CHAPTER 7

Allie | Sterling Tower | February

Allie smiled at the way Ezra and Graham couldn't take their eyes off each other as they walked across the stone bridge to the island where she and the other witnesses waited. She'd participated in several bonding ceremonies now, and they never failed to freak her out.

It was beautiful and sweet and all the things it was supposed to be, but it was always a stark reminder that someday—perhaps even someday soon—she was going to lose Aidan forever.

"You okay?" Aidan murmured behind her. His hand pressed against her back in that way he did whenever he was near. She leaned into him, her entire body attuned to his. She wanted to say that nothing could ever come between them again. They were on the same page now, in almost every way. But something still wasn't right. Some unknown thing kept them from moving forward.

Eventually, someone would tear them apart. Already, Aidan sensed his own Complement. She'd never experienced the tiny glimpses others had of their Complements. Not that she would be able to tell them apart from the things her Clairvoyance showed her every day. But Aidan was ready for it. He never mentioned it, but he was so ready for his forever. That it didn't include her shattered her heart every time the thought crossed her mind.

Allie liked what they had now, and if she had it her way, she would choose him every day for the rest of her life. But Immortals didn't get a choice. It was made for them, and when it happened to her, she'd be happy. She knew that much was true. But she was happy now and didn't want anything to change. She couldn't fathom ever loving anyone else.

She feared the moment when Aidan would be ripped away from her to become someone else's forever. She knew it in her soul. Her gift had revealed it in no uncertain terms that Aidan would recognize his Complement first. And then she would shrivel up and die watching it happen.

"I'm fine." She took his free hand, watching the happy couple approach the pergola Santi's grandfather had carved for her wedding—bonding ceremony. The ceremony she had in Naeemah's gardens in the underground back home on Kelleys Island without said pergola.

Mr. Santiago had been happy to let Graham and Ezra use the beautiful canopy for their ceremony, but eventually, when Quinn and Santi had a house of their own, they would move it to their garden. Santi already had plans for her children to have their bonding ceremonies in the garden she didn't even have yet.

Barring any of them had a future that would allow for such things.

"Stop thinking about bad things," Aidan whispered, his breath warm at the nape of her neck.

"Who says I'm thinking about stuff?"

"I can see it in your eyes, babe. You're stressing about the future."

"I'm trying to be in the moment." She pushed away thoughts of the looming darkness, the threats coming at them from every corner, and focused on the two people in front of her.

"They're the cutest, aren't they?" She sighed, enjoying the sight of Graham getting his happily ever after. Even if he was just a baby himself.

"They're perfect." Aidan wrapped his arms around her, resting his chin on top of her head.

Graham and Ezra stood under the pergola, their hands clasped as they fell into their own little world for a while. She wondered what it felt like to surrender their power to each other. She supposed she wouldn't really understand the difficulty until it was her turn, somewhere in the distant future, after she'd dealt with Marcus, the unknown darkness, and the Senate. After she finished rebuilding Soma into a refuge for young Immortals. After she'd come to terms with her role as the First Princess and eventually Queen of Indriell. After ... *if* she survived her Proving. Then maybe she could think about her Complement. Whoever he was.

A glimmer of silvery-blue light enveloped Graham and Ezra.

"It's begun," Wes murmured beside her, clutching Chloe's hand. His eyes grew tight with worry for his Syntrophos. It had to be difficult to watch Ezra go through something like this without him.

Allie took Aidan's hand, moving to place her other in Chloe's. They were all here to support their friend today. All the old Kelleys Island kids together again, linking hands to protect one of their own. Sasha, Quinn, Chloe, Allie and

Aidan, and Wes too, all linked hands to watch over these two precious souls as they united on a level few could even comprehend. It was beautiful.

But sometimes, even beautiful things could be terrifying.

Chapter 8

Allie | Sterling Tower | February

Allie and Aidan wandered hand in hand along the grassy slope dotted with wildflowers of every sort. A tent sat among the flowers, shimmering in the fading light of a beautiful sunset.

"Hal really outdid himself this time." Aidan tugged her close, his warm hand resting on her hip. "It's a perfect reception, babe. I'm sure they're going to love it."

"I hope so." Allie was eager to see the look of surprise on their faces when the newlyweds arrived for their surprise reception. Neither Ezra nor Santi and Quinn were expecting the elaborate party Allie and Graham had cooked up.

"Mortals do this kind of party when they get married?" Aidan's eyes scanned the activity below. Everyone from Soma was dressed in their finest, eager to greet the happy couples. The kitchen staff had outdone themselves with the food and wine, and there would be dancing and gifts for the newlyweds later.

"It's called a reception." Allie looped her arm through Aidan's, leaning her head against his shoulder—the part she could reach anyway, anyway. She stifled a yawn. Watching over a Complement bonding ceremony was boring work, but also exhausting. Graham and Ezra's bonding was the quickest one yet, but it had still taken most of the day to complete.

If she was this tired, she couldn't imagine how they must feel.

They walked along the path down to the tent. Other couples and groups were making their way down to the warehouse for the reception, but Allie was enjoying the quiet moment with Aidan. The rest of the evening would not be quiet.

"It's uplifting to see our friends find their forevers, isn't it?" Aidan seemed so relaxed and at ease after the bonding.

"If you say so." Allie sighed.

"It's not a bad thing, Allie." Aidan chuckled.

"I know. They're just so young. It's going to be hard for them, trying to become adults together when they're ages away from their Provings, and they still have so much to learn as individuals... I just can't wrap my brain around trying to do all those things and be married at the same time."

"You're thinking like a mortal. They're ready for this, otherwise they would still see each other as friends."

"You say that, and it makes sense, but then I look at them and I just feel ... responsible somehow."

"Responsible?" Aidan stopped, turning her toward him. "Explain." He frowned down at her and she almost laughed. She hadn't seen that look from him since they were kids, and she was the newbie Immortal fresh out of her Awakening.

"My gift sees it, Aidan. If it weren't for me and that frigging prophecy, none of this would be happening. The Syntrophos pairs linking up all around me and now the

Complements, too. It's like I'm ..." She threw her hands up in the air. "A chaos magnet, pulling all these people together to make them more powerful. And if it weren't for me, their lives would take a more natural course to all this marriage stuff."

The corner of Aidan's mouth twitched up into a half smile. "That's kind of what prophecy does, Allie. It still doesn't make it a bad thing. When we are ready to see our Complements, we're ready, and nothing else matters. Yes, our circumstances factor into when that happens. But you are not a puppet master, making everyone dance to your tune. You're one of us, babe. All of this is happening to you, too, and you handle it all with grace." He grinned. "Most of the time."

"I still don't like it." Allie took his hand, and they continued their walk down to the tent where some had already started dancing.

"Aidan!" Neela and Ivy came running up to meet him. "It happened! Can you believe it?" The two young Syntrophos clutched hands, waving frantically for two of Quinn's dream walkers to join them. Rocco and Maddox were a little rough around the edges, and neither were big talkers, but both wore pleased smiles as they joined the girls.

Rocco couldn't seem to keep his hands off Neela, and Maddox had eyes only for Ivy. Allie had seen those looks before.

"Just now?" Aidan grinned at his favorite Syntrophos pair from the Milan Initiative.

Neela nodded, beaming. "I'm the anchor between Rocco and Ivy."

"And I guess that makes me the spare." Maddox bobbed his head, grinning like a fool in love.

"Not exactly." Aidan took on his teacher's voice. "You will bring them balance as an integral part of this unusual relationship. That makes you the keystone that holds it together. I've just never seen it happen all at once like this. It will be interesting to see how that helps you all adapt."

"Well, it looks like you're going to need some new girls to make you crazy." Ivy batted her eyes at Maddox.

Aidan took her hand. "I have every confidence that you and Neela will forever make me crazy." He reached for Ivy, pulling the girls in for a hug. "Congratulations, you two." He turned to the walkers. "And ..." Aidan ran a hand through his hair with a grin. "You guys have no idea what you're getting into with these two troublemakers. So good luck with that." He reached to shake their hands. "And congratulations."

"Congrats!" Allie smiled and hugged the girls, who had so often made Allie's life difficult. Aidan had asked them to watch over her in the early days after they first came to Soma, and the girls had taken the job seriously.

The new Complements dashed off to celebrate with their friends.

"Two more weddings to look forward to." Allie sighed, leaning into Aidan. "Am I the only one who finds all this bonding exhausting?"

"Definitely not. It's tiring, but it's also a reminder that there are still wonderful things in this world." He wrapped his arm around her.

"Does it ever ..." Allie trailed off unable to voice her fears.

"Does it ever what?" Aidan pressed. "Tell me what's bothering you."

"Does it ever terrify you that one day a total stranger

might rip us apart?" She ducked her head as he turned her toward him, tilting her chin so he could look into her eyes.

"That is never going to happen, not like that," he added quickly. "I love you, Alexis Ann." He gave her a devilish smile that curled her toes. "You are all I see, and as long as we're together, I don't have eyes for anyone else.

"Allow us to introduce the happy couples." Aidan spoke into the microphone as Ezra and Graham arrived. "Please welcome Mr. Graham Loukas and Mr. Ezra Loukas!"

The Soma crowd cheered for the newlyweds as they entered the tent, hands clasped and raised over their heads. Graham broke away to approach Aidan, taking the microphone in hand.

"Ladies and Gentlemen, thank you for coming to celebrate with us tonight." He held his hand out for Ezra to join him. "But tonight isn't all about us. That's why we've gone all out with the festivities. Another couple was recently bonded, but they didn't get to have the ceremony they planned. They gifted it to us instead." Graham turned toward the entrance where Quinn and Santi had just arrived, looking perplexed.

"Tonight, we are also celebrating the bonding of my brother, Quinn, with his beautiful Complement, Santi. With Allie's help, this party is our gift to you both. May you always be as happy as Ezra and I are at this moment."

Santi's eyes filled with tears, and she rushed forward to hug Graham and Ezra. Quinn joined them, shaking his head at the wonderful surprise.

"I don't know about everyone else, but I'm starving." Graham spoke into the microphone. "Let's eat."

Allie laughed, taking her seat next to Aidan at the grooms' table where the guests of honor joined them, looking happier than she'd ever seen them.

See, you ding-dong, Complements are a good thing. Allie had tried so many times to convince herself of this, but she still saw it as a lack of choice. That some unseen force would make one of the biggest decisions of her life for her. She knew very well she was being stubborn and unreasonable, but she supposed until it happened to her, she would never fully understand it.

"Try to act like you're happy for them." Aidan nudged her under the table.

"I am happy for them."

"Tell that to your face."

"Sorry." She plastered on a smile, eager for the meal to be served. Like Graham, she was starving.

"You look creepy when you fake smile." Sasha sat down beside her.

"Ugh." Allie reached for her glass of wine. "I'm trying here, people."

"She just doesn't get it," Chloe said, seated across from Graham and Ezra. "And that's okay."

"Thanks Chlo." Allie started to relax.

"You'll get it when it happens to you. But you should probably try to wrap your mortal brain around the whole Complement thing someday, or you'll never be ready, and your poor guy or gal will be suffering in silence." Chloe gave a longing look at Justice seated with their Scholar friends at another table.

"Sorry. You're right." Allie leaned back for the waiter to serve the first course, and she was really hoping it wasn't going to be salad.

"Ouch," Chloe snarled.

"You okay?" Allie looked up to see Chloe leaning over to rub her leg under the table.

"Yeah, just caught my foot on something." She glared at Aidan.

"Any news from Jayesh?" Sasha asked, her tone airy and forced.

"Not yet." Allie popped a bacon wrapped fig into her mouth, excited for the full plate of hot appetizers Graham had chosen for them. "I'm really sorry I had to send him into the field. I know you were counting on attending the ceremony with him."

"It's okay." She smiled. "We'll get back out there together soon enough. He still thinks its creepy to be seen together socially. He's afraid everyone will think he's an old man creeper." She sipped her glass of wine. "One of these days, he'll decide I'm not too young to date."

Allie cleaned her plate in record time, eyeing Aidan's untouched appetizers. "Well, the age difference is huge, Sash." She leaned toward her best friend. "Maybe you should try dating someone else for a while. It might give Jayesh the kick in the pants he needs to get over it."

Sasha nodded, picking at the bacon she probably wouldn't eat. "I'm not sure he'll ever see me as anything but the young student he's taken under his wing."

"What are you two whispering about?" Chloe moved her chair to sit closer to them.

"Jayesh." Sasha sighed. "But I shouldn't complain." She reached for Chloe's hand. "It could be so much worse."

Chloe put on her fake smile. "We'll get there someday." It had to be hard for her, seeing all these couples bonding around her when Justice still didn't see her. That must be the absolute worst kind of heartache. To know and it not be reciprocated.

"I'll send someone else next time." Allie turned her attention back to Sasha.

"It's okay. I know he misses me when he's gone, but he just won't admit it."

"Absence makes the heart grow fonder and all that." Aidan gave Allie a playful nudge.

"I just wish the stubborn man would acknowledge that I feel so much older than I am." Sasha rolled her eyes.

Sasha was older in ways most people could never understand. Years ago, when she returned from the Chola Valley Temple, she wasn't the same. Her time there happened within the span of six weeks in the "real" world, but it left her out of sync with others her age. She was twenty-four physically, but mentally she was much older.

"Jayesh?" Sasha shot out of her chair so fast it fell over behind her. "He's back." Her face lit up like the sun at the sight of him racing for the grooms' table.

"Allie, I need to speak with you." Jayesh sank into a crouch beside her. "It's about the escaped prisoners."

Allie | Sterling Tower | February

"They made landfall on the island of San Salvador in the Bahamas." Jayesh sat hunched over in a sleek leather chair at the conference table back in Allie's office. They'd left the others to their festivities, though Sasha, Aidan, and Darius had insisted on coming with them.

"They had a boat?" Allie couldn't fathom how such a large group of ancients would have known how to navigate a modern ship.

Jayesh shook his head, wiping a weary hand over his eyes. "They swam."

"From somewhere in the *Bermuda Triangle*?" Allie's jaw dropped.

"They really wanted off that prison island." Jayesh gave an odd shiver.

"It was an awful place," Sasha murmured, her concern for Jayesh seemed to supersede the current situation. "I was only there for a few days when we first went to stop the prison break, but I never want to go back. I can't imagine what those poor people went though there."

"They came ashore along Bonefish Bay," Jayesh continued his report. "Hundreds of them, just rising from the water like demons. The beaches were crowded, full of tourists. I imagine the big hotels probably frightened the ancients. It was a bloodbath." He shook his head. "We don't even know the full extent of it yet.

"But it's been weeks since their escape. I believe they must have found a smaller island somewhere to recuperate. And now that their power has returned and they are stronger, they're seeking a place to ... assimilate."

"But the modern world must be so terrifying for them." Allie had known from the moment she heard about the escaped prisoners that this was bound to happen sooner or later. And it was probably for the best that it happened on a small island in the Bahamas, but she could not allow herself to become distracted by this mess. It was exactly what Marcus wanted.

"They've taken the whole island of San Salvador." Jayesh leaned his elbows against the table. "Dozens have been killed in their terror. They don't understand this world. The last time any of them were free, the world belong to the Immortals. They don't know to conceal their power. Some of them don't even know what a mortal is."

"I can't imagine how they must be feeling, but we have to contain this situation before the media gets ahold of it." Allie pinched the bridge of her nose, trying to stave off a headache.

"It's only a matter of a day or two before this ends up on world stage news," Jayesh said.

"That cannot happen." Chloe barged in, Fei Long scooting in behind her, immediately going to Allie's side. Chloe's dragon adored Allie, and the feeling was mutual.

"I believe Chloe's gift is attuned to whatever is happening with the escaped Immortals." Grandma Alísun came in behind Chloe, closing the door to the conference room.

Fei Long laid her head on Allie's lap, her snout nudging her hands for head scratches.

"Not now, Fei Long." Chloe swatted her away. "Whatever you're deciding right now, we can't afford a wrong move."

Allie nodded, trusting Chloe's gift to guide them through this newest minefield. "These Immortals need kindness and understanding. But we cannot let this situation leave the island."

"I don't think that is our biggest concern." Chloe took an empty seat next to Aidan, her smoky eyes pulsing with the power of her gift. "If mortals find out what's happening there, they'll attribute it to some tragedy or another, at least at first."

"She's right," Jayesh agreed. "In my experience, mortals are quick to blame these kinds of tragedies on an act of terrorism. That could buy us a little more time."

"Marcus would expect us to use force with these poor creatures." Alísun joined them at the table. "He's waiting for us to put all of our resources into keeping them quiet."

"While he makes big moves to take over the world like the megalomaniac he is." Allie leaned on the table, exhausted from the stress of playing her role. She was supposed to save them all.

But how? How am I supposed to stop him?

"I think it is important that you hand this problem off to someone else, Allie." Aidan laid a hand on her knee under the table. "He expects you to go after these prisoners with everything you've got. To get to them before the Senate does. But you need to keep your focus on him. Chloe too." He nodded at Chloe and her dragon. "You two are our best chances of staying two steps ahead of Marcus, but neither of you can afford the distractions he's throwing our way.

Allie nodded. "You're right." She turned to Chloe, who seemed to be somewhere else. Her eyes shone bright with her power, and Fei Long moved to her side with a throaty growl. "I need to deal with the Senate." Allie sighed. "As long as we remain divided and distracted, Marcus wins."

"Wise decisions." Chloe's voice rang with the power of her gift. It was an odd thing to witness. One moment Chloe sat there, far away on some Scholar-like plane Allie would never know, and the next she was back with them, having gained some sort of insight.

"I don't want to treat them like criminals unless they give us a reason to." Allie fumbled with a ball-point pen she'd left on the table during her last meeting. "These people have been imprisoned for far too long. I want to give them a chance to slowly integrate into the modern world. To get their lives back. But I also don't want to unwittingly unleash a monster on the world. We have enough of those." She gave a weary sigh. "We have to ... process them before they can be truly set free."

"That will be the most difficult part of this," Aidan said. "Once we have the situation on San Salvador in hand, we need to find a quiet place where they can feel safe until they are ready to rejoin the world in full. Whether that's here in the Warehouse or somewhere else, we need to have a plan in place for where we will send them."

"Jayesh and Sasha, will you gather your team and go to San Salvador?" Allie asked. They needed to get feet on the ground there immediately.

"Yes," Sasha said before Jayesh had an opportunity to say it was too dangerous for one so young.

"I think it will be important for your Syntrophos to join you, if Quinn is up for it."

"He will be. He'll want Santi with us. She makes us stronger." Of all the new Syntrophos pairs, theirs was the first to gain further completion now that Santi and Quinn were fully bonded Complements. Quinn was the anchor at the center of his relationship with Sasha and Santi. Their Syntrophos bond would be complete only when Sasha bonded with her Complement, which would bring them balance. But at every stage of completion, each member of the three gained in power. Together, they were a force to be reckoned with.

"That's a good idea. She can help bring peace to those who struggle to come to terms with the years they've lost."

"I'll talk to Mom and Dad, see if we can make arrangements for some of the prisoners to stay in the Yard back home until they're ready for more." Aidan pushed back from the table, digging his phone out of his pocket.

"Good idea." Allie nodded., turning to her grandmother. "Grandma, could you and Gramps go with them? These Immortals will need someone they can rally around, and I can think of no one better than our Queen and the Scholar."

"Of course, darling. You are probably right. They will need something familiar." Alísun nodded.

"Gather your team." Allie turned to Sasha and Jayesh. "You will leave immediately for San Salvador Island. Keep me in the loop with what's happening down there."

"We will leave tonight." Jayesh nodded.

"Are we good, Chloe?" Allie asked her talented friend. "Any decisions we've made look iffy to you, you'll tell me, right?"

Chloe stared at each face around the table, her own

impassive, until she gave Aidan an indecipherable frown. "We're good for now. I'll keep studying the situation and discuss it with Dad. His gifts are a great source of guidance for mine." She stood to leave, patting her leg to call Fei Long to her side.

"By sweet girl." Allie gave Fei Long a final scratch behind her ears. "Be a good girl and don't make Chloe crazy."

Chloe snorted like it was far too late for that and left them to find her way back to her apartment. She spent most of her time there these days. The common areas of Sterling Tower had proven to be too hard on her heightened senses, so Darius had soundproofed her apartment to give her a quiet place to study.

"We'll report back when we're ready to leave." Jayesh stood, opening the door for Alísun and Sasha.

"Darius, give us a minute?" Allie asked after the others had all gone.

He gave her a pained look but stood and crossed to the door. "Don't give her a hard time. You have no idea the stress she's under."

"Darius, you have no idea what I know." Aidan's voice hit that deep tone that told Allie he didn't find Darius' meddling amusing.

"Come find me if you need me." Darius gave his brother another wary look before he left them alone. He wouldn't go far. He never did. Sometimes, Allie's Syntrophos was like a personal bodyguard for her emotions. He couldn't help his need to keep her safe and happy. She felt the same for him. She'd inserted herself into his relationship with Pilar on a number of occasions, but Pilar had worked with the Syntrophos of the Milan Initiative long enough to know her way around the intricacies of their odd relationships.

"I know, I should have sent you." She sighed, pushing away from the conference table. "You and your Syntrophos army would be perfect for this job. Not that Sasha and Jayesh can't handle it."

"Then why didn't you?" He scooted his chair closer to hers, reaching for her hand.

"I'm sorry." She chuckled softly to herself. "I know it's stupid, but I just ... I'm not ready to lose you again."

"You wouldn't be losing me if you sent me on assignment. It's not like Germany."

"I know! Logically, I know that." She propped her elbow up on the arm of her chair, letting her chin rest against her hand.

"I know I hurt you when I didn't come home from Germany like I promised—"

"Aidan, that's all ancient history now. I don't hold it against you, you know that don't you?"

"Of course I do."

"I'm just being silly."

Aidan held up a hand to stop her. "No you aren't. I love being here with you." His voice softened. "I love getting to watch you become the amazing, strong woman I've always known you were. And I love that I get to be the man beside you. Don't think for one moment that your power and position somehow makes me feel..."

"Emasculated?" She cringed at the word.

Aidan gave a deep chuckle that had her thinking about all the pleasant things they could be doing rather than having this discussion. "Have no fear of that." He tugged her chair next to his, draping his arm around her. "I believe everything happens for a reason. I ended up in the Milan Initiative because those kids needed me. They still do. You are right, my Syntrophos would be perfect for this job, and they need the experience."

"Then I should just get over my fears and send you?" Her eyes widened and she fought off the threat of tears.

"No, that's not what I'm saying at all." He ran a hand over her shoulder. "I'm not ready to leave you yet. But someday soon, we aren't going to have much of a choice. You're going to need my team, and you and I need to be ready to say our goodbyes when that happens."

Allie leaned into him, needing to feel the reassurance of his presence. "That sounds awful."

"It does." He leaned his head against hers. "But when it happens, you have to trust that I will come back." His fingertips traced over the vine tattoo along her arm, leaving a trail of gooseflesh behind. "I'm not saying I want to go on a month's long assignment, but a few days? We can handle a few days apart. At least I think we can." He laughed, raking a hand through his hair.

"It shouldn't be this hard." She laughed along with him.

"Just don't be afraid to give me a job. I am pretty good at certain things, you know. And I can be a useful tool as well as the First Princess' doting boyfriend."

"You are so much more than that." Allie breathed him in. "I know you're right. I will do better next time." Though she didn't know how she would manage it. Allie lived in fear of letting Aidan or Darius out of her sight. She couldn't function well without either of them, and that was a dangerous thing. She'd dealt with needing Aidan too much in the past. She could deal with it again. Perhaps it was time for a little tough love from her big brother.

CHAPTER 10

Sasha | San Salvador Island | Late February

It was odd to see the empty runway below. The island airport was certainly small, but from Sasha's vantage point circling above, it looked like a ghost town. The whole island was deserted.

Alísun and Alexander murmured behind her, talking about the situation below.

"Where is everyone?" Sasha buckled her seatbelt, trying not to think about what awaited them once they landed.

"Our team has boots on the ground somewhere over there." Jayesh leaned over her, pointing to the jungle toward the south of the small island. She tried not to let his nearness distract her, but that was impossible around Jayesh. He was a distracting sort of man, but they made a great team. Almost as good as she was with Quinn, who sat across the aisle with his newly bonded Complement. She didn't like them putting themselves at risk so soon after their bonding, but they were needed for this mission. Santi would be a key player in helping them get close enough to the Immortals to speak with them. And Sasha just performed better when her Syntrophos was by her side.

"They've made camp near the Great Lake at the center of the island. We'll make our way there first and find out what's happened while I've been away." He looked worried.

"Where are the mortals?" Sasha frowned, studying the pristine white beaches along the row of high-rise hotels and beach homes for the super rich. Not a soul was in sight.

"I don't know." Jayesh took her hand in his. "I just hope they haven't killed them."

"And the locals?" She worried about them, hoping they were able to take shelter from all the chaos of the prisoners' arrival.

She was born in Haiti, just a few islands south of San Salvador. Now that she knew she came from a mortal surrogate mother—a Banished Daughter like Lily Carmichael and Kayla Pierce—she found herself wondering about her from time to time. Was she down there somewhere?

"We will find out soon." Jayesh buckled his seatbelt as they prepared to land the private jet. It once belonged to Jayesh, but he'd given it to Soma. Now that he was free of his past, he wanted to wash his hands of everything Marcus Servius ever gave him.

Jayesh emerged from the plane first, armed and ready for whatever they might find. They still didn't know how many Immortals they were here to collect, but from what Jayesh reported of their initial arrival, it was at least forty or fifty, if not more.

She couldn't imagine how scared and overwhelmed they must be in such a modern world compared to the one they remembered. And they had only seen the small towns here on San Salvador Island.

Sasha, armed with a German MK-556 rifle outfitted

with loadstone ammo and her assassin's blades, moved behind Jayesh, eyes alert for any movement. Dust kicked up along the end of the runway and she smiled. "Looks like our ride is here." She waved the others forward. Santi, and Quinn were armed as well, guarding the Queen and the Scholar.

An old jeep raced across the tarmac, skidding to a halt in front of them.

"Can't keep the plane here, Jayesh." Ephraim stood up in the passenger seat, huge forearms resting against the Jeep frame. "The mortals saw you fly over. They'll think help has arrived and swarm the airport. We don't want to be here for that."

Jayesh signaled to the pilot to take off. She would wait for them in Nassau until they were ready to leave.

"Quickly, Miss Sasha." Abel, the driver, waved her over to the Jeep. "We need to get going yesterday."

"Abel, we've been over this." Sasha climbed into the back of the Jeep, scooting over to make room for Alísun and Alexander. "Drop the Miss and just call me Sasha."

"Will do, Miss Sasha." He gave her a toothy smile, and she swore he called her that just to annoy her. The two African men were her favorite people on their team. Like Sasha, they were also assassins, trained by Mother Raghavan herself at the Chola Valley Temple.

They were brothers who looked a lot alike but couldn't be more different in personality. Abel was the quiet, respectful one. His younger brother Ephraim was the talker.

Jayesh, Santi, and Quinn all climbed into the cargo bed in the back of the Jeep, and Abel took off before any of them had time to get settled.

"Good of you to join us, brother." Ephraim slapped the side of the Jeep as they raced back across the runway.

"We made it back as quickly as we could." Jayesh leaned forward. "Catch us up."

"It is a disaster." Ephraim flung his hands up, his melodic accent making everything he said sound beautiful. "The mortals are freaking out, huddling in the jungle thinking aliens have landed and are taking over the world."

"They really think that?" Sasha laughed. "Aliens?"

"It is probably because my brother suggested it," Abel said, deadpan as he drove along dirt paths through the jungle.

"Seemed like as good an excuse as any." Ephraim chuckled. "Better than the truth."

"And where are the prisoners?" Jayesh asked.

"They're holed up in one of the hotels. They have a leader, and she doesn't want to talk to any of us. Says she will only talk to the queen. She doesn't want to hear that we haven't had a queen for a few thousand years."

"We brought her with us." Sasha gestured at Alísun and Alexander squished in beside her.

"What?" Ephraim turned in his seat, regarding Alísun for the brief moment it took to sense the mantle of power in her presence. With a grin, he turned back to his brother, whistling a happy tune. "We got us a queen, Abe. Everything might turn out all right after all."

"I noticed that when she got off the jet, brother. If you shut up once in a while, you might learn something."

"How have we kept this off the news?" Sasha asked. "I half expected helicopters and camera crews to be on this place like flies on honey."

"No power," Abel said, as if that explained it all.

Ephraim shook his head. "One of the old ones came up out of the sea, like some creature from the deep, screeching like a banshee. After that, anything with a computer system up and died. No lights. No phones. No, nothing. All the rich people cars don't work, and their phones don't either. Nothing that was here before is getting off this island after all that screaming."

"Sounds like an EMP blast," Quinn said, hanging over Sasha's shoulder. "Probably not a bad thing for the time being."

"Maybe it will give us an opportunity to deal with the situation before the Senate gets wind of it."

"The hotel has power. They have those solar panels on the roof." Abel made a sharp turn down a narrow path. "It blazes like the sun at night. I don't think they know how to turn all the lights off."

"When can we approach the hotel?" Alísun asked, clutching her Complement's hand. "I feel responsible for these poor people. After so many years cut off from their power, they must be overwhelmed."

"Well, they have it now." Abel shuddered.

Ephraim nodded, picking up his brother's stilted conversation to fill in the blanks. "We think after they escaped the prison island, they found somewhere else to recuperate. Another island, perhaps. Now, they are stronger, and their power has returned, but I do not think their minds have healed yet."

"Physical damage heals quickly," Alísun murmured, looking out into the jungle. "The deeper scars we can't see will take much longer."

"We will regroup at camp with the full team and go from there," Ephraim said. "We can attempt to make contact at the hotel tomorrow morning." He turned to face the queen. "I sure hope their leader will speak with you, madam. Otherwise, I don't know how this will end."

Sasha was eager to reconnect with the other members of her team. Since she'd returned to Sterling Tower, she hadn't had a chance to work with them in recent months. She much preferred being out in the field and not cooped up at Soma, unable to contribute much. This operation, though, this was right up their alley. It was their job to round up all the escaped Immortals on San Salvador Island and get them whatever help they needed. She just hoped that wouldn't involve actually hunting them down or using her weapon.

Abel drove along a gravel road circling a huge freshwater lake, stopping on the other side where they had set up a camp for those who had survived the arrival of the Immortals. The locals were holed up in their homes and villages, staying far away from the tourist areas and hotels.

Sasha could imagine how crowded the beaches must have been when the Immortals came ashore. It must have been a terrifying sight to behold—on both sides.

"It was a blood bath when they arrived." Ephraim pointed toward the largest tent. "We had to set up a makeshift hospital for the injured. We got here as quickly as we could, but the first couple of days were violent. We lost a lot of people. Whole families just gone."

"How many?" Santi asked, scrambling out of the back.

"Forty injured, more than a hundred dead. All of them terrified." Abel shook his head. "I wish there was a way to set them at ease."

"I can do something about that. I'll be at the hospital if anyone needs me." Santi grabbed her gear, kissed Quinn on the cheek, and set off to do what she could for those most affected by the situation. Her calming influence would be put to good use there.

"Be careful," Quinn called after her. "Don't overdo it."

"I won't." She turned, walking backwards. "You worry too much."

"Someone has to." Quinn shook his head, laughing. He watched her go and then turned to Sasha. "We should have brought Dad. We're going to need every mortal here to believe they were caught up in some freak accident."

"We have Roman." Sasha grabbed her duffle bag from the Jeep. "His gift isn't like Daniel's, but he can mesmerize a whole group at a time and talk them into remembering events in a way that will make sense to them."

Quinn nodded. "Perfect. Let's get settled and I'll do my best work tonight when everyone is sleeping."

"Peaceful dreams will go a long way to help the injured get through this."

"Where's our tent?" Jayesh asked.

"We're on the ground by the lake." Abel led them through the sprawling camp.

"We left the tents for the families." Ephraim walked beside Jayesh.

"Call everyone together. It's time to figure out our next moves."

"Sasha!"

Sasha turned at the familiar voice. "Wren!" She ran to meet her friend. Wren was older, but she was the only other woman on their team of assassins. She was the mama hen of the group, but she was also kind of scary.

"Missed you, little girl." She wrapped her arms around Sasha, squeezing her tight. "You get enough of the easy life in that tower of yours?"

"I'm so ready to get back to work." Sasha fell in step beside Wren as they made their way down to the campfire by the shore. "It was wonderful to be home with family and to get to see my friends' bonding ceremony, but I'm glad to be back."

Sasha loved her team. The six of them were like a family. A family of assassins who had all gone through the same brutal training Sasha had, only at a much older age. She was the baby of the group.

"Little sis." A stocky man with the widest shoulders she'd ever seen stood from his seat on an old tree stump. Holding his arms wide, he caught Sasha up in a sweaty hug.

"Roman." She hugged him back. "I missed you the most, just don't tell the others because I told them the same thing." Roman was exactly that. An ancient Roman soldier who had never stopped being a soldier of one kind or another. In many ways, he reminded her of her father.

"Finally, the whole family is back." Roman led them over to the smoldering fire pit where there were plenty of makeshift seats. Sasha and Jayesh sat on a felled log, making the introductions all around.

Roman leapt to his feet again to give the queen a formal bow. "My mother spoke of you often, my queen." He held a hand over his heart. "She and my father were there at the sack of Carthage when you were taken prisoner. They feared you and the Scholar were killed. They will be happy to know that was not the case."

"Your mother was Laelia and your father, Magnus, right?" Alísun gave his hand an affectionate squeeze. "I remember them fondly."

Roman touched a hand over his heart again. "They will be honored to know you remember them."

"Enough pleasantries." Jayesh stretched his legs out toward the cooling fire pit. "Give us a full report so we know what we're dealing with."

Roman returned to his seat with a weary sigh. "It is very sad, my friend. These Immortals are confused and frightened. From what I have been able to tell, they have no notion of how much time has passed during their imprisonment. They do not yet realize the world they once knew has passed them by. I fear when they finally realize it, they will be inconsolable. And very ... very angry."

CHAPTER 11

Allie | Sterling Tower | February

Allie thumbed through her sketchbook, studying the drawings she'd made the previous night. Leaning against Aidan, she gave a satisfied sigh, snuggling up close to his side on the couch. These quiet nights at home together were rare. Even rarer still for them both to be home with nothing to do on a non-sleeping night when their Syntrophos partners were busy with their own lives.

"What are you studying?" Aidan flipped through playlists on his phone and landed on his favorite *Paganini's Twenty-Four Caprices*.

"Dream scribbles." Allie reached for her glass of wine, enjoying the music. "I need to compare them to my actual visions waiting in the wings."

Aidan set his book on the arm of the sofa, moving to drape an arm around her, so he could see her drawings.

"Anything potentially scary in there?" He eyed the page of fuzzy drawings shrouded in shadows. "Is that Marcus?" He pointed at a vague profile sketch.

"Don't know. It could be anyone, but he does play a significant role in my dreams these days."

"Hey, little one." Liam's booming voice shattered their

peaceful evening. "I brought ice cream and cookies." He sauntered into the kitchen, making himself at home.

"Hey Liam." Allie scowled at her brother rummaging through her drawers for spoons. "What brings you here so late?"

"Liv is hosting a sleepover for Kahlynn and her screaming little minion friends. I managed to escape." He moved to set a bag of chocolate peanut butter chip cookies on the coffee table. "I'll be a dead man when I go home, but I'll be a dead man who managed to keep his hearing to the very last." He handed Allie a pint of chocolate ice cream and moved into the living room to sit on the couch, right between Allie and Aidan.

Aidan just managed to move out of the way before Liam sat on him. "All right, guess I'm moving to the chair," Aidan grumbled.

"Oh, hey Aidan, didn't see you there." Liam dipped a spoon into his pint of strawberry.

"I can take a hint." Aidan stood, retrieving his book and glass of wine.

"Sorry." Allie tilted her head back with a smile. "I did ask him to help me with the whole needing you too much thing."

Aidan grinned, leaning down to take a bite of her ice cream. "It is a wonderful thing to be needed." He kissed her nose, his lips cold from the ice cream. "But we probably do need to learn to function better as individuals."

"That was the general idea. Seems like a bad one right now."

"I'll be at Naomi's if you need me. She's on a date, so I'll take advantage of the quiet at her place." Aidan gave her a quick peck on the cheek.

"Oh? Who's she on a date with?" Allie's eyes widened

at the idea. She would get so much more Aidan time if his Syntrophos found a new relationship.

Aidan scratched his head. "Yeah, not sure." He turned to Liam much too quickly. "Thanks for crashing my date."

"Any time." Liam licked the cookie crumbs from his spoon and reached for a fistful of cookies to crumble into his ice cream.

"You've been around Allie too long." Aidan rolled his eyes, leaving them to their evening.

"Love you, babe." Allie tossed her sketchbook aside in favor of her ice cream.

"Love you too." He winked. "Study those visions, Allie. Don't let them pile up another day."

"Yes, Mom." Allie waved him away with her spoon.

"Night." Aidan stepped through the door into the hallway, leaving her with her brother.

"Real subtle." Allie tucked her feet under her, grabbing a row of cookies from the rapidly diminishing bag.

"I'm here to perform a service. It's wonderful being in love, little one—even if it is with my nephew—but you have to make sure your relationship is healthy enough to handle a little space from time to time."

"Which is the only reason I'm not taking your snacks and kicking you out right now."

"You can't keep him under your thumb forever."

"I know, and I don't want to smother him." She set her half-eaten ice cream on the coffee table. "This is so much harder than it should be. Can't we learn to function as individuals together?"

"I'm not even going to dignify that with a response."

"I know you have a point. Darius stays close to me, but he also manages our investigations on a level no one else could achieve. He has a purpose here. Aidan deserves the same opportunity to do his part."

"So, you will send him on an assignment?"

"Maybe a close one." Allie reached for her spoon. "Just for practice until we're both ready for it."

"You're never going to be ready for it if you don't push yourself out of your comfort zone. It's the same problem you had when you were kids, and you couldn't sleep without him by your side to keep the dreams away. And you learned to control that how?"

"By pushing through and putting my big girl PJs on and sleeping by myself until I could control the dreams myself."

"And this time?" Liam pressed.

"I'm going to do the same thing. Small steps every day until we're not so co-dependent." She stuck her tongue out at him.

"Now about those visions?"

An hour later, Allie sat on the sofa alone, relaxing her rigid focus until the ghost-like visions she fought to keep at bay wandered the living room at will. Some grew in detail, their surroundings becoming more defined. Others stayed vague and indistinct, not ready for her attention just yet.

A familiar spectral figure fought for her attention. Red hair flaming like a beacon. "Oh good, it's Gift-Allie." She rolled her eyes at herself. She'd seen this version of herself in the past. She came to her in dreams when she was younger. Now, the decidedly un-funny version of herself pushed and shoved through the crowd to stand in front of Allie, arms crossed over her chest.

"Fine." Allie sighed, letting the last of her control slip

away. A chorus of voices shouted for her attention. "I took you off mute, say what you need to say before I lose my sanity." Allie grabbed her wine glass and took a big gulp to steel herself for whatever Gift-Allie had to say.

"You're not paying attention." She growled.

"What do you call this?" Allie spread her arms wide.

"You're getting lazy." Gift-Allie glared at her.

"Fine, what am I missing?" Allie let her eyes wander around the room. Visions scrambled on top of each other, vying for her attention. She had let it pile up too much lately. It was like an inbox with more email than she could reasonably be expected to wade through.

"Okay, you're right." She finally relented. "Show me what has your knickers all in a twist."

Gift-Allie pointed across the room where a group of shadows lingered near the floor-to-ceiling windows. "Focus."

Taking a deep breath, Allie pushed some of the other shadows and wispy figures back into her peripheral vision. She would study them later once they had fully formed.

Massive oak trees morphed into existence, their green leaves just beginning to take shape after a long winter. Sunlight dappled the hard-packed earth beneath the canopy.

Allie lost herself to the vision, pacing across her living room until the hardwood floors faded to the red-clay ground where grass had long refused to grow.

She knew that Georgia red dirt well, but this place was none she'd ever seen before.

The rich dark clay was a vibrant orangy-red.

"Stained with blood," she heard herself whisper.

Allie turned in a circle, chills sweeping down her spine as a white plantation-style house grew from the mist.

Sweeping lawns stretched out in all directions from the beautiful mansion. But these grounds were tainted with the blood of those who had trained here.

"Focus." Gift-Allie stepped up beside her, pointing away from the house. She could just make out a high brick wall surrounding the property.

Her eyes told her everything she saw was beautiful, but her power also told her this place was not just a home. It was a prison.

"It can't touch us." Gift-Allie stared at her with vacant eyes.

"Well, what the heck does that mean?" Allie demanded, but her gift faded into a golden mist.

The dappled sunlight vanished, and all that remained was a golden circle of light surrounding her like an embrace. The light so brilliant, she could hardly see the figure walking toward her.

Allie shielded her eyes from the blazing light, like molten hot gold. Familiar laughter filled her ears.

"Aidan?" She took a step forward. She would know the sound of his voice anywhere. She could just make out the width of his shoulders and the glint of his smile.

"What is this?" She searched for clues, but this was different from all the other waking visions she'd ever had.

In her experience, they were often vague and indistinct until she gave them her full attention. Just like with the plantation house, once she focused, the details came into view. She didn't yet know what it meant, but that would come in time. Other visions were tinged with the green light of her power, an indication that she needed to pay attention to a vital clue that would set her on the right path. Others came and went with various levels of detail and sounds.

This was none of those things, which meant it was

something new. And new things were never easy to decipher when it came to Allie's Clairvoyance.

The golden light burst into an explosion that left her momentarily blind. She caught a brief glimpse of a tall man facing away from her. His arms reaching out for something she couldn't see. And then it was gone.

The light faded until Allie stood alone at the center of her living room, an overwhelming sense of loss and loneliness tugging at her soul.

She was certain she'd just seen a vision of Aidan, but what could it mean?

CHAPTER 12

Aidan | Sterling Tower | March

"You think you can get a hit on me, Mate?" Ezra taunted his Syntrophos, dodging Wes's quarterstaff, stabbing his own into the mat and spinning away from his opponent in a move Aidan hadn't been able to teach anyone else.

"Stop jumping around like a chimpanzee in a tree and fight like you're supposed to." Wes leaned into a crouch, preparing to pounce.

"Hey, defense is defense. It doesn't matter how I move as long as you can't touch me with that stick of yours. Wow, that sounded dirty." Ezra's laughter had Aidan shaking his head.

"Marriage agrees with them." Naomi circled the mat, studying their students with a practiced eye. She liked the progress she saw in them. So did Aidan.

Aidan stepped between the sparring Syntrophos. "It seems Graham has had a positive effect on both of you." It was crazy how laser focused Ezra was since he'd completed his bond with Graham. He was stronger and faster and more powerful than he had ever been before. It was becoming clear to everyone that Ezra was the anchor in their relationship. But even Wes was stronger than he was before. And he would be stronger still once he bonded with his own Complement.

"My husband is the best." Ezra bowed to his Syntrophos, barely breathing hard from his workout. "He's so good with Wes and the weirdness of our relationship."

"Weird is the keyword there." Wes lowered his quarterstaff. "But I'm happy for us. We're an odd little family, and I haven't had that in a long time."

Aidan shrugged out of his t-shirt, taking up a quarterstaff from the wall of weapons at their corner of the massive gym. All across the room, students worked with their teachers and trainers just as Aidan worked with his Syntrophos.

His and Naomi's role as their teacher had continued naturally from their time with the Milan Initiative. Of course, their methods had changed, and all of their students were flourishing here at Soma. With the absence of a few. Rowan and Spencer, along with Rowan's Complement had left Soma only days after the takeover. It was for the best. The others could never forget the torture those two had inflicted on them during their time with the Initiative. Aidan only hoped they'd found peace somewhere else far, far away from Marcus and anyone else who would use them for their power.

"Wes, you're with me." Naomi took up her weapon, and Aidan faced off with Ezra.

"You've come a long way from the gangly kid who didn't know the difference between a dagger and a sword." Aidan sank into a defensive crouch, waiting for Ezra to make his move.

"Of course, I know that now." Ezra rolled his eyes, shifting his staff as he launched his attack, landing the blow behind Aidan's knee. "The dagger is the short, pointy one."

Aidan locked his staff behind Ezra's jumping back to avoid tripping as his opponent intended. He grinned and the two lost themselves to blow after blow, their wooden staves cracking against each other, echoing across the gym.

"Mr. McBrien? May I have a word?" a young woman called from the side of the mat.

Aidan pulled himself from the sparring match, shaking off the adrenaline a really good fight always gave him. "Good job, Ez." He returned his staff to the wall. "Work on your forms with Naomi and Wes." He clapped him on the back and went to retrieve his shirt from the floor.

His skin glistened with a sheen of sweat, and his breath was labored from the intensity of the match. Ezra was indeed improving if he could even give Aidan a run for his money.

"How can I help you, Miss...?" Aidan tugged the shirt over his head. He recognized the teacher, but he still couldn't put names with faces yet.

"Gloria." She cast her eyes down at the mat, unable to meet his gaze. Aidan took a step back from her to give her some space.

"Of course, Gloria." Aidan nodded. He remembered her now. Gloria and her Complement worked with some of the younger teens, helping those who'd had little to no training before coming to Soma.

"My husband and I teach a large class. We're kind of overwhelmed with students these days, so it's hard to give everyone the attention they need."

Aidan crossed his arms over his chest, nodding. "I can speak to the board, and I'm sure we can find someone to assist you."

"Oh, no, that's not necessary." Her cheeks flushed. "We

teach a very basic course to prep students for more rigorous training. It's just...we have two students that need some special attention. I can't quite put my finger on it but they're different. More powerful than most of our students. I'm not sure we're giving them everything they need. I was wondering if they might be a better fit for one of your classes?"

Aidan nodded. He knew where this was going. He'd had conversations just like this several times now. "What are their names?"

"Haylee and Jason. Haylee is eighteen and Jason is seventeen, but something has changed for them recently. I don't understand it. They're suddenly inseparable. It's very strange."

Most Immortals didn't understand the Syntrophos bond, and it wasn't something any of them were prepared to broadcast to all of Soma. Over the last six months, Syntrophos pairs had popped up here and there among the students in residence. He supposed it was to be expected when a large group of young Immortals lived and worked together. For generations, the young trained at home with their families and didn't venture out into the world to gather in large numbers with their peers.

Now that they were all together, bonds were forming up all around them. Pilar had already brought four new pairs of Syntrophos into their ranks, and it looked as if she would have another pair joining her soon.

"Are they here?" Aidan glanced around the gym.

"Follow me." Gloria tossed her dark hair over her shoulder and led him across the gym where her class was gathered for basic sparring instruction with her husband. She waved the boy and girl over, and Aidan quickly picked up on their bond. Others would sense it as something unusual, but most wouldn't immediately recognize it as a bond.

"Not to worry, I have just the right class for them." Aidan gave them a reassuring smile.

Jason reached for Haylee's hand. "We don't want to be separated."

"And you won't be, I promise. Would you come with me?"

The two exchanged a look that spoke volumes, communicating with each other in that way only Syntrophos could. Hesitantly, they nodded, and Aidan wondered how long they'd managed to hide their bond from their teachers.

He leaned toward them, his mouth tilting up in a half smile. "You can come back if you hate it." He winked and they visibly relaxed.

"Gloria, thank you for bringing this to my attention. We need more teachers like you at Soma."

She gave him a flustered smile and reached for her students, wishing them well and murmuring words of encouragement.

"Where will you take us, sir?" Jason stood with his hands clasped behind his back.

"We're just going to go peek in on another class and see if you like it." Aidan led them to the nearest exit. All across the gym, others were taking notice of him taking notice of Haylee and Jason. He knew how people saw him. Boyfriend to their First Princess. He was a curiosity. Something to gossip about.

He didn't care about all that. Let them talk. It would all work out in the end. Whenever Allie got her head screwed on right.

"You're really powerful," Haylee blurted when they stepped into the quiet hallway.

"So are you two." Aidan forced a smile, guiding them to the elevators. Pilar would kill him, but he wasn't in the mood for explaining all the ins and outs of Syntrophos. That was what her class was for and it just started.

"What are we?" Jason asked, refusing to step onto the waiting elevator until Aidan answered him.

"Hop on and I'll give you the short version." Aidan stepped back, giving them what little space he could to get away from him. It had been a long time since Aidan had dealt with that particular reaction to his power.

With a sigh, the doors closed, and he launched into an explanation of what Syntrophos were.

"So it's completely normal?" Haylee's shoulders slumped in relief as she stepped off the elevator a few life-altering moments later.

"It's a rare kind of bond, but it's normal for those who have it." Aidan took the quickest route to Pilar's classroom, knocking on the door before he peeked inside. "I have a surprise."

"Don't tell me it's another one?" Pilar glanced up from her seat at the head of a semi-circle of students. Eight of them. They would join his class once they were up to speed. And eventually, his army would grow to include some or all of them.

"Congratulations, it's a girl ... and a boy." Aidan grinned, holding the door wider for Haylee and Jason. "They are newly bonded and very confused."

Murmurs of sympathy rose up among the others.

"Then they're in the right place." Pilar stood, grabbing a pair of chairs to add to their semi-circle.

"My job here is done." Aidan sighed, turning to Haylee and Jason. "You're in good hands with Pilar."

"Thank you." Haylee chanced a smile as she studied the

others, no doubt sensing their similar bonds and feeling relieved they were no longer alone.

Backing out of the room, Aidan turned toward the gym. He enjoyed teaching here at Soma, continuing the work that began, however misguided, with the Milan Initiative. He just worried he was growing complacent.

Was he losing his edge? All while Marcus was out there, growing more and more powerful. Aidan was without a doubt Allie's equal and her Complement—even if she didn't recognize him yet. He had a duty to her and to their people. He just wasn't sure where that duty might take him.

CHAPTER 13

Sasha | San Salvador Island | March

Sasha and Wren took the lead, walking down the long drive to the massive high-rise hotel the prisoners had commandeered for themselves. There was an air of foulness about the place that just didn't sit right with Sasha. Maybe it was the piercing silence in a place that should be crowded with people. Either way, it was off-putting.

Staring down the barrel of her MK-556, she kept her marker set on the front door of the building, waiting for an emissary to come meet them.

"There is something twisted about this place," Wren murmured, not taking her eye from her scope.

"I feel it too." Sasha motioned for the rest of their team to close in as they neared the front entrance. They were a team of six, but they didn't need large numbers to handle big situations. If they wanted, they could slip inside unawares and start picking them off one by one, but these people didn't deserve that. At least not all of them.

"Santi, you with me, girl?"

"Yep, right behind you ready to roll." Santi's special gift might be the difference between success and failure today. She could offer them a sense of peace that would likely help ease them into trusting Sasha and her team. They just had to be cautious in the extreme.

The prisoners could prove to be dangerous, but they believed the vast majority of them were victims of the Coalition. They had to remember that when dealing with them.

"Hey Ephraim, how about putting out some *non*-threatening vibes?" Sasha kept her voice low and even.

"Sorry. This place gives me the willies." Ephraim gave a shudder and some of the tension rolling off him subsided. Ephraim generated some pretty intense pheromones—mostly warning signs to other Immortals to back off. Not the vibe they needed today.

"That's better." Ephraim also guarded Alísun and Alexander, letting his pheromones mask their overwhelming presence.

Quinn moved right beside her, his own weapon focused and at the ready. His gift for controlling others with a command would be invaluable if things got out of hand. But the last thing Sasha wanted to do today was shoot someone who hadn't really done anything wrong.

As one, the group paused when the front doors opened, and a lone Immortal came to greet them. He was unarmed, but Sasha didn't trust it. He had to be the oldest Immortal she'd ever met. Even older than the Scholar. Tall and lanky with dark skin and gray-streaked braids down to his waist. As unthreatening as this man appeared, his power was likely a weapon. Probably the likes of which Sasha had never seen.

"The Lady Xera will not speak with you." The man stood before the doors, as if to bar them all by himself.

Sasha had no doubt he could do just that.

"What is your name, sir?" Wren asked, lowering her

weapon just enough to show they were willing to speak peacefully.

"I am not a sir." He stood like a soldier, his hands behind his back. "I am Leandro."

"Leandro, I am Sasha and this is Wren." Sasha lowered her weapon a fraction. "We just want to talk."

"You are touched by the sun, Lady Sasha." He nodded, as if to tell her to go on.

"Well, I am no Lady, but I would gladly speak with your Lady Xera if I may. We only want to help you."

"You are touched by the sun." He gave a respectful nod of his head.

"I don't know what that means, but I believe we have a great deal we could learn from each other."

"I am afraid my Lady will only speak with her queen." He turned to go back inside.

"We have brought the queen with us," Sasha called after him.

"Where is she?" He peered past her, searching for Alísun. It occurred to her that he might even recognize her. The weight of just how many years these poor people had lost really hit her in that moment.

"Leandro?" Alísun took a step forward, clutching Alexander's hand. "Is that really you?" Her face broke into the most brilliant smile Sasha had ever seen from the stern queen.

"Little Alí?" The man's hard exterior began to crack, but he seemed confused.

"It's me." Alísun took a few hesitant steps forward before she flung her arms around the older man.

"But ... where is your mother?"

"She and father died a very long time ago." Alísun

pulled back, holding Leandro's hands in hers. "She always said you were her most loyal soldier."

"Dead?" He frowned. "It cannot be. She has named you her heir?" He turned to Alexander, giving him a once over. "And it seems the Scholar is now our king?" His frown deepened. "This is all so confusing."

Sasha felt sorry for him, but something was ... off about all of it.

Alísun nodded, gripping his hands tight. "I would be honored to meet your Lady Xera if she will see me and my friends."

"Of course, your Majesty." Leandro gave a formal bow. "The one touched by the sun may accompany you and our king. The others may wait just inside this strange building."

"What does that mean?" Sasha lowered her weapon again. She ran a hand over the golden streaks of her hair. She'd heard such murmurings before—that the gold of her hair marked her as some sort of nobility—but when Leandro said it, it seemed to imply much more.

Alísun turned toward her, leaning in to whisper, "It means you are descended from the highest of Indriell nobility."

"Come this way, Majesties." Leandro stepped back toward the entrance and fumbled with the glass doors.

Sasha followed, slinging her rifle over her shoulder. Her hand rested on the hilt of her assassin's blade holstered at her hip.

"Be careful, Sasha," Jayesh followed her inside. She knew he didn't like her going further without him, but he also sounded certain she could take care of herself.

"Yeah, watch your six, bestie." Wren didn't sound nearly as certain.

The sense of wrongness increased once they were

inside. Jayesh and the others stayed in the lobby while Sasha followed the royals into what was once the hotel banquet hall. Now, it was basically a campsite, complete with a fire pit they'd dragged in from the pool and parked by an open window.

Didn't they know there were hundreds of rooms on the upper floors? Surely, they'd at least found the stairs if they hadn't figured out the elevator yet.

"Leandro?" A musical voice carried across the room, but Sasha couldn't tell who had spoken. The room was full of unwashed bodies and bedrolls lay scattered across the floor. The pungent odors of cooked fish, campfire, and too many humans was overwhelming.

They hadn't even bothered to set up tables for seating. Several ancient Immortals lounged on the floor around a central figure.

A powerful force seemed to radiate behind Sasha. A smile tugged at her mouth as she let Santi's gift fill her with a sense of peace. She hoped the prisoners would let her comfort them as well.

"Who have you brought?" The figure rose like Venus rising from the sea in a Botticelli painting. She was beautiful despite the tattered dress she wore and the layers of filth covering her golden tawny skin, nearly the color of Sasha's. Her dirty hair fell in a tangled mass of chestnut brown waves down her back. She was very old, yet her years did not show like they did with Alísun and the Scholar, or even Leandro. She appeared not much older than Sasha.

"I have brought our queen, my Lady." Leandro sank into a deep bow before the willowy woman.

"Eiselynn?" Blank staring eyes searched the room. "Is that you, my friend?"

"I am her daughter." Alísun managed in hardly more

than a whisper as she approached the blind woman. "My mother and father passed a very long time ago."

"Strange." The woman's head titled in a bird-like gesture. "May I?" She lifted her hands, stepping toward Alísun.

"Of course, you may." Alísun's voice sounded somewhat stronger, but it was clear to Sasha the great queen was shook. She reached a hand back, grasping for Alexander's as the Lady Xera ran her fingertips over the queen's face.

Xera's face puckered into a deep frown, and she staggered away from Alísun.

"I do not understand." The strange woman shook her head, sinking back to the floor, as if she could no longer stand. "Please sit, your Majesties. Tell me what news you have of the war. Of our daughter, Lecia?"

"Lecia?" Alísun moved to sit beside the Lady. "Now, there's a name I have not heard in a long time."

"I left her in the care of my Syntrophos when I was taken. He would never let anything happen to her."

"She lived well beyond the last days of the Great War, though I'm afraid I have no news of what's become of her since. She did have a daughter—"

"A daughter?" Xera scowled. "I do not understand. Lecia is just a girl." A delicate hand fluttered across her youthful brow.

"How were you blinded, Lady Xera?" Alexander asked in a firm voice, sharing another look with his Complement that did not give Sasha the warm fuzzies.

"Those vile creatures on the island prison. They must have taken my eyes a hundred times before my sight failed to return. My eyes healed, but I am left in darkness, though of late, it seems to have enhanced my other senses now that my power has been restored." She turned her avian-like gaze on Sasha. "Why have you brought an assassin into our presence?"

"We weren't certain what to expect." Alexander spoke for his wife. "The queen must be protected, no matter what."

"Of course." Xera dipped her head into a slight bow. "It is only natural for the First Princess to become queen in her mother's stead."

Judging by the way others deferred to her, Sasha surmised this woman once stood among the highest ranking nobility of Indriell and was unused to bowing to anyone.

Alísun took Xera's hand, giving it a gentle squeeze. "How long were you there on the island?"

Sasha sucked in a breath, realizing at that moment why there was such a sense of wrongness about these people.

"Many years. Too long, but I am eager to get back to my life. My daughter will need me, and I must find my Complement. Vitor was severely wounded in battle. He wasn't with me the day I was taken. He will be lost without me. And if my daughter has a daughter, then I have missed much."

None of them had a clue how long they were imprisoned on that island. Sasha's eyes burned with tears for them. The time they had lost was devastating.

"Xera." Alísun turned to gaze across the room at the dozens of Immortals hanging on her every word. "All of you. I am so sorry for what has been done to you." She shared a heartbreaking look with her Complement before she went on. "I am afraid I have some startling news for you. I believe you were on that island for far, far longer than any of you realize."

Alísun paused, as if searching for the right words. "Am I

correct that you were all taken during the war with the Enlightened?"

"Yes. Has the war finally ended? You speak of it as if it has passed." Xera's voice grew excited with this news, and her people began murmuring amongst themselves.

"Yes. The Great War is over." The queen took a deep breath as a cheer of victory erupted around the room. The ancient Immortals celebrated with back slapping hugs and enormous smiles.

Alísun waited patiently for the din to die down before she lowered the boom.

"My mother and father were executed at the hands of the Enlightened. My mother had already named me heir when I was very young. Not long after they passed, we were able to bring an end to the war." Tears slipped down the queen's face. "But that was more than ... seven *thousand* years ago." She dropped her head as if speaking the words aloud had cost a piece of her soul. Alexander kept his hand locked around hers to give her comfort and courage.

"It cannot be," Xera whispered as alarmed whispering buzzed around them and more than a few Immortals sank to their knees. "My daughter. My Complement and Syntrophos ... I am their anchor. What? How?" Xera's blind eyes seemed to search for answers to questions she couldn't comprehend enough to express.

"I do not know how such a thing could happen." Alísun's voice wavered. "But I do know how you feel on some level. I was also a captive for more than a thousand years. I lost my daughter during that time. And so much that I will never get back. I promise you all, I will make this right for you."

"I cannot hear any more." Xera lifted a shaky hand. "Not yet." She took a great gulp of air before she continued.

"We have seen how much the world has changed and it frightens us."

Sasha feared this small resort island was just the tip of the iceberg for these poor people. They would need a quiet, safe place to go until they were ready for the modern world. Maybe this resort was the right place for them. At least for now.

"Your Majesty?" Sasha spoke in the silence.

"Yes, Sasha?" Queen Alísun turned to her, tears glistening on her face.

"Would it be okay if my team shows them the rooms upstairs? We can help them find all the things they need right here in the hotel."

"Yes, thank you. That would be wonderful. I think clean clothes, baths, beds, and food are the immediate priorities." Alísun's gaze wandered over to the fire pit, where signs of cooked fish seemed to be the only evidence that they had eaten recently.

"Leandro? Will you go with Lady Sasha and see what she has to show us?" Xera tilted her head toward her right-hand man.

"Yes, my Lady." Leandro gave a bow and followed Sasha from the room.

"How far have you explored here, Leandro?" Sasha asked when they stepped into the lobby outside the ballroom.

"We came in from the strange small lake that lacks fish into the large room. We have not ventured elsewhere. We have been very ... tired. Like we have only just woken from a long sleep."

Sasha laid a hand on his arm. "It will be okay. You are with friends now, and we will help you. I'm going to show you some things, and you just let me know if it gets to be too much." She guided him to the elevator bank and pressed the button to call the car.

The old man nodded, looking like he'd aged a thousand years in the last moments. Seven thousand, to be more exact.

Chapter 14

Allie | Sterling Tower | March

"The aldermen are up to something, Allie. I can feel it." Graham paced the length of the penthouse living room.

Allie pulled herself away from the newest set of building plans she'd received just that afternoon. Construction on the lower floors would begin soon, and she was nervous about letting a mortal construction crew into the building, but it had to be done.

"Shouldn't you still be on your honeymoon, Graham? I know you guys couldn't actually take a vacation, but you two should be in a happy little bubble somewhere not caring about the rest of the world."

"I can't shake this feeling." Graham stood with his hands on his hips, glaring at her in a way few would dare these days. But that was Graham. He had never felt intimidated by her power like so many others their age did.

"Okay, but can you be more specific?" Allie watched him return to his pacing, the twin spheres of his gift racing around the living room to keep up with his nervous steps.

Finally, Graham flopped onto the chair across from her. "I don't know. I'm too far removed from the League. I think I need to get back in there."

Allie dropped her construction documents. "You want to go back to the League of Ancients? No. It's too dangerous." She was already putting Sasha and Quinn and their teams at risk. She didn't like treating her friends like pawns on a chessboard.

"I'm useless here, Allie." Graham sighed, fidgeting in his chair. "I know I can't go back to being the Grim in the New England League. I left too suddenly, and I refused the job Marcus offered me, but I know how they operate. I could find a way back in."

Allie shook her head. "It's too dangerous. Don't think for a second that Marcus doesn't know you're here with me. That man doesn't miss anything."

"What if I infiltrated the League all over again?" Graham leaned forward, his elbows on his knees. "What if I worked my way back in under a new guise and find out what they're up to? I have the tools to disguise myself. I might not fool Marcus into accepting me again, but I could get close to another group. Those who know what his next moves will be."

Allie spent a great deal of her time worrying about all Marcus Servius had planned for a future of his making. Since taking control of Soma and taking on the responsibility for everyone under its roof, she'd made it her business to stay abreast of every move Marcus made. Yet, the League of Ancients was a dark spot in her intel.

"See, you think it's a good idea too." Graham scooted to the edge of his chair.

"I didn't say that."

"No, but your face did."

Allie scowled at him. "It's not fair you know my face so well."

"Tell me it's a bad idea then."

Allie reached for her iced coffee on the white marble-topped table beside the white leather couch she was never comfortable sitting on. She really needed to Allie-proof the decor in her sister's old apartment.

"I won't say it wouldn't be nice to have more information on the League's activities, I just question whether you're the right person for the job since Marcus knows you so well."

"He knows the Grim. I never let that man get to know the real me. He's never even seen my face—no one in the League has. We hide behind masks, remember? And my masks are far more than they realize."

"But he knows your real name."

"Doesn't matter. I would use a fake name anyway."

"Well ... I don't like it." Allie stuck her tongue out at him.

"The boy has a point." Darius came down the hall from the gym, a towel draped around his bare neck. "Names can be easily changed. Especially when you're me with a talent for forgery."

"The *boy* has a name." Graham threw his empty water bottle at Darius. "And he's right, Allie. Dare can give me a whole new identity, and I can create an online history for my new name. These people hate technology. They won't know to be suspicious. Aunt Gabrielle and I can make a new mask that will conceal my identity, and she can help me create a new persona."

"You're not going back." Allie tucked her bare feet under her and leaned forward. "At least not to Salem. And not alone, either."

"What are you suggesting?"

"What did you tell me they call Porcia?" The woman who raised Livia was not at all what Allie had expected of

Marcus' Complement. For one, she was on their side, working to undermine all of her husband's plans. And she reminded Allie so much of Livia. It was good to see nature verses nurture at play within her sister. Marcus made her a hard woman, but Porcia had taught her how to love.

"The Lady Gray," Graham said. "Her persona is an enigma within the League. They respect her but fear her as a woman as influential as the Master. She is able to move among the different groups with ease."

"So Porcia could likely return without causing a stir?"

"We were careful to never be seen together. It's nothing for her to disappear for long periods of time only to resurface somewhere new out of the blue."

"Perhaps she could accompany you?" Allie chewed on her bottom lip.

"It's a good idea." Darius moved to sit beside her. "We need to know what the whole point of the League is for Marcus' end game. He didn't create it for nothing."

"The aldermen will play an essential role in whatever new world Marcus has planned." Graham's eyes held a determined edge that reminded her of Emma. There was no arguing with either of them once they had their minds set on something.

"How will you prove your membership? Or do you plan to go through that awful initiation again?"

"The Lady Gray will vouch for me. I can easily become part of her entourage. We have been studying the Savannah Alderman and a few others who might prove useful."

Allie nodded. "Make a plan. Though I'm not saying yes yet," she added in a rush. "I just want to know what we're sending you in there to do before we do it."

"I can work with that." A weight seemed to vanish from Graham's shoulders. "This is important, Allie. I can feel it."

Something in his eyes told her he needed this. To do his part. Like it or not, her equals all had roles to play. This was Graham's, and she had to give him whatever he needed to see it done.

Allie's vision went green, a sure sign that she was on the right path. She would still check with Chloe before fully agreeing to this mad plan, but Graham was right; they needed to know more about the League of Ancients.

"Okay, make a solid plan and name your team," Allie relented. She worried for Graham like she would for a little brother, but he was more than capable of handling this.

"Porcia, Uncle Lou and Aunt Gabrielle, and Brooks." Graham rattled off their names without pause. "They each know the League and how to operate within it."

"Do you really think Ezra is going to be okay staying home while you go risk your neck out there?" Allie smiled, thinking of Graham's feisty Complement and what his reaction might be if he were left behind.

"Probably not." Graham grinned. "It will be harder to get him inside, but he would be an asset."

"They." Darius scribbled all their names on a pad of paper. He would have a lot of documents to forge in the creation of so many new identities, but they would be the best forgeries. Not even the most sophisticated mortal equipment or detective could tell Darius' fakes from the real thing. "Syntrophos come as a package. Wes won't be left behind either."

"Sasha and Quinn have gone on different missions before," Allie said. "It can't be easy, but sometimes it's necessary."

"When's the last time we were more than ten feet apart?" Darius gave her a knowing look. "If I had to leave for an indefinite period, what would you do?"

"Sneak into your luggage." Allie sighed. "I guess it's different for Quinn and Sasha."

"Something about their long history makes it easier for them." Darius shrugged. "Maybe we'll all get there in time, but most of us are still too new at this to handle separation as well as they do."

"They don't like it, but it's somehow not as painful for them as it is for Wes and Ezra." Graham's eyes glazed over as he went to that place where he communicated with his gift. "I'll try to talk Ezra into staying behind, but if he doesn't go for it, Wes will have to come too."

"I'll get their papers ready just in case." Darius added their names to his list.

Fuzzy shapes shifted in Allie's peripheral vision. Things she needed to pay attention to before they piled up again. "I need to consult my crystal ball but make your plans." She sighed, releasing her visions to walk across her living room, letting them morph from indistinct shapes and colors into corporeal forms she would study when she was alone.

Sometimes, she felt like a mother eagle, pushing her babies out of their nest before they were truly ready to fly on their own. She needed to trust her chicks more.

Who was she kidding? She was more like a chicken clucking around the yard than a brave eagle trying to soar.

"Where did she go?" Graham's laughter drew her out of her reflection.

"She's looking at her visions when she makes that face." Darius chuckled. "It's best to ignore her muttering."

"What?" Allie blinked, returning to the moment with her friends.

"You said something about clucking like a chicken."

Graham grinned. "I think we need to hear the rest of whatever conversation you just had with yourself."

"Shut it." She threw her pillow at him. "You should know by now I'm weird."

"Weird and sorely missed when I'm gone." Graham stood to go. "This needs to happen sooner rather than later."

"Duly noted." Allie picked up her construction documents, wondering how it would all ever get done.

Chapter 15

Allie | Sterling Tower | March

"You ready for this, Chlo?" Allie, Darius, and Chloe stepped off the elevator in the lobby to meet with Raina, the walker on duty for the afternoon. "It's your first big diplomatic meeting with the Stupid-Senate. I should warn you. It will be like talking to a pile of bricks."

"A pile of bricks would be more amenable than our current Senate." Aidan reached for Allie's hand as she joined him and Navid for the meeting.

"I still don't know why I'm here." Chloe tucked a strand of purple hair behind her ear. Dressed in dark jeans and a simple black sweater, she looked like the old Chloe—except for the tattoos, the dragon at her side, and the brow piercing.

"I love how she thinks she's not useful." Allie shook her head.

Their meeting with the Senate representatives would take place in Peidmont Park across the street. The idiot-squad wanted access to Sterling Tower but it wasn't happening. Not on her watch.

"I think I once told you, you were going to be an amazing blend of warrior and scholar. Was I wrong?" Allie searched Chloe's face. She didn't like how little Chloe thought of her contributions. She still didn't see how much she'd grown.

"I don't know about the amazing part, but you were right about the rest." Chloe absently scratched at Fei Long's ears.

"Hey, Fei Long?" Allie crouched down beside the smallish dragon. "Do you think you could be a little fiercer looking today?"

The dragon growled, flames shooting from her tiny nostrils. Today, she was the size of a golden retriever, darting around Chloe's feet like she was just excited to go out for a walk.

"Oh, don't be insulted." Chloe rolled her eyes. "She just meant bigger and intimidating. You know, more you."

Allie stepped back as Fei Long seemed to stand up to her full height until her head bumped the top of the double doors. She had to stoop to pass through the doors, and her rear end got stuck on the way out.

"Yeah, we probably should have done that outside." Chloe sighed. "Give her a push with your foot, Aidan."

"I don't think so. She's got really sharp-looking teeth."

"She's a big baby."

"Scary looking baby." Allie marveled at the dragon stuck in her door. With a wiggle of her butt, Fei Long slid through the opening, her tail and wings flicking behind her. She let out a deep roar, breathing fire across the vast plain of the dream world.

"She's going to want to fly before we go back inside." Chloe watched Fei Long waiting patiently for Navid and Raina to escort them into Piedmont Park. Since making Sterling Tower her permanent residence, Allie had cleared a small corner of the park for their use. Briggs used his gift to repel mortals from this area, so they could be assured of a private corner whenever they needed it.

"Are we completely certain mortals can't see Fei Long?" Aidan asked.

"Hundred percent." Chloe fell in step beside Allie. "And she's kind of scared of them anyway, so if one gets too close, she's going to vanish."

"I kind of want to go first so I can see the look on the Senate losers' faces when they see her." Allie giggled. "Once they're gone, she can go for a quick flight right here in the dream world." The wide open plain was grassy and a little spooky with dark skies and that not quite real quality that always reminded Allie of a painting.

"Can I ride your dragon, Chloe?" Raina bobbed along beside them in the tall grass, ever oblivious and a little disturbing in her child-like exuberance.

"You'll have to ask Fei Long if she's in the mood for it. She normally doesn't even let me ride her."

"We're buds." Raina skipped ahead to talk to the dragon.

Aidan and Darius moved to flank Allie and Chloe as they reached the park where Navid and Raina would open a rift to let them out.

"Remember, if they try anything funny at all, you're coming right back inside." Darius stood with his arms crossed over his chest, like he didn't approve of any of this. "We're not taking any chances."

"I know the drill, Dare." He was even more protective than her own mother. "You do know I could just melt them where they stand with my solar zappy."

"You need better names for your gifts." Aidan shook his head. "How about your solar glare? That sounds a lot more intimidating."

"I like zappy." She shrugged. "That's the kind of thing that makes them underestimate me. They can roll their eyes at my silly names when their faces are melting off their skulls."

"Good point." Aidan chuckled. "Don't ever change, babe." He elbowed her.

"Don't intend to, big guy." She winked at him.

"Enough flirting." Darius glared at them both. "She needs to focus. We don't know what the Senate had planned for this visit."

"Jeez Allie, what did you do with my irresponsible brother? This one's turned into a wet blanket."

"It makes me nervous when she's outside the protection of Sterling Tower." Darius pinched the bridge of his nose, looking just like Naeemah when her children were trying her patience.

"I think between the five of us, we can keep her safe. She's pretty capable on her own, you know."

"Of course, she is. I just don't like it. It makes my Syntrophos vibes all wonky when she could be in danger."

"Now you sound like Allie."

"Enough, you three." Chloe raised her voice. "You're all like an old married thrupple."

"Ew. No." Allie wrinkled her nose. "Take it back, Chloe."

"I just call it like I see it." She grinned and whistled for Fei Long to return to her side.

"They're here, Allie." Navid stood beside the opening the barrier he and Raina created.

"How many did they bring?" She peeked through the rift into the park.

"Looks like four or five, but it could be more," Raina said over her shoulder, her arms held high to keep the rift open. "I imagine they have several out of sight so be vigilant, your Princesship." The girl cackled, completely in her own little world.

Stepping outside the boundaries of Sterling Tower for this first time in weeks felt like escaping a prison. Part of Allie wanted to run and not look back. But the Senate was literally knocking on her door, and she had about a thousand kids counting on her.

"First Princess." A woman dressed in a boring gray skirt and matching suit jacket gave a curt nod, the only concession the Senate would make regarding Allie's position. To them, she was First Princess in name only.

Allie felt underdressed in her messy bun, jeans, and fuzzy teal sweater with her favorite black boots. Her sai were tucked into the tops of her boots, and she had at least a dozen other weapons on her person. She was what Immortal princesses looked like in the modern world.

"Who am I talking to?" Allie moved to sit on a park bench with Aidan and Darius. She didn't miss the shade the five Senate reps where throwing at Fei Long.

Chloe and Fei Long stood behind Allie with Navid and Raina on either end of the bench.

"We are the senior undersecretary to the chairman." The woman lifted her chin with her Complement standing beside her, armed to the teeth with a variety of assault weapons and mob gear. What did these people expect from her?

"And your names are…?" Allie waited patiently. When it came to the elite members of their government, they liked to prop themselves up with titles that meant little to Allie.

"Ida Jameson." The woman smoothed a hand over her skirt as her husband stepped forward. "Ivar Jameson." The tall, broad-shouldered man sent out some fairly intimidating Viking vibes.

"Ida and Ivar, that's easy to remember." Allie gestured to the bench across from her. "Please have a seat." She turned to the other three. "And your friends?"

"This is our secretary, Valentina and Patricia Navarro."

"Wait, you two are secretary to the chairman of the senate. And you two are their secretary?" Allie nodded. "That's a great idea. I never thought of getting a secretary for my secretary. The poor thing is swamped."

Focus, Allie. Aidan's thoughts echoed in the far reaches of her mind. They didn't often speak this way, but in these moments, it was an important tool.

Right. Sorry! Allie turned to the fifth member of their party. "And you, sir?" She kept a bright tone in her voice, but this man was much older and wiser. Everything about him demanded respect.

"Just a bodyguard, Princess." He gave her a nod.

"Not just a bodyguard, daughter." Navid leaned forward. "Ibrahim is a dream walker. A very old, talented walker who hasn't shown his face in our world in many long years."

"I have made a point to stay out of the conflict brewing in the dream world." Ibrahim stood, stoic with his hands folded in front of him.

"The conflict has been resolved." Allie tilted her head to the side. "But you would know that if you could enter the dream world. Has something blocked you?" Allie knew very well that a walker could no sooner resist entering the dream world than she could resist a slice of chocolate cake. If this man had abstained for so many years, there was a reason, and it wasn't will power.

"If I recall correctly, and I do," Navid began, "Ibrahim

has been … indisposed for at least a century. I was called to perform the punishment myself."

"I see." Allie nodded. Her Judgment gift came to her through her mother's ancestral line, all the way back to King Ían who obtained the gift from Marcus, known then as Lord Teigan. But the manifestation of her Judgment gift was heavily influenced by her father's own brand of judgment. Navid could determine a person's guilt and sentence them to a coma-like state for a period of time equal to the crime committed. That would be the only thing that could keep a dream walker from the dreamworld for any length of time.

"I was paroled for good behavior." The walker shrugged, leaving Allie to wonder who woke him up.

"Not important." Ivar raised his voice. "Introductions have been made. We have important matters to discuss with the princess."

"It does matter." Navid's cool gaze focused on Ivar and Ida. "You bring a walker to my daughter's doorstep, and we take that as a strategic move against her."

"It's okay, Dad." Allie nodded. "Let's just hear them out." That was all she intended to do anyway. Listen and then return to business as usual.

Chapter 16

Allie | Sterling Tower | Early March

"For three months, the Chief Justice and the Chairman of the International Senate have repeatedly asked you to grant us access to Sterling Tower and the young residents inside. It is vital that we are able to assist our young Immortals through the most trying times of their lives. We are no longer asking permission to enter Sterling Tower."

Allie held up her hand to halt Ida's yammering. "Let me stop you right there. We have been more than willing to work with the Senate, yet you refuse to compromise. You've ignored my orders for an immediate election to fill the vacant Chief Justice seat. Yet you expect me to stand back and let you take control of Sterling Tower?"

"You have no authority in this modern world, Princess. The Senate has declared you and your family figureheads and nothing more."

Allie called on the mantle of power her grandmother had bequeathed to her not so long ago, letting it slide around her like a cloak. It wasn't something she lorded over people. She didn't like the way most reacted to it.

Ida Jameson's eyes widened as the full force of Allie's authority hit her. Allie leaned forward. "Your Senate is broken, Ida. Until the people have the right to vote for those they wish to lead them, there is no official Senate. Your Chairman is trying to fill a role they were never elected to."

"Yet you do the same here." Ida spread her hands wide.

"Soma is a school, not a seat of government. It is a safe haven for all who wish to be here. Anyone who would like to leave at any given time is free to do so. But as long as these children and young adults are under my roof, they will be protected—even if that means from their own government."

"It is not *your* roof, my dear," Ivar said, his voice like steel. "You seized Sterling Tower illegally, and you have no right to preside over it. You are all squatters."

"I hold a deed to the building along with a bill of sale from the original owner that says otherwise."

"How is that possible?" Ida frowned. "You staged an illegal coup."

"Funny, I recall Chairman Thomas calling it a 'mere corporate takeover.' But if you must know, the previous legal owner of Sterling Tower was my sister, Livia McBrien. When she decided she no longer wanted to lead Soma, she sold the building and the business it houses to me. I can submit the documentation if you'd like. It's all legitimate, even by mortal standards of property laws."

Ida's face paled in the cool afternoon sunlight as she grappled for a response.

"So, it seems I do have the right to bar you from my property as Soma is and always has been a private institute."

"Perhaps," Ida relented. "But this is not the mortal world, my dear. I realize you were born and raised among them, but our government does not operate the same. When it comes to the lives and safety of our young, we can and will step in to supervise. I believe your friend Sasha McBrien is well acquainted with the Senate's supervision in her training."

Be nice, Allie, she's baiting you. Aidan's warning helped sooth her anger, but only just.

Allie pasted on a smile. "Well, Ida, that is where we will have to agree to disagree. You say you're advocating for young Immortals, but I say you're abusing them for their abilities that far outstrip yours. We are a powerful generation. Like it or not, I am the First Princess of Indriell and with that comes an ancient mantle of power you couldn't possibly understand." Allie stood, ready to leave this pointless conversation.

"Please sit for a moment longer, your Majesty," Valentina spoke for the first time. "Allow us to deliver our message from the acting Chief Justice."

"Fine. Get to it then." Allie returned to her seat between Aidan and Darius, grateful for their calming presence.

Valentina nodded to her Complement, and Patricia stepped forward with a thick document.

Patricia cleared her throat. "I will read the highlights, but you will receive a copy."

"Lovely." Allie restrained herself from rolling her eyes.

"The First Princess will allow a council of eight Senate representatives to reside inside Sterling Tower where they will oversee all Awakenings and Provings hence forth."

"We will consider it." Allie folded her arms across her chest. "Is that all?"

"There's quite a bit more, madame. May I get through it quickly?"

"If you never call me madame again, yes." Allie nodded, and Patricia stifled a laugh.

"The First Princess will step down from running Soma until she is of an age to handle such a responsibility, or another leader is assigned in her stead." Patricia looked up from her document. "That would likely be after your Proving, many years from now."

"Of course, years and years." Allie nodded, grateful the Senate didn't know that would likely happen in a few short months.

Patricia flipped a page and continued reading. "The First Princess may appoint a leader of her choosing to direct Soma for the interim. This leader must be one of the eight Senate officials provided to assist in the running of Soma."

Allie snorted a laugh. "I'm sorry, go on." She shook her head. That one was never going to happen.

"The First Princess will have her dream walkers remove the dream world barrier surrounding Sterling Tower, and she will submit a dossier for each student and employee residing within Sterling Tower. Any student deemed a warrior will be allowed to stay and train if they so choose. Any student deemed a Scholar, Tech or Prophet will be transferred to another facility specializing in such training. Any Syntrophos pairs will return to the Milan Initiative immediately. As a gesture of good faith, this will exclude the First Princess and her own Syntrophos, one Darius McBrien.

"Any young Complements who have not yet Proven must submit a petition to the Senate for approval before any legal bonding ceremonies can occur. All currently bonded young Immortals must report in person to the appointed Senate officials upon their arrival at Sterling Tower.

"Failure to comply to these requests will result in further action from the Senate. Measures that will include forceful removal of the First Princess and her family should they fail to cooperate with the governing Senate of the Immortal community, up to and including imprisonment.

"In exchange for her cooperation on all these matters, the Senate is thrilled to offer the First Princess a voice within our government as a Junior Senator, representing the youngest generations."

Patricia lowered her copy of the document and stepped back. Allie noted a hint of apology in her eyes. If she wasn't mistaken, this woman and her Complement were on her side.

"Is that everything?" Allie sighed.

"For the moment." Ivar nodded. "The Chairman would like an immediate response of your cooperation on these matters."

I could be inclined to agree to some of their demands as my own gesture of good faith, but I'm afraid to even give them that much. Allie shared a look with Aidan, noting the look of defiance in Darius' eyes. It was clear what her Syntrophos thought, and she agreed with him. This was absolute bull.

We need to buy some time to discuss this, but you're right about possibly hosting the reps, but that's probably going to set us up for a huge headache and another distraction we cannot afford.

I think I have to agree to step aside until my Proving. But I will appoint someone I trust to take the reins.

That might be the only thing we could give them today since we know it won't be long.

Allie nodded. "Very well. That's quite a list you have. I am willing to consider hosting your representatives, but I will need to discuss it with my own council first.

"However, once we have reached an agreement on these issues, I am willing to step down as leader of Soma until I have Proven. I believe that is a reasonable request, but I will choose my successor from those I trust to care for the best interests of our students.

"The dream world barrier isn't going anywhere. That is a hard no." Allie shook her head.

"Then we must—" Ida tried to interject, but with nothing more than a look from Allie, her words died in her throat.

"I gave your secretary my undivided attention, and you will do the same while I am speaking." Allie sounded just like her grandmother, and it would have been funny in any other situation.

"The point of Soma is to protect our students from those who would abuse their power. There will be no dossiers on my students, but if our employees are willing, they can submit their own dossiers. I will be happy to provide one for myself that the Senate may use however they like." Not that it would be a complete dossier by any stretch of the imagination, and judging by the look on Ivar's face, they knew it.

"Soma is equipped to teach all manner of young Immortals, whether they be warriors, Scholars, or any other kind of Immortal, so all students who wish to stay will stay.

"If any of the Syntrophos pairs would like to return to the Milan Initiative, they are perfectly free to do so, but I will never force them. The same for all young Complements as well. If they choose to submit a petition for approval, I will be the first to provide them with the materials to do so. I hope you see a pattern of free will emerging here because that is the whole point of our endeavors with Soma.

"As for the offer of junior Senator, I respectfully decline on the grounds of it not being legal. All Senators are voted into office by their constituents. Should I ever wish to become a Senator, junior or otherwise, I will run for official election."

Allie rose from her seat. "We will be in touch regarding the few terms we will be considering."

"Alexis Carmichael." Ida's voice fell over them like ice water. "We are not done here."

"What more is there to discuss?" Allie remained standing.

"There is the matter of the dragon." Ida glared daggers at Fei Long. "This is an unprecedented gift. This young woman is registered as Chloe Long, natural daughter of Jin Jing and Ming Lao Long. A Scholar. But this gift has not been registered, and it's clearly not a scholarly gift. I'm afraid she will have to come with us."

"I'm afraid she won't," Chloe and Allie said at the same time.

"Your dragon could be a reckless and dangerous weapon. She must be photographed and her markings recorded for legal purposes."

With a snort that sounded an awful lot like "Bye," Fei Long faded into a puff of golden mist.

"She's a coward as you can see." Chloe stood with her arms folded in front of her, her eyes blazing gold and fiery. She stepped forward with a menacing smile on her face. "Besides, I'm the one with the power. She's just a manifestation of it." A stream of white-hot fire shot from Chloe's mouth, setting the grass at Ida's feet on fire. "Use that in your report."

"We are done here. But rest assured, you will hear from me again." Allie turned to leave, shoving Chloe in front of Darius and Aidan. Raina waited to let them into the dreamworld while Navid stood guard between the representatives and Allie's group.

Chloe stepped around her, letting out another stream of fire, creating a burning wall to hold the diplomats at bay as they retreated into the barrier.

"What a load of crap," Allie muttered as she followed Raina back into the building. "And that dreamwalker dude." She fumed. "That was a threat if I ever saw one. Where did he even come from?"

"We're going to need a backup of some sort." Aidan stood at the glass doors waiting for Navid and Raina to finish sealing them off from the outside world again. "They're going to send that Ibrahim guy in to force their way in."

"And we'll be ready for them." Chloe snorted, a puff of black smoke and sulfur filling the air. "Did I ever tell you guys Dahlia created the perfect security system for us back in Westbrook?"

"Do tell." Allie linked her arm through Chloe's as they made their way back into the building and across the lobby to the elevator bank.

"She's going to get us all murdered in our sleep, isn't she?" Darius shook his head.

"I heard that." Allie held the elevator doors for them.

"He isn't wrong." Aidan sighed. "We're going to need to up our defensive game because my people are never going back to the Milan Initiative." Aidan punched the button for her office floor.

As the doors closed, Allie leaned against the wall. "I just upped the ante in this war with the Senate, didn't I?"

"Doesn't matter." Chloe shrugged. "We're just not going to cower in fear of their threats. If they want to bring it, let them. We're more than capable of fighting back."

"What can Dahlia do?" Darius asked. "We're going to need a strong backup if they have a walker who can just waltz in."

"He will still have to get past us." Navid said. "And Ibrahim has a lot to answer for with the elder dream walkers. For the time being, I'll increase the number of walkers we have on duty.

"I'll get Dahlia on backup right away," Chloe said. "She can make the building itself refuse them entry. Even if they do get through the dream world, if the building doesn't recognize them, they aren't getting in."

"I knew I liked that girl." Allie grinned, reaching to meet Chloe's fist bump.

CHAPTER 17

Allie | Sterling Tower | Late March

"Will they buy it?" Allie stared at the elaborate mask in her hands. It was heavy with layers of various metals, cogs, and wheels. There were even working gears and old-fashioned goggles to cover the eyes. She stared at Graham seated across from her at the conference table, uncertainty in her eyes. "You don't think these are a bit over the top?" She gestured at the beautiful masks he'd laid out on the table. She hadn't realized he'd set up a forge in the warehouse, much less that he'd been busy with this project since shortly after his arrival at Soma.

He shook his head. The twin spheres of his gift zoomed around her office; little balls of blue light taking in all the data they could absorb from her conversation with Graham and their surroundings. With his gift at work, there was no detail Graham missed. He was the right man for the job he wanted to take on.

"I don't like it." Livia scowled at her mother seated beside her, refusing to look at the masks Graham had spent weeks crafting.

"No surprise there, dear." Porcia patted her arm in a patronizing gesture.

"This is kind of the League's thing." Graham shrugged. "The more outlandish and mysterious the persona and costumes, the better." He gathered the dark brown leather leash that attached to the matching collar he would wear around his neck.

The stained leather of the collar made Allie shudder. It looked like it was crusted with dried blood. The cogs and wheels of the clasp whirred with an unseen energy source, and Allie surmised the old-fashioned mechanics were some kind of lock only the Lady Gray could control—and hopefully Graham, too.

"It feels extreme. You're planning to take on the persona of a ..." She was at a loss for words.

"A circus freak? Something to gawk at?" Yes, that's the idea." Graham ran the length of leather through his hands. The leash he would willingly wear. "The more demeaning the costume, the more I will be underestimated. They have no respect for technology and even less for Immortals like me. They'll see me as nothing more than a curiosity belonging to the Lady Gray—an accessory for her eccentric costume. While all eyes are on her, and with the power Quinn and I have given this mask, I can fly under the radar, seen, but ignored."

"He is correct." Porcia took the mask from Allie's hands. Her dark features clouded with some emotion Allie couldn't identify. "These people view themselves as elite nobility. They have proven time and again to underestimate technologically gifted Immortals like Graham. I intend to see it as their downfall."

"Mom, I don't like you going back into that world without me," Livia said, lifting one of the other masks from the table. Adorned in an array of blue peacock feathers, it was a beautiful piece of art.

"Darling, I've done this many times. I know how to manipulate the League because I know how to play their game. I don't need a bodyguard."

"I still feel like I'm sending you both into the lion's den for too little gain." Allie tapped her pen against the black onyx table.

"You kind of are but we've volunteered." Graham flashed her a mischievous smile.

"I don't like it either, Allie, but this is the best use of his gifts." Livia finally leaned forward to examine the other masks on the table.

"I know you're more than capable of doing this, Graham. I just worry." Allie dropped her pen on the table with a clatter. "What about these other masks? Did you really make them all?" There was something sinister about their rictus grins and vacant eyes that gave her the heebie-jeebies, but she couldn't deny the artistry was exquisite.

"Yes, with Aunt Gabrielle's help. Each is imbued with a layer of protection and power that can't be detected. The Jester's mask calls for attention, allowing Brooks the opportunity to keep all eyes on him while I do what I need right under the League's nose."

Allie shook her head in amazement. "Your creative gifts are like nothing I've ever seen before." She studied the peacock mask with an artist's eye. She couldn't tell what powers it possessed, but she knew it and the others would protect Graham and his team through the insane task they had taken on for themselves.

"We've got this, Allie," Graham assured her.

"She's going to worry no matter how prepared you are," Livia said in a bored tone. "We all will, even though you're well prepared for this mission. But what do you think you'll find on this Alderman's estate? Why him?"

"His name is Albert Abernathy." Graham propped his elbows on the table. "He's a relic of the old south and prides himself on being the consummate gentleman, but he's kind of a weirdo. A bit of an outcast the other League communities disdain."

"He's an oddly peculiar man I've had my eye on for months." Porcia sat back in the dark leather chair like it was a Grecian throne. "On the surface, he's the least of Marcus' aldermen. The others view him as a social climbing oaf with strange predilections. The members he presides over are small in number, but equally baffling in their behavior."

"And you think that's all a ploy?" Allie asked.

"Marcus does love to outsmart his foes as well as his allies." Porcia smiled. "He prefers to be the only one in the room who knows what's really happening." She tapped her index finger against the table, lost in thought for a moment. "I have a strong hunch that Marcus has hidden his most important henchman behind a ruse." Porcia's thoughtful and direct manner reminded Allie so much of her sister it set her at ease. She still didn't know Porcia very well, but this was the woman who'd raised Livia, and she trusted her sister implicitly.

"You think this man is that important to Marcus' end game?" Livia asked. "For whatever he's been working toward for only God knows how long?"

Porcia nodded. "I do."

"Your mother and I have been studying all the aldermen since we've been here," Graham said to Livia. "Along with Aunt Gabrielle and Uncle Lou and the rest of our team. We're all but certain that this Albert Abernathy is the key to whatever Marcus has planned next. If our skills can help you beat him, Allie, this is where we need to be."

Porcia leaned forward, placing her delicate elbows on

the table. "If we can infiltrate Abernathy's headquarters, we will be that much closer to getting ahead of Marcus before he does something that can't be undone. I believe we are running out of time."

"So do I." Allie sighed. "When do you want to leave, and what do you need from us?"

"We'll leave tonight." Graham gathered his masks. "The sooner the better because it will take time to infiltrate his circle and gain his trust."

"What happens if you're caught? I'd feel better if you had an exit plan in place." Allie knew she needed to chill and let him do his thing. It just killed her that she had to sit here where it was safe while other people took the risks for her. Because of her. *What kind of child of prophecy hides in her tower? Some bad ass princess I've turned out to be.*

"We've got this, Allie." Graham and Porcia stood to leave. "I will get a message to you once we're settled."

"Well ... good luck." Her words sounded about as empty and hollow as she felt watching him walk out that door to put himself at risk.

"Stop it," Livia said as soon as the others had gone.

"Stop what?" Allie pushed away from the table, turning to gaze out the window.

The door behind her opened and Darius and Aidan waltzed into her office. She could see their reflections in the window.

"She's probably sitting there thinking: this is *all my fault* and *I should be the one taking the risks*," Darius said in a high-pitched Allie voice.

"You don't even know what we're talking about, and I do not sound like that." Allie sat back in her chair, folding her hands in her lap as she slowly turned back to face the room. "But he's right. This is just one more thing that makes me feel useless, stuck inside my tower while everyone else does the hard work."

"You're the only one who sees it that way, Lex." Aidan sank down into a chair, shuffling through a pile of paperwork he'd brought with him. "But who's the one doing the hard work this time?" He nudged her playfully with the toe of his boot.

"Graham. He's asked to infiltrate the League of Ancients Community in Savannah."

"He'll be good for that." Darius slumped into a chair beside Allie. "He's basically James Bond without the cool car and good taste in clothes."

"She worries too much." Livia rose to go. "Distract her with something non-work related, boys." She gave Allie's chair a whirl and left to go find her husband and daughter.

"I hate to agree with my brother, but he's got a point. No one thinks you're hiding up in your tower except you." Darius gave a massive yawn and a stretch.

"And maybe Marcus," Allie muttered under her breath.

"You not getting enough sleep, Dare?" Aidan's eyes widened.

"What, you worried about my health?"

"No, just wondering if you're feeling all right. You know you just agreed with me, right?"

"Shut it." Darius rolled his eyes. "How are my kiddos doing? You didn't rough them up this afternoon, did you?" he asked. He'd taken to teaching a class for a select few ... troublemakers who had a knack for the art of forgery, much like Darius himself. He was great with them, but they'd spent the afternoon with Aidan for a little tough love, strength training session they were sorely in need of.

"They're a bunch of little punks, but we're making

progress." Aidan closed his eyes with a shake of his head. "Slow progress."

For the last several weeks, Aidan and Allie had started helping Darius get his "kiddos" into fighting shape. They were woefully undertrained.

"They have no manners." Allie snorted.

"Of course, they don't. Their parents were never around to teach them any." All four of Darius' "kids" were under seventeen and were products of Soma's underage "school" once known as the Fold. They grew up in the system with very little contact with their families and not nearly enough real training.

"They're just getting used to spending more time with their parents, and they're acting out a bit. Give them some time to adjust. They all had a rotten upbringing."

"Well, you're doing a great job with them, Dare." Allie leaned her head back against the headrest, wishing it was time to go home, but hers wasn't the kind of job that ended at five o'clock every day.

"Yeah, even I have to admit it." Aidan grinned. "You speak delinquent, so they trust you in a way they haven't trusted any of their other teachers. It's cute."

"Hey, speaking of people doing a great job," Allie interjected before Darius had a chance to respond to Aidan's baiting. "That list of demands the Senate gave me needs our attention. I need to attempt to show some cooperation, so let's revisit that bit about me stepping down until my Proving." Just the mention of the word had Allie's stomach tied in knots. She wasn't ready, but she could feel it coming toward her like a freight train with faulty brakes. The idea of stepping down worried her, but at the same time, she needed to focus, or she was going to fail. And if she failed her Proving, she could lose her power, and then what would happen to Soma?

"Not it." Darius pushed away from the conference table, moving his chair over to the tall windows looking out over Peidmont Park.

"You can't call not it," Aidan said.

"Why not? It's like shotgun. He who calls "not it" first is out of the running for whatever she's trying to pull here."

"Why not? Because I was going to call not it." Aidan pushed his chair back, rolling to a stop beside Darius. "We're both calling not it, babe."

Allie crab walked her chair over to theirs. "Then if all three of us aren't it, who can we push this on to? Livia would sooner shoot me in the face than take on her old role."

"And I don't think Jayesh would even consider it again," Aidan added.

"We need fresh meat." Allie sighed.

"What about Liam?" Darius suggested.

"I've thought of that." Allie propped her feet up against the glass window. "He would be great, but I don't know how Liv would feel about it."

"Well, I've got somewhere else to be." Darius shot out of his chair. "Good luck with that."

"Tell Pilar I said hello." Allie waved over her shoulder, watching the people down below walking along the sidewalks and going on about their lives, never knowing what kind of monumental decisions were being made twenty floors above their heads.

"No time like the present." Aidan stood, offering her his hand.

"For what?" Allie laid her hand in his, letting him pull her up from the chair.

"Finding your replacement. I'll walk you down to Liam's classroom."

"Now?"

"Yes, now." He guided her across the room, giving her a little shove into the hall. "You're Proving soon, and I'd feel a lot better about it if you had a little less on your plate. Let's get this giant albatross off your back so you can breathe."

"Fine." Allie squeezed his hand as they walked down the hall to the elevator bank.

Allie pressed the button for the basement. Liam didn't like to teach inside if he could help it. He much preferred the Warehouse for his students. Nearly everyone in Allie's world taught at Soma now. Some more than others. Liam was one of the former. He'd taken on teaching a large group of kids Kahlynn's age, and it was about the most adorable thing Allie had ever seen.

Somewhere around the fifteenth floor, the elevator screeched to a halt and the lights went out.

"What the—" She didn't have a chance to finish her question before Aidan's warm hands hauled her up against him. His lips found hers in the darkness, and she melted into him, eager for more. He didn't often initiate such delightful activities, nor were they alone often enough to make it possible.

Allie's hands ran up the length of his body, finally sinking into the thick inky darkness of his hair. She suppressed a moan as his hands wandered up the back of her shirt.

"I can never get enough of you, Lex." He broke their kiss, trailing his lips down her throat before he buried his face in her hair. "Do you know your scent has changed over the years?"

"Has it?" she murmured, still too drunk on his kisses and his nearness to make much sense of his words.

"You're more potent now." He pressed into her, and her back flattened against the elevator wall, the handrail digging into her. "You used to smell like honey and citrus, sweet and clean. A lovely scent." His mouth grazed her earlobe. "Now, you're like that, but you smell like winter blossoms and cinnamon, too. It drives me insane."

Allie searched for his face in the darkness. Finding his lips again, she claimed his mouth, taking in his scent and searching it for new depth. "You don't taste like dirt anymore," she blurted, trying to stifle her laughter at the memory of their first discussion of such things.

Aidan's breath was warm in her face as he laughed. "I hope not."

"You've always had an earthy, woodsy scent. It's one of my favorite things about you." She laid her head against his chest, wrapping her arms around him to take in as much of him as she could get in this rare moment they never had time for. "Like cedar wood and cool spearmint."

"Is that all?" He sounded amused.

"Maybe a little eucalyptus, too, but I don't always catch it. I just know the combination is uniquely you." She tried to kiss him again, but he broke the kiss off almost immediately and put some space between them.

"We better get moving again." He reached for the elevator button. And like always, Allie reeled from the punch in the gut that was his rejection.

"Or not." Allie stopped him from pressing the button. "We can always talk to Liam later." She tried to step back into the circle of his arms so she could run her palms up his chest, but it was like he'd lost interest. "We could play hooky this evening and go home to an empty house." She sounded desperate even to her own ears. The only person she'd ever been intimate with was Aidan and not in years. Since his return, he thwarted her every single time she tried to lure him back into her arms. It left her feeling confused over his mixed signals. She knew he loved her, but she often wondered if that was enough for them.

"You have to settle things with Soma. Whether that's handing Liam the reins or someone else that's not me." Aidan stepped back and sent the elevator on its way.

"You're right." She forced a smile she didn't feel, her eyes stinging with the threat of tears. "We'll ... uh, continue this another time. Or not." She shot out of the elevator as soon as the doors opened. To her horror, the burning tears began to fall, and Aidan pulled her back onto the elevator, letting the doors close before he hit the button to hold the elevator.

"What's wrong, Allie?" He wiped the tears from her cheeks with his thumbs.

"Not a thing." She shook her head. "I don't want to talk about it."

"I'm sorry." He sighed, moving to the opposite side of the elevator. "I have a question for you, but you have to be honest with me."

"Sure." She shrugged, trying to get control of her emotions. "Whatever."

"Have you ever had a glimpse of your Complement?"

"No. You know I don't dwell on that stuff. Why do you ask?" She met his gaze, and for an instant, she saw something there that looked like guilt.

"Just curious." He gazed down at the white marble floor, refusing to look up.

"But you have." She wrapped her arms around herself, trying and failing to keep the jealousy from her voice.

"You've been seeing your Complement, and you're feeling guilty for fooling around with me when you should be looking for her."

"No, Allie. That's not it at all." He pushed away from the wall. "Believe me, there is no one else I think about. It's always you."

"Then why don't you want to be with me for more than a short make out on an elevator with a quick escape?" She was so tired of it. Something was wrong with them, and he was never going to tell her what it was.

"I need you to trust me, Lex. This is the way it has to be right now. Just please know I love you, and I'm ... doing the best I can right now." He glanced away again, defeat hanging heavily in his slumped shoulders. "I'm trying to find my way back to a version of me I can tolerate." He scrubbed a hand over his face, the scruff of his stubble rasping in the silence that hung between them. "Marcus messed with my head. You know that. Any hesitation on my part has nothing to do with you and everything to do with me.

She nodded, not feeling much better. "I don't like having secrets between us." She hit the release button on the elevator, not sure what else to say.

"We are okay." He pulled her into his arms for a brief moment before the doors opened, and they were met with a chorus of adolescent giggles as a sea of girls joined them on the elevator.

"Going up, Princess Allie?" The tallest girl reached to punch the button for the sixteenth floor.

"Not this time, girls." Aidan grabbed Allie's hand, and they darted through the closing doors to a chorus of more giggles.

Draping his arm around her, Aidan sighed. "Let's go find your brother."

Once again, Allie forced a smile and shoved unpleasant thoughts from her mind. Aidan had been through a lot in the years they'd spent apart. Especially at the hands of Marcus Servius. She doubted she would ever know exactly what happened between the man she loved and the man she despised.

Whatever he'd done to Aidan was just one more thing on the list of reasons why Marcus had to be stopped.

Walking hand in hand, Allie and Aidan stepped through the unassuming metal doors into the vibrant landscape of the Warehouse. The terrarium changed from time to time, on the whims of the old hermit who lived up on the mountain.

"Hagrid's been busy cleaning up after we got all the kids moved back inside." Allie gazed around the green hills dotted with tulips and what looked to be a new grove of birch trees near the lake.

"You know his name isn't Hagrid." Aidan moved his arm from her shoulders to her waist. "I believe it's Hal."

"He reminds me of Hagrid." She shrugged. "He's like our very own gamekeeper."

"Oh no, it looks like Liam's teaching the kids to swim." Aidan turned them toward the lake. The shoreline had morphed into a sandy beach since she was last here. And the much-used cabins along the edge of the forest looked clean and brand new.

"You don't think there's like snakes and leeches in there, do you?" Allie cringed, thinking of all the emails she was going to get from ticked off parents.

"Let's hope not.

"Does it look more like he's teaching them how to drown each other?"

"I don't even want to know." Aidan groaned. "Maybe we should ignore it. If we don't see it, it's not happening, right?"

Allie met his high five as they walked out onto the dock. She hoped her brother had a very good point to this lesson.

"Dunk her, Kahlynn!" Liam shouted, egging his students on.

"He's teaching them to spar in the water." Aidan chuckled. "We should have put a pool in the underground at home years ago. This would have been a lot of fun trying to drown Sasha when we were kids."

Allie cupped her hands around her mouth and shouted, "Liam!"

"What? Oh, hi, little one. Be with you in a minute." He turned back to his students. "Jackson, use your superior swimming skills to your advantage. Your opponent can't stay under water as long as you can. Remember that."

Allie watched the ten-year-old kid zoom under the water like a fish. He was going to be one to watch as he reached his Awakening in a few more years.

"Auntie Allie!" Kahlynn floated on her back beside her sparring partner, Kyleigh Reynolds. The two nine-year-olds were inseparable. "Ky taught me to swim backwards."

"Pay attention to your lessons, girls." Allie gave the mild reprimand, though she might have a bigger one for her brother.

"What brings you down to the Warehouse?" Liam pulled himself up onto the dock, lake water streaming down his tall form.

"What in God's name are you teaching these kids?" Allie asked, trying not to sound like a bossy boss, but technically, she was the leader of Soma, and he was one of her teachers.

"We're working on sparring techniques in an unusual fashion." He wiped the water from his face and shook out his hair, sending droplets of water in Allie's direction.

"I got the unusual part. It's the trying to drown each other part I'm not so sure we can explain to concerned parents. These kids aren't manifested yet."

"Exactly, so sue me for letting them have some fun while training. This way, I keep their attention longer, and they go home tired after a good workout."

"Just ... don't let anyone get hurt." Allie sighed.

"Kahlynn, honey, focus a little more on your grappling and a little less on chatting." He shook his head with a grin. "That kid of mine could talk the horns off a goat if it sat still long enough."

"Allie has come to talk to you about something important." Aidan gave Allie a none-to-gentle shove toward her brother.

"I'll get to it." Allie shot him a glare over her shoulder.

"Aidan." Liam eyed his nephew with pursed lips before he turned his attention back on Allie. "Always with one of your boys, aren't you?"

"They aren't boys." Allie crossed her arms over her chest and stood to her full height. All five foot, almost four inches of it.

"Until they've managed to survive for at least a thousand years, they will still be boys to me. When's the last time you performed a task without one of them underfoot?"

"I'm just going to leave you to navigate *this* task without me. Good luck, Lex." Aidan sauntered off down the dock to the trail leading around the lake.

"You know, both of them belonged to you first." Allie

moved to sit on the dock beside Liam, letting her feet dangle in the water as he barked orders at his class. None of whom were paying them the least bit of attention. "Oh, just let them have fun."

"They might be my nephews, but you're my sister. You come first." Liam nudged her with his shoulder. "You rely on them too much. It's almost like you can't function unless they're right there with you."

"It's a problem I am fully aware of and have every intention of working on. Once I figure out how to do that." Syntrophos especially struggled with the need for each other. But she and Darius still hadn't mastered the art of being apart and pursuing separate endeavors.

"You came to see me, and I really hope it wasn't to talk about boy trouble. Something on your mind, little one?"

"Yes." She let out a breath. "I have to step down from leading Soma. It's something the Senate wants me to do until my Proving. They just don't know how soon that's going to be."

"And you figure that's an easy thing you can give them to show you're cooperating?"

"Exactly. So will you do it?" She blurted, turning to him in desperation. This was a big job. One no one really wanted, considering it no longer came with a huge paycheck like it once had when Livia was in charge.

"Me? Why me?"

"You really need to ask that?"

"I guess I would have thought you'd ask Gregg or Naeemah to step up. They have so much more experience."

"As governor, they're too close to the Senate. And I've caused them enough trouble in the past. They can't become embroiled in another association with me. At least not such a public one. Besides, you were my first choice."

"Not one of your boys?" Liam arched a brow at her.

"They called 'not it' before I could ask them."

"Stupid boys." Liam shook his head. "You know you can do a lot better than my nephews, right? They're both idiots."

"Let's not talk about my Syntrophos or my boyfriend. We're talking about you taking over as director of Soma."

"I'll have to talk to Liv about it. I won't do it unless she's comfortable with it. It took her a long time to agree to let Kahlynn train here after school a few times a week. She's determined our daughter's going to have a normal childhood at a normal school." Since relocating permanently to Atlanta, Kahlynn attended a mortal elementary school with a few other day students who lived locally. It was the best thing for both Kahlynn and Livia. There would be time to increase her training in the years to come.

"And if Livia agrees, you'll take it on?"

"Temporarily. This is your gig, little one. No one is going to run this place as well as you do. You're passionate about it and everyone respects you."

"I hear a but coming."

"But you're young, and you've got to focus on yourself for a little while. And part of that means you need to break your habit."

"Habit? You say that like I've got some kind of addiction."

"You do." Liam's eyes returned to the water where his students had stopped all pretense of sparring and were actively playing now.

"And you're about to tell me exactly what my addiction is?"

"Yep. You spend too much time with your boys. You need them too much. Just like you did when you were sixteen and couldn't sleep without Aidan to keep your dreams away. You broke the habit then, and you can do it again with a little focus. It's not healthy to need them to the detriment of all your other relationships."

"You think I'm neglecting my other friends and family?"

"When's the last time you had a girls' night with Santi, Sasha, and Chloe? Or spent time with Lily and Carson, just the three of you?"

"A really long time." Allie sighed. She didn't like what he was saying, but she could see his point. "I wouldn't even know where to start." Allie studied the water swirling around her feet. The thought of putting distance into her relationships sent a wave of sadness through her. Followed by a bout of panic.

"You can start by kicking at least one of them out of your house. You have too many people living there anyway."

"I can't do that." She recoiled at the idea of having Darius or Aidan so far away.

"They can move down one floor. It would be good for Pilar and Darius to have more time together, and then maybe Aidan and Naomi could share her place."

"So, it's fine for Aidan to be close with his Syntrophos but not for me?"

"They don't have this dependency problem. They were forced to live apart for a long time. They don't wilt and die the way you and Darius do if you have to spend an afternoon apart."

"We're not *that* bad."

"Okay. What would happen if Darius had to suddenly go to California or Europe for a few weeks? How would you react?"

"I'd stow away in his luggage." Allie twisted her hands

together, nervous at the pretend idea of having her Syntrophos gone for any length of time.

“If I take on Soma for you, you’re going to deal with this problem. Start by kicking them out of your house.”

“Both of them?” Allie squirmed.

“Yes.”

“I’ll think about it.”

“You have one week. If you don’t do it by then, I’m staging an intervention. A public one you won’t like.”

“Ugh, you suck.” Allie buried her face in her hands.

“Maybe, but you also know I’m right.”

Chapter 18

Aidan | Sterling Tower | Late March

Aidan paced across Naomi's living room, trying to psych himself up for another long evening with Allie. Another evening of pushing her away when that was the last thing he wanted.

"I shouldn't have done it." His hands shook as he reached for the doorknob for the third time, letting his hand drop once again before he could actually get the stupid door open.

Then the door opened in his face and he almost came away with a bloody nose.

Naomi stepped inside, dropping her gym bag on the floor. "What are you doing lurking inside my apartment like a creeper?" She kicked the door closed behind her.

"I'm an idiot." He crossed the space between them and bent to press his forehead against her shoulder. "Tell me to stop being an idiot."

Naomi slapped the back of his head and then pulled him into her arms. "But you're allowed to be an idiot when it comes to that girl of yours." She ran a soothing hand across his back. "What happened this time?"

"I kissed her."

"Like you should, since you're kind of her boyfriend and that's your one job." She sighed. "Haven't you been working on your control? You've got to be able to at least kiss the girl without forcing the bond on her."

"Yes, but it's not improving. I thought I could handle it." He backed away from his Syntrophos and moved to sit on the red leather sofa that only Naomi could pull off in a way that didn't look cheesy.

"Tell me what happened." She came to sit beside him.

"We were in the elevator."

"Well, that was your first mistake. I told you to try nice big rooms with wide open spaces and windows. Keeps the pheromones from collecting in one small space."

"Yeah, the elevator was a dumb idea." Aidan wiped a hand over his face. "But it's like every time we're together, whether we're just talking or kissing or touching, the bond starts to well up inside me. I've been sleeping opposite days to her so I can avoid staying in her room all night. And I feel like a complete jerk every time I have to lie to her, or tell her half-truths."

"Have you thought about just ... controlling the situation?"

"What, like actually tell her? No. I could never do that." He gave his Syntrophos a horrified look.

"I don't mean it like that. Not entirely." She scooted around to face him, her legs crisscrossed in front of her. "Allie doesn't know why you're holding back, and it's causing you way too much grief."

"Understatement." Aidan's shoulders slumped. "I can't stand the look on her face when I have to put some distance between us. I can see it in her eyes. She thinks she's losing me."

"She's no closer to figuring it out than she was when we

first came back, so maybe give her some rather strong hints. This is Allie we're talking about." Naomi leaned forward. "The girl who never reacts the way you think she's going to. So, you lead her into it. Let her figure it out. She won't know or care that it's not the way we usually handle these things."

"That's not the point, Naomi. She might not see how ... disgusting a thing it is to force a Complement to see it when she isn't ready, but *I do.* I won't do that to her. No matter how long I have to wait."

"You might have to break up with her then. Just about anyone in your situation would tell you to leave and try again in a few years."

"I can't do that either." Aidan shook his head. "I can't hurt her like that ever again."

"But you're torturing yourself. When you're with her and the bond starts to form because you can't control it, it's killing you a little more each time. Allie's a stubborn girl. It may take her a lot longer than you could imagine, and you're already at the end of your rope."

"I will not force the Complement bond on her. She deserves the chance to come to the realization on her own and plan whatever kind of bonding ceremony she wants. Can you image if you were with Briggs one night, and you think you're just having some fun? And then the next thing you know, he's initiating the Complement bond with you when you're not in that place yet. No. That's the worst thing anyone could do to their Complement." The very thought of it made him ill. And the memory of the bond beginning to form when he last kissed her shamed him to no end. Why couldn't he control it?

"This isn't about me and Briggs. It's about you and Allie and that mortal brain of hers taking its sweet time to see what's right in front of her."

"You know she's probably going to scratch your face off when she finds out you're dating Briggs."

"She won't care. I don't know why he's freaked out about it. She was never that into him, and she only has eyes for you."

"She's got to be close, right?" Aidan turned to his Syntrophos, wishing she had all the answers.

"I don't know." Naomi sighed. "But you do know what she's going to say when she finally does figure it out, don't you?"

Aidan leaned back against the sofa, banging his head against the wooden frame with a dull thud. "Yeah. She's going to want to know why I didn't just tell her."

"Exactly my point."

"I'm just going to have to keep lying to her until I figure out a better approach."

"And we're back at a non-solution. Don't you have a date to get to?" Naomi checked the time on the clock in the hall.

"Yes. I'm just trying to collect myself. I have to get through tonight without another incident like this afternoon."

"You can do this. For her. And if you have to get out of there, just blame it on me. I can be the bad guy."

"I can't do that either." Aidan gave her a half smile. "You two are finally not hating each other. I don't want to mess with that."

"I'll get Pilar to call you with a fake emergency in an hour in case you need it."

"No. I can get through one night with my girlfriend. She has to be close. I can feel it. I can hold out a little longer." Aidan took a deep breath and made his way to the door. This time he managed to get it opened. "Wish me luck."

"Hey you." Allie met Aidan at the door to the penthouse they shared with Darius and occasionally Pilar. Santi and Quinn had moved out after their bonding ceremony. They had a small apartment on one of the lower floors now. Not that they were home often enough to have settled in yet.

"Hi." Aidan tugged her close for a brief moment, dropping a kiss on her cheek as he moved to shed his jacket.

"Have you eaten yet, or do you want to head down to the dining hall?" She returned to rummaging through the fridge. "I suppose I could try to make us something, but I don't know if either of us wants to open that Pandora's box again."

"Babe, as long as we live, you never have to cook ever again, unless you just really want to. And you can probably count on me to be busy that night."

"You've got yourself a deal, best boyfriend ever."

A genuine smile slid across Aidan's face as he watched her. He could handle anything if it meant staying close to Allie. "Let's just order up something from the dining hall. I don't feel like going out tonight." Truthfully, he didn't feel like going out most nights—not that out meant outside the safety of Sterling Tower. He'd rather spend every free moment with just the two of them here in their private little bubble, blocking out all the bad things coming at them from every corner. But that was a lot harder than it should be.

"Rough day at the office, honey?" She slammed the fridge closed, a half-eaten slice of cold pizza clutched between her lips. He loved the way she snacked *while* she was looking for food.

"Something like that." He kicked off his shoes and sank down onto the couch. "I'd rather just snuggle with you and eat some junk food that's bad for us."

"Music to my ears." She hopped onto the sofa next to him, munching her pizza. "What should we order? Nachos or pasta? Or wings?"

"Wings. And that horrible fried cheese stuff we like." Aidan propped his feet up on the ottoman. "And some wine."

"Oh, are we being fancy tonight?"

"If wine is your idea of fancy, then we're fancy just about every night."

"True." She dialed down to the kitchen to place their order.

Oh, get some tater tots, too. With the spicy cheesy sauce I like.

Sure, you want it with bacon and ranch? She didn't miss a beat while she was talking to the concierge.

No, I'm watching my figure.

Allie snorted at that, and Aidan quickly closed his mind to hers. There was just too much she could see in his thoughts that he couldn't explain. Not yet. He longed for the day when he could let their thoughts mingle like they used to. These days he let her in just enough so she wouldn't get too suspicious, but never for more than a few moments at a time.

As she ended the call, she tucked her feet up under her and leaned against him.

"This is nice," she murmured. "Just us."

"It is. This hardly ever happens. Where's Darius tonight?"

"He's at dinner with Pilar. I'm sure they'll be back later."

"Of course, he will. He can't stay away for more than a few hours." It didn't bother him the way they needed each other. Not like he thought it would. Knowing Allie was his Complement made her relationship with his brother a lot easier to bear. That and he wanted to get a jump on their future together. It wasn't like Darius was going to go away. Ever. The three of them were going to have to make it work. So, Aidan did whatever he could to make it easier on them.

"That's kind of a problem, isn't it?"

"What?" He looked down at her. "Darius? No. You know I get it more than most boyfriends would. I have Naomi, you know."

"Yeah, but you don't *need* her the way I need Darius. You guys can function as individuals."

"Yes, but we didn't have any other choice. We had to learn how to be independent of each other."

"Don't you think Darius and I should learn that too?"

"You will. In time." He draped his arm around her. "We had to learn the hard way. You two can take a little more time with it."

"What if that's a mistake?" She sat up, turning toward him, her eyes wide and worried.

"What's this about, Lex?"

"You don't think I need him too much?"

"Maybe." He shrugged. "But it's entirely normal for new Syntrophos to need some time to adjust to the demands of the relationship."

"It's been five years. I don't know if we can call us *new* anymore."

"Are you thinking of sending him away?"

"No, no. Nothing like that. I was thinking we might

start pushing ourselves to spend time apart. Like days rather than hours. Or maybe a single day to start with. No, maybe half a day," she rambled.

"That's not a bad idea if you're feeling up to testing your boundaries a bit."

"I think it's important," Allie hedged.

Allie was never very good at concealing her worries. Her emotions always played out across her face. Something was bothering her, and it wasn't Darius.

"What is it, Allie?" He took her hand in his.

She swallowed and looked up to meet his gaze. "Darius isn't the only one I lean on a little too much."

"You mean me?" A jolt of fear ran through him at her words.

She nodded. "I love you. I love you both, but I can't function without you. When you're gone—either of you—it's like I can't take a full breath until you return. I can't focus on anything other than that you're gone."

That was the unfulfilled Complement and Syntrophos bonds at work. She just didn't realize it yet, though it was a good sign for Aidan that she was feeling this way. They would all feel out of sorts until all the bonds were complete when Darius and Nomi found their own Complements. Allie and Aidan were Complements, but they were each anchors within their Syntrophos bonds as well, making their relationships even more complicated than anyone else realized.

"That's not necessarily a bad thing, Lex. Lots of Immortal relationships are intense." He held his breath, hoping he hadn't said too much. He desperately wanted her to see him and for them to be bonded forever, but he had to be patient. Though he wasn't above giving her a slight nudge now and then.

"Unfortunately, I'm not like most Immortals. I'm about to face my Proving and I am not ready for it."

"You'll be fine." Aidan reached to cup her face, turning her chin so he could see her eyes. "What's really bothering you?"

"I think you should move out." The words came out like a garble of nonsense, and her eyes filled with tears. "Just for a little while. I need some space to learn how to just be me. No Darius and no Aidan. Just Allie." She sucked in a breath and held it.

"You're serious?" He pulled his feet down from the ottoman and sat forward. "You want me to move out?"

"I need you too much, Aidan," she whispered. "And I'm so afraid that's going to be my downfall. It's like when we were kids, and I couldn't sleep without you. I needed to learn to face my dreams on my own. Right now, I need to learn to function without you. I need to focus on my Proving and figuring out what to do about Marcus."

"And you don't need me in the way." Aidan's tone sounded petulant and immature to his own ears.

"That's not it and you know it. Maybe I'm not saying this right, but Liam said I needed to break the habit—"

"So, I'm a bad habit? One you've been discussing with your brother?" Aidan reeled back as if she'd slapped him.

"No, this is coming out all wrong." She shook her head, resting her hand against her forehead. "I love you, Aidan. Don't lose sight of that, even if I don't have the right words to tell you how I'm feeling."

"You just can't live with me?"

"Not right now," she whispered. "I don't want anything to change between us. Except our addresses—and only by a few feet of hallway and some stairs."

"Okay." Aidan nodded, taking a deep breath. She

wasn't close. Not by a long shot. He'd fooled himself into thinking he could do this, but it was just too ... soul-crushing. "You just want to take a step back from us."

"No. That's not what I'm saying at all."

Aidan forced a smile. "I understand." He stood. "Let's start now. I'll go stay at Quinn and Santi's tonight, and we'll see each other tomorrow. Or the next day. It'll be fine." He didn't even know what he was saying. The only thought in Aidan's mind was that he had to get out of there.

"Aidan, please don't go. Not like this. I didn't mean to upset you." Allie shot to her feet, trying to get between him and the door. "Let's just have dinner and we'll forget everything I just said."

"It's okay, Allie. I do get what you're saying, and you're probably right. We should spend a little time apart." And he did get it, logically. But his heart had just taken a blow he wasn't prepared for.

"The same with Darius, too." She pleaded with her eyes, begging him to understand.

"Maybe we do need each other a little too much. It shouldn't hurt like this when your girlfriend asks you for a little more free time."

"Don't hate me." She reached for him hesitantly, regret written all over her face.

"I could never hate you, Allie. But please don't ask me to hug you right now. I can't bear it." He turned and fled the apartment, not even stopping long enough to get his shoes.

Aidan couldn't be in the same room with her right now. He was holding back the urge to bond with his Complement, but he was losing that battle. If he'd stayed a second longer, he would have failed her in the worst way possible.

He took the stairs, running down several flights, like he couldn't get away fast enough. But running from Allie wasn't going to help his situation. She wasn't ready to see him as her Complement, and she wasn't going to be ready for it any time soon. He'd let himself believe she just needed a few weeks, or months—maybe as long as a year—and it would happen for them. But what if it didn't?

Aidan had left her once because he couldn't stand her not knowing, and that time apart had been the hardest thing he'd ever done. Until this. Leaving Allie was an impossible choice, but staying was so, so much worse.

CHAPTER 19

Aidan | Sterling Tower | Late March

Aidan walked aimlessly through the building. Floor by floor. Wandering downstairs, hearing nothing but the words Allie had said.

I think you should move out.

His shoeless feet shuffled across the carpeted hallway of a residential floor. One of the floors with bigger apartments where the most talented students used to live, but Allie had moved much of the new faculty to this floor during renovations.

I should be happy. She'd just given him the perfect excuse to protect himself from the dangers of getting too close. Now, they could be together like a normal boyfriend and girlfriend without the pressures of living together and the level of intimacy that came with it.

But he was devastated—not because she'd asked for space. It was what that request represented. The timing for them to come together was all wrong. He was back to square one, and he wasn't sure he had it in him to keep going. To keep waiting for their life together to start.

"Come inside, Aidan." A familiar voice sounded behind him. "No sense in pacing up and down my hallway if something is bothering you." Emma stood in her doorway, Parker peeking out from behind her.

He hadn't even realized he'd been pacing this hall, but Emma was the one person who could advise him in this, so it was only natural his subconscious had led him to her door.

With a nod, Aidan followed her inside the small residence Emma and Daniel kept for their frequent visits to Atlanta.

"I think someone is late for his bedtime." Daniel scooped Parker up into his arms. "Not that he actually sleeps."

"Ever." Emma rolled her eyes. "I swear this kid of ours is part vampire."

Aidan stood with his hands in his pockets until Daniel closed the door to Parker's nursery.

"Sit." Emma pointed to the black leather sofa in the center of the living room.

Like a puppet, he moved to sit at her command, his mind blank.

"What's she done this time?" Emma sat beside him.

"She's never going to see me." Aidan leaned forward, letting his head fall into his hands. "I don't know if I can do this, Emma." Emma had known he and Allie were Complements even before he had. Her gift allowed her to see the Complement bonds of those around her.

"I told you coming back was going to be difficult." She laid a hand on his back. "But I also told you there was no reason not to be with her if you were prepared to wait however long it took."

"She asked me to move out."

"Did she have a reason?"

"She thinks she needs me too much. That she needs

Darius too much. It all makes perfect sense and she's right. It's probably for the best." He heaved a weary sigh. "If she were one of my Syntrophos students, I would commend her for recognizing the need for strong boundaries."

"But it's a reminder to you of just how far she is from recognizing you."

"I really thought she was close." He shook his head. "I swear I could almost feel it coming. Any day now."

"You are both so young, but circumstances seem to be accelerating everything for this generation. You see your friends coupling up all around you. It's only natural that you would be anxious for the same."

"But this is Allie we're talking about." He managed a sad smile. "I knew I was in for a long wait. But my heart ... I don't know how much more of this I can take."

Emma leaned back, tucking her feet under her. "You know what I'm going to say."

"I can't leave her." Aidan sat back, giving Emma his full attention. "I did that once, and it was awful for both of us."

"I'm not on the inside of this, so correct me if I'm wrong, but are you any less miserable?"

"I don't... yes, it is better to be with her than without."

"Despite her request, Allie is comfortable with you. She's happy with your relationship as it is."

"But she doesn't want to live with me anymore."

"That has nothing to do with you and everything to do with her need to be her own person without you and Darius sucking up everything she is."

"Ouch."

"All I mean is this. Allie is *never* going to be ready for her Complement as long as you're right there being the perfect boyfriend. Put yourself in her shoes for a minute.

She loves you. Adores you. She doesn't want anything to change because she doesn't want to lose you."

"But she doesn't have to lose me if she'd just open her eyes to the possibility." Aidan's hands balled into fists in his lap.

"In her mind, she has to be ready to give you up to receive her Complement—A Complement she has no reason to believe is you. Now tell me, would the Allie we know be willing to do that when she's perfectly happy with the way things are?"

"No," Aidan admitted reluctantly. "But how can I leave her when I know it would break her heart all over again?"

"Then don't leave her."

"You're not helping, you know that, right?"

Emma gave him a patronizing smile. "Maybe you should let her know that you're okay with moving out. Maybe you let her know you're so okay with it that she'll relax the death grip she has on this relationship she's terrified to lose, and then she'll be the one to send you away."

"Send me away?" Aidan nodded. "Like on an assignment?"

"Exactly. Then you get the distance you *both* need, but you can still be together, and no one has to get hurt."

Aidan took a deep breath, nodding again. "Okay, but how do I make that happen?"

Chapter 20

Sasha | San Salvador Island | April

"What are we going to do with them?" Wren sank down onto the sofa in the double hotel suite they'd taken for their small group. She looked as tired as Sasha felt.

None of them had slept much in the last few weeks, but for the first time, the prisoners were calm and settled. No one was freaking out about running water, reflections in mirrors, or trying to figure out how toilet paper worked. Sasha had removed the hairdryers from all the rooms the ancient Immortals were using. It had become clear after one lesson that they were not ready for hairdryers or electric lights. The generators were working for the hotel while the rest of the island was still without power. Given the fragile state of the ancients, they were choosing to use very little electricity.

"I don't know." Sasha ran a hand through her tangled hair. She needed a shower herself. And some decent sleep. Then maybe she could come up with a plan to help them. She couldn't think of Xera and her people as escaped prisoners anymore. If any of them had ever done anything wrong, they'd paid for it a hundred times over and then some.

Jayesh and Quinn stepped into the room, gently closing the door behind them. Jayesh leaned against the door looking haggard. "It's like having newborn quintuplets."

"Are yours sleeping?" Wren asked. "I got mine down about twenty minutes ago, but I can't make myself go to bed yet. One of them's going to wake up the second I do." Wren leaned her head back onto the couch, closing her eyes. "And then I'm going to have to shoot them."

"We can't keep this up." Quinn dropped down onto one of the double beds. "I thought this might be as good a place as any to help them acclimate, but they aren't getting any better." He rubbed a hand over the week's worth of beard he'd been too busy to shave. "Even the mortals out at the camp are in bad shape mentally." He and Santi had been dividing their time between the camp and the hotel, doing what they could to help both sides through this mess.

After they got the Immortals settled into rooms on the second floor—they couldn't handle the elevator, so they used the stairs for everything—Sasha and her team each took on four or five of the ancients to help them with all the things they needed. And they were a needy bunch. Sasha had to instruct them on the use of everything from towels and flushing, to sheets and pillows. It was exhausting.

"We need a few simple, super basic houses with zero distractions," Wren suggested.

"Zero distractions, yes. But I think we need a familiar location. A place they might understand," Jayesh said.

Wren snorted. "They've been locked up for thousands of years. Anything familiar has crumbled to dust by now."

Jayesh shared a look with Sasha. "Not every place."

Sasha shook her head, standing up to retrieve a bottle of water from the mini fridge. It wasn't that she hadn't had the same thought. "Don't even suggest it." She paced nervously, sipping the water she didn't really want. Her hands had started to shake, and she had to set it down on the bedside table.

Sasha sank down on the bed beside Jayesh. "I can't do it, Jay," she whispered.

"You don't have to go. I'll take them." But she clutched his hand at the thought of him leaving. Of him going there without her. "No."

"No, Sasha." Quinn's eyes widened when he realized what Jayesh meant. "You're not going back there."

"What are you guys talking about?" Wren sat forward, her eyes full of questions. "You look like he's just suggested we take them to hell and set up camp."

Sasha gave a humorless laugh, shaking her head. "You're not far off."

"Okay, tell me what's going on. Right now," Wren demanded.

"We have to take them to the Chola Valley Temple," Jayesh said.

"And where is that?" Wren scowled at him. She was the only one of their group who had not trained with Mother Raghavan.

"India," Sasha said. She couldn't say more. It wasn't allowed this side of the valley. When one went to the Chola Valley for the first time, it was without certain knowledge of the place.

"Name another location where they could recover in peace without the mortal world threatening to suffocate them?" Jayesh asked.

"You're right." A tear slid down Sasha's face, and she wiped it away. "It's the best place for them." She turned to him, her eyes full of misery. "How do we ask the Mother if we can bring them?"

"It's done. I've already asked."

"And?"

"She's expecting us in a few days."

"How long this time?" It was a loaded question, but he knew what she meant.

"Just a few months."

"All right," Sasha said, resolved. "If we're doing it, then let's get some sleep. We're going to need it."

"I'll go tell Santi where we're going." Quinn moved to leave.

"You're not going." Sasha wouldn't allow it. She'd miss her Syntrophos, but she couldn't ask him to follow her into the valley.

"That's not how this relationship works, Sash. If you're going, so are we."

"I can't ask you to make that kind of a sacrifice."

"Sacrifice? Okay, this place sounds like a bad idea," Wren said, looking from Sasha to Jayesh and Quinn. "I'm going to need more information about this valley." Wren crossed her arms over her chest, giving them her best glare.

"We'll tell you more about it on the way." Quinn narrowed his eyes at Sasha, refusing to budge. Finally, she nodded. It looked as though they were all going to India.

CHAPTER 21

Aidan | Sterling Tower | April

"Focus, Sam." Aidan tried to mask his impatience. He had a newfound respect for his parents and teachers who had showed endless patience—most of the time—when he was growing up.

"I'm trying." Samantha slammed her fist into the mat before she stood up. "Does it have to be so high?" She stared up at the balance beam he'd just raised to six feet. She'd fallen off it a dozen times already.

"Yes, it does," Pilar answered for him. "You have perfect control over your power, but you're not progressing as you should at your age."

"That's why we're going back to the basics." Aidan placed a sympathetic hand on her shoulder. "Believe me, I know from experience exactly how boring and monotonous that stupid beam is. But you have to get back up there.

"Fine. I just don't remember the *basics* being six feet off the ground," she muttered as she climbed back up to the beam to work on her balance and fighting forms.

"Look at it this way," Aidan said, digging up one of his father's old lines and dusting it off. "The extra height is more interesting. It's just a challenge you need to conquer."

"I miss Bennett." She stood at the end of the beam—her feet planted firmly for the exercise she was trying to perfect.

"I know that's rough too. The separation will be good for you."

"Says the guy who never leaves his Syntrophos' side." Samantha stood with her hands on her hips.

Aidan stared her down. "I left Naomi in Milan for nearly two years. I think we've earned a little time together. We had to learn how to be apart when it was forced on us. I don't want any of you to ever know what that feels like. And he'll be back in another month."

"I don't understand why I didn't get to go with him." Her voice raised in a whine that was very unlike her.

"Because with Ben's elemental gift, he needs to work closely with someone else who has an affinity for water. Jin Jing has been acting as his mentor, from Cleveland, but they need to spend time together, and Jin is busy at home. That's why we had to send Ben to him. He'll be back soon."

"I could have gone with him and helped." Samantha sighed.

"Distracted. Helped. Same thing," Pilar said, pointing at the center of the beam where Samantha was supposed to be.

Samantha stepped out onto the beam, her balance just right

"Now focus." Aidan let the first targets loose. The clay spheres the size of his head launched toward her as she flipped across the beam like an Olympic gold gymnast. Using her destructive gift, each target exploded when they came into range.

"That's it." Aidan clenched his fist, willing her to make it through the second round of targets. She hadn't done this well all day.

She wobbled a bit on the last target, but she had time for a second shot at it and obliterated it as her feet landed at the edge of the beam.

"Yes!" Aidan's fist shot into the air. "That's how you do it."

Samantha grinned at her success. Moving to sit on the beam, she let her legs dangle toward the floor.

"Nicely done," Pilar said, and that was as much praise as Aidan had ever seen her give out.

"Thanks. But what's all this for anyway? I know how to use my gift."

"Then why have you struggled to hit your targets?" Pilar asked, arms crossed over her chest.

"Because I'm not perfect." The way she said it sounded like a question.

"And training will help improve your odds of being darn near close to perfect when it matters," Aidan said.

"But I'm rock solid with Bennett. We never miss."

"And he might not always be there." Aidan moved to set up new targets for another round. "It's important you both learn to function without the other. Yes, you can choose to be together as much as possible, but circumstances might not always allow for that."

"And then what are you going to do when that happens?" Pilar stared her down with a shrewd gaze. "Fall apart, or kick some butt?"

"Kick some butt." Samantha groaned, standing up for another run at the beam.

Aidan stood back and admired her hard work. She was missing her Syntrophos in a bad way, but in the end, it would make her stronger.

So why had he taken Allie's suggestion to move out so hard? Wasn't she trying to do exactly what he was teaching his student to do? Function well in his absence so when it truly mattered, she wouldn't fall apart without him.

In her eyes, he was a boyfriend she depended on a little too much. In reality, he was her Complement, and that made her struggle every bit as difficult as the one she faced with her Syntrophos.

Samantha wasn't the only one learning a lesson today. It was time he took his own advice and not make Allie feel bad for doing what she needed to do.

"Your mother sent us a meal kit subscription box," Allie called from the kitchen the second Aidan walked through the door. He breathed a sigh of relief that she sounded normal after their previous disagreement.

"Has she met you?" Aidan raised a brow at the mess she'd managed to make unboxing the ingredients.

"That's what I said!" Allie threw her hands up in the air. "This is supposed to feed four of us dinners for a week, but I don't know what goes together."

Aidan picked up the card that came with the box. "Oh, there's a note from Mom. She says this kit is for Darius, Pilar, or me to manage, and it's meant to feed us decent food at least once a day. She wants to know if we like it once we've used it for a week, and she'll send us more. Oh, and she said you're not allowed to cook it. You were supposed to just put the meal boxes in the fridge, not open them all."

"Oh." Allie frowned at the counter covered in vacuum sealed bags of fresh ingredients. All of them were mixed up with no hope of ever figuring out which ingredients went together. "Want to just order a pizza?"

"Sure." Aidan chuckled softly, gathering up an armload

of bags and shoving them in the fridge. "By the way," he called over his shoulder. "I'm going to room with Chloe for a while. I just talked to her this afternoon. There aren't a lot of available apartments with all the construction happening on the lower floors, and Wes just left with Graham and Ezra for Savannah. It's kind of a perfect arrangement."

"Okay," she answered hesitantly. "And how do you feel about that?"

"I'm sorry I was a jerk about it when you asked me to move out." Aidan moved back to the counter, gathering up more vacuum-sealed bags, stacking them in neat piles. "I know you didn't mean it the way I took it. I—it just scared me." He gave her the most honest answer he could.

"You're not mad at me?" She stepped around the counter toward him.

"Of course not. You just asked for space. I can give you that."

"I don't really want it." She wrinkled her nose. "But I want us to be a healthy couple. Not so codependent."

"I realized that's what you were asking for somewhere between leaving in a rush and forgetting I didn't have on shoes. And I won't be far." He forced a smile. "Just a few floors down."

Allie slid her arms around his waist, laying her head against his chest. "Baby steps." She giggled. "That's as far as I can handle you going."

Aidan ran a hand over her hair. "That's as far as I'm willing to go for the moment, but I was thinking all of this over today." He wrapped his arms around her, resting his chin on top of her head. "I'm not ready for this yet. But you are right. We don't function well without each other and that's not healthy. My reaction to your suggestion is proof of that."

"So, you really get what I meant? You're not just saying what I want to hear?"

"I get it, babe. We're going to do better. And I was thinking it might be time to send me—and maybe even Darius—out on an assignment soon. Just something small that would take one of us away for a day or two."

Allie nodded, biting her lip. "I hate that idea so much."

"I kind of do too, if we're being honest." He pressed a kiss to the top of her head, breathing in her scent. He loved this girl with everything he had. It was torture being away from her even for a day.

"But it's a good idea. Something's bound to come up that you or Darius could handle."

"What can I handle?" Darius walked in, tossing his gym bag on the floor by the bar.

"Take your gross gym clothes to your room. You know that drives me bonkers when you leave your smelly crap sitting around for days, reeking up the whole place." Aidan kicked the bag toward the living room. "At least get it out of the kitchen. This is where we eat."

"That's odd." Darius ducked into the fridge to grab a beer. "I heard a rumor that you didn't live here anymore."

"Boundaries," Allie snapped at him. "Stay in your lane, bestie. And get your stinky clothes out of here."

"I may not live here anymore, but I still eat here," Aidan called after him.

"Snappy comeback, bro." Darius skipped down the hall to his bedroom.

"I'm not going to miss that," Aidan said, grabbing a beer for himself and Allie.

"I am rather looking forward to less brotherly bickering." Allie followed him into the living room. "We actually talked about him moving out. It didn't go too well. He had a bit of a panic attack."

"Did not!" Darius shouted from his room.

"It was messy. Lots of crying and pathetic sniveling. Mine, not his. We decided to get through the hurdle of you moving, and for the time being, he's going to stay at Pilar's a little more often."

"Baby steps all around then." Aidan sank down to the couch beside her. "After dinner, I'll pack up some of my things and head out early to hang out with Chloe and Dahlia. Give you some Syntrophos time."

"What about Naomi? She hasn't been around much lately."

"She's seeing someone."

"Really?" Allie's smile widened. "Anyone I know?"

"Uh, not sure." Aidan avoided the question. "Let's order that pizza." He grabbed Allie's phone just as it rang. "Hey, it's Sasha."

"Put her on speaker phone, and I'll get snackies to tide us over till the pizza gets here. I think I saw some healthy hummus in the meal box, and I've got some not so healthy crostini bread soaked in olive oil to go with it."

"Hey Sash," Aidan answered the phone. "You're on speaker. Allie's hunting for food in the kitchen."

"Good, I'm glad I caught you both." She sounded tense.

"What's going on down there? We heard you guys were making progress with the prisoners."

"We have, but it's not enough." She sighed. "These poor people are in bad shape mentally. They have no idea how long they've been imprisoned, and everything modern just freaks them out. We finally got them settled in hotel rooms with the basics of food, showers, and plenty of sleep, but they're scared of the elevators and don't get me started on the hairdryer fiasco."

"What are you going to do?" Allie dropped down onto the couch beside Aidan, her arms full of snacks. "You sound like you have a plan."

"We do. It's just not one I particularly like."

"Spill it. Maybe we can help you come up with an alternative," Aidan offered.

"They need a place to go to recuperate. Some place peaceful and familiar."

"We could set them up in the Warehouse," Allie suggested.

"I thought of that, but I don't know enough about most of them to trust them completely around the kids at Soma. I mean, we're talking about escaped prisoners after all. Their power is extremely volatile right now."

"True." Allie popped open a tub of hummus and set it on the coffee table next to her beer.

"Not that I think any of them are a real threat. They're just overwhelmed and confused," Sasha added.

"So where do you want to take them?" Aidan asked.

"Want is a strong word, brother." Sasha blew out a breath. "We're taking them to the Chola Valley. We've already arranged it with Mother Raghavan."

"No," Allie and Aidan said together in a rush.

"There has to be a better solution than that." Allie shoved the food aside.

"I don't think there is one. The valley is a safe haven where they can take all the time they need to get back on their feet without losing even more time than they've already lost. The valley is a beautiful place outside of time. No matter what era you're from, the valley feels like home."

"How long will you be gone?" Allie asked.

"Only three months," Sasha said.

"Which could be an actual three months, or it could be a hundred years for you." Aidan reached for Allie's hand, sharing a worried look with her.

"Don't go, Sash," Allie whispered. "Send them to Mother Raghavan and come home."

"She's right. You don't need to make that kind of sacrifice." But Aidan knew his sister. She would go, and there wasn't much he could do to change her mind now that she'd made the decision. This was just a call to let them know where she was going.

"I can't abandon them, guys," Sasha said in a strangled whisper. "They trust me, and I owe it to them to see them safely through this transition. They're like babies in a world that makes zero sense to them. I have to go."

"You need to call Mom and Dad. A few weeks won't be too hard for them, but you need a chance to say goodbye." His throat tightened at the thought of what she might be facing. "Just in case."

"I already called them." Sasha choked on her words. "I have to go, guys. I love you, and I'll see you soon, okay?"

She hung up before either of them could respond.

Chapter 22

Sasha | Chola Valley | April

"I never thought I'd be here again." Sasha stared down at the ancient mosaic floor of the pavilion leading into the Chola Valley. It seemed as if a lifetime had passed since she was last here, ignorant of what lay across the threshold to the Valley. Really, it was just a handful of years.

The sun faded along the horizon, illuminating the pavilion in the dazzling shades of sunset.

"I've said that every time I've stood here." Jayesh sighed. "I really mean it this time. This is the last time." She took his hand just as Quinn and Santi came to stand with them.

"You two sure about this?" Sasha asked.

"We're in this to the end." Santi gripped Quinn's hand, glancing back at the group of prisoners behind them. Getting them here had been a chore, but they'd made it.

"You guys are freaking me out." Wren stood behind them with Ephraim, Abel, and Roman guarding the ancients. They'd each been here before with Jayesh, but they wouldn't be crossing into the valley this time.

Wren had tried to insist she accompany Sasha and Jayesh, despite knowing there was some grave detail she hadn't been told yet, but Sasha refused to drag her along.

"Let's go, so we can get this done already." Jayesh tugged on her hand, and together, they stepped across the threshold.

"I totally thought you guys were about to disappear or something." Wren laughed as she watched them from the safe side of the pavilion.

"See you when we get back." Sasha turned her back on her friend, letting her head fall back as she took in the twinkling stars overhead. It was the dead of night now, where a moment ago, the last rays of the sun had warmed her face.

Jayesh stood aside as each of the ancients crossed into the valley. The sudden leap from day to night seemed to alarm them less than the jet had.

Just as it had before, the temple appeared in the valley below. Except this time, it shone under the moonlight like a beacon of tranquility. Like a monument of ages past come to life, it should offer the ancients something familiar to cling to in their time of turmoil.

An old stone pathway led down into the valley toward the northern gatehouse standing eight stories high and carved with fantastical relief sculptures of the Immortals who built this place.

"It's beautiful," Santi breathed.

"It's a magical place," Sasha murmured. Now that she'd made the decision to enter the valley, she was looking forward to experiencing it again—hopefully a much different experience awaited her this time.

Even from here, Sasha could smell the beautiful flowers that bloomed in the gardens behind the walls of the temple. She'd only ever seen those flowers here.

Fifteen stories of carved stone stood at the center of the grounds, surrounded by four quadrants of smaller temples and pavilions with cloistered paths connecting the walkways and gardens.

Jayesh cleared his throat, pulling everyone's attention back to him. "As you can see, the Chola Valley Temple is a special place. You will find peace here, though you will each face hard lessons before you can leave." He hung his head for a moment, and Sasha moved to stand with him.

"Mother Raghaven will guide you each through your individual journeys until you are ready to rejoin the modern world," Sasha said.

"What aren't you telling us?" Xera asked, her head titled to the side.

"We have left the river of time," Sasha said gently. "While only a few months will pass in the real world, for us, it could be much longer." She hated telling Xera and her people such a thing. Especially after they had experienced a reversal of the valley in the prisons where they were held far longer than they could comprehend.

Jayesh spoke above their confused murmuring. "This is the safest place we could think to bring you. None of you are ready for the modern world, but the Mother will help you, so you can move on with your lives. She will not allow any of us to leave until we have learned what she desires to teach us." He turned toward the group. "And don't think for a second that she has nothing to teach you. When she believes you are ready to leave, you will return to the world where only a short three months have passed for everyone else, yet you will be better for the time you have spent here. However long that might be"

Xera nodded, taking in a breath. "Then let's get moving."

Sasha followed Brother Rabishan along the narrow halls of the temple. The way was familiar, one she'd walked a thousand times before.

"Your rooms, Miss Sasha." The monk gave her a slight bow before he stepped aside to let her in.

"My sister stayed here last time." Sasha left her shoes at the door and gazed around the familiar room that somehow looked as though Imogen had just left it. Larger than the stark dormitory she'd stayed in during her last visit to the valley, Sasha realized she was in a much better position than before. She was a veteran of the temple now.

"It is good to see you again, my dear." Brother Rabishan opened her windows to the cool night air and waved another monk into the room with a tray of fresh food with fruits, cheeses, soft bread and butter, and the sweet honey and nut pastries she associated with fond memories of her time here.

"You too, Brother Rabishan." Sasha gave him a respectful bow. Perhaps it wouldn't be such a bad thing to take some time for herself here. Life at home was a constant wave of chaos and activity. She would have time to think and meditate here. Time to gather her strength of mind and body before she returned to the hustle and bustle of life at Soma.

"Mother Raghavan will see you in her garden at midnight." Brother Rabishan backed out of the room, leaving Sasha to her meal and the overwhelming silence of the temple at night.

Chapter 23

Allie | The Warehouse | April

"Ms. Carmichael!"

Crap. Allie managed to get all the way onto the elevator before Mrs. Mitchell caught her this time. "Yes, Martha?"

"We have a few matters that need your attention." She stared at her, unblinking.

"Is anyone dying, at risk of losing a limb permanently, or is the building on fire right this minute?"

"No." Mrs. Mitchell still gave her a twitchy look that said she didn't think Allie was very funny.

"Then it can wait until morning." Allie stuck her elevator key into the slot and turned it, closing the door in her assistant's face. "Sorry." Allie winced at the disappointment in Mrs. Mitchell's eyes.

Allie had learned the hard way that she had to take time for herself when it really mattered, and right now it mattered. Her head throbbed with the effort of holding back her visions. They swarmed at her peripheral vision, demanding her attention.

Hijacking the elevator so no one would stop her on the way down, she rode quickly to the basement. When the doors opened, she yanked her key out and returned it to the chain she wore around her neck for that purpose. She only had a few more minutes before the curfew she'd insisted upon was in effect. Every evening at six o'clock, the Warehouse closed for three hours along with the gyms and all of Soma's educational facilities. This forced all students and faculty to take those three hours for rest and relaxation. This was the time when most flocked to the dining halls and the various fun activities Soma offered its residents. The point was to ensure everyone had ample downtime to just be kids out watching too much TV and eating too much junk food.

And it was the best time for Allie to make use of the Warehouse for her own purposes. It had gotten to where she couldn't go there during normal hours because her presence was too much of a distraction to the students who adored her.

"Dad! Wait," Allie called as she jogged down the hall to the large double doors leading to the Warehouse. The ones her father had just locked.

Navid smiled as she neared. "Breaking your own rules again, sweetheart?" He withdrew a ring of keys from his pocket. Only a select few people Allie trusted had keys to the Warehouse and other important places within the building. It was Navid's week to lock up and ensure the only one left inside was Hal, the hermit who lived on the mountain. Hal cooperated with the new rules. He was the only one who had the ability to tell who was inside at all times, and he enjoyed the opportunity for silence within the world he'd created.

"Very much." She nodded. "Care to join me?"

"I could just get you your own key, you know?" He unlocked the door and held it open for her. "Seeing as the building belongs to you."

"My name might be on the deed, but the Warehouse belongs to Hal. Besides, I'd lose it, and everyone knows it." She clutched her elevator key around her neck. "This is the only one I can be expected to keep up with." Allie hated getting stuck with a car full of students on the elevator. She loved the kids of Soma, but her gift couldn't handle being around them in such close quarters.

"To the lake?" Navid tucked her arm around his. "Harold has made some new adjustments I think you're going to love."

"Lead the way." Allie leaned on her father, enjoying the rare quiet moment with him. With so many things needing her attention and so many people pulling her in a thousand different directions, she didn't often have much time left over for the most important people in her life. She really hoped the changes she was trying to make in her relationships with Aidan and Darius would make a difference in her other relationships.

"How are you doing, daughter?" Navid gave her one of his searching looks. She'd been on the receiving end of that look for as long as she could remember, even when she was a child and didn't know he was her birth father.

"Tired," she admitted.

"You look a bit strained. Are you sleeping?"

"Not much." She shook her head. "It's the visions. They needed my attention about a week ago."

"You need to take better care of yourself."

"I need more hours in the day."

"Says the woman who doesn't sleep much, and when she does, still manages to work in her sleep."

"It's a big job, this saving the world thing." She leaned her head back, enjoying the warm sunshine on her face.

"If I could take all your burdens onto my own shoulders, I would."

"I know." Allie sighed. "You know what bothers me the most?"

"Oh, I know you well, daughter, mine. The not getting to leave this tower is driving you mad." Navid chuckled.

"I just want to go shopping with Sasha or to a movie in an actual theater where they serve the best popcorn with lots of butter. Just something normal and not here."

Navid pulled her to a stop along the hillside. "Your sense of normalcy is refreshing." He cocked his head, searching her face for something. "I think that's the thing that will truly save us all in the end."

"My appetite for buttery popcorn?" she teased.

"Your ability to see the mundane as extraordinary." They moved to the top of the hill where the lake now rested in a sweeping vista below.

"An island?" A smile spread across Allie's face as she turned to her father in question.

"It's just for you."

"I get my own island?" It was small. With a sandy beach tucked inside a secluded cove and a strip of jungle along the sheer cliffs. Atop the cliffs seemed to be a flat, rocky plain with trees and sparse shrubs. From here, it looked like a tiny toy island she could pluck out of the water like a bath time rubber ducky.

"Just a small one." He winked. "A gift from Hal to the *little miss*. You're going to love this." Navid guided her to the edge of the lake, much bigger than the one she'd first seen upon her takeover of Soma.

"What's this?" Allie studied the simple wooden sign that bore her name.

"Press your hand against the sign."

"No way. It's got palm recognition?" She placed her hand over the rough wood and waited expectantly. The water began to churn at her feet, stretching across to the island. "What's happening?" She stepped back.

"Well, you need an easy way to get onto your island." Navid smiled, gesturing at the rough wooden bridge rising from the water.

"Holy moly." Allie gave a little hop. "This is exciting." Water poured off the sides of the narrow foot bridge as it ground to a halt at her feet. She took a tentative step forward, turning to Navid. "You coming?"

Her father shook his head. "This is your sanctuary. None but you and your mentor can access it."

"What's stopping the kids from swimming out to it?" she asked.

"Immense power," Navid said. "I will be here if you need me." He moved to sit on the grassy edge of the lake.

Nervous, Allie stepped out onto the bridge. It wasn't far, perhaps forty yards to the little island. Except the walk took a lot longer than it should have, and when she stepped onto the sandy beach, the island was much larger than it had a right to be on such a small lake. Once again, Hal's ability to defy the laws of physics astounded her.

Turning back, Navid was just a speck on the opposite shore. "Thank goodness Hal's on our side." She shivered at the magnitude of his power, coupled with his humble nature. The only thing the man wanted was a place where he could live quietly and alone. When asked about his Complement, the old man just shrugged and said he wasn't ready for that kind of commitment yet. She could relate to that.

Tilting her head back to search the cliffs, Allie saw a

line of stone steps near the top. She would have to figure out how to get up there another time.

Allie froze on the sandy beach. The gentle waves lapping at the shore the only sound in the peaceful afternoon. "I can only come here with Emma," she gasped, taking another look around, letting Navid's words sink in. Hal had prepared this island for her Proving.

A shiver of fear raced down her spine. It was coming so fast, and if she wasn't careful, it was going to catch her by surprise like it had for Naeemah. Though, when it came for Naeemah during her time with the Shaolin Monks, she'd had more than a century of experience behind her.

"I'm so screwed." Allie walked along the beach, enjoying the tropical feel of the environment here. Kicking off her shoes and rolling up her jeans, she tiptoed closer to the water.

"It's seawater," she murmured in awe, inhaling the unmistakable scent of the ocean. Perfect shells dotted the beach, stretching back to the jungle she couldn't wait to explore.

But Allie had work to do and not a lot of time to do it. Now that she had such a private expanse of nature, she could come here any time she needed the open sky and lots of space to let her visions wander unhindered.

A chaise lounge waited for her, set back from the water with an umbrella overhead, along with a wicker side table offering an icy pitcher of lemonade and a plate of cookies. A dressing tent billowed in the breeze behind. "Someone who knows me super well helped Hal with this." She ducked into the tent and changed into a swimsuit, sun hat, and lightly tinted sunglasses.

Settling back in her lounge, Allie poured herself a glass of lemonade and sat back to soak up some much-needed sun. This little slice of paradise just made her pretty fantastic world a whole lot better.

"Okay, visions, go do your thing. We've got about three hours." She took a deep breath and released the control she'd worked so hard to attain. Spectral figures burst from her peripheral vision, morphing into more corporeal forms as she relaxed. The longer she let them wander, the more defined they became.

They drifted off in blobs of twos and threes, moving to different points along the beach where they stretched and transformed into specific places with details she couldn't afford to miss.

The first vision to coalesce was one of Aidan. She had those frequently. He was so close to her it wasn't unusual to see bits and pieces of his future. She sometimes saw flashes of insight concerning Darius and Chloe and others she loved dearly. The more she studied her clairvoyant gift, the more details she was able to gather. Aidan's visions were always golden, like the color of his power. Chloe's were orangish-red, like the fire she and her dragon breathed. Others were just beginning to find their color. And then there was Marcus. His visions were always a dull sepia, as boring and bland as the man himself.

Allie watched the simple view of Aidan talking with Emma in her apartment. She studied it from every angle, looking for anything important she might glean from the ordinary glimpse into his life.

"Nothing." She shook her head, letting the golden vapor dissolve as she dismissed the vision.

She saw another nondescript view of Chloe struggling along the beach farthest from her. She existed within a dark bubble, nothing of her surroundings coming into view. Her friend was grappling with a decision, which meant it involved Chloe herself. The only decisions Chloe ever second guessed were her own.

This one warranted further study, so Allie let her continue to wander the beach, hoping more detail would come to light soon.

Familiar faces swarmed the beach now. Allie studied them each, giving them her undivided attention. Some faded into nothing as she dismissed the ones she deemed unimportant for the moment, filing away the information for another time. Others continued to grow as details were filled in.

Eventually, only one remained for her to study. The sepia-colored form mocked her, as he often did in her dreams.

"Marcus." Allie took a careful sip of her lemonade, losing any appetite she might have had for the plate of sugar cookies still warming in the sun. The man terrified her. Mostly, because she knew it was up to her to defeat him, yet she still had no clue how to do it.

She watched him pace along the beach, looking for hints of his surroundings. Finally, the details began to come to her. An old white plantation home loomed behind Marcus, its wide wraparound porch marking it as authentic to a time long forgotten.

Sweeping green lawns receded into the distance behind high brick walls secreting it away from the public eye. Ancient oaks and pecan trees rose like sentinels around the perimeter, and a natural pool sat closer to the house, a more modern addition to the palatial home.

A glimmer of gold and faded sepia caught Allie's eyes and she stood, taking her sunglasses off as she let herself wander the landscape of her vision.

"Aidan? What are you doing here?" She watched, startled as a phantom of her boyfriend came into view under a giant oak tree. He sparred with an indistinct form. But judging by the drab color of the form, it could only be Marcus Servius.

Aidan fought well as Marcus pushed him harder and harder. A drop of crimson blood shone brightly against Aidan's pale skin as it ran down his cheek.

"He's sweating blood." Allie sank down to her knees, horrified to witness a ghost of the pain Aidan must have gone through during his time with Marcus. As the bright drop of blood fell to the ground, what Allie thought was the dappled shadows of the sun shining through the trees morphed into a sea of blood staining the ground. Aidan's blood.

Familiar rage coiled inside her, but she had better control of it now. One day, she might have to use her Judgment gift with purpose, but that day wasn't today.

The spectral figures faded into nothing, but the house was still there. She turned in a circle, taking it all in and wondering what her gift was trying to show her. Green light called her attention to the rear of the property. She followed, barely aware of her true surroundings as salty waves lapped at her ankles.

Allie's heart sank in her chest as new surroundings came into focus. An old military battery came into view. A crumbling stone structure was built right into the more modern brick walls. It looked like a relic of the civil war where cannons might have once occupied the upper deck, and empty doorways stood open on the ground entrance. Except for the jail cells that bore shiny new bars.

Allie gulped for air as the hairs raised on the back of her neck. New figures emerged as she approached. She saw a ghost of herself along with two others she couldn't identify. Marcus stood between them and the cells.

"Mom?" Allie heard the vision of herself cry out. "Dad?"

The gaunt figures of Lily and Carson Carmichael flashed before her just as the vision collapsed into the sand.

CHAPTER 24

Sasha | Chola Valley Temple | The Beginning

Midnight looked just like any other hour after the sun had set in the valley. Sasha walked on slippered feet, wearing the traditional clothing the Mother preferred. The loose linen pants and matching tunic in a shade of rosy pink with yellow and soft green embroidery were likely the same ones she'd worn before. The clothes seemed to remember her, contouring to her form like a pair of much-loved jeans.

The cool stone pathway led from the temple into the familiar gardens that occupied the grounds in every available corner and alcove. The Mother's favorite garden faced the northern gates overlooking the valley. The gnarled old woman waited for her on a stone bench that had probably been there since the beginning of time. Sasha genuinely believed Mother Raghavan had been there just as long.

"Young Sasha." The Mother rose from her bench, her back still straight and strong as ever, despite her advanced years.

"Mother." Sasha reached for her, embracing the petite old woman like a favorite grandmother. "I've missed you."

"Have not." The old woman harrumphed and returned

to her seat. "Sit." She tapped the bench beside her with her cane.

"Have too." Sasha swatted her cane away before the old woman could rap her on the knees. For that, she got a rare smile.

Mother Raghavan looked at her expectantly.

"I am ... very tired." Sasha sighed.

"You're too young to be so weary."

"What have I come to learn, Mother?" Sasha asked.

"We will speak of that soon. You've brought a horde of lost souls to my doorstep."

"Yes." Sasha nodded, turning her attention to the fountains glinting in the moonlight. "I did not know what else to do for them."

"They have lost much."

"My soul aches for them." Sasha felt helpless in the wake of all they had endured.

"Sweet child." The Mother nodded. "They will do fine here. It's best to show them what they have gained rather than focus on what they have lost."

It was a relief to hand over the responsibility for so many, but Xera particularly tugged at her heart.

As if reading her mind, which Sasha was convinced she could do at will, Mother Raghavan spoke of Xera. "The blind one needs you."

"I think so, too. She is important, but I'm not sure why." Sasha couldn't shake the feeling that no matter what happened, she could not abandon Xera.

"We will find out. You will work with her, yes." The Mother nodded. "She has lost important memories. You will guide her along her journey to discover them again."

"How am I to do that, Mother?" Sasha asked. "When I am so young, and she is thousands of years old."

"Ha." The Mother snorted. "She's a scared child still. All the time she has been imprisoned doesn't matter when she has not lived it. Help her, child. I fear you are the only one who can."

"I will do my best."

"You will start tomorrow."

"Yes, Mother." Sasha bowed her head in respect, though she had no clue how she was going to help Xera reclaim her memories.

"Jayesh has his own journey. A reckoning he must prepare for."

Sasha jerked her head up as a bolt of fear shot through her. "I will help him."

"You will not see him or your Syntrophos until your own journey is complete."

For a moment Sasha couldn't breathe. "You demand too much, Mother." She stifled a sob. She would not argue with Mother Raghavan. It was pointless. No matter how much she might miss them, she could look for Jayesh and Quinn under every stone of the temple and still not find them if the Mother didn't wish it.

It could be years before she would see either of them again. That was the way of the Valley. She would feel every moment of the time she spent here, yet when she left the temple behind, it would be as if she'd only stepped away for a short time.

"Your mentor was Ming Lao Long, yes?" Mother Raghavan asked.

"Yes, Mother. She died a few years ago."

"And who have you been working with since?"

"Several of my teachers. My father mostly."

The Mother shook her head. "That won't do. You need a strong mentor who isn't a parent or sibling. Someone who will guide you with a firm hand when the time comes."

Sasha's breath seemed to stall in her chest, choking her. "When the time for what comes?"

"Your Proving, child. A darkness taints our future, and if you are to do your part, you must be Proven. When it is upon you, I will be your guide."

Chapter 25

Allie | Sterling Tower | Late April

Liam: My office, now.

The group text message lit up Allie's screen and she groaned, regretting handing over the running of Soma to her brother.

Allie: It's two AM, go home!
Liam: It's important.
Livia: You hired him to replace you. That was your first mistake. If I have to suffer, you have to suffer. Get down here.
Allie: Fine.
Darius: Does this apply to me?
Aidan: And me? I was sleeping.
Naomi: I'm not coming.
Pilar: Me either.
Liam: ALL OF YOU GET DOWN HERE!
Darius: Fine
Aidan: Fine

Naomi: Whatever

Pilar: Fill me in tomorrow. I'm too old for this.

Allie paused to shove her bare feet into slippers and shuffled into the hall.

"Your brother is a tyrant," Darius grumbled, his hair sticking straight up.

"He's your uncle," Allie muttered, heading to the kitchen for some iced coffee.

Her phone chirped again.

Liam: And don't stop for coffee, I have some here.

Allie snorted, grabbing the pitcher of iced coffee from the fridge. "That crap he gets at Walmart isn't coffee." She poured cream and sugar into her travel mug and headed out to the elevator in her PJs.

Aidan and Naomi met them in the hall outside Allie's old office. In the few weeks since Liam had taken the reins, Allie had enjoyed having someone else handling the day-to-day running of Soma, but she was afraid she'd created a monster. Liam was or-gan-ized. And he ran a tight ship.

"Get in here," he barked, sending them all scurrying into the conference room where Livia waited, still in her workout clothes from earlier.

"Sit." She pointed to the chairs. "Where's Pilar?"

"She's not coming." Darius cleared his throat. "I'll fill her in. She hasn't slept in days."

"Fine."

"Why do I feel like we just got called to the principal's office?" Allie whisper-shouted and followed Aidan closely, taking a seat at the table. A sea of photographs littered the surface. Ugly ones of brutal crime scenes.

"What's going on?" Darius fell into his detective voice, sorting through the photos with a practiced hand.

"We've had some alarming reports come in over the last two days." Liam lowered himself into the chair at the head of the table where Allie used to sit. She'd thought it would be weird to give up that seat, but she didn't miss it at all. She still got to do a lot of the work she enjoyed, but she didn't have the weight of Soma resting on her shoulders—and for the moment, the Senate was off her back.

"These look like murders. Brutal murders." Naomi looked up from the photos. "Where is this happening?"

"All over," Livia said. "We can't pinpoint a source, or sources."

"It's one source," Darius said.

"How can you tell from the pictures?" Liam asked.

"I was a homicide detective. I know things."

"Right." Liam nodded. "We think we're dealing with the escaped prisoners."

"The ones Sasha and Jayesh just took to the Chola Valley Temple?" Aidan asked.

"No." Livia pulled a map from the pile of photos. "We think this is a different group who escaped from the same prison."

"Show me." Allie leaned forward.

"The murders started here." Livia pointed to a tiny island just north of the Bahamas. "Grand Cay island. Four families were murdered in their beach houses one night a week before we heard about the prisoners on San Salvador island. A few days later, there were similar murders in Daytona Beach. Then Tallahassee and Pensacola. From there, the murders moved across Alabama, Mississippi, Tennessee, Arkansas, and Missouri. Always at night and always in a northwestern path."

"Is this on the mortal news?" Naomi asked.

"Yes, but they haven't connected all the murders yet. It's only a matter of time before they realize they have a serial killer on their hands."

Darius nodded, still studying the photos. "Just not any kind they've ever seen."

"How do we handle this?" Aidan asked. "Are they killing with their power or with their hands? Is it one person or a group?"

"Good questions." Liam sighed. "We don't know, but we need to find out before the Senate tries to cover it up like it never happened. If this is the work of escaped prisoners, we don't want the Senate involved. The less they know about that island prison the better."

"They'll just make a mess of it if they get involved," Allie said. "They're refusing to see what's really going on." She had very little faith in their farce of a government. They refused to see all the damage Marcus had done. She wasn't even sure they were still looking for him, not that he would ever let them find him.

This was just what Marcus wanted. Chaos. The more chaos he stirred up the less attention fell to him. And before the International Senate could figure out what he was doing, Marcus would have already done it.

"We have to send out a team to investigate these murders," Livia said. "This has to stop, now. We need to know who this Immortal is and if Marcus has charged them with a task, or if they're just meant to distract us."

Allie finally worked up the nerve to look at the crime scene photos, and she wished she hadn't. Families, men, women, and young teens torn apart in a rage. Blood stains on walls and unidentifiable human remains. No mortal hands could do such a thing. This came from some place dark and full of hatred.

"These wounds are self-inflicted." Darius' voice trembled with power, and his eyes pulsed with his gift. He was seeing a vision of the event leading to the death of a young girl in the picture he held. "She did this to herself."

Allie gasped, her stomach churning with bile.

"So, we're dealing with a psychological ability," Naomi said.

"A powerful one. This Immortal hasn't actually committed these crimes with their bare hands. They're using their persuasive powers to torture their victims and their families. They're playing." Darius set the photo back on the table, his jaw clenched.

"I think Aidan should be on the team tracking this Immortal," Allie said in a rush before she could change her mind. Just saying the words filled her with dread and she thought she was going to be sick, but it was time and this was the right mission.

"I agree." Aidan nodded. "I know we talked about me going out on assignments that would only take me away for a few days, but this is something I can do. This is exactly what I was trained to do, but I could be gone for weeks."

"I know." Allie choked on the words.

"*We* could be gone for weeks," Naomi corrected him. "I'm going with you. And I think we should take Neela and Ivy and maybe several of the other Syntrophos too. If this is just one escaped prisoner broken off from the larger group, then there are likely more. I don't think this is going to be a one-off incident."

"My thoughts too." Liam nodded.

"Darius needs to lead this investigation." Allie only barely managed to get the words out before her eyes started to burn. She would not cry. She bit her lip to hold it in. She could cry after they left.

"No, Allie. I'm not doing it." Darius shook his head stubbornly.

"Of course, you're going," Liam barked. "You're a homicide detective, and this is about a hundred homicides." His hand swept across the table at the photographic evidence.

"He's right, Dare. You're the right man for the job. You both are. Those victims and their families need you guys more than I do. They need justice. I'll be all right. I'll just miss you." Her voice wobbled, and she knew she didn't sound very convincing.

"I've never left you for more than a day. We suck at this, Allie." Darius' eyes were frantic. "If I'm going, you're coming with me."

"I can't. I'll just be a distraction. The minute I'm seen outside of Soma, the Senate and Marcus will have their spies on me. That is the last thing any of us needs. You have to go." She turned to Aidan. "Both of you."

"She's right." Liam glared at his nephews. "Now, go put on your big boy pants and pack. You're leaving in a few hours. And wake Pilar up. She's going with you. You all need adult supervision."

Chapter 26

Aidan | Sterling Tower | Late April

Aidan was anxious to get going, and it left his self-loathing a little worse than usual. He wasn't just eager to hunt a killer, though that was part of it. Mostly, he was anxious to leave Allie.

To say his emotions were confusing was an understatement. He had promised to never leave her again, but as he packed his gear into a duffle bag, the thought of having a break from the stress of keeping his biggest secret from the woman he loved was kind of invigorating.

He was just so sick of lying to her. Allie had taken a huge step in asking him to go on this assignment, but she probably thought he would be home within the month. Aidan knew once he was out there, if there were other Immortals like this one on the loose, he couldn't come back until they were all behind bars again.

"You have everything?" Allie asked, tiptoeing around Chloe's apartment like she shouldn't be there.

"I think so." He zipped his duffle and gave a last search for anything he might need on the road. He liked to travel light.

"This will be good for us." Allie lifted her chin, putting

on a brave face. "Good for you and your team to put your skills to use."

"We'll be back as soon as we can—"

"No, you won't." Allie sighed, taking a step toward him. She tugged on his belt where an array of weapons were sheathed. "This is bigger than us, so do what you need to do to catch this guy and any others out there. Don't worry about me. About us. We'll be fine. I know this isn't like Germany."

Aidan gathered her hands in his, a smile tugging at his lips. "I promise to do my best not to get blackmailed into another Milan Initiative."

"I will hold you personally responsible if that happens again. And this time, I won't wait four years to come after you."

"Heaven help the person who comes between us again." Aidan cupped her face in his hands, memorizing every line and angle.

"Cheers to that," she whispered, her lip trembling as she stepped away, tugging him along behind her. She led him into the hall by the elevators.

"Take care of yourself, Allie." Aidan dipped his head, pressing a gentle kiss to her lips, wishing he had more time to say goodbye.

"Don't worry about me. You just watch your back."

"That's my job." Naomi stepped out of her apartment down the hall, a pack tossed over her shoulder. "Just hold down the fort, Princess. I'll make sure he comes back with that pretty face intact." She gave Aidan's cheek a gentle pat as she walked by.

The elevator doors opened to reveal a very disheveled looking Darius pacing back and forth. "I can't do this, Allie." He lunged for her, wrapping his arms around her middle and laying his head on her shoulder. "I have to go but I can't. I think I'm having a brain hemorrhage trying to be in two places at once."

"We're going to be okay, Dare." Allie hugged him back, her voice trembling despite her attempt at bravery. Of the two of them, Darius was clearly not handling the impending separation very well.

"Pull yourself together." Naomi slapped him on the back of the head. "We were never this bad, were we?" She glanced at Aidan.

"They've had the luxury of spending more time together." Aidan shrugged. "I'm sure we would be just as pathetic if it hadn't been forced out of us."

"We're not pathetic," Darius mumbled into Allie's shoulder.

"It's okay, Dare, they just mean you." Allie stroked his hair, but Aidan could see the pain in her eyes. Losing them both at the same time, even just for a few months, was going to be really hard on her. She understood the bond she had with Darius, but the unanswered bond with Aidan would confuse her.

"Time to go." Pilar came up from the stairwell from her apartment one floor down. "I heard the caterwauling all the way downstairs. You okay, tough guy?" She laid a hand on Darius' shoulder.

"This is too hard." Darius stepped away from Allie, his dark blue eyes studying her face as intently as Aidan had. "Call me if you need anything. Day or night."

"You, too." Allie clutched his hand. "I'll ride down with you guys."

"Better not." Pilar punched the call button for the elevator. "This is hard enough for him here in the hall." She slipped her hand into Darius'. She wasn't a touchy feeling kind of girlfriend—at least not in public. But Aidan could see it on her face. She was worried for Darius, and she loved him enough to give him the space he needed for his unusual relationship with Allie. Maybe it was her work with the Syntrophos of the Milan Initiative, or maybe it was something more, but she had endless patience most girlfriends in her position wouldn't have when it came to the Syntrophos bond.

"You're right." Allie couldn't seem to make herself drop Darius' other hand, and she hovered close to Aidan's side. "Best be on your way." She let out a shaky breath. "The sooner you leave, the sooner you get back."

The doors to the elevators dinged and slid open. Darius threw his arms around Allie for a quick second, and then Pilar dragged him onto the elevator.

"Love you," Aidan whispered, brushing a last kiss on her lips before he stepped onto he elevator. If he didn't go now, he wasn't going to have the strength to leave.

"Love you, too. Both of you." Allie took a step back. "Go catch that son of a—"

The moment the doors closed in Allie's face, Aidan reached for Naomi's hand. A crushing loneliness hit him at the thought of how long it might be before he saw Allie again. Naomi gave his hand a reassuring squeeze. A gentle reminder that he wouldn't be alone.

Taking a deep breath, Aidan let Allie go. He had to if he was going to survive what was next. "Let the hunt begin," he whispered.

Chapter 27

Allie | Sterling Tower | May

"Mom? Dad?" The question echoed through Allie's mind. Her gaunt and emaciated parents stared at her with hollow, vacant eyes.

Slim, skeletal hands gripped the bars of a prison cell. The same hands that had comforted Allie as a lonely child who'd never understood why she didn't quite fit into the world around her.

"How long have you been here?" the ghost-like Allie asked, ignoring the looming figure of Marcus Servius standing between her and her parents.

"It doesn't matter, Allie-girl." Lily Carmichael's voice was strong, despite whatever horrors she'd been through.

"Leave this place." Carson gripped the bars of his cell right beside his wife's.

"No." Allie shook her head stubbornly.

"Sweetheart, he is using us to get to you. Don't let him win," Lily pleaded, the momentary strength fading from her voice.

Allie watched herself refuse her mother's words.

"If I leave, he will kill you both. You know that."

"You have to let him." Carson's voice came out in a

harsh whisper. "Walk away while you can, Allie. We are mortal." He shook his head sadly. "We are prepared to die."

"If I walk away, he still wins." The green glowing vision of Allie pulsed with anger and frustration. "If I sacrifice the people I love, if I turn my back on you now, I'm no longer the daughter you raised, but a creature not much better than the one who seeks to destroy our world. We might not be mortal, but that doesn't make us better or more important than those who are. It just makes us different." Ghost-Allie closed the distance between her and her parents, searching for a way to free them from their prison.

Allie had watched this play out a number of times since the first dream. She still didn't know how to free them. Instead, she turned her attention on the hovering figure of Marcus. He wasn't actually there with ghost-Allie and her captive parents, and the two other figures she still didn't recognize. But he watched from the sidelines, waiting for the perfect moment to strike.

Colors swirled around her in shades of indigo and fiery orange. Heat radiated from those colors, pushing her away from the scene unfolding before her. Like always, ghost-Allie couldn't free her parents from their prison, and a menacing laughter echoed around her.

She sucked in a sharp breath when the sepia colors faded, and Marcus Servius stepped through the swirling colors in all his mundane glory. He dressed in shades of gray and brown as indistinct as his own coloring, but every detail was laser sharp.

"Come now, Alexis. Don't you think you're running out of time?"

Allie sat up in her bed, gasping for breath and shaking, covered in a sheen of cold sweat. She always woke up this way now. The damp sheets twisted around her body, and she reached for Aidan and the comfort he represented, but he wasn't there. He was out hunting a psychotic murderer.

Lunging for her phone where it charged on the bedside table, she Facetimed her mom.

"We're fine, Allie-girl." Lily's sleepy voice sent a wave of reassurance through Allie.

A light flickered on, chasing away the darkness filling her screen. "I'm sorry I keep doing this." She wanted to reach through the screen to hold her parents. She hated being so far away from them.

"We're going to be just fine, kiddo." Carson leaned over his wife's shoulder so Allie could see him. "Everyone is working hard to keep us safe." He took the phone from Lily and crossed the room to the windows, letting Allie see for herself the Immortal keeping watch over them from the driveway. One of Gregg and Naeemah's lieutenants.

Allie chewed her bottom lip. "I don't think it's going to be enough. Underestimating Marcus is the worst thing we could do right now. I'm not ready to face him, but if he tries to harm you—"

"Then we will deal with it when the time comes—*if* it comes," Carson said.

"Humor me and remind me of the plan," Allie said, just like she did every night when she called them after having the dream.

"We will immediately call Gregg and then our guard on duty will escort us to the entrance to the underground in the garden shed out back," Lily said. "From there, we will go to meet Naeemah in the common room and stay there until it is safe."

"Thank you." Allie drank in the sight of her healthy parents. If Marcus should get to them, according to her vision, she wouldn't find them for months and months.

Long enough for them to be half-starved and weak by the time she arrived to save them. But she knew where the plantation estate was already, thanks to her sister. As soon as she'd described the place she'd seen in her vision, Livia was quick to tell her it was the home where she'd grown up, right there on the outskirts of Atlanta. If he managed to get his hands on Lily and Carson, Allie knew exactly where to go.

"We love you, sweetie," Lily said. "Try to get some sleep."

"I will. Sorry to wake you again in the middle of the night. It's kind of an impulse I can't really control." She usually had the phone in her hand and them on the line before she'd fully left her dreams behind.

"Call us any time you need us, Allie," Carson said. "Day or night."

"Love you." Allie blew them a kiss and ended the call. Unfortunately, there was no going back to sleep after that. Instead, Allie pulled out her sketchbook and went to work drawing everything she could remember of the dream. She wrote down every word spoken. She even added the specific array of colors to each scene.

Just as dawn started to lighten the sky, Allie looked at her latest drawing and realized her subconscious had filled in more details. That happened almost every time she sketched now, each drawing evolving from the previous ones.

She ran her hand over the page where a fiery-looking Chloe, rendered in reds, oranges, and yellows, stood by Allie's side.

Chapter 28

Graham | Savannah, Georgia | May

"We're ready, Porcia." Graham tossed the leather mask onto the table. It was just a prototype. He'd nearly finished casting the bronze version his husband would wear to protect him once they were back inside the League of Ancients.

"I don't think we are." Porcia paced across the second-story great room they'd commandeered as a training room in the rented mansion that sat along the marshy river country outside Savannah, Georgia. Plans covered the walls, from Porcia's first introduction to the Alderman in Savannah a few weeks ago, to their exit plan only a few weeks hence. And a thousand steps in between. They'd gone over it a dozen times just today. They were ready.

"Porcia, time is of the essence." Gabrielle sorted through the costumes she'd designed for the Lady Gray's entourage. They each had at least five formal costumes and several daily outfits that fit the personas they had perfected in recent weeks.

Graham had only one costume. It would be the only one he needed for his role.

"This Alderman skims the bottom of the Master's hierarchy," Uncle Lou said. "Whether that's due to Abernathy's circumstances or by design, it doesn't matter. Nothing that happens way out here will get back to anyone we know. These people don't even have landline phones, much less social media accounts."

"That we know of," Porcia interjected. "Nothing is ever as it seems within League circles. You know that as well as I."

"We'll be in and out before any of the old guard of the Boston circles even hears about the Lady Gray and her band of misfits taking up with Abernathy," Uncle Lou continued his argument. "Besides, this lot here in Savannah are a peculiar sort the others look down on." Uncle Lou clutched the Venetian mask Graham had cast from solid gold over a porcelain base. His face would be concealed with golden filagree enhanced with green painted scroll-work to adorn the eyes. The lower half of the mask was hand-painted porcelain with a rictus blue and gold grin that was meant to be off-putting. The costume Gabrielle designed matched perfectly with the golds, green, and blues, complete with fitted brocade jacket, a high green and gold Venetian collar, and a wide-brimmed hat sporting ostrich feathers and sprigs of foliage.

Gabrielle's mask and costume matched in color, with a peacock headdress and an enormous fan of peacock feathers. Each of the other's costumes were equally ostentatious representations of animals. Ezra and Wes would wear reptilian masks and matching livery of scaled leather. Ezra was the dragon, and Wes was the crocodile. And Brooks would be the blind jester. His mask was simple, but no less beautiful. Forged of silver with only the barest hint of eyes and mouth, he would be silent and sightless, accompanying the Lady Gray wherever she went. Graham had given the mask special powers that would allow Brooks to see things others would assume he couldn't.

Porcia would wear the mask she was known for. Pewter and adorned with smoky gray crystals and intricate scrollwork, her mask hid her features well. Accompanied with a high collar and silk headdress, it emphasized her persona as the Lady Gray. Her costumes and clothing came in every shade of gray one could imagine.

"We have to be careful about our entry into the Alderman's estate. The Lady Gray is a highly regarded member of the League. I've only taken on her persona in recent years."

"And you will do her justice," Graham said. "Because we will help you through it. I know you prefer to plan these ventures for weeks before you attempt to infiltrate, but we don't have that kind of time." He understood her caution. Many other women had come before her as the Lady Gray. An enigma, she drifted from one alderman's estate to another, bringing wealth and prestige with her. Most believed that to have her favor was as important as having the Master's, yet none knew who she was behind the mask. They only knew she traded in secrets and her favors cost a great deal, though it wasn't money she sought, only information—which was exactly what they were looking for this time.

"Alderman Abernathy's ranking within the League is a joke. Others make fun of him, calling him Napoleon behind his back. But Marcus doesn't give favor to just anyone. He's carefully selected each alderman to serve a purpose." Porcia continued her pacing. "We cannot underestimate him. And we don't know enough about him to infiltrate his estate yet."

"We will discover what we need when we get there." Graham intercepted her, placing a gentle hand on her shoulder. "That's why we're coming with you. You won't be alone this time."

"We've already received his invitation," Brooks added.

It had arrived only two days after they'd settled into the rented mansion on the outskirts of old Savannah along the rivers and marshlands. The Alderman had invited the Lady Gray to visit at her earliest convenience.

"Tomorrow." Porcia finally nodded. "We will go for tea in the afternoon for a short visit."

"Shall we take the barge?" Ezra asked, excited for the chance to sail down the river on the newly renovated houseboat.

"Yes. We will leave at noon." Porcia moved to the rack of costumes that belonged to her, selecting an old-world afternoon dress that might have been fashionable sometime during the Italian Renaissance.

"We'll be ready," Graham assured her. He was eager to discover what he could of the Master's intentions with the League. Marcus created it for a reason, and he meant to find out what that reason was. Only then could he destroy the League of Ancients from the inside out.

CHAPTER 29

Allie | Sterling Tower | June

"You want to do what, now?" Chloe blinked at Allie over her steaming mug of tea.

"I had the dream again. It's been almost a month of it every night. For my own peace of mind, I think I need to go check on my parents, and I think I need your help to do it."

Chloe cast a glance at Justice painting in the corner of the studio apartment they now shared since Aidan's departure. Allie couldn't fathom how difficult it must be for Chloe to live with her Complement when he still hadn't recognized her.

Justice was in his own world, painting furiously on a large canvas, his brush dripping with vibrant colors and his eyes blazing with the strength of his prophetic power.

"Just ignore him, he's been at it for a few days." Chloe fluttered a hand in his general direction. "He'll come out of it soon enough."

"How does he take care of practical things when he's like that?" Allie watched him, wondering if that was what she looked like when she sketched in her sleep. Somehow, she doubted she looked nearly as cool as Justice did right now.

"He generally doesn't. He won't eat unless I leave something within reach, and even then, he often won't find it until he starts to come out of his prophetic state. I usually just leave him a plate of peanut butter and jelly sandwiches so it doesn't spoil and make him sick. And sometimes, I have to guide him toward the bathroom to take care of business."

"And he won't ... hear anything we talk about?" Allie chewed nervously on her bottom lip.

"He's basically a plant sitting in that corner right now. He's not aware of anything outside his own head. We could walk around naked, and he wouldn't notice." Chloe sipped her tea, waiting for Allie to get on with it.

Allie clutched the mug in her hands, resting the soothing herbal tea against the sketchbook in her lap.

"All right, so tell me again about this nightmare you keep having." Chloe took a hesitant sip, blowing on her tea to cool it.

"Not a nightmare." Allie was grateful her friend wasn't sleeping tonight. It was just after eleven, but Chloe had been working on her journals while keeping a close eye on Justice when Allie had knocked on her door still wearing her pajamas.

"Then we're dealing with a vision." Chloe set her mug on the coffee table. "I have lots of experience with prophecies, so visions can't be all that different."

"From what I understand, clairvoyant visions have a bit more urgency to them than the average prophecy." Allie thumbed through her sketchbook to the latest drawings she'd done tonight.

"True. With Prophets like your grandmother, their predictions tend to be more of a long term what if, but some Immortals with prophetic abilities like Justice's can behave more like clairvoyance with a little more immediacy." Fei

Long slept on the floor between the coffee table and the sofa, curled up like a contented cat. She was even cat sized this evening. She sat up with a yawn and laid her head on Allie's knee and drifted off again. She was currently snoring, tiny sparks shooting from her snout now and then.

Allie scratched Fei Long behind her ears, taking a sip of her tea before setting it on the coffee table beside Chloe's.

"This one is hitting a little too close to home for my comfort." Allie laid her sketchbook open on the sofa between them for Chloe to study.

Chloe leaned over the drawing of both girls facing Marcus at the battery where Lily and Carson would be confined—if Allie couldn't prevent it. Everyone told her it was going to be okay—that Gregg and Naeemah would handle it and keep them safe—but Allie couldn't shake the feeling that it wasn't enough. In this, she would not underestimate Marcus Servius' ability to get what he wanted, and right now, he wanted Lily and Carson.

"What do you think it means?" Chloe asked.

"Exactly what it looks like. He's going to use my parents to lure me out of this tower."

"Right. I guess I don't have to look for the hidden meaning." Chloe scratched her head as she studied the sketches. "Who do you think this gray blob is?" Chloe pointed to the indistinct figure standing between Marcus and Allie.

"No idea."

"Give me a minute." Chloe took the book in hand and flipped through the sketches from the last week. Every drawing Allie had made since the first night the vision came to her expanded on the one before it.

Chloe's eyes dilated, and the power within began to shine through her smoky quartz eyes. Allie watched her and Justice both. Neither were really there with her any longer.

They each had traveled to a higher plain, letting their power guide them to the answers they sought.

"I'm such a hack compared to these two," Allie murmured to Fei Long, who grumbled in her sleep.

"This isn't good, Allie." Chloe came back to herself a moment later.

"I know. I'm really scared. I can't let anything happen to them, Chlo. They're my parents. I love them, and I owe them everything. For sixteen years they kept me safe. I won't let anything happen to them."

"I can't see a clear path yet, but I don't think this is something to be passive about. He's waiting for you to make a mistake."

"Liam and Livia don't agree with you. They're determined to let others take care of this threat and I'm supposed to be a good little princess and stay in my tower."

Chloe shook her head again, studying things in Allie's aura she couldn't fathom. "It's a mistake to ask for help. Marcus is trying to lure you out from the protection of Sterling Tower and your council."

"And I know I shouldn't let him," Allie sighed, running her hand over the warm scales of Fei Long's back. She'd slowly made her way up from the floor onto Allie's lap.

"No." Chloe frowned, cocking her head to study Allie again. "That's not the right path either."

"What do you mean?"

"Ask me a direct question with two distinct options."

"Huh?"

"Just do it," Chloe insisted.

"Okay. Should I sit back and let my council deal with the potential threat to my parents, trusting them to provide the protection they need?"

"Or?" Chloe pressed.

"Or do I take matters into my own hands and deal with the threat myself?"

Chloe's eyes went blank for a moment before she responded. "Well, when you want something done right, you have to do it yourself."

"That's what I thought." Allie leaned forward, dumping Fei Long onto the floor with a spark of flames and a hiss, as she grabbed her sketchbook from the table.

"Allie? When did you get here?" A groggy voice had her yelping in surprise. She'd forgotten Justice was there.

"Justice? You okay, buddy?" Chloe leaned over the back of the couch, doing her best to seem like the concerned friend and not the love of his life she would be some day.

"Yeah." He rubbed his eyes, still opaque from the power of his gift. "I'm glad you're here, Allie. You need to see this." Justice had made a lot of progress since arriving at Sterling Tower where he got to work with other prophetic students with similar gifts. There weren't many, but they had an excellent teacher in Queen Alísun.

Allie crossed the room, still clutching her sketchbook because she had a feeling some comparisons were in her near future. The green glow of Justice's aura told her there was likely another reason she'd sought out Chloe tonight.

Justice turned the large canvas around.

"That's Kelleys Island," Chloe whispered.

"And those are my parents with Marcus in my mother's garden." Allie took a step forward, searching the painting for clues. This wasn't the battery at the rear of Marcus' estate. This was her home. Which meant things had escalated.

"I don't know exactly what's happening here." Justice moved to stand behind her. "At least not yet, but I think the circumstances of this event depends on what you decide right now."

"Tell us the prophecy behind your work," Chloe urged him.

Allie suppressed a shiver as Justice's eyes grew opaque, and his voice rasped in his throat. "The two will converge this night. If the child of prophecy fails to deliver in this, she will fail all."

"Well, that ... just friggin ... sucks, doesn't it?" Allie sank into the nearest chair, wiping a clammy hand across her brow. "I was hoping for some actual direction."

Justice snorted. "Prophecy is never direct."

"Allie." Chloe sank down to her knees beside her. "You okay?" Can I get you a glass of water? You look like you're two beats away from a stroke or something."

She shook her head. "What does 'fail all' mean?" She looked up at Justice.

"All means all." He shrugged.

"But *all* as in everything I'm supposed to do? Or does it mean I fail my Proving? Or fail all the people I'm supposed to protect?" She pleaded with him for concrete answers, but with prophecy, nothing was ever as it seemed.

"I think it means a-all ... of that," Chloe stammered, taking Allie's hand in hers.

"Then I have to find out when this is happening, and I have to go." Allie clutched Chloe's hand like a lifeline. She needed to ask her friend for something, but she was afraid to put her in danger.

"*This night*, means tonight," Justice said softly, studying his painting to be certain. "That much I am sure of."

"Oh my God, I have to call my parents now. They have to get to the underground." Allie searched for her phone, but she'd left it on her nightstand.

"No, Allie. You can't interfere with this." Chloe's eyes grew warm as she studied Allie's options with her gift. "I'm afraid you're going to have to let this happen. You have to go, now."

"He will torture and enslave them if you don't." Justice stared at his painting, like it was a window into the future.

"What? I-I'm not ready to face him." The blood drained from her face, and she began to tremble. "I still don't know how to end this." She was a heartbeat away from completely losing it. "I need Darius. And Aidan." She clutched at her heart where she could feel her Syntrophos' heart beating right alongside hers.

"Tonight isn't about the end," Justice said in his creepy prophetic voice. "It's about the beginning of the end. Tonight's events will set the Master's plan in motion."

"Chloe." Allie turned her attention to her childhood friend. "You don't think Marcus is ... manipulating our gifts to lure me out without protection?"

"Prophecy can't be manipulated," both Chloe and Justice said at the same time.

"It just ... is," Chloe whispered.

"And what we do with the knowledge it gives us can be a tricky business," Justice added. "Trust me when I say what you see rendered here in paint is not a literal illustration of what will happen. Prophecy rarely takes context into consideration."

"I need to get Darius and Aidan on Zoom and ... and I need to call my council in for an emergency meeting. Can I use your phone?" Allie couldn't stop trembling.

"No!" Chloe's voice held a note of panic, and Fei Long lumbered up from her spot on the floor with an irritable growl. "No, that is not the right path. I think in this, we have to be your council." She shared a look with Justice.

"The queen would understand," Justice offered. "She is a genuine prophet."

"And so are you." Allie laid a hand on his arm just as a soft knock sounded at the door.

"Speak of the devil and she appears." Allie rose from her seat on unsteady feet and crossed the room to let her grandmother in, not surprised when she found Navid waiting beside her.

"Allie, dear." Alísun's face told her everything she needed to know. She had her family's support in this.

"Your Majesty." Justice bent into a proper bow, and Allie tried not to roll her eyes.

"Do we need to catch you up to speed?" Allie asked.

"No." Navid moved to her side. "Your friends have done their jobs to perfection."

"Okay, so who's going with me?" She glanced from her grandmother to her father.

"They can't." Chloe stood to her full height. "Marcus will see it as a sign of weakness. He is testing you."

"She is right, Allie." Navid laid a protective hand on her shoulder. "I would go with you in an instant if I could, but I fear my presence would provoke him."

Allie's trembling turned into full on shaking. "I'm not ready for this."

"I think he only wants to talk to you," Justice said in a quiet, uncertain voice. "Take your measure for himself, so to speak."

"But what about my parents?" Allie wiped at the tears threatening to spill.

"If you want to see them again, you're going to have to get to them before he does." Navid wrapped her in his arms. "And if it's any consolation, you *are* ready for this, daughter.

You are so much stronger than he knows. And more prepared."

"Your father is right, dear." Alísun moved to place her hands on Allie's shoulders. "I wish I could have given you more time, but Marcus' actions have only come to me within the last hours. Rest assured, he will expect a child with too much bravado and not enough sense, and you haven't been a child in a very long time."

Allie stepped away from her family and turned to Chloe. "I have no right to ask, but will you go with me?"

"Nothing could stop me," Chloe said without a moment's hesitation.

"Okay." Allie took a deep breath. "All we need now is to figure out who this is supposed to be." She turned their attention to Justice's painting and her drawings. Both showed Chloe with her at both locations. Both also depicted an indistinct figure accompanying them.

"It's a dream walker," Navid said, studying each form carefully.

"How can you tell?" Allie moved to stand beside her father in front of the painting.

"It's the way he moves in the shadows, like he's not really there. And see here, the way Marcus focuses on Allie and Chloe like he doesn't even see the person standing between them. It's a walker shrouded in the dream world."

"How could we have time for a walker to construct a boundary of protection around us with Marcus right there? He might already be there now." Allie flipped through her sketchbook, studying the way Chloe's form slowly developed from an indistinct blob into a replica of the face she knew as well as her own.

The walker figure was always in shadows from the beginning, never fully forming into a recognizable person.

"It's Briggs," Navid announced. "I'll ask him to go with you, but Marcus won't see him."

"What? How?" Allie glanced from her father to her grandmother.

"The dream world behaves differently with Briggs, like the veil between the worlds is ... thinner, and more malleable for him. He's able to come and go easily and with fewer repercussions. He still has a threshold of how long he can be there at one time, but his threshold is almost as long as Quinn's."

"Then he will take you both through the boundary and travel with you to Cleveland." Alísun pulled her phone from her pocket. "I'll order the jet for you now. It will be waiting when you arrive at the airport."

"I still don't understand how Briggs is going to help?"

"He will explain it on the way," Navid said. "Come now, Allie. You need to get ready. I think we're already running out of time."

Chapter 30

Graham | Savannah, Georgia | June

The river barge floated low in the water, and the gentle breeze chased the sweltering heat of the day away. Graham crouched beside Porcia under a large umbrella Wes held over their heads, casting most of the upper deck in shade. He looked menacing in his crocodile mask and scaled leather jacket and breeches.

In the month since they'd arrive in the Savannah river country, it had grown hotter and hotter and their time with the Alderman had gotten them nowhere. He still hadn't invited them into his inner sanctum, but Graham hoped today was the day.

Lou and Gabrielle manned the rear deck, guiding them toward the Alderman's estate over the smooth surface of the water. Below, the houseboat was equipped with several staterooms, a galley, and salon large enough to house them comfortably while attending Alderman Albert Abernathy.

As they approached the estate landing, Graham secured his mask in place. It was heavy. Made of cogs and wheels, springs and bolts, it blended well with his costume of faded leather breeches and threadbare linen shirt with billowing sleeves. A leather vest hugged his chest, displaying patchwork pockets filled with an inventor's tools and supplies. Even now, he worked with a coil of wire and a web of fine lace he'd treated with an acrylic soak to make it stiff and malleable.

"Is there a point to the things you're fiddling with, or is it just for the facade?" Ezra asked from his perch behind Porcia, holding a tray of iced lemonade that did little to chase the heat of the afternoon away.

"Both." Graham worked the lace into the shapes he desired.

"Are those wings?" Wes asked.

"It will be a tiny clockwork dragonfly for the Mistress." Graham twisted the wire to hold the lacy wings.

"And what will I be doing with this dragonfly?" Porcia held her gaze along the horizon, ignoring her minions and those who waited for her arrival along the docks they approached.

"It's a drone, meant to be worn as a pin on your lapel. It can record conversations and video. And when no one is looking, you can leave it behind to buzz around collecting information."

"If we ever managed to get past the front parlor," Wes muttered.

"It's going to be today." Graham was certain of it. In the last weeks, he'd gathered data from the Alderman's estate and spent his nights analyzing it. Based on probabilities and a statistical analysis of their time thus far, Abernathy was poised to invite them into his circle.

"Well done, my pet." Porcia's voice lifted as they reached the docks and she stroked his hair. Already in character, she slipped the jeweled end of his leash around her wrist.

Graham crouched beside her, casting his eyes down on

the trinkets he worked for his mistress. He had fully committed to playing the degrading role. He was a prized creature of the mistress's menagerie. A novel accessory to her own eccentric persona. The more she treated him like a pet, the more the Alderman and his attendants ignored him, and that was exactly what he wanted.

Let them ogle him and then promptly deem him unimportant. As far as the League was concerned, the Lady Gray's entire entourage were merely decoration.

"Careful, everyone," Porcia whispered. "Once again, the game is on."

The barge slid smoothly in place along the docks, and Uncle Lou tossed the lines to the attendants there to greet them. Each of the Alderman's servants wore colorful livery and simple masks of painted leather to conceal their identities.

Porcia waited until the barge stilled beneath them before she rose from her lounge. "Come, my darlings." She tugged on Graham's leash. He walked hunched over behind her, fiddling with his trinkets and mumbling to himself.

Ezra and Wes helped the Mistress down the portable steps to the dock.

"My Lady." A gentleman dressed in the finest livery bowed, offering her his arm. He wore a painted mask of leather as well, yet his was adorned with red and orange feathers and swirls of gold leaf—clearly a phoenix. "The Alderman is delighted to receive you this beautiful afternoon. I trust you are all enjoying your time here along the old river country. It's a breath of fresh air to leave the chaos of the mortal world behind, is it not."

"It's been wonderful, though it's dreadfully hot today and I'm afraid I cannot stay long, Phoenix." She took his arm and they headed up the path to the estate. "I have another engagement this evening I must attend."

"Perhaps afternoon tea would suffice?" the man suggested, his gaze drifting down to Graham where he stood crouched beside his lady, tinkering with his invention.

"That would be lovely." Porcia dabbed a delicate handkerchief over her lip as they took the brick steps up to the entrance. "Come along, Tinker." She tugged on Graham's leash and made her way up the steps with Graham in tow. "Let us escape this infernal heat."

The Phoenix was quick to reach the door before her, making a show of inviting them inside his master's humble abode. He ushered them quickly into the same old parlor they'd visited a dozen times before on their brief visits to the estate.

Graham shuffled after them, showing little interest in his surroundings. His newest mask suppressed his presence and that of his power, making him always appear as the weakest Immortal in the room, and therefore not a threat. Even now, as he called on his power, the Phoenix spared him little attention, allowing Graham the opportunity to call on the twin orbs of his gift and send them whizzing around the room to gather data he would analyze later.

"Mr. Abernathy has other guests?" Porcia placed a hand against her throat as she acknowledged the voices floating down the hall from the great room at the back of the mansion. "Should we come another time?"

"Not to worry, Mistress." The Phoenix moved to open the heavy drapes of the parlor, letting the sunlight in. The room had an air of disuse about it, as though few guests were greeted here. "The Alderman always has many guests in attendance. He has been anticipating your arrival today.

If you will excuse me, I will let him know it's time to join you."

"Thank you, Phoenix." Porcia nodded at the butler as he left them.

"I swear that man thinks he's in an episode of *Downton Abbey*?" Ezra murmured softly, and Porcia gave him a glare.

"Pretend *you're* in an episode of *Downton Abbey* and you'll be okay," Graham said, giving his husband a wink.

"Hush you two." Aunt Gabrielle added her glare to the mix just before the Phoenix returned. "I think the Tinker is right, today is different." She let a note of breathy excitement into her voice, just in case someone was listening to their conversation.

"His Grace, Alderman Albert Abernathy at your service." The Phoenix gave a deep bow and stepped aside to allow the diminutive man behind him to enter the room. The Alderman was perhaps the least intimidating Immortal Graham had ever encountered—at least of such an advanced age. He had a multitude of centuries behind him, and his stature spoke of a time when most mortal men were much smaller than they were now.

During their first encounter with the Alderman, he reminded Graham strongly of Napoleon Bonaparte. He wore an elaborate Baroque pirate mask of bronze and burnished gold covering his entire head like a helmet. The face itself was smooth and unadorned except for the cheeky smirk etched into the facial features. Intricate scrollwork formed the bronze curls of a traditional wig, and a wide brimmed tricorn hat with plumed feathers completed the mask. The thing must have weighed fifty pounds or more, but the Alderman seemed accustomed to its weight.

"Lady Gray," he greeted her warmly. "I'm delighted to see you again."

Porcia smiled and nodded, giving him her full attention. Moving around the room, she removed her charcoal gray gloves, dropping them on the floor at her side for Graham retrieve. "You have such a lovely home, Mr. Abernathy, I would love to see more of it."

"Shall I ring for tea, sir?" the Phoenix asked in a hushed tone.

"Yes, yes." The Alderman nodded, following Porcia around the room. "Please, my dear, have a seat. I believe we will finally have time for that tour today." The nervous little man shifted uncomfortably in her presence.

"Excellent." Porcia flounced down on the hard-backed settee, and Graham crouched on the floor beside her, muttering to himself about the tools he kept stored in the leather gauntlets he wore around his forearms.

Clearing his throat, Abernathy made an effort to ignore Graham and turned to greet Lou and Gabrielle perched on a more comfortable looking sofa under the wide windows. "I hope my Lady Peacock and the Ostrich are settling into the area." He gave a gracious nod. "Have you had any luck procuring a permanent home?"

"Not yet, your Grace," Uncle Lou said. "Nothing that is suitable for our needs."

"At least nothing that doesn't need extensive remodeling," Gabrielle added. "We aren't opposed to remodeling, but it would be wonderful to find an estate that has been well kept. Either way, we have fallen in love with the community."

"Excellent. Wonderful to hear it." The Alderman nodded, a note of relief in his voice when the Phoenix entered with a tea cart. "Might I offer you some refreshment?"

"Please." Gabrielle nodded, her peacock feathers fluttering like butterflies around her face.

The butler made quick work of serving the Alderman's guests with rich dark tea and an assortment of delicate sandwiches and pastries. He ignored Ezra and Wes standing guard behind the Lady Gray, and avoided Graham altogether.

Porcia sipped the tea from an elegant porcelain cup designed with an elongated rim to accommodate their masks. She heaved a dramatic sigh as she set her cup on the side table. "Unfortunately, I will be spending a few more weeks in the Savannah area while my friends look for a place that serves their needs. The weather this time of year is intolerable, but I would like to see them safely settled and moving in the proper circles." She let a note of impatience creep into her voice.

"But of course." The Alderman turned to Lou and Gabrielle, a bright smile lightening his voice. "I have decided you are most welcome to join us... as guests for now and perhaps something more permanent in the near future. Once we've established proper vetting, of course."

"Of course," Uncle Lou said eagerly. "We understand completely."

"Lovely." Gabrielle clapped her gloved hands in delight. "We are just honored, your Grace.

"I have but one ... concern before we leave this awful room." The Alderman chuckled softly, turning his attention back on Porcia. I must ask, my dear Lady Gray ..." he trailed off. "Your young man here..." He watched Graham tinkering with his inventions as cogs and gears whirred and clicked from some unseen power source, unsure what to make of him. "He is a Tech." Graham could hear the disdain in his voice. "We do not allow such Immortals within our inner sanctum."

"Here my darling." Porcia broke off a piece of her pastry and fed it to Graham, who lapped it up with a toothy smile. She ran a loving hand over his hair as she met the Alderman's curious gaze. "He is my favored pet, of course." She played into the eccentricity of her persona. "Of all my collection, he amuses me the most with his little inventions."

"I see." The Alderman shifted uncomfortably in his seat.

"What are you making, my lovely?" Porcia's voice took on a sweet tone, like she spoke to a beloved dog, rather than a powerful Immortal with a degree from MIT.

Graham smiled and lifted the pliable leather and canvas he'd spent weeks perfecting. It took a bit of ingenuity and a lot of cheating to get it to work how he wanted. He lifted the thin leather and blew air into the makeshift balloon that actually hid a real balloon inside. Tying it off with a coil of wire, he inserted a key into the attached mechanism and wound the internal workings. With a puff of steam, the mini dirigible balloon took off, floating around the Alderman's head.

"Brilliant!" Porcia clapped her hands in glee, watching the dirigible hum and click as it chugged and belched steam for a brief moment of entertainment.

Graham let a braying laugh escape him as he clapped along with his mistress.

"What a clever toy." The Alderman studied the contraption, a note of disapproval in his voice.

"He is a clever boy, isn't he?" Porcia leaned forward, a teasing tone in her voice as she laid her trap for the Alderman. "He's one of those dreadful young things so prevalent these days. He is weak in power but amusing with his gift for tinkering with useless mortal technology. Isn't that right, sweetheart?"

"Dreadful." The Alderman nodded, his disapproval instantly shifting to interest.

"Who's a good boy?" Porcia patted Graham's head and placed a plate of sandwiches and treats on the floor for him.

Graham scrambled to sit on the floor and busied himself with the food as if he had little interest in the conversation.

"His gifts aren't useful, but they are endlessly entertaining." Porcia poured herself another cup of tea from the tray. "He isn't good for much else, to be honest, but I love him so."

"He serves our mistress well." Gabrielle laughed as the dirigible began to lose steam and drifted to the floor beside her where she kicked it aside.

"I am relieved to hear it. We don't hold with mortal technology in our community here," the Alderman said proudly. "We believe in the old ways of power and prestige.
"

"I find that a refreshing sentiment, Alderman Abernathy," Uncle Lou said, nodding his approval. "The mortals have their ways of coping without the abilities that come naturally to us. It is not for us to adapt to them. The idea that our power could evolve into one such as this is distasteful in the extreme."

"My thoughts exactly." The Alderman nodded eagerly. "Perhaps I could interest you all in a tour of my home." He moved to stand. "My real home," he added with a hint of mischief in his voice.

"Just a quick tour." Porcia wiped her hands on an embroidered napkin and took up Graham's leash. "I'm afraid we will have to be going soon."

"It will be my pleasure to show you the great room just down the hall, madame." He offered his arm to Porcia, and the Lady Gray's menagerie scrambled to follow.

Graham shuffled behind his mistress, keeping his head down and his hands busy with the dragonfly drone he'd nearly completed. So focused on his character and selling the ruse, Graham somehow missed the moment they left the aged wooden floors for the soft carpet of primroses that now cushioned his step. He looked up, turning around in complete awe.

They hadn't gone outside.

Behind them lay the wide hallway they'd just traversed. Through a pair of beautiful carved oak doors, the Alderman revealed the great room. It looked like something out of an epic fantasy novel.

The room was huge and circular, its borders clearly defined by walls of bark. Window openings held no glass but looked like the natural hollows of a very old tree. The ceiling towered overhead with bark covered stairs sweeping up to the floors above.

"It looks like the inside of a tree," Gabrielle whispered in awe.

"It is, madame." The Alderman gave her an indulgent smile.

Lights twinkled from every surface, yet Graham could tell these were no mere electric lights. They pulsed with power. Everything within the great room fairly hummed with Immortal power.

"It reminds me of tales of Indriell." Porcia shook her head, trying to keep her cool indifference in place, but struggling to keep the surprise from her voice.

"Indeed." Alderman Abernathy guided the Lady Gray

across the fantastic room where a fire crackled with blue flames in a hearth adorned in river rocks.

A cool breeze embraced them as they stepped closer to the hearth. The blue flames sparked and burst with clouds of frost and pops of icicles.

"I've never seen anything like it." Uncle Lou crouched in front of the cooling hearth.

"Ahh, here we are." Abernathy called their attention to a wandering servant shuffling past with a tray of wine. "Might I offer you some cool refreshment?"

"Yes please." Porcia forced a bright tone, ignoring the servant—the very mortal and very distressed servant.

With the attention on Porcia and the others, Graham studied the mortal's vacant eyes and slack mouth. He moved like a mannequin with stiff arms and legs, like some unseen force held him upright long after he'd lost the will to stand on his own.

"Something seems to be amiss with your servant, Abernathy," Uncle Lou said in a tone of jest.

"The Phoenix and Mrs. Jessop, the housekeeper are my only Immortal servants." The Alderman lifted his glass of crisp white wine. "Mrs. Jessop is quite useful in *training* our mortal servants to do as they're told. They are quite useful in this way. They don't talk, or sleep, or even eat much for that matter."

"I can't imagine they'd last too long in such a state." Aunt Gabrielle chuckled behind her enormous, feathered fan.

"They last long enough." Abernathy chuckled, moving on to show them the rest of the spectacular room.

Holding his arms out wide to encompass everything they could see, the Alderman turned in a slow circle. "Nothing you could ever want is impossible with our power." He pranced around like the peacock Gabrielle was supposed to be, proud of his accomplishments. "I don't remember the days of Indriell myself, but my great-grandmother used to tell me stories about it when I was just a boy. She talked of the grand palaces in the forest cities where Immortals lived in trees and homes built to blend with the natural world around them, rather than destroy it. We've recreated something of those days right here on my estate." Abernathy stood with his arms clasped behind his back as they each marveled at the enormous structure towering over them.

Panic clutched at Graham's chest as he studied the stairs leading to various floors and off shoots of the tree-like structure from his vantage point below. It could take months to explore all the hidden secrets that might be ensconced within this one room. He had no doubt the Alderman would have other such places on his estate. They could be stuck here for months and never find the information they were here to uncover.

"How magnificent." Porcia's voice echoed what Graham was feeling. "It goes on for days." She turned in a circle, staring up at the domed ceiling far above them.

He'd noticed the dome from outside on their way up to the mansion from the river, but what lay under the roof seemed to occupy much more space than normal physics would allow.

That the interior would still mimic what was found on the exterior told him there were physical limitations to this place. Still, discovering what they came here to find was going to be ten times harder than Graham had expected.

CHAPTER 31

Allie | Cleveland | June

> **Allie:** I love you both and I miss you so much. I have to go do a really stupid thing tonight. (Don't freak out, I'm not alone and I have Grandma's support.) Just thinking of you both and hoping you're safe. I'll call you soon. I'm getting on a plane now so my phone will be off.

Allie hit send, hoping Aidan and Darius weren't quick to respond, but the dancing dots told her she was probably in trouble.

> **Darius:** Why are you on a plane? You shouldn't leave the safety of the tower. It makes me nervous.
> **Aidan:** Be careful. I love you and I miss you. Try not to do anything extra. You have a penchant for being extra when you're doing crazy things. You have your mother's sai? (Leave her alone, Dare, she's perfectly capable of protecting herself.)
> **Allie:** Yes, I have my sai and several other forms of

protection that might also include a fairytale dragon. (Don't bicker you two!)

Allie: And you're the one who's extra.

Aidan: Tell Chloe I said hi. You two will be fine together.

Aidan: Am not.

Allie: 😘

Darius: I know she can take care of business. She just shouldn't have to without us there to help. Where are you going? Can you call me when you get there? I'm not feeling so great. I think I'm going to be sick.

Allie: Someone hold Dare's hand. I can't say where I'm going on here. You never know who's paying attention. Just know I'm doing what I have to. I didn't want to worry you, but you were both bound to figure out I was up to something.

Darius: Just be careful.

Allie: You be sure to return that favor. Love you both.

Allie's hands shook as she slipped her phone into her pocket just before the private jet took off for Cleveland. This time it was a commercial jet.

"Did your seriously old grandma actually spring for a last minute jet rental through an app?" Chloe asked, taking in their luxurious surroundings.

"Seems like she's always prepared for anything before the rest of us even know what's going on." Allie checked her phone for the time. It was just after midnight. Grandma Alísun had worked a miracle getting them out of Sterling Tower and to the airport in record time.

She managed a snort of laughter at the thought of her ancient grandma tackling technology head on. iPhones and even jet apps, apparently, never seemed to slow her down now that she had the hang of it. She was amazing the way she never stopped adapting and moving forward. Nothing seemed to scare her.

"I want to be just like her when I grow up." Chloe eased back into her seat, kicking her feet up on the footrest.

"Same." Allie pushed back in her lounge, letting the footrest pop out. "We'll be kick-ass grannies when we're her age." Allie tried to fist bump her friend, but she was still shaking.

"You okay, Allie?" Briggs turned in his seat on the other side of the narrow plane.

"Scared to death and nauseated, but I'll be all right once my parents are safe."

"Are you sure no one is going to like court martial me for kidnapping the princess and sneaking her out of her castle?" He kicked out his footrest and stretched back for the short flight to Cleveland.

"Promise." Allie tried to get comfortable in her seat, but the plane started to spin and she had to close her eyes.

"You're on the verge' of hyperventilating," Chloe warned. "Take some slow, steady breaths."

"She's right, you look like you're headed to the executioner's block," Briggs said.

"Aren't I?" She sucked in a deep breath and let it out slowly, but it didn't make her feel any better.

"Here, take a few sips of this. It'll mellow you out." Briggs handed her a shiny silver flask from his pocket.

"What's this?" Allie took the flask and sniffed at the contents. "Oh my God, is that battery acid?"

"It's some of Gregg's Bruichladdich whisky. It's a

hundred-and-eighty-four proof and aged eighty years in an oak barrel."

"Alcohol doesn't really affect me." Allie took a tentative sip, and she nearly choked at the burn sliding down her throat. "Holy crap, that's rough." The whisky made her sound like a pack a day smoker.

"Hon, I've only ever seen you drink a glass of wine with dinner. This isn't that." Briggs tipped the flask back, urging her to keep drinking. "It'll take the edge off for a little while so you can settle down. It's going to be a long night."

"Careful, Allie," Chloe warned. "That stuff will hit you like a charging elephant in about thirty seconds."

"It kind of grows on you after the first sip." Allie took another drink from the flask before she handed it back.

"You all right?" Chloe eyed her.

"Give her a minute." Briggs watched Allie.

"I'm good." Allie sat back in her seat feeling a little more relaxed. A smile tugged at the corner of her mouth as warmth trickled through her. "I'm real good." She let out a giggle-snort.

"There she is." Briggs held the flask up and took a sip for himself.

"Yeah, I'm super fine," Allie said, feeling like all her earlier worries had just vanished. "I think the nature of my dream visions just freaked me out. It'll be fine." She waved it away like it was nothing. "We'll just go talk to Marcus. He's just a man like any other, right? We can just reashon wif him." Her words started to slur, and she fell into a fit of giggles.

"Enjoy your buzz while it lasts." Chloe sighed. "Because it's never quite long enough."

"With any luck, she'll fall asleep and wake up feeling a

little more in control." Briggs tucked the flask back in his pocket.

"Great idea, get the clairvoyant tipsy so she can fall asleep and have another terrifying vision of her parents being tortured." Chloe shot him a glare.

"Come on, you two." Allie flung her hand out and patted Chloe's face. "Be nice. You know I used to date him?" She pointed at Briggs and whisper-shouted, "He's hot, right?"

"Miss me, do you?" Briggs winked.

"Not really." Allie shrugged. "I have Aidan." Her smile fell. "At least I think I do. Something's bothering him." Her shoulders slumped. "I think he couldn't wait to leave me."

"Allie, why don't you take a nap?" Chloe suggested.

"No, no, no. No!" She shook her head. "I have the besht idea. You two should go on a fate." The grin returned to her face. "A fate. No. No." She threw her hands out as if to steady herself. "A D-ate!"

"Let's not go down that road, shall we?" Chloe picked up the unopened bottle of water the flight attendant left for them and tried to shove it into Allie's hand, but she dropped it and watched it roll across the narrow aisle.

Allie hiccupped, pushing Chloe's hand aside as she turned to Briggs. "Chloe's got a dragon." She giggled.

"A fact everyone inside your tower knows already."

"I hate that tower," Allie grumbled. "Want to buy it?" She leaned over Chloe's chair, resting her head on her friend's shoulder. "I'll sell it to you for fifty cents."

"No thanks. I'm all set on towers." Chloe patted her head gently.

"You're no fun," Allie muttered. "Fei Long would totally buy my tower. Hey, why didn't we fly to Cleveland on her?"

"Because she's got a terrible sense of direction, and we'd probably end up in Miami." Chloe pressed another bottle of water into her hands.

"I knew it. She's a cute drunk." Briggs chuckled.

"Let's just hope she sobers up before we get to her parents' house." Chloe's voice drifted far away as Allie burrowed into her seat.

"S' comfortable." Her head fell back against the buttery leather cushion.

And there she goes." Briggs checked his watch. "Took maybe five minutes from the first sip. She's a total light weight."

"Am not." Allie murmured.

"Never give her whisky again," Chloe shouted at Briggs, her shrill voice bouncing around the inside of Allie's head like a drum.

"Shhhh!" Allie forced her eyes open. "Oh, we're walking." Her stomach heaved at the movement.

"Finally." Chloe wrapped a steadying hand around Allie's waist.

"Wha's happening?" Allie's insides trembled, and she thought she might puke any second.

"We're in Cleveland trying to get you into the rental."

"What rental?"

"Alísun texted me with the details. We have a car waiting for us."

"Come on, Princess, we need to keep moving." Briggs held Allie braced against his shoulder as they walked through a sea of boring little black sedans to the lavender-gray car at the end of the lot.

"Oh no." Allie closed her eyes as the world went green, her gift's way of telling her it was time to pay attention. "That is not a car." She stumbled forward. "I'm okay." She threw her hands out as her friends lunged to catch her. "I'm good." She stood up straight, and the parking lot started to spin again. "But I'm not getting in that death trap."

"It's what Alísun ordered for us." Chloe clicked the key fob to unlock the tiniest car Allie had ever seen.

"It's a toy car." Allie fumbled with the passenger door. "Were they all out of real cars?" She pointed back to the lot filled with safer looking vehicles.

"It's a compact, it's fine." Chloe sighed, losing her patience.

"Just get in." Briggs moved to push the seat forward so Allie could get in the backseat.

"Nope, that backseat looks like a coffin." She backed away. "I'll feel better if I drive."

"That's so not happening, Alexis Ann Maree Carmichael. Get your butt in this car right now."

"Ooh, four named. I'm in trouble." Allie shifted unsteadily on her feet, her head throbbing with the worst headache of her life. "Shotgun." She shoved Briggs toward the backseat.

"Come on, Allie, you're like four feet tall. The backseat is sized just for you."

"Are *you* claustrophobic?"

"I don't think Immortals get things like that." Briggs stood his ground, folding his arms across his chest.

"Trust me, this one does." Chloe slid into the driver's seat. "And we don't want her having flashbacks. Just get in the back, Briggs. We'll be at the ferry dock in a few minutes, and you can get out to stretch your legs."

"Uh-oh. Wait a minute." Allie lurched toward the rear

bumper, her stomach roiling as she puked up what was left of the sour whisky.

"She's the only Immortal I've ever seen who does that." Briggs peeked out of the back seat. "You okay, hon?"

"Peachy." Allie slid into the front seat and buckled her seatbelt.

"Let's get you home so you can rest off the last of that hangover, you know, after we deal with saving your parents from Marcus."

Allie waited until they pulled onto the highway before she corrected her friend.

"Take seventy-one downtown to Tower City."

"What? Why?" Chloe changed lanes, casting a quick look over her shoulder.

"Because." Allie sighed. "We're going home the hard way."

"No." Chloe's shoulders fell. "Why?" The word came out in a whine.

"Tell me I'm wrong." Allie glanced at Chloe; her profile glowed green with the only affirmation Allie needed.

A moment later, Chloe slammed a fist into the steering wheel. "Ugh, I hate it that you're right. It's our best course of action. What made you choose that?"

"The car selection is a clue from my grandma." Allie chugged the last of her water from the plane. She was sober and clear headed now. It happened from one breath to the next. She went from hungover and loopy to calm and collected—almost. Her stomach still churned with nerves, and she didn't feel quite herself.

"You guys are creeping me out right now," Briggs muttered from the back. "What's the hard way?"

"We can't go that way with him here." Chloe gave Allie a nervous look. "It's protocol. Only family."

"I'm not family?" Briggs sounded more relieved than offended.

"We're breaking protocol. Marcus is already there waiting for us."

"How do you know?"

"The teeny car. There's only one reason Grandma Alísun would have rented this thing, and it wasn't to save money. She's telling me we have to take the tunnel. And we have to take the tunnel because someone is waiting for us at the docks."

"Oh." Chloe turned her focus back onto the road, gripping the steering wheel tighter. "But why do we need such a small car? We've gone through in SUVs before."

"It's the rainy season." Allie cringed and shared a look with her friend.

"Okay, tell me about this tunnel right now," Briggs said.

"Should we blindfold him?" Chloe asked. "Or put him in the trunk?"

"No. No, we shouldn't." Briggs sounded nervous now.

"I think he's already in the trunk," Allie said, ignoring Briggs.

"I will gladly close my eyes, thank you very much." Briggs hunched down in his seat and tugging his hoodie over his eyes. "I don't need to know anything about where this tunnel is, but I have a very bad feeling I'm not going to like this jaunt to the island if it involves a secret tunnel.

"No, you're not," Allie sighed.

"Especially in the rainy season," Chloe added with a sigh of her own.

"How did I get roped into this again?" Briggs muttered.

True to his word, Briggs kept his head down and his eyes shut as they headed through downtown Cleveland to Tower City. The parking garage was nearly deserted at this late hour, so it was relatively easy to find the entrance to the tunnel along the tracks at the underground train station. Allie darted out of the car and punched in the code in the analog box hidden in the wall.

"Let's get this over with." Allie hopped in the car as the wall slid back, revealing a very damp, dark, and narrow tunnel.

A few miles into the bumpy drive, Allie turned in her seat. "You can get up now. We're in."

Briggs sat up from his cramped position curled in the back. "Well, this looks like a really bad idea." He eyed the windshield wipers running at high speed. "It doesn't usually rain inside tunnels, does it?"

"Nope." Allie turned back to face the darkness looming before them. They could only see as far as the wimpy headlights allowed, but there was at least four inches of water on the uneven ground, and they still had more than twenty miles to go.

"So that little waterfall running down the side of the tunnel up ahead ... that's the lake?"

"Yep." Chloe sucked in a deep breath.

"Okay, next time either of you asks me to help you do something like this, I'm going to need these kinds of details before I say yes."

Allie focused on the beam of light ahead, trying to get her mind settled on what she was about to do. For years, she'd known she would have to face Marcus eventually. She just wasn't ready for it at this very minute. Not that she ever would be ready.

Am I supposed to end this tonight? She laid her head back on the headrest, wishing they could go faster, but at the same time, she didn't want to get there too fast.

"When we get there..." Chloe trailed off, glancing at Allie before she returned her focus on the road ahead.

Allie took a deep breath. "Yeah, I don't have a plan."

"I need you to make solid decisions so I can stay a few steps ahead of you. You're sure he's already there with your parents?" she asked.

"Positive. He's waiting for me." Allie had known the minute her vision went green when she saw the tiny car.

"Okay, so we park this thing at the crypt. And then what?"

"Crypt?" Briggs groaned from the backseat. "This is the worst trip ever."

"We're already geared up, so we'll take the tunnels to my house. It's the best chance we have of sneaking up on him."

"He'll sense us coming," Chloe said.

"He just won't expect us to be moving underground." It had been a long time since Allie had used the tunnel entrance in the garden shed behind her parents' house, but it was going to come in handy tonight.

"What's that?" Briggs pointed ahead.

"That is a cave in." Chloe gripped the steering wheel tight.

The tunnel narrowed as a mountain of rubble came into full view. Water gushed from several large cracks in the wall.

"Dad and I are going to have to fix that." Chloe rolled to a stop.

"We're going to get stuck." Briggs leaned forward.

"I think there's enough room to go around." Allie rolled her window down to check the level of the water. "We might be floating through." She pulled her head back into the car. "We better hurry."

"What if we get stuck?" Briggs asked again.

"Then we'll climb out through the sunroof and run the rest of the way." Chloe opened the sunroof as a precaution before she inched forward.

"Or swim," Allie added, bracing her hand against the dash.

"How deep is it, Allie?" Chloe moved as far to the side of the rubble as she could.

"More than two feet."

"The engine's going to flood," Briggs warned.

"We're going to floor it in a second." Chloe continued to maneuver the car forward, easing past the pile of rubble until she was certain they could get through.

"Careful!" Briggs yelled just as Chloe hit the gas, and they went surging through the water, missing the big chunk of limestone blocking their path. They were out the other side without a scratch.

"Wow, I thought for sure we were going to get stuck." Briggs looked back as they shot forward, leaving the mess behind them.

"There couldn't have been more than a quarter inch of space on either side of us." Chloe let out an anxious breath. "Alísun is the coolest ever."

"Right?" Allie grinned, hoping she'd get to thank her grandma very soon for choosing the exact size car they needed to get through this.

The rest of the trip went much too fast and before Allie was ready, they came to a stop inside the crypt.

"What *is* this nightmare place?" Briggs stared around at the gloomy stone cavern with its arched openings leading to different places within the underground.

"Pretend like you don't see anything." Allie headed up the steps.

"You know someone's going to be here at this hour, right?" Chloe raced up behind her.

"Hopefully Grandma's paved the way for that too." Allie cracked open the door at the top of the stairs, peeking into the common room.

Familiar pale blue eyes peered back at her, and she nearly jumped out of her skin. "Gramps!" she shrieked. "You scared me to death." She pushed open the door to find her grandfather waiting on her.

"Alísun sent me ahead a few hours ago. The way is clear for you and your friends." He stood back for them to enter the common room.

"You're coming with us?" Relief flooded through her at the thought she would have the Scholar with her tonight."

Alexander shook his head. "No can do, Allie-girl. Marcus has been after my hide for centuries. And I'm told my presence would hinder whatever Alísun sees happening tonight. You three must face him without outside interference."

Allie flung her arms around her grandfather, dangerously close to tears.

Alexander wrapped her in his loving embrace, and a sense of peace washed over her. "You know I will be there in my own special way, sweet-girl. I wish I could do more."

"How am I supposed to do this?" Her voice trembled. "I don't have a plan. I'm afraid he's just waiting for me to show up before he kills them."

"Tonight is a parlay," Chloe said softly, her eyes smoldering with power. "You're to do the best you can, but only you will know how to navigate this event to save your parents."

"She's right." Alexander gripped Allie's shoulders.

"Follow your instincts and trust in your power to guide you, and in the two you've selected to join you tonight."

Allie nodded, sniffing back her tears. "We have to go now." She stepped away from her grandfather and the safety he represented. Somehow, it helped to know he was so close.

"Good luck, granddaughter." He lifted a hand as they left the empty common room for the vaulted hall leading to her tunnel. She knew it was hard for him to let her face Marcus alone, but she had to stop hiding behind her family.

Turning toward the green-lit tunnel, Allie put her game face on. It was time to rescue her parents.

CHAPTER 32

Aidan | Wichita, Kansas | June

"Well, this is deeply disturbing." Aidan stepped through the house, careful not to touch anything. Unlike the previous crime scenes, this house was a moderate middle class home in a suburb of Wichita, Kansas. Every other location had been the home of someone wealthy and influential. A number of them held local political offices. A few were elected state officials. None of them seemed connected in any logical way, yet Aidan was almost certain there was a pattern to the murders.

"Quiet. Let him do his thing." Pilar's eyes were glued to Darius as he made his way through the crime scene, following the path of the killer.

Aidan couldn't deny his brother at work was an impressive sight. He knew far more about this killer than the FBI they were continually avoiding. But he was distracted tonight. With Allie off handling some catastrophe on her own, they both were.

Aidan didn't like it any more than Darius had, but she was nothing if not capable. He just wished they could be there with her. They were a team—or would be when the bonds were completed. It was only natural that they would want to be with her.

Tonight was the first Darius and his group had entered a crime scene before it was reported, and they had to be careful not to leave any evidence of their presence behind.

The bodies were seated at the dinner table in a gruesome scene Aidan would never get out of his mind. He'd seen a lot of such things in the time since they'd left Atlanta on the trail of a killer.

"Not self-inflicted," Darius murmured, stepping around a blood-covered chair Aidan refused to look at. He also didn't want to see whatever bloody thing it was displayed on the serving platter. Nor the blood dripping down the chins of the victims. He didn't want to see the expressions of horror forever frozen on their faces.

"Our killer used their gift to torture the family with their three teens while they were having dinner." Darius' voice held a tremor of power as he spoke, his eyes sill swirling with the visions he saw.

He'd explained how his gift worked during their first crime scene investigation. He could see a replay of particularly violent crimes, seen from the eyes of the killer, though he never actually saw the murderer.

"The killer forced them to harm each other with their steak knives. Cut after cut." Darius mimed a slash of the knife. "I won't tell you what this sick psycho made them eat."

Aidan could imagine. Most were missing various features. Remnants of fingers, toes, ears, and noses lay scattered across the table. Aidan was just grateful there was no sign of an infant or small child. Bad enough the youngest teen was hardly old enough to be in high school, but Aidan wasn't sure how he might react if there was a small child wrapped up in this horror show. He already wanted to permanently kill this Immortal with his bare hands.

"There's something deeply personal about a murder like this," Pilar said gently as she watched Darius, taking in every detail he did. "This isn't just a killing spree—not like the others. This time it's passionate. Vengeful."

"I agree," Naomi said, stooped over a corner of the room where a bloody bare footprint was etched in the carpet. "I think we're dealing with a female killer." She snapped a picture of the print.

"What makes you say that?" Pilar asked. "I can't imagine a woman would be this vicious—against a family she doesn't even know."

"She's angry," Naomi murmured, standing up from her crouch. "Have you noticed how she attacks families with a little more hate than the crime scenes without young victims? When it's a whole family with a mother and father and children, it's like she has an extra special kind of hate for them than all the others combined."

"I think you're on to something there." Aidan forced himself to study the victims, shoving the horror aside so he could see the details. "Whenever it's a man or woman alone or just a couple, the murders are more calculated."

"Emotionless," Pilar added.

"Still gruesome, though." Aidan shuddered.

"She's angry because they have what she doesn't," Naomi said. "They have what was taken from her, and she's after vengeance ... and she has small feet." Naomi passed Aidan the picture of the footprint.

"She's right. This kind of killing comes from some deep well of hatred and loss." Darius came out of his trance, his eyes back to their normal dark blue. "Which means this is likely a crime of passion and not premeditated like the others. This time she wasn't crossing a name off a list. She was just ... reacting to something she saw."

"Unless this is a different killer than the one we've been tracking," Pilar suggested, but Darius was already shaking his head.

"It's the same killer. The power that did this comes from the same person. There's just a lot more hate here."

"So the important detail we need to figure out is her path." Aidan pulled out a map with all the crime scene locations labeled. "And where she is going."

"Exactly." Darius nodded. "That's how we catch her."

"Then let's get out of here before the cops show up." Pilar snapped a few more pictures, and they all followed her out, careful not to touch anything.

Once outside, they removed the cloth booties from their feet, making a quick escape through the backyard shadows to the car parked a few streets over.

Aidan shucked off his latex gloves and shoved his hoody back, letting the cool night air calm him. He couldn't save the victims, but he was determined to make it so this woman never did this to another family ever again.

"What's wrong Darius?" Pilar crouched beside Darius. He was buckled over, leaning against the car.

"It's Allie. I think she's sick." He shook his head.

"What do you mean she's sick?" Aidan came up beside him, trying to get a sense of his brother's pain with his healing gift.

"I don't know. Something's wrong, but I don't think she's aware of it yet. She's ... distracted."

CHAPTER 33

Sasha | Chola Valley Temple | A Season of Memories

Just as she had every morning for the last several months, Xera waited for Sasha in the pavilion along the northwest quadrant of the temple grounds. It was where she had trained with Jayesh for so many years.

Xera was amazing with her ability to get around despite her sightless eyes. She moved through the maze of the temple gardens using her other senses. It took her a while to learn the layout of the temple, but she was far more at home here than she had been at the resort hotel where Sasha and her team had found them.

"Good morning, Lady Sasha." Xera sat at the top of the ancient stone steps in her meditative position, the warm breeze blowing through her long silvery hair. It wasn't age that had marked her hair as Sasha had first thought. Xera's silver was much like the strands of gold in Sasha's curly brown hair and Allie's copper, silver, and gold strands mixed in among her red locks. Sasha was beginning to understand how such things had marked the nobility of Indriell. The silver ranked Xera as somewhat less than

Sasha's gold. And Allie's trifecta put her at the top of the list. Not that such things mattered anymore.

"Good morning." Sasha moved to sit beside her, adopting her pose. They sat together in silence for a time. Time was one thing they had plenty of here in the valley.

"Yesterday, you told me how you became separated from your Complement after a great battle against the Enlightened. Have you pushed through your memories of what came after?"

Xera sighed, lowering her head. "I don't know. Something happened after that battle." She shook her head, frustrated. "It's like a wall in my mind I can't get through."

"What is the last thing you remember?" Sasha had spent a great deal of time inside Xera's memories. It had taken them a while to develop a solid relationship built on trust and mutual respect before Xera was able to take Sasha into her memories. Happy times, they were not.

Xera frowned, closing her eyes as she rocked back and forth. "The battle was like nothing I'd ever seen before. The Enlightened turned the pure power into a weapon, and the skies over the battlefield grew blood red from the ... wrongness of it all."

"And where was Vitor?" Sasha hoped and prayed that when they left the valley, she would be able to find out what happened to Xera's Complement. Surely someone among her parents' friends would know of him.

"I don't ..." Xera trailed off. "He was with my Syntrophos." Her eyes snapped open. "I think they escaped together."

"And then the Enlightened took you?"

"No. Not yet." Her brow wrinkled. "I was injured. I ... sent Vitor away. Someone had to care for Lecia. She was just a girl, not yet master of her immense power. She was such a special girl. Others sought to use her. She had to be protected during those days. It was such a dangerous time for the young ones."

"Can you take me there? To that moment when you sent Vitor away?"

"I don't know if I can recall it in enough detail." Her blind eyes seemed to pulse with power unlike any Sasha had ever seen. Xera was a relic of the old world. Her power was purer, still tainted by the Great War, but whatever prison she'd been in had protected her and her people from the lasting effects of the war. "I will try."

Sasha braced herself for the venture into Xera's memories. It wasn't like visiting her mother's memories—a gentle drifting from the present into the past. With Xera it was ... jarring. And her word was so alien to Sasha's, it was difficult to believe they were the same world separated only by time.

"I will guide you." Xera held her hand out, palm up, and Sasha hesitated a moment before she took it.

As soon as their skin met, Sasha's entire body shattered into a thousand tiny pieces, twisting into a cyclone of agony where she felt herself dissolving into nothing.

An instant later, she crashed onto the ground, solid and once again whole. The earth beneath her seemed to exude power, and she scrambled to gather her wits about her.

"Take my hand." Xera loomed over her, younger and her eyes a clear blue, the color of ice on a winter's day. A silvery blond braid hung over her shoulder. "We have to keep moving or we'll miss it."

Sasha took her hand, trying to wrap her mind around the things she saw. They were surrounded by rolling green hills, dotted with rocky outcroppings and natural stone arches that looked as though they'd been there for thousands of years. A tranquil river flowed down from a mountain range where a castle kept watch over the valley below. Trees unlike any Sasha had ever seen towered over them, and luscious pink flowers bloomed larger than cabbages as they walked along a worn pathway into the shelter of the forest.

It was a glorious sunny day with blue skies filled with puffy white clouds.

"Where are we going?" Sasha rushed to keep up with Xera's steady pace.

"The battle."

The ground trembled beneath her feet, and boulders tumbled from the mountains into the valley where they walked. Sasha's heart pounded in her chest, and though she knew this was only a memory and nothing could harm her, it was far too real to her in that moment.

As they passed through an ancient archway, the feeling of being torn apart and put back together passed through her again, but only for an instant.

Gasping for breath, Sasha lay a hand over her heart. "You have to warn me about that next time."

"What?" Xera looked over her shoulder with a frown, but Sasha turned back to gaze behind them. The valley looked strange behind her, and she was disoriented. The landscape was similar, but everything was in the wrong place.

"The castle was just over there and now it's there." She pointed to the pathway behind them where the mountains receded in the distance, the castle a smaller break in the horizon.

"We traveled," Xera explained.

"Clearly, but how?"

"You don't have ways of traveling great distances quickly?"

"Yeah, it's called flying. Remember? We did that when we traveled from the island to the valley."

"That wasn't fast." Xera turned back to the narrow road that stretched into the distance and up a series of hillsides to another archway. "That took hours and hours."

"It was a very long way."

"The archways are faster. We'll reach the main battlefield once we travel through the next gateway."

"Um, did we just teleport?"

"I don't know what that means, Lady Sasha." Xera picked up her pace, marching up the pathway into the hills. They reached the old archway at the apex of the highest hill, and Sasha scrunched her eyes shut as she stepped through the gateway.

It wasn't as bad now that she expected it. It was painful but mercifully brief, and she was convinced she literally had shattered into a million tiny particles inside the archway and reformed again as she exited another just like it, miles from where they'd started.

This time, the landscape was more brutal. The ground fell away from the archway, rolling down a steep slope littered with stone and wiry shrubs that managed to sprout from the space between boulders. The mountain was so high, foggy clouds rolled by within reach.

As they darted from one stone to another, they made their way down the steep slope toward a row of massive hills of the same mottled gray stone.

"It has begun," Xera said. "We have to hurry."

The clouds began to clear, and Sasha thought she saw one of the hills move. She rubbed her eyes, blinking rapidly, but the hills were all moving now.

"Are those ... dinosaurs?" Her feet continued to move, but she couldn't stop staring.

"The beasts of war?" Xera shook her head. "They are abominations created with stolen power and used to destroy the people of Indriell who can no longer protect themselves."

One of the massive beasts roared, throwing its head back and revealing rows of sharp teeth. It reminded Sasha vaguely of a T-Rex, but it seemed to understand its masters driving it and its companions across the marshy ground. The battlefield stretched across a wide-open plain at the base of the mountains.

Thousands of soldiers marched in rows with the beasts, and Sasha caught sight of a lumbering creature with a long neck. It looked an awful lot like a brontosaurus, only slightly smaller, and faster than she would have imagined something of that size could move.

Men and women slipped in the marsh, their boots mired in the mud.

As they drew closer to the rear of the army, Sasha realized it wasn't a marshland. The ground was soaked in blood. Rivers of it ran across the plain where the opposing army prepared to strike. The enemy had what looked to be dragon-like beasts soaring in the air, though they screeched like some prehistoric creature Sasha had studied in high school.

"There." Xera pointed to the head of the army they stood behind where the sky glowed a bright red. A woman with familiar silvery blond hair rode atop a white horse-like animal, far larger than any horse Sasha had ever seen.

"You're leading the battle?" Sasha turned to the version of Xera she'd come to know through their travels into her memories. She looked more like the woman on the battlefield, but in the ancient's eyes Sasha could see the older woman she'd become.

"I was a high-ranking noble woman and the anchor of my Syntrophos. I served the queen's army as a general." She pointed down to the young Xera riding between two men. Her Complement and her Syntrophos. Sasha had missed them when she first saw Xera, but she couldn't ignore them now. Together, the three were an insanely powerful entity. Even from her vantage point, Sasha could feel their collective power.

Without warning, Xera pulled her back into the cyclone of her memories, shredding her to pieces and spitting her back out again. This time, they landed in the midst of battle at the front.

Power raged like an electrical storm between the foes. Lightning crashed and thunder boomed as the world fell into chaos around them. The ground shook and broke apart beneath their feet. A river that wasn't there a moment ago now separated the opponents, crashing and surging with impenetrable rapids that reached up from their banks like hands and swept soldiers into its depths.

The world had come alive with all the horror of a nightmare, and Sasha didn't know which way to turn. She ran, keeping up with Xera as they charged across the field to reach the Syntrophos pair riding together through the destruction. The battle was not going their way. Xera and her soldiers were losing, and Sasha had no doubt if they were taken, they would be slaughtered without a moment's hesitation.

The ground surged up, rolling beneath their horses like a wave on the ocean. Sasha watched as the young Xera tumbled from her horse. Scrambling away from the unstable ground, she gained her feet, drawing her sword as a cloaked figure emerged from the storm clouds.

"Vitor!" Xera shouted for her husband standing on the

opposite side of the wide canyon that had opened between them. "Go to Lecia!" She brandished her sword, preparing to meet the enemy head on.

"Rhaegal?" Xera lifted her sword, and it blazed with the fire of her gift. "Face me as you are. No tricks or perversions of the power."

An evil voice laughed, the sound bouncing off the mountains, amplified by the power coursing within him. He was one of the Enlightened who had risen from nothing, taking power from others until it had corrupted him beyond redemption. "Now, why would I do that?"

A boulder nearly the size of Sasha and Xera combined shattered into splinters as long as her arm. The man guided the sharp fragments, turning them toward Xera.

"No!" someone shouted just behind Sasha, but they were too late.

Rhaegal let out a maniacal laugh. With a flick of his hand, the shards of stone ripped through Xera's body. A thousand razor sharp blades sent her stumbling to the ground.

"Xera!" Vitor shrieked from the other side of the canyon. He was still trying to get to her despite her worries for their daughter.

"Lecia!" she cried, blood spurting from her mouth as she rolled to her side. "She needs you." She coughed and gasped for breath.

"Save your daughter, you fool." The voice Sasha had heard before sounded closer now, but she couldn't place its owner.

"Poor little Lecia," the Enlightened said in a mocking tone as he sent the rest of the shards darting across the canyon where they rained down on Vitor as he tried to escape.

Xera lay bleeding and struggled for breath.

"Leave her." A wave of power washed over Sasha, and she turned toward the source.

For a moment, it seemed as if the Enlightened would turn and leave, but he fought to shrug off the impulse to obey. "She is done. I will have her and her *Complement.*" The Enlightened man sneered, spitting on Xera with disdain for her bond. "Run now while you can, coward."

Sasha almost missed him again. The man was so plain and unassuming he blended into the sea of soldiers staggering across the battlefield.

"No," Sasha whispered, forcing herself to get a good look at him.

"You should have sided with us, my *Lord.*" The Enlightened gave a mocking bow. "You could have risen to greatness with the rest of us."

"I could not turn my back on Xera." Xera's Syntrophos crashed to his knees beside her. "And I won't leave her now."

Their voices grew garbled, and the memory fell away into a cloud of smoke.

Sasha stumbled back onto the steps of the pavilion in the temple gardens. The sun shone brightly overhead, warming her face and chasing away the chill of the memory.

"That is all I can recall." Xera panted beside her, her face covered in sweat from the effort of remembering. "I assume Vitor escaped with my Syntrophos. Otherwise we both would have died that day."

"Who was that man?" Sasha placed her hands on the ground to still herself in the moment as her mind whirled with what she'd just witnessed.

"Rhaegal was one of the original Enlightened. He attacked hundreds of the nobility, taking their power to bolster his own. It was never enough for him. He craved more and more, until he was nothing more than a monster."

"Not him." Sasha gripped the sun warmed step she sat on. "The other one. Your Syntrophos."

"Teigan." Her voice trembled with sadness. "I believe that was the last time I saw him. I cannot remember anything beyond that moment. I can only recall the vaguest of memories of my arrival at the prison of the Enlightened. And then nothing."

"Lord Teigan of Indriell?" Sasha gasped. "The man who was betrothed to Princess Eiselynn before she bonded with her Complement, Ían? He is your Syntrophos?"

"Yes, how in the world could you know anything of my Teigan? It's been thousands of years. I don't even know if he lives. I haven't been able to feel him, but it's been so lon—"

"He lives." Sasha interrupted, struggling to take a breath. "He goes by the name Marcus Servius now."

Chapter 34

Allie | Kelleys Island | June

"So, we're just going to run in there like gangbusters?" Briggs sprinted behind Allie along the tunnel to her parents' house.

"Pretty much." Allie pushed them faster. A sense of urgency had given her determination to get through this, even if she had to wing it.

"You just do your dreamworld thing and keep us and my parents protected from Marcus and whatever muscle he's brought with him. And I need you to remember my mom and dad are mortal. Protect them first before anyone else. Especially me."

"Roger that." Briggs began to pull on his power, and the air around them went thick like molasses, slowing them down.

"What's happening?" Chloe shot a glance over her shoulder at Briggs.

"I need a minute to call on the dreamworld." He slowed to a halt. "It's not something I can do in a heartbeat."

"This feels weird." Chloe lifted her arms, watching as they swayed and drifted, like she was suddenly submerged in water.

Allie's hair fanned out around her, and for a moment, she felt weightless.

"Ready," Briggs called from the darkness over her shoulder, but she couldn't see him.

"Where are you?" Allie whispered, searching for him in the narrow tunnel.

"The dreamworld," Briggs' voice sounded ethereal and ghost-like.

"Cool." Chloe grinned and turned back toward Allie's house.

Allie followed, her confidence bolstered by Briggs' brand of protection. "No one can see you, right?"

"Right."

"And Marcus won't even sense you?"

"Nope. The dreamworld shields me from detection. I've pulled a thin barrier around you and Chloe, so he can see you. If he turns his power against you, it'll work, but not well."

"That's so amazing." Allie ran faster. "Remind me, I'm going to owe you big time for this."

"Oh, I will not be letting you forget." Briggs faded further into his protection until she couldn't sense him at all, but his voice was a gentle whisper in her ear. "Take care of yourself, Princess."

"Fei Long is close, right?" Allie whispered as they neared the ladder entrance to her parents' garden shed.

"Right on the surface." Chloe nodded, her eyes pulsing with the fire of her dragon.

Allie reached for the ladder, but something knocked her back on her rear.

"What was that?" She scrambled back to her feet.

"Sorry." The ghost of a whisper coiled around her. "Sometimes, I forget how much stronger I am this way."

Briggs moved past her in a chilly blast of air. "I'm going up first."

"You need the code." Allie hurried behind him, unable to sense where he took up space.

"Punch it in." His breath brushed against her face.

"You're creeping me out." She punched in the code, and they all scrambled through the hatch in the floor of the shed.

"She's here." A smooth voice echoed in the night. "Find her."

"Game on." Allie pointed for the door leading into the garden, which occupied the space between the main building of the old church her parents had renovated into their retirement home and the guest house Liam and Kahlynn had once lived in back when Allie's life was a lot simpler.

Allie followed Briggs into the cool spring evening, a riot of familiar scents filling her with a sense of homecoming. Sage and basil along with roses, lavender, and chamomile from the world's most unorganized garden. It was the scent of home and that put her even more at ease as she stepped onto the moonlit path, glowing with the green light of her gift.

"Keep going with your gut, Allie," Chloe whispered as she followed closely behind.

"Alexis, welcome." Marcus gave an indulgent chuckle from his perch on one of the patio chairs under the umbrella. "You never cease to disappoint me with your ability to do exactly as I expect. Though, I suppose those pulling your strings from behind the scenes deserve some of the credit."

The insult rankled, but she was all too willing to let him underestimate her.

"You don't need to involve my parents in this." Allie's eyes went right to her mother and father, sitting quietly on the swing opposite Marcus. They weren't moving, except for the slight motion of their breath. But they saw her, their worried eyes shifting nervously between Allie and Marcus. They couldn't seem to speak at all. She tried to reassure them with a smile, but the fierce looking Immortal woman standing behind them was a cause for worry. What more could this woman do beyond subduing her parents?

Another Immortal stood behind Marcus, whispering to him, his voice like a gentle hiss.

"Mortals." Marcus shook his head. "I'll never understand what Kassandre was thinking when she abandoned you with them."

"She didn't abandon me." Allie took a bold step forward, Chloe following, gripping her bladed bo staff in her fist.

Allie gripped Kassandre's blades in her hands, eager for a chance to use them to defend the parents she'd chosen for her daughter.

"And who is this brave little soldier behind you?" Marcus gestured for Chloe to come forward, like she was a shy child hiding behind her mother's skirts.

Chloe's eyes pulsed with fire, and he gave a soft chuckle, sitting back in his swing like they were all attending a garden tea on a summer afternoon.

"She moves with a shadow, Master." The rail thin man behind Marcus hissed. "It is a power not her own."

"Ah, the unseen protection of Mr. Quinn Loukas, no doubt." Marcus smiled. "Come out to play with us, dear boy."

"Quinn isn't here," Allie said. "But I am. You've orchestrated everything to perfection so I would arrive here without the protection of my elders or the support of my council. What do you want?" She chanced a look at her parents, and she gripped her sai blades tighter in her hands.

"No need for those tonight, dear Alexis. I only wanted to talk. To take your measure on your own. You have powerful friends shielding you, my dear. I merely wanted to meet you as you are. No games. No coup. Just you and I, one to one. Will you join me?" He gestured at the curved iron bench her mother found at a flea market. It was a rusted mess when she'd brought it home, but together, Allie and Lily had breathed new life into it with a little elbow grease and paint.

Allie moved to sit on the bench, and Chloe took up her stance beside Allie. Standing with her weapon at the ready, but noticeably not behind her. Chloe was making a statement that she didn't serve Allie in the way Marcus' people served him. She stood beside Allie as an equal.

"Say whatever you came to say and let's be done with this." Allie shoved her blades back in their sheaths at her waist. A surge of fear rushed through her mind, and she gripped the edge of her seat, wincing at the effort to resist Marcus' power. Even behind the shelter of the dreamworld Briggs had offered her, the pressure mounted, and a spot of blood dripped from her nose to splash on her hand.

"How do you resist me?" Marcus leaned forward, studying her aura.

"What do you mean?" She pretended ignorance, though she was nearly certain of what he'd just done ... or tried to do.

"You guard your mind better than most adults a hundred times your age."

"Talent." Allie held her power close, like a hedge of protection she could hide behind.

"Not hers," the Immortal behind Marcus was quick to add. "At least not hers alone. The shadow protects her."

"I didn't say it was just my talent." Allie shifted on the bench. She ached to go to her parents, but she couldn't afford any sudden moves. For all she knew, the Immortal guarding them held them on the brink of death already.

As she relaxed against the bench, feigning a calm manner she didn't feel, the green light of her gift settled around her like a blanket, giving her courage. Allie sensed the whisper of Briggs nearby and stilled her fidgeting.

"You're stronger than I thought." Marcus frowned. "But you're still just a child."

"I'm just a girl trying to live her life. What did you expect?" Allie shrugged, trying to get a read on his intentions for this meeting.

"He's trying to get inside your head," Briggs murmured gently in her ear. "Don't let him."

"Though, you probably shouldn't underestimate my generation," Allie said, glancing at Chloe. "Some of us are much more than we appear."

"Yes, yes, your generation is talented," Marcus said in a bored tone. "But you lack experience, which is why the Senate will never bend to your demands."

"You have some inside tips for me, Senator Sinclair?" Allie leaned forward, her tone mocking, despite the tremor of fear she felt at the probing sensation entering the darkest corners of her mind. It was a very familiar sensation. One she'd felt often when communicating with Aidan. But this intrusive force was alien and wrong.

Marcus smiled. "Your early election will never happen, dear girl. It was a good thought, I'll give you that, but Immortals are creatures of habit, and we only have a few years before the next scheduled election. Why rush it now?"

"Because we do not have a fully functioning government and the people know it. A lot of damage can be done in a few years with a corrupt government in charge." Allie was grateful for Briggs' protection. Without it, she had no chance of resisting Marcus' gift at work. Few had ever seen him use his powers directly. Even fewer knew what they were. Not even Livia or Porcia knew everything he could do.

"You know, this *is* interesting." Allie's voice shook slightly from the effort of resisting him. "You usually hide behind the gifts of others while you lurk in your mundane shadows."

"One could say the same of you, my dear." Marcus' eyes smoldered with the power of his telepathic gift, but Allie had years of experience controlling her own telepathic mind. She'd worked tirelessly to protect her mind and her private thoughts. She would not succumb to Marcus.

"Steady," Allie whispered to Briggs for encouragement. He was undoubtedly taking the brunt of Marcus' mental attack.

Chloe let out a growl of irritation, and Allie raised a hand to steady her.

Marcus' shoulders shook with a patronizing laugh. "Like kittens frolicking in the grass."

The assault Marcus pressed against Allie's mind doubled in intensity, and she grappled with her control. Sharp, stabbing pain ripped through her head, and she gasped.

Did you think it would be easy? His voice rattled in her mind. *To face me all on your own?*

"No," Allie spat the word out through gritted teeth as

she grappled to keep him out. Marcus wasn't just a telepath. Not like her. He was something much scarier. Even now she could feel him worming his way through the edges of her thoughts, planting doubts and lies he wanted her to believe. His power was slick and oily. Repulsive. She pushed him out, sealing her mind off as best she could.

It left her weak and unsteady. Her stomach heaving from the effort.

Allie wanted to put herself between Marcus and her parents, but she didn't have the strength to stand. "You've given me little choice, dragging me here in the middle of the night." Her voice was small and insignificant against the weight of his mind pressing into hers. "Get on with it, old man." Her teeth clenched and she thought she might faint from the effort of holding off his psychological assault on her mind.

With a stab of shooting pain through her head, he was back inside her thoughts, slipping past her mental barriers like smoke.

You would sacrifice yourself to save these mortals. It wasn't a question, so Allie merely met him gaze for gaze. *Your love for them will be your downfall, Ms. Carmichael.*

Fear flowed like molten lava through Allie's veins, and she wanted to give into the urge to run. To leave those she loved behind to face her enemy on their own. The minute she fled he would kill them. She knew it for certain, yet she still wanted to run.

Allie shook her head, grasping for her power and the control she'd worked years to perfect in order to have the privacy of her own thoughts. Thoughts that would never even consider abandoning her parents.

Oh, you have power, Alexis, his voice hissed in her mind. *Great power. But you are too weak of mind to use it.*

"No." Allie pressed back, recoiling from the fear and thoughts that weren't hers. Lifting her head, she finally managed to stand and moved between Marcus and her parents. The fear didn't belong to her. It was only Marcus' influence. It wasn't real. Neither were her thoughts of abandoning her parents, yet she finally understood why others bent to his will. But she wouldn't give in so easily. She couldn't. "You can't make me abandon them," Allie's voice was like gravel in her throat, but she fought on, resisting him with everything she had.

Brave girl. He gave her a nod of respect. *But I have so many questions.* He sifted through her mind, searching her for weaknesses, but Allie threw up a mental block, pushing him away from the most private corners of her mind. She'd learned to compartmentalize her thoughts when her telepathic connection with Aidan first developed. She could do that again now, keeping the core of who she was protected against Marcus.

"Did you ... ever think ... to maybe ... just ask me your questions?" She struggled to speak. "Like a normal person."

"Touche." The force beating at the edges of her mind receded, and she took a deep breath, throwing her hands out to catch her balance. He scared the bejebers out of her, but she would stand her ground or die trying.

"All right, I'll play by your rules for the moment. Exactly what do you intend to do to fulfill your little prophecy?" Marcus steepled his hands under his chin, his elbows propped on the arms of the chair where he sat.

"Nothing if I can get away with it, but that's entirely up to you." Allie stood with her feet firmly planted on the ground, her hands resting on the sai blades at her hips. Chloe had moved to stand with her, keeping a careful eye on her parents.

"You think of yourself as the savior of the world because an old prophecy claims you're the only one who can stop this 'darkness' from coming."

Allie laughed. "Not even a little bit. I'm clairvoyant, and even I don't know what the future holds. But you and I both know that prophecies are subjective. A lot of wordy waffle that doesn't have to mean anything literal. If my grandmother's prophecy is fulfilled, it will be entirely due to your actions. Self-fulfilling prophecies never really work out well for those involved."

"You and I could work so well together, Allie."

"Is this the part where you lure me over to the dark side?" Allie was grateful to have Chloe by her side, but she could sense the heat surging within her friend. She chanced a glance at her, urging Chloe to keep Fei Long at bay a little longer. The last thing Marcus needed to see was the dragon, yet they needed the reassurance of Fei Long's presence if things went sour and they needed a quick escape. Allie could just barely sense Briggs standing between them and Marcus, but knowing he was there gave her confidence. She just had to trust him to help her parents when the time was right.

"I could just take your gift now, kill your parents, and be done with you all." Marcus let his hands fall apart like that was the only other option. "Or, perhaps I could take you on as my personal executioner. Your gift will always work better for you than it would for me—even though you inherited it from the man who stole it from me thousands of years ago."

"Neither of those options work for me. My Judgment gift doesn't work at my will."

"Semantics." Marcus shrugged. "I can train you to overcome that limitation. Just ask your boyfriend. Aidan has benefited quite well from my training."

"You take your *training* too far." Allie's hands balled into fists at her side. This man had messed with Aidan's head so much she wasn't sure he'd ever be himself again. Not entirely.

Marcus gave her a sour look. "You aren't ready. It's a pity Aidan wasn't the child of prophecy. It's not often anyone manages to fool me. He is above and beyond anything you can ever hope to be."

"Then we agree on one thing. He will always be the better person, no matter what he faces."

Marcus laughed. Not a gentlemanly chuckle, but a full-bodied, tears in the eyes, kind of laugh, like he'd just realized something and found it utterly amusing. "Go back to your tower, Princess. You're no good to me yet." He gave another amused chuckled and nodded to the woman standing guard over Lily and Carson.

The ear-splitting screams of her parents nearly ripped Allie's heart to shreds.

"Mom! Dad!" Allie fumbled for her blades, but some unseen forced pinned her in place.

"It's not working, Master," the woman shouted over their screams. "Something is blocking me."

"It's the shadow." The thin man hissed. "He weakens our power with his shield."

"Interesting." Marcus lifted a brow. "Very interesting. Winifred, kill them the old-fashioned way."

"No!" Allie shrieked, trying to reach her parents, but her limbs wouldn't work and the woman already had a dagger to her father's throat. "No, please! Briggs!" Her voice broke and she slid to the ground.

Chloe stood immobile beside her, but her eyes burned

bright with dragon fire. "Help them, please." Allie begged and Chloe nodded.

Fei Long spiraled out of her in a cloud of golden vapor and raging fire spewing from her maw. She burned the Immortal woman to a crisp in an instant.

Lily and Carson slumped to the ground, shaking and gasping, but seemingly all right.

The Immortal woman wasn't. Her charred corpse was intact. She would recover, but it wouldn't be today.

The thin man standing guard over Marcus stepped from the shadows of the garden umbrella, but Marcus held him back. "See to Winifred." He dismissed his companion.

"What do we have here?" Marcus stood up, studying Chloe, her eyes blazing with the surge of her power. He took a step toward her, his eyes glued to Fei Long who now stood guard over Allie's parents. Nothing could harm them as long as Chloe's dragon was with them.

"You do surround yourself with the most talented people, my dear Alexis. Such a pity I can't see your shadow bodyguard." He shook his head.

Allie could see it in his eyes: he wanted to add Chloe to his collection, and he wanted her badly. Briggs too.

Marcus crossed the grassy lawn between the haphazard garden beds. "You are the daughter of the Immortals Ming Lao and Jin Jing, yes?" He asked Chloe.

She met his gaze and gave a single nod as he approached her. She waited until he was within arm's reach, and a stream of dragon fire spilled from her mouth and hit the ground at his feet.

"Release us."

"Very impressive." He took a step back, tapping his shoes against the grass to put out the fire. He studied the angry Fei Long, roughly the size of a small house with fury lighting the obsidian orbs of her eyes.

"Are you even aware of how your dragon was formed, dear girl?" He ignored her demand but feeling returned to Allie's limbs and she crawled across the garden to her parents' side.

"I made her as a tribute to my mother." Chloe's voice was rough and garbled with the strength of her dragon's power.

"A very dangerous thing. And a very unusual one. Not many full-grown, Proven Immortals could have managed it, and so well, I might add."

"Briggs." Allie hissed.

"They're okay. See to Chloe." Briggs' voice brushed softly against her ear. "Get up and face him. I've got you all shielded."

Allie climbed to her feet, checking over Lily and Carson while Marcus was distracted with Chloe.

"Something of your mother's spirit resides within your dragon." Marcus stood with his hand in one pocket as if they were discussing politics.

"I know." Chloe held her bo staff in front of her, keeping his attention on her.

"Are you okay?" Allie crouched beside Lily and Carson. She searched them for lasting signs of distress, but with the Immortal Winifred now incapacitated, they seemed to be fine at first glance.

"We're okay." Lily's voice shook with the effort of speaking. "Or we will be when you're safe." Allie helped them to their feet, noting the subtle signs of aging that hadn't been there before. Her mother's hair was a little grayer, and the fine lines around her father's eyes were deeper. Sucking in a strangled breath, she wondered how many years this Winifred had cost her parents in the brief moments she'd used her power on them. Thank God for Briggs or there might not be anything left of her parents now.

She couldn't think about that right now or she really would lose her temper, and that wouldn't be good for Chloe or Briggs.

"Stay with Fei Long, she'll protect you." Allie patted the fiery-red dragon scales as Fei Long stretched out her wings and roared her fury at Marcus. "Get ready to run when I say."

"I'm not sure running is going to happen." Carson's voice sounded weary, like he might collapse at any moment.

"Ming Lao hasn't gone far, you know?" Marcus watched Fei Long. "It's not a natural thing for an Immortal to die. It happens, of course, but when it does, the spirit often lingers, unsure of where to go."

"What are you saying?" Chloe took a step toward Marcus.

"Chloe don't listen to him," Allie tried to call her back. "He will mess with your mind."

"Your mother is still with you, my dear. She can come back."

"Chloe." Allie wanted to lash out at Marcus for giving her hope. "We have to go, now." Allie urged Lily and Carson toward their escape through the garden shed. Marcus and his remaining buddy didn't seem too worried about them now that more interesting things had their attention.

"Every gift has a yin and yang, girl," the thin Immortal said.

Marcus crossed the garden to stand with Chloe. "Exactly, an opposite side of the same coin."

"What are you saying?" Chloe's voice was the most dragon-like Allie had ever heard.

"My daughter has bonded with her Complement, hasn't she?" Marcus directed the question at Allie.

"*My* sister is happily married, yes." Allie put herself between Fei Long and Marcus.

"Certain ... effects of some gifts ... very powerful gifts, can often be reversed." He leaned down to Chloe's level. "And I know how it's done."

"You're saying you can bring her back?" Chloe asked, and Fei Long shrieked in outrage, like a mother trying to protect her child. She tried to get between Chloe and Marcus, but Chloe had learned to control Fei Long and refused to let her.

"Not to her body. But there are ways she can return."

"She wouldn't want that!" Allie screamed the moment she realized Chloe would fall for it.

Chloe turned toward Allie, the fire of her dragon raging inside her. "Go."

White hot fire erupted from Chloe's mouth, scorching the ground between them. "Chloe, this is how it will happen," Allie shouted over the roar of the flames. "Remember Justice and his painting." But Chloe shook her head, turning back to Marcus. Fei Long faded into a wisp of golden vapor, and it was just Allie and her parents standing by the garden shed.

"Going somewhere Ms. Carmichael?" Marcus sent his remaining minion after them, taking Chloe with him.

"Hurry." Briggs' form shimmered in and out of focus. He reached for the trap door in the floor of the shed. "I can't hold onto the dreamworld much longer."

"Mom, Dad, you go first." Allie's hands trembled as she tried to punch in the code. The room swam around her, and her head throbbed. Something was wrong. She didn't feel right.

Lily and Carson ignored her, moving around the shed, flipping switches and punching in codes on panels she'd never seen before. She watched mystified as they retrieved magnetized weapons from the garden box where they kept fresh soil.

"We need to move quickly." Lily tossed Allie a flashlight, but it clattered to the ground before she could catch it.

Thick metal slabs slid from the walls, enclosing them in a steel box before Marcus' bodyguard could get to them.

Darkness flooded the room, and as soon as she knew they were safe, Allie collapsed to the floor.

CHAPTER 35

Sasha | Chola Valley Temple | A Season of Revelations

"I remember what happened." Xera charged into Sasha's room in the middle of the night, but she wasn't sleeping. Sasha was still trying to figure out how she was going to tell the poor woman that her Syntrophos had become a monster in her absence.

"What?" Sasha sat up in her bed, feigning confusion.

"I remember it all." Xera slumped down on the bed beside her. "I died on the battlefield that day. Rhaegal took me as a prisoner of war, knowing I would rise again.

"Where did Rhaegal take you?"

"He didn't." Xera shook her head. "I was useless to him without Vitor so he turned me over to the Enlightened prison camps. I was there for a long time, cut off from my power and the rest of the world by their wicked barriers that made us sick. We lived in squalor with barely enough to eat or drink. I grew weak, but Leandro was there with me."

Her shoulders shook with laughter. "This is the first time I have been away from him since. I've spent more time with him than with my own family." She wiped the moisture from her opaque eyes.

"We were transported to a prison in Indriell where we stayed for many years while the war still raged around us. My memories of that time are vague and distant. I believe we were there far longer than we were on the island prison, though I don't know if that's true or not."

"Trust your instincts," Sasha whispered, laying a comforting hand on Xera's shoulder.

"I think someone tried to make us forget those years." She stood, crossing the room to the untouched tray of food on Sasha's desk. She picked at a bunch of grapes before she turned back toward Sasha. "My memories are just out of reach, but I keep grasping at them. Some moments I remember the Indriell prison and all the years we existed there, all but forgotten. Then nothing." She threw her hands up in frustration. "Just a white room. And nothing. Nothing but white. Silence and isolation."

Sasha nodded, rising from her bed to stand with Xera. "I've heard of this white room." She took Xera's hands in hers. "My Syntrophos was a captive once." She didn't want to go into great detail about Soma or the Coalition. It would just confuse her more. "He was tortured, and his memories of that time weren't real. As he explains it, he spent a great deal of time in a white room. Isolated and alone. It nearly drove him mad."

"Yes." Xera's eyes widened as she clutched Sasha's hands. "What is it?"

"It doesn't matter right now. Can you tell me what you remember after the white room?"

Xera shrugged. "The island. I don't recall how we got there. The white room faded, and we were just there." Xera's knees buckled, and Sasha pulled her back to the bed, forcing her to sit down and drink a glass of water.

"That's not all I remember," Xera said, her whole body

trembling. "The island was a brutal place. We suffered there. But we were not alone."

"The guards?" Sasha had visited the island herself. It was a strange place with buildings that were centuries old, pitifully small cells made of natural loadstone and heavily rusted iron bars. It was the island itself that felt like the prison with miles of vicious jungle, few sources of fresh water, intense heat, and nothing but open, shark infested waters surrounding the small island.

"There were guards in the beginning. Mortals oddly enough. It was the first time any of us had encountered such creatures. Some were almost kind, others seemed to hate us. They taught us your language. Forced us to learn it, actually. I remember one once said it was a waste of time, but the ... Margrave ordered us to learn."

"I wondered where you learned English." Sasha nodded for her to go on, schooling her face not to show any emotion. The prison, at least in the beginning, was a Coalition prison. It made sense, since Marcus had infiltrated and taken over the Coalition in the sixteenth century. He must have taken a special interest in the island and the ancients who inhabited it, but how had he never realized his own Syntrophos was trapped there?

"Eventually, the guards died and none came to replace them. We were confined to cells for too many years to count. Starving, weak, and cut off from our power, but we eventually escaped when the building began to crumble around us. But it was the island that was the true prison. There was no escape."

"Why?"

"An invisible barrier kept us trapped so we couldn't reach the sea. We discovered it was the barrier itself that left us weak, cutting us off from our power, so we were defenseless and sick. Resources went quickly, and that's when we turned on each other."

Sasha nodded. A powerful magnetic barrier would certainly keep them there. "If there were no guards, who else was there with you?"

"The bad ones." Xera shivered. "Cruel and evil to the core."

"Who were they?"

"Rhaegal and the other Enlightened who survived the Great War. They were powerless, driven insane from their thirst for the power they could no longer touch. They hunted and tormented us."

All the blood drained from Sasha's face. "Xera, if they were there on the island with you, where did they go once you escaped?" Sasha and her team had scoured every inch of that island searching for any remaining prisoners, but they hadn't found a single soul, and there was no magnetic barrier to speak of.

"They escaped when we did." Her voice trembled with fear. "One day the barrier was just gone, and we fled across the sea to a nearby island. We did some healing there, waiting for our powers to return. It wasn't enough. My mind..." she shook her head. "Everything was a mess. I didn't trust my own thoughts. I'm so sorry."

"Then these others—the Enlightened—are out there? Roaming free in the modern world?" Sasha wanted to throw something in her frustration. It wasn't Xera's fault she hadn't thought to tell Sasha of these others. She'd been through too much to make sense of it all. But there was little Sasha could do about it now.

Xera nodded. "My memory is becoming clearer here in the valley. Things that made little sense before are falling into place. I think someone let us out, Sasha. I think they wanted us to ... destroy the world until there was nothing left."

"How many of the Enlightened were there?"

"At least half our number, though they were as ruthless as an army of a hundred well-trained warriors. After all this time, cut off from their power, they will be thirsty for more."

"We have to get this information to Allie as soon as possible."

"Will Mother Raghaven allow us to leave now?" Xera asked.

"I will talk to her."

"Lady Sasha," Xera began in a hushed whisper. "Who would do such a thing?"

Sasha sighed. "Someone who has been plotting revenge for a very long time." Sasha took Xera's hand in hers. "I'm afraid the man behind all your suffering is very familiar to you."

"Who could it be?" Xera's blind eyes searched her face and Sasha was loathe to break her heart with the news.

"A man who calls himself Marcus Servius. He is an ancient who once went by the name of Lord Teigan. Your Syntrophos."

"She isn't ready, child, and neither are you." Mother Raghavan rapped Sasha's knees with the butt of her cane as she perched on the edge of the stone bench in her garden.

"It's imperative we get back to Sterling Tower to deliver the information we've uncovered. Xera is Marcus' Syntrophos. Do you know what that means?" Sasha wanted to rip the cane out of the old lady's grip and see how she liked the be on the receiving end for a change, but she had far too much respect—and fear—for the Mother to give into her fantasy.

"Of course, I know what it means, girl." She held her cane in a tighter grip, as if she could tell what Sasha was thinking. "You think because I live here in the valley, I don't know what's happening in the real world?" The old woman snorted a laugh. "I know more than you do, child. And I know Xera could be the key to Marcus' undoing. He doesn't know she lives. He believes she died that day on the battlefield with her Complement. Vitor survived, but he spent years trying to find Xera. No one has seen Vitor in a thousand years. But he left his child in the care of Lord Teigan. Can you imagine what he's done to that poor girl?"

Sasha shivered at the thought. That Lecia could have ended up like Livia hadn't even occurred to her. But if the girl was powerful, Marcus wouldn't have let her out of his grasp.

"Losing Xera is what sent him on the path toward what he's become," the Mother said in a kinder tone. "If she should return to the river of time now that her power is fully restored, he will begin to feel their bond again. That cannot happen yet. It needs to happen at the right moment, and when it does, it will kill him when he realizes he's the one who imprisoned her on that island. When he sees the disapproval and rejection in her blind eyes, it will destroy him."

"How did he not know she was there?"

Mother Raghavan shook her head. "I don't know. But there is a reason he tried to eliminate the mortals of the Coalition. They had fulfilled their purpose. I believe he has strategically taken control of every Coalition prison across the world, and when the timing is right, he will free all those within who serve him. Just as he did with the ancients he sequestered on that island of horrors."

"We can't let him do that, Mother," Sasha said. "I *have* to get back."

"And you will, when I'm done with you. Whether you leave now or in a year hence, you'll arrive home a short time after you left it. You know how this works, girl, so stop acting like you're a novice when you haven't been such in a long time." She moved as if to strike Sasha's knees again but tapped her cane against the ground instead. "You will leave after your Proving and not a moment before."

"Yes, Mother." Sasha bowed her head in respect for the Mother's wishes. "I just ..." she trailed off, biting her lip.

"Spit it out, child."

"I miss Quinn." The longing in her voice was only a hint of the pain she suffered being separated from her Syntrophos. "If I could just see him now and then, it would make this so much easier."

"I know the separation is difficult. I am sorry for that. You two have had more than your fair share of suffering, but Quinn and Santi are hard at work, building something wonderful with their collective gifts. A place that will be sorely needed in the coming age. Because that is what we are facing child, the dawn of a new age for our people."

Sasha nodded, holding back her tears. "I understand, Mother."

"No you don't." She chuckled, rapping Sasha's knees with the tip of her cane. "But you will. Did you know the rules of the dreamworld are slightly different here in the valley?"

"I did not."

"The boy can spend much more time there, doing what he is best at, from this side of the valley."

"I see." The tension in Sasha's chest relaxed some at the

news of her Syntrophos. That he was hopefully doing something he loved.

"The valley is old. Older even than me, and that's quite a feat." The Mother laughed. "Immortals much more talented than you or I built this place. It lies on a plain somewhere between the river of time and the dreamworld, safe in its own little bubble."

"Then I can imagine having a dream walker here in the valley would be beneficial," Sasha said.

"It is." Mother Raghavan nodded. "But there are only so many I can help here. The Coalition won't recover from the recent attacks. Some might try, but there aren't enough of them left to make a go of it."

"Does that mean the prisons across the world aren't manned?" Sasha gasped.

"Those that are functioning are hanging on to control by a breath. It's only a matter of time before all those prisoners are freed. Whether they escape or they are liberated doesn't matter. Most of those poor souls never did a thing wrong. They will need a place to recover. I can do that here, but the valley wasn't designed to take on that many lost souls."

"You want to send them to the dreamworld? With Quinn?"

"Yes and no. Quinn is the most talented dreamwalker born in thousands of years. He is a true Commander. Even the dreamworld itself recognizes him as such. The talent for building places like this shouldn't be lost. Quinn and Santi are building a refuge—one that will dwell partially in the dreamworld and partially *inside* the river of time. The valley is a wonderful place to reconnect with one's self. It is also a place where certain skills can be learned, as you well know. But the sacrifice of time ... hurts a little too much for some."

"It can be a necessary sacrifice," Sasha said sadly. "It hurts, but it also heals."

"You speak truth, young Sasha. Yet some, like Xera and her people, could benefit from a different sort of place, don't you think?"

Sasha nodded. "I do. And I have no doubt Quinn will create something wonderful."

"And not just for his ability as a walker—though that is a remarkable gift—but Quinn was blessed with other gifts he's struggled to understand."

"He's always been hard on himself, believing his gifts were evil."

"They can be." The Mother tapped her cane against the hard packed ground beneath her feet. "But with practice, his gift for ... manipulating mental health can easily swing toward the positive and away from the negative."

Sasha's eyes burned with tears. "Oh, Mother Raghavan, you have no idea how much that would save him from himself." She threw her arms around her teacher. "The weight of his gifts is so much more than he can bear sometimes."

"He is learning how to heal minds, dear girl. With a little instruction Santi is actually guiding him through it. Her gifts will also go a long way in healing those who have suffered. Together, they are doing great things. You will become part of that in time. He is your Syntrophos after all. But first, you must Prove.

"Yes Mother. Thank you for the insight. It does my heart so much good to know how he is doing. I can be patient while he trains and works toward a future that will be so much better for everyone, including him.

"Off to bed with you." Mother Raghavan swatted her with her cane. "You've kept an old lady up far past her bedtime."

"Goodnight, Mother." Sasha rose from the bench, offering a deep bow of respect to her teacher before she turned back toward the temple.

With a deep sigh, Sasha wondered if she could survive the crippling need to take action while she was stuck in the valley. The thought of her Proving still seemed so very far away.

Chapter 36

Allie | Sterling Tower | June

Allie woke up on the plane and immediately puked in an airsick bag.

"Ugh." Allie blinked, shielding her eyes from the bright sunshine. "What happened?" She peered up at four concerned faces—two of them her parents—and it all came rushing back to her. "Chloe!" She sat up, and the plane seemed to choose that exact moment to drop a few thousand feet, and she wanted to hurl again.

"Briggs told us what happened." Grandpa Alex helped her sit up. "Chloe went with Marcus, but we don't understand why."

"He tempted her away with promises to bring her mom back." Allie shook her head, immediately regretting it. The hangover had come back with a vengeance. "But Chloe's too smart to fall for that."

"Marcus can be very persuasive." Grandpa Alex frowned.

"Yeah, he's some kind of monster telepath." She shivered at the memory of his voice in her head. "But it's more than that. It's like he can manipulate you with his thoughts. But Chloe has a strength of will like no one else I know. She went with him, but I don't think she'll fall for his promises. Something she saw with her gift led her to make that choice."

"She is young, and he is a difficult Immortal to resist," Alexander insisted. "We will help her find her way home again."

Allie wanted to protest that Chloe wouldn't have fallen for such an obvious ploy, but her head pounded like a drum, and she couldn't think straight.

"Honey, you don't look so good." Lily handed her a bottle of water. "I think you need to rest."

"I'm fine." Allie took the water and drained the tiny bottle in a few gulps. "Are you guys okay? He didn't hurt you, did he?"

"We're okay, sweetheart," Carson said, but Allie didn't like what she saw when she studied their faces. They looked so ... old. It was a subtle change, but they both had more gray in their hair and deeper lines in their faces. She didn't like it.

"We have bigger things to worry about right now than us." Lily pressed her to keep drinking water.

"We have to go back for Chloe." Allie couldn't imagine returning to Sterling Tower without her.

"Not a good time for that, hon." Briggs sat beside her looking exhausted, like using his gift had drained him of every last ounce of energy.

"We can't just leave her."

"I'm afraid that's exactly what we have to do, granddaughter." Alexander moved to the seat across from her.

Allie choked on a breath as a stabbing pain hit her like icepicks through her skull. "What's going on?" She clutched her head.

"How are you feeling?" Grandpa Alex cupped her face in his hands to study her for a moment before he let her go.

"Not great." She raked a hand through sweaty hair. "What happened after we got into the underground?"

"You passed out cold," Briggs said over a mouthful of the chicken salad sandwich he was devouring. "Went down like a boulder. For a second, we thought you died." At Allie's eyeroll, he clarified, "Not permanently. We just thought Marcus gave you a heart attack or something you'd have to regenerate from. Like some kind of sicko parting gift."

Allie rubbed her chest, giving her body a mental checkup. "I feel like I've got the flu. Everything hurts. 'Specially my head."

"What's wrong with her?" Lily ran a motherly hand over her brow, checking for a fever. "She's never been sick a day in her life."

"It's time." Grandpa Alex gave her hand another squeeze.

"So soon?" Carson sounded afraid, and her dad didn't scare easily.

"Wait, what are you guys talking about?" Allie tried to focus on them as they each gave the other a knowing look. "Time for what?"

"We've got to get her back to the tower as soon as possible," Grandpa Alex said.

"I'll radio ahead for Daniel to meet us at the airport with the chopper." Briggs stuffed the last of his sandwich in his mouth and headed to the cockpit.

"Radio ahead for what?" Allie's nerves started to churn in her stomach. "Mom." She reached for Lily, suddenly needing her mother more than she ever had before. Lily took Briggs' vacant seat next to her, draping a protective arm around her.

Carson crouched beside her, taking her hand. "It's time for your Proving, sweetheart."

Alexander didn't even flinch when the mortal man showed just how much he knew about their world. But of course, Grandpa Alex—the Scholar—knew everything.

"No." Allie shook her head. "I'm not ready." Tears filled her eyes. With her parents right there beside her, she wanted nothing more than to return to the little girl who knew nothing of the Immortal world. The girl who didn't understand why the mortals around her didn't seem to like her very much. It had been lonely then, but the world of her childhood represented safety. Safety she hadn't felt in a very long time.

"It wouldn't be happening if you weren't ready, darling." Lily hugged her tightly.

"Your parents are very wise." Alexander took a seat on the sidelines of this monumental moment. Lily and Carson hadn't been able to be part of Allie's Immortal milestone moments, but she was really glad they were here for this one.

"I don't know how to do this." Allie trembled. She'd just faced her greatest enemy—the world's greatest enemy—and she'd made it through. She'd rather face Marcus again than what lay ahead of her now.

"That's the way it is for us all," Alexander offered. "You will do the best you can, and you'll make it through."

"What if I don't?"

"We will cross that bridge when we come to it."

Allie shook her head. "If I fail, what happens?"

"Your power will begin to die, and you'll grow weak. It won't kill you, but it's a difficult transition for some Immortals. That's why they live in remote colonies together. It's no small thing to be powerless and Immortal at the same time. Though we offer a great deal of protection for such colonies."

"Let's not dwell on what ifs," Carson said.

"When will we land?" Allie asked, trying to pull herself together. "I need Emma."

Briggs returned. "She'll be waiting for you at Sterling Tower. We'll land in about twenty minutes, and Daniel will be waiting to take us home. You'll be with your mentor in less than an hour."

"Okay, good." Allie let out an anxious breath. "Grandpa, will you get Mom and Dad settled in my apartment?"

"Of course, Allie-girl. Don't worry about a thing."

She turned to Lily and Carson. "I can't let Marcus try to use you against me again. You're going to have to stay with me for a while."

"We've been prepared for this." Carson nodded.

"We knew it was only a matter of time," Lily added. "Though, we'd hoped it would be a few more decades before all this came to fruition."

Allie's head rushed with white noise, and she had to focus on not passing out again. How long had she been feeling like this? When Darius went into his Proving, he'd felt out of sorts for at least a week. But these things had always moved faster with Allie. She should have expected it to go this way. Though she'd felt trembly and headachy for a few days. But events had masked her symptoms.

Nausea hit her hard when she realized she'd faced Marcus just as she was entering the early stages of her Proving.

Did he sense it? She wondered if that was why he'd

laughed and said she wasn't ready yet. Once she'd passed her Proving—if she passed it—she would have mastered her power, making her Judgment gift ripe for the picking. The next time she saw Marcus Servius in the flesh, one of them wouldn't be walking away.

CHAPTER 37

Sasha | Chola Valley Temple | Many Seasons Later

Sasha ducked down, whirling into a sweeping kick as she raised her staff to block Xera's advance. The blind woman stepped back, avoiding Sasha's kick, causing her to overcorrect and lose her balance.

"How do you do it?" Sasha laughed, dropping her staff with a clatter against the stone floor of the pavilion where they trained. "You know what I'm about to do before I do it. Is it your gift?"

"It's my ears and my nose." Xera smiled, leaning down to offer Sasha a hand up. "When you lose one sense." She pointed to her eyes. "The others come alive in a way you'd never imagine. I can hear the sounds your body makes as you move."

"You're a good teacher." Sasha took her hand and hauled herself up. In the last months since she'd finally resigned herself to however long she would be here in the Chola Valley, she'd trained daily with Xera. The activity was good for both of them and gave them an opportunity to help each other.

"Come, let us relax in the sun while you tell me more stories of the modern world."

Sasha smiled as she returned their weapons to the shelves that housed every possible weapon they might need for training. The sparring was good for their physical well-being, but the true training happened when they talked. The ancient couldn't get enough of Sasha's stories.

"What did we talk about last time?" Sasha crossed the shaded pavilion to sit beside Xera on a stone bench in the sun beside one of the many natural pools of the gardens. During her last visit to the valley, Sasha had spent much of her time in meditation. This visit was different. She was both teacher and student.

"You told me about your intelligent small computers I still don't understand."

"Smart Phones," Sasha corrected her.

"Yes, that's what I said. Tell me again, what they are used for?"

"A million different things. You can make phone calls. We talked about that, but you can also take pictures with the camera and play games."

"And the internet?" Xera cocked her head in confusion. "That is where you tell the pocket computer what you want to know, and it gives you the answers."

"Basically, yes. We'll have to wait until we're home before I can show you what that looks like. It's hard to explain to someone who's never seen a calculator, much less a computer."

"What's a claculator?"

Sasha laughed, not bothering to correct her this time. "It's a device that helps you solve math problems."

"Like an abacus?"

"Yes, but more compact and complex."

"Everything in this modern world is small, yes?"

"Some things. Others are much larger. Like buildings." Sasha moved to sit on the grass, stretching her legs out in front of her. "We have cities with buildings that seem to scrape the sky."

Xera nodded. "I have seen such castles."

"Not castles. Imagine a large house with multiple rooms, and then stack a hundred of them on top of each other."

Xera's eyes widened. "Such a thing would surely topple over without the power to keep it steady."

"Mortals have a remarkable way of discovering new things that weren't possible a generation ago."

"A strange thought for such a short-lived people." Xera frowned, leaning down toward Sasha. "If they have these scraping buildings, with houses stacked on top of houses, how does one reach the top? It would take hours to walk up so many stairs."

"Remember the elevators at the hotel?" Sasha asked. There were only five or six floors there, but Xera never left the banquet hall.

"The moving boxes?" Xera shuddered. "It was difficult to comprehend such things when we first arrived at the hotel. And without my sight, it was even harder."

"An elevator is like a closet that goes up and down from floor to floor, taking people where they need to go without the use of stairs. It's much faster."

"Faster seems to be the only way these mortals move."

"Exactly. They have a lot to accomplish in their lifespan and not a lot of time to do it. Saving time is essential for their daily lives."

"I see." Xera nodded. "Poor souls. Do they get to enjoy the beauty of life during their brief time here?"

"Some never learn to slow down and smell the roses. They like to stay busy."

"That sounds like someone else I know." A man's shadow fell over them.

"Jayesh!" Sasha scrambled to her feet, her heart racing at the sight of him. For months she'd only seen Xera and the Mother and occasionally, Brother Rabishan. Her eyes were starved for the sight of someone familiar. Someone who reminded her of home.

She rushed to greet him, throwing her arms around him in her excitement. "I've missed you!" She pressed a kiss to his cheek, her heart warm in her chest, and a real smile lighting her from the inside out.

"Missed you too." He took a step back, holding her at arm's length, like he couldn't stand to be so near her.

She clutched his hands, not wanting to let go as she searched his eyes for the source of his hesitation. If he was hurting, she needed to know what caused it.

If he hurts, I hurt. The thought came unbidden to her mind.

"The Mother has sent several of my students back to the real world. Roman and the others will see them safely back to Sterling Tower." He continued to babble about why he was still here and not leaving with his students, but Sasha was trapped in his gaze. A prisoner of those beautiful brown eyes flecked with shades of blue. Had they always been so beautiful? She wasn't sure she'd ever fully appreciated their depths before now. Stars danced in her own eyes and she felt faint.

"Breathe, Sasha." Jayesh startled her back to reality. She dragged in a breath, chasing the stars away from her vision. "Are you okay? What's wrong." He tilted her chin up to meet his eyes. "Are you sick?"

"No." She shook her head, smiling. "I'm perfect," she whispered.

"Why does she sound so odd?" Xera asked, but Sasha barely heard her.

Jayesh let out a gasp of surprise, and his hands slid down her arms, his palms warm against her skin. She'd never felt anything so divine. *He knows.*

"What's happening, Sasha?" Jayesh whispered as she leaned into him, hardly aware of Xera's movement when she left them to their moment.

"You know." She couldn't wipe the smile from her face. "How long have you known?"

"*You* know?" His words were breathless, and his hands shook as he pulled her closer. "You do know." His breath was warm against her face.

She nodded. "How could I not see it before? I've always had a thing for you. I should have seen it."

"You were too young. You weren't ready." Jayesh pulled her close, wrapping his arms around her. "I've known since the day I took you up to the cliffs for target practice not long after we arrived here the first time. I demanded your trust, and you flew into a towering rage. I still don't know what you said that day." His hands moved to cup her face as he smiled down at her. "But that moment changed everything for me. You were far too young for me then—you still are—but I vowed that day, that the moment you truly looked at me and saw me as yours, I would be a man you could be proud of. Worthy of your love."

"You are mine, Jayesh Basu." She closed her eyes, taking in the scent of him. Her Complement. "And you have always been worthy of my love."

CHAPTER 38

Allie | Sterling Tower | June

"We're nearly there, sweetheart." Lilly and Carson held Allie firmly between them. They were so warm, and they smelled of home, comforting and reassuring.

"What's happening?" she murmured. "It's so hot." Flames engulfed her from the inside as her power churned, spreading like liquid heat through her body, leaving scorch marks behind.

"You're going to be fine, Allie," Carson assured her. "You've got a tough hill to climb, but it's the natural next step on your journey to becoming what you were always meant to be."

"I'm scared." Allie shivered despite the heat boiling in her core. "I'm not good enough."

"Oh, Allie-girl," her mother whispered. "This isn't about becoming what everyone else needs you to be."

"Your mother is right," Carson agreed. "This is about becoming your true self. Nothing more and nothing less. Don't be scared, honey. We'll be right here for you when your journey is done."

"I love you." Allie held onto them, taking strength from their presence.

"We are so proud of you." Lily kissed her burning forehead, smoothing her hair back the way she'd done countless times throughout Allie's childhood. No matter what happened in life, no matter where her immortality took her, Lily and Carson were her constant. They were her true north.

"We're landing now." Carson wiped a tear from Allie's face. "You're going to go with Liam. He's going to take you to Emma."

"Stay with me?" Allie looped her arms through each of theirs. "I can't do this alone."

"You have to, baby." Lily tried to pry her arm away from Allie. "This is where you go on alone. We'll be waiting for you when you're done."

"Grandpa Alex?" Allie had to force herself to let go of her parents.

"Yes, my girl?" Alexander leaned over her as they floated down through the dreamworld barrier, approaching the helipad on top of Sterling Tower. "What do you need?"

"Take care of them," she whispered.

"Of course, dear one." He squeezed her arm. "I'll take your parents right to your apartment to get them settled."

"No." She gripped his hand tightly. "If I don't make it through, if I fail, you take care of them. Always."

He gave her a grim look and nodded.

"Thank you." Her head whirled with things that weren't truly there. Images of what was to come, and her visions wandered about unhindered.

She appreciated her grandfather's careful nod. That he didn't tell her it was all going to be all right. That she wouldn't fail. She needed to know if the worst happened and her power withered and died and she had to fade from the world, that someone would be there to care for her family.

"Little one." Liam lifted her into his arms, cradling her against his chest as he ran for the elevator to take her down to the warehouse where Emma prepared to guide her into her Proving.

"What happens next?" Allie closed her eyes and breathed him in.

Just like her parents, he smelled of family and safety.

"Once your mentor is with you, things will happen quickly," Livia answered her question as she punched the button for the basement floor. Her sister wore a mask of strength to cover her worry.

"It's different for everyone, so there's not much we can say that will prepare you," Liam said, his chest rumbling against her ear.

"You are strong, Allie. And no matter how awful you feel right now, you are prepared for this." Livia laid a hand on her shoulder. "I hate that we can't go with you. Just know that we've all been there." She shared a glance with her husband. "And if we can come out the other side whole, then you will too."

"Thanks." Allie watched the numbers light up as they moved from floor to floor, the elevator seeming to move too slow and too fast at the same time. "Why am I so tired?" She felt like the weight of the world pressed down on her, and all she wanted was a nice long nap ... and her two favorite people in the world.

She'd always assumed Aidan and Darius would be with her when her Proving came upon her. Naturally, fate had other plans.

"It's the stress of the beginning. You're very close." Livia hammered on the basement button, as if that would make it go faster.

The elevator dinged, and Liam ran toward the double doors to the warehouse. Livia was right there with him, shoving the doors open for them.

"Be careful, little sister," Livia shouted as Liam left her behind. "You've got this." Her voice faded in Allie's mind as she fell into a deep, dark pit where not even her visions accompanied her.

"Safe journey, little one."

Cool hands lifted her from Liam's arms and a warm kiss brushed across her forehead as her brother left her cradled in Emma's arms.

Water rushed and roared in her ears as Emma murmured soft words of encouragement.

"You're so young." She stepped carefully onto the bridge that would take them to the island prepared specifically for Allie's Proving. "You should not have to face this now, brave girl. I've done all I can to prepare you, and I'll be here with you every step of the way."

"Emma?" Allie whispered, struggling to find her way back to the surface of this overwhelming darkness.

"I'm here." Emma's strong arms held her close. "We're going to get through this together."

"What do I do?"

Emma's steps faltered for a moment as they left the bridge and crossed the sandy beach. Emma sat her back down on her own feet, keeping an arm braced around her. "You take it one step at a time, and you listen to me. Even when you can't see me, listen for my voice. When it gets rough, and you feel like you're in your darkest moment alone, know that I am right by your side." She gripped Allie's shoulders tightly. "Look at me," she commanded.

Allie let her head fall back until she locked eyes with her mentor.

"I will not let you fail. Do you hear me?"

Allie nodded.

"Take a deep breath for me." Emma's voice sounded distant, like some ethereal part of the gentle waves lapping at the shore.

Allie sucked in a breath, and the sharp brine of the ocean air brought her clarity. Light whirled around her, chasing the darkness away. Her mind cleared, and she blinked in the bright sunshine overhead.

"Oh." She held onto Emma's shoulder, but she had her feet solidly beneath her again. "Okay, I feel better." She took another breath. "What just happened?"

"We've prepared this place for your Proving." Emma's hand slid down her arm to grip her hand. "This is a place only you and I can access. It helps to ease into your Proving when no outside forces can interfere. It's meant to give you a sense of peace and security so you can focus."

Allie nodded. "I do feel more in control." She cast a glance around the white sandy beach and across the water to the distant shore. Dark clouds brewed overhead, looming like a storm about to descend upon them. She didn't need an explanation to understand that once those clouds reached them, she would be well into her Proving. "What's next?" She returned her gaze on her mentor.

"A Proving is instinctual. Whatever happens next is for you to decide." Emma held her hand, waiting for Allie to make the next move.

Lightning flickered across the water. Green lightning. She turned in a circle, taking everything in before she headed for the jungle. "We have to go up there." Allie pointed to the flat top of the mountain at the center of the island, just beyond the jungle.

"All right, let's do this." Emma took a deep breath of her own.

The path was narrow once they left the beach behind, and the light grew dim under the canopy of trees. It was cooler here and Allie's confidence grew.

"What was your Proving like?" Allie asked.

"I was on a ship." Emma walked close behind her. "It was a place kind of like this. Not a dream, but not entirely real either. I faced my demons. Struggled with some. The journey was long, but I eventually reached the shore."

Allie nodded. She wasn't sure what shape her demons would take, but it was something she'd thought about a lot over the last year. Ever since Emma explained that her Proving was near and what it would entail.

Her power swelled within her. Unrestrained and wild. The logical side of her brain told her she had to rein it in and get control over it, but this was the one time she had to let her power take the lead. She would have to conquer it before this was over, but first she had to push herself to the limits of her ability. Only then could she fight her way back and master her power for good. After this, she would no longer struggle to keep her immense power under control. She would own it.

Sweat rolled down Allie's face. The momentary coolness of the shade passed quickly. It wasn't humid and hot like she'd imagined a jungle would be. It was hot like nothing she'd ever experienced before. And dry, like a desert. Her mouth tasted like ash as she trudged along the pathway.

Pushing past a group of huge ferns, the scent of sulfur and acrid smoke filled her lungs. Heat radiated from the path ahead. Fire blazed hot and bright, yet it didn't burn the jungle.

"What do we do here?" Allie searched for a way around.

"The only way is forward. No matter what you see or feel." Emma's voice held strength and confidence.

Allie took another step, right into a wall of flames that singed her hair and made her eyes water. Her flesh bubbled and blistered under the scalding heat. It was difficult to take a breath, but she dragged oxygen into her lungs. It tasted fresh and full of the scents of the jungle. No smoke.

This isn't real. The thought came to her mind. Of course, it wasn't. That didn't change the fact that the flames threatened to burn the flesh right off her bones.

A shadow moved within the flames, taking on a familiar form she'd know anywhere. Allie rushed forward, leaving Emma behind.

"Aidan?" Allie called out to the shadow as it disappeared at the end of the trail where the mountain loomed large.

"Allie, stay with me!" Emma darted through the flames behind her.

Allie looked back over her shoulder but couldn't see her mentor. She was alone, surrounded by fire that wanted any excuse to consume her. As her skin tightened and blisters swelled, Allie's steps faltered.

In another instant, she was back in the cool shade of the jungle, the flames dying down to embers under her feet.

"Pathetic." A familiar voice emerged from the vines. Her hair was as familiar as her voice, though her youthful face set Allie's heart thudding like a jackhammer in her chest.

The girl's hair sparked like flames, like fire itself.

Allie sucked in a breath. "What are you doing here?" She stared at a version of her own face. One she hadn't seen in years.

"You need a reminder of where you came from." The pale green eyes looked at her with disapproval. They lacked the smoldering fire of her power, just as her hair lacked its luster. A riot of red curls framed the younger Allie's face, but there was no trace of the golden, silver, and copper threads that marked her as unusual even among the extraordinary.

This was Allie as she'd seen herself in the mirror thousands of times before her Awakening changed everything. This was the Allie who thought of herself as nothing special. The lonely girl who never had friends and never understood why.

"It's been a while," Allie said hesitantly, unsure where this might lead, for surely this was the first of her demons.

"You really let them call you *Princess*?" The girl sneered, her knees peeking through the tears in her paint-splattered jeans. "How did that even happen?"

"To tell you the truth, I don't know." Allie folded her arms across her chest, hunching her shoulders as if to protect herself.

"You let it happen." Another voice joined the first as several more versions of her young self stepped from the shadows of the jungle. Each stared at her with accusation in their eyes as they closed in on her and Allie thought they might rip her apart if she didn't answer them.

"You don't understand. I had to take my title." Allie backed away from the angry mob. Versions of herself who would never understand how circumstances had led her to become the First Princess of Indriell.

"*Your* title." One of the Allies wearing her favorite old

suede jacket with ink stains around the pockets shared an eyeroll with another. "Listen to her. She even acts like a princess."

"I stepped up to save Aidan." Allie's voice took on a hard edge. "That was the only reason."

"And he didn't even need you to do it," the original Allie said. "He had his own plan to escape the Milan Initiative, but you thought you knew better."

"I had to try." Allie lifted her chin. "Every single one of you would have done the same." She didn't need to justify her actions to phantoms who weren't there when the hard decisions had to be made.

"Maybe if you hadn't been so high and mighty and all princessy, you'd have realized he would save himself and come home in his own time, when he was ready."

Allie stared down at the swarm of angry girls closing in on her. There were dozens of them, tearing at her clothes and clawing at her skin. Shame swept through her, and she wanted to run from their accusations. They were right. She'd meddled in Aidan's life and screwed up all the plans he'd set into action to save himself and the other Syntrophos from the Milan Initiative. He hadn't needed her to claim her title. Hadn't needed her to respond to the Senate's summons when they'd taken Naeemah in for harboring an unknown, unregistered Immortal child. He would have saved his mother. He'd have probably done a better job of it too.

She'd left a bloody mess in her wake. One that still needed cleaning up.

"Focus Allie!" Emma's voice found her ears over the din of girls shouting about all the ways she could have stayed out of it and let Aidan find his way home. They had answers for everything. All the ways Allie could have acted that wouldn't have led to her assuming her title and becoming the First Princess.

"What are you here for?" Emma stepped into the fray with her, laying a cool hand on her burning face. "Fight back. Tell them they're wrong."

"Right." Allie lifted her chin and pushed all the negative thoughts from her mind. Standing tall, she let them come at her.

"I did what needed to be done and every single one of you would have made the same choices. You see what happened, and you have a million ideas of how I could have done better. Yet, where were you guys when I was on my own, making the best choices I could, given the information I had?"

The girls cast wary glances at each other. Some of them faded back into the jungle where they'd come from.

"If I could have found a way to help Aidan without taking on the influence the role of First Princess gave me, I would have done it. At the time, that was the only path available to me. I did it for him, and if I hadn't, he might have found his way home eventually. He is strong and capable. Of course, he would have saved himself and those he felt responsible for. But at what cost? Where would the Syntrophos of the Milan Initiative be right now if I hadn't done what I could to help? What more would they have had to endure if they stayed? Maybe Aidan would have gotten them all out in another year or two. Maybe I could have done a better job of helping. But unless one of you has a time traveling gift, we're stuck with the way things are. So, I'm a princess." Allie threw her hands up in the air. "Get over it. I have. Mostly."

Allie's confidence grew as more Allies faded with every

word she spoke. Finally, only the first version of herself remained.

Letting her voice take on a gentler note, she stared into the eyes of her former self. "Our lives changed the moment Aidan came into it. Yeah, it got really complicated, but I'd do it all over again without a moment's hesitation. You know why?" Allie took a step forward, eager to be on her way.

"Why?" The girl in the paint-splattered jeans lifted her chin in equal defiance.

"Because he's the best thing that ever happened to us, and we'd do anything for him. Because he would do the same for us. That's what people who love each other do, Allie. He's the best friend we never had when we were alone and lonely. He is everything. Yeah, I made a mess of it, but he's home now. He'll never recover from what he went through at the hands of Marcus Servius, but at least he isn't there with him right now, suffering still."

"But you *let* them call you princess." The young Allie shook her head. "The girl you were would never allow that word to pass anyone's lips."

"It's just a word." Allie smiled. "This girl has learned not give an old title too much power. I'm not perfect. I'm so not the royal type, and I never will be. But this isn't about us, kiddo. It's about so much more."

The angsty version of herself faded along with the others.

But the stinging pain of her burns came back with a vengeance. Allie fell to her knees, her skin pricking in the salty air, like the worst sunburn she'd ever had.

A cool breeze rushed through the jungle, and Allie wiped the sweat from her brow as she searched for the way forward.

"Well done, Allie." Emma's voice drifted to her through the jungle.

"What now?" Her shoulders slumped, and exhaustion weighed her down. She wanted to lie down and rest, but they'd only just begun.

"This will get harder." Emma came to crouch beside her, no longer just a voice in the wind. "You have to keep moving."

Allie searched the pathway ahead. It seemed to disappear into the jungle with no clear direction. Frowning, she stood with Emma's help. "It's not there."

"What's not there?" Emma asked.

"The green light of my power. It usually lights the way, so I know I'm on the right course."

"Allie, what have I spent the last year trying to beat into your head?" Emma's clear eyes shone in a beam of sunlight that broke through the canopy of trees.

"That I'm a stubborn child who knows nothing?" Allie suggested.

"The other lesson." Emma rolled her eyes.

Allie sighed. "My power isn't some foreign entity with a will of its own," she said by rote. "It's me. I'm the power. I'm the one with all the information I need to make my choices. The green light is just a physical manifestation of what I already know." She nodded, taking a few steps forward until the path became overgrown with huge green ferns and vines. Sweeping a fern frond aside, a sheer cliff rose upward to meet the mountain that sat at the center of the small island.

The green light of her power flickered along a twisting path up the side of the mountain.

"Time to climb." Allie reached for the first handhold, urging her power to light the way.

"Trust in yourself, Allie. The light you see is your own mind marking the way." Emma watched her climb, leaving Allie to her journey to the top.

She made headway quickly, refusing to look down at how far she'd already come.

"Who thought up this whole thing?" Allie reached for a handhold that was more of a stretch than she was currently willing to make. With her feet perched on a precarious ledge, she managed to brush her raw fingertips against the next grip her gift told her was the safest of the available places she might use to pull herself up a few more inches.

"If you're listening, oh great leaders of the Immortals, this test of yours is sadistic!" She tried to grasp the ledge and missed. Her arms swinging wildly to correct her balance, Allie's gaze fell to the few thousand feet of open air below her. She immediately pressed herself against the cliff, ignoring her gift's insistence that she reach for the ledge she couldn't grasp hold of.

"Never mind." She leaned into the rock. "I live here now." She sucked in a breath and closed her eyes, hoping the world would decide to stop spinning.

"You're going to fall."

"Shut up." Allie groaned. "I thought I told you to leave me alone." She peered up at herself. Another version of herself. This one identical right down to the clothes she wore. Except this Allie had managed to stay clean. And she was also really mean.

"Can't do it, loser." The annoying Allie shrugged, holding onto the wall as if she were at some local rock-climbing center with all the safety gear she could ever want. "You can't reach that." She pointed out the obvious as the real Allie tried once again to reach for the ledge.

"It's green. That means I can." Allie stretched her arms

as far as she could, but once again she as she just managed to touch it, her blood smeared hand slipped away just short of her goal.

"Come on!" Allie groaned.

"You're going to fall."

"No. I'm. Not." She studied the other possible hand holds around her, wondering if she should try something a little closer.

"You can't do it that way."

"I know." She sighed, her feet growing numb from standing in one place too long.

"You should go back down and find a safer way up."

"No." Allie pressed her forehead against the coolness of the stone, trying to block out Ms. Pessimistic. It was like this version of herself wanted her to fail.

"Fine, fall to your death and fail our Proving."

What was the worst that would happen if she did fall? She'd probably break some bones and fail her Proving, but she wouldn't die.

"Ohhh." Allie wanted to smack her forehead. "You're my mortal brain!" She grinned up at herself. "I get it now." She moved up on her tip toes.

"That's not smart, you know. You're totally going to fall." The mortal side of Allie sounded nervous now. "You can't afford to take a big risk here. Look for something safer to grab onto."

"No." Allie refused.

"But you're going to fall and..."

"And what?" Allie looked up at herself. Fear written all over her face. "It'll be okay. If I slip, I'll find another hand hold on the way down." She peered down the slope of the cliff. "Or I'll land on some of those ferns way down there."

"It's too much of a risk, Allie. You aren't a rock climber."

"No, I'm not." She maneuvered away from the wall. "But I am Immortal. And I'm stronger than any mortal in the same boat. We'll be all right."

"Don't do it. You're going to die."

"Eh, well, I'll come back." Allie reached for the ledge with her left hand, releasing her death grip with her right hand.

"Don't!" the scared Allie screamed just as the real Allie got her left hand firmly on the handhold. She hung there for a second until she got her left foot and then her right settled under her and she inched up, placing her right hand on the next handhold far above the one she'd finally left behind.

"See. Not so bad, yeah?" She looked up, but the mortal Allie faded away. "All right then." Allie moved faster, scaling the next hundred feet with much less drama. "Note to self. The mortal brain gets in the way of progress. I probably need to remember this little convo with myself in the future."

"Just don't forget me." The scared voice sounded like a whisper on the wind.

"No worries, girlfriend, I won't be parting ways with that mortal brain of ours anytime soon. We just need to learn when and where it's useful and when it's probably best to ignore you."

Panting with the effort, Allie pulled herself onto a ledge wide enough for her to sit. "Oh, thank the Lord." She groaned, eager for a quick respite. Leaning against the cliff with her legs dangling over the side, she studied how far she'd come.

"Whoa!" Allie pressed her back against the wall. "That's a long drop." She couldn't believe how far she'd come and all on her own. Well, she'd had some company along the way. Extremely unhelpful company—except for Emma.

"Your journey has been easy thus far." Emma's amused voice reached her on whatever plain she'd ascended to in the throes of her Proving.

"Easy? We need to work on your definition of easy." She glanced up to see how far she was from the top and groaned. "Are you fricking kidding me?" She was nowhere near the top. "I swear this stupid mountain is growing."

Allie carefully got to her feet, keeping her back plastered to the wall behind her. "Where to next?" She studied the cliff, searching with her gift for the right way up. Focusing, she pulled on her power, letting it flood her core, but she still didn't see the way.

Turning, she glanced back down at her feet, and the green light of her power flickered. "Oh, it's going to be like that is it?" She inched along the narrow ledge, moving laterally until the ledge grew larger, and she could walk without worry of falling over the side.

"This works for me, oh great testers of the Immortals." But Allie knew in her gut that things were going too easily for the moment, and it wouldn't last.

When this pathway widened into more than a ledge, a crumbling set of broken stairs began to rise up the side of the mountain. Each step was no wider than a foot, and there was no railing to speak of.

"Crap on a crapstick." Allie paced along the clearing, trying to work up the nerve to keep going. Nausea rose within her, and she had to sit.

Sweat trickled down her face as the sun beat down on her relentlessly. The heat intensified until she was engulfed in the flames she thought she'd left behind on the jungle floor.

The world whirled around her, making her dizzy. Allie closed her eyes, praying for the spinning to stop. When she opened her eyes, she was no longer on the side of the mountain.

She lay on the ground, staring up at an angry gray sky with churning clouds tinged with red billowing smoke. Tall grasses sprouted up around her, swaying in the wind. She couldn't move, her arms and legs bloodless and heavy, like dead weight.

The place was familiar. A safe haven she'd retreated to time and again as a teenager.

"I'm home." She tried to sit up as the rooftop of her tower bedroom took shape around her. She only had to cross the grassy wildflower garden to the door and retreat to the safety of her childhood home.

Allie managed to sit up as a pins and needles sensation swept her body.

"Oh no," she lay back against the grass, her head swimming with memories of her Awakening. "This is so not fair." Her body tingled with the pins and needles ache that would surely have her screaming before much longer.

"It's not real." She sucked in a breath, focusing on the warmth of the power in her core. "This isn't going to be like my Awakening."

Except it was. The itch buzzed just beneath her skin, and no amount of scratching brought her relief. Soon, she was a bloody mess from clawing at herself.

Alone and scared on the rooftop garden, Allie watched the storm churning overhead, wondering if it would consume her this time.

"Focus on the power, Allie." She forced herself to stop scratching, to save her energy for what was to come. She fell limp against the grass she knew wasn't really there. Maybe she was still on the side of the mountain. Or maybe all of this was happening in her head. Maybe she was safe in the warehouse on the small island Hal had created for her. A safe haven where she could make her way through her Proving.

Warm blood oozed from her arms and legs where she'd scratched herself raw. It puddled and cooled beneath her.

"Keep fighting, Allie, you're stronger than this!" Emma urged her to get a hold of her mind and her power.

Heat swept her body, throwing her into a blazing inferno that charred her from the inside out, burning away all traces of the young woman she'd fought so hard to become.

Faint echoes from her Awakening came back to haunt her.

Stay with me, Lex!

Remember this girl, this version of yourself.

You've got this!

We have all been exactly where you are right now.

Allie gulped the warm air, grappling with her power for control. She bolted upright, her gut roiling as she spewed the contents of her stomach into the grass beside her.

Her sight blurred and dimmed as she stared at the ominous sky. A red fog descended over her. Thunder clapped in the distance, the eerie golden-green light of her power flickering in the sky.

Memories flooded her vision. She saw a figure standing against the brick parapet of her tower. Aidan, his eyes filled with anguish as he spoke with Emma. This wasn't the boy she remembered seeing during her Awakening. The one preparing to leave for Germany so many years ago. This was the man. Her Aidan. The one who had only recently returned to her. He still looked broken. There was an anguish so clear in his face she wondered how he ever managed to hide it from her.

In a flash of green light, she saw herself with her family. Livia and Allie laughed as they watched a little boy and girl playing with their grandparents. The sight of them tugged at her heart, but she didn't know them yet.

Liam sat nearby with his blue-eyed daughter. An older Kahlynn who looked just like Kayla did when she was a teenager. This Kahlynn was on the cusp of her own Awakening. Aidan and Darius laughed at the children's antics.

A much older Lily and Carson entertained the children with a light of youth long past in their eyes. They were old, but they were whole and healthy, and so very happy. Even her mortal sister, Josceline, was there with her husband and teenage daughter. It had been so long since she'd seen her sister it saddened Allie that the vision of her was crackled and faded like an old photograph. Like her mind couldn't conjure up a clear image of what her older sister and her small family might look like in this distant future.

Her family faded away with the ghost of their laughter. Just seeing them had given her new strength. Strength she knew she'd need in the coming moments. It was the same future she'd seen in her Awakening. More distant now than it was then. Everyone was a bit older than they were the first time she'd visited them. And that was okay. It was still there. It was still a possibility. One she wasn't quite ready for yet. It gave her hope to know that her future was there. And it was a happy one.

Visions of times not yet known dissolved into a golden green light, replaced with more recent memories.

Allie saw herself standing defiantly before the International Senate with Gregg, Aidan, and their friends standing boldly behind her.

In another instant, the old Livia flashed before her eyes. Fear and loneliness clouding her stormy eyes for a moment before she morphed into the version of her sister she knew now.

With a violent jerk, the new visions and familiar memories faded, and Allie's head exploded in agony. Grappling for control, she forced her eyes open, searching for something corporeal she could grasp.

No longer in the tower garden, the cold sandy beach chilled her fevered body. Allie grasped at handfuls of the blood-soaked sand beneath her. Waves rushed over her, and she cried out as the water swept her out into the depths of the cold, dark lake.

She knew what came next as she slipped into the void.

You didn't think it would be easy, did you? Marcus' voice filled her mind.

"Leave me." She spoke the words aloud, but she couldn't hear them. "You have no place here."

You are weak. You have always been weak, relying on others to build you up, making you into something you aren't.

"I will not listen to this. Not now and not ever." Allie clawed her way through the void, the glacial lake waters pressing her down to the dark depths of oblivion.

You are nothing, Alexis Carmichael. I expected so much more from the one marked by prophecy.

"No!" She reached for her power, fighting toward the surface, but she didn't know which way led to the sweet air she longed for and which way would lead to her ruin. If she failed now, it was all over. Marcus would win, and she would never find the quiet life she craved.

"Leave me, this is my fight." She willed Marcus to fade from her mind, but he refused.

Who do you think you are?

"I'm just me." She found the strength to laugh at herself. At him. "Just a girl who's going to make you wish you'd never heard that prophecy." As she laughed, Marcus dissolved into the void, and the green light at the surface guided her forward.

Allie had never been normal. She was never going to be normal, and that was okay. She was exactly who she needed to be. Imperfect, simply doing the best she could with what she had.

Gasping, she broke the surface, dragging in the crisp, fresh air. She floated in the cool water, searching for land and found nothing but open water in all directions.

"Just keep swimming," she hummed to herself. She chose a direction and started swimming. She'd find a way home eventually. That was all anyone could do. Mortal or Immortal. Whatever circumstances she found herself in, she only had to pick up her feet and keep moving forward. The details would take care of themselves in time.

The lake waters washed away, leaving her on dry ground once again. The hard stone grew hot beneath her. When she opened her eyes once more, she was back on the side of a mountain she still had to climb.

Rising to her feet, the crumbling stairs ascending into the distance didn't look half as intimidating as they had before.

Shaking her head, she put one foot in front of the next. "Dorie was right. Just keep swimming."

CHAPTER 39

Sasha | Chola Valley Temple | A lifetime of Seasons

Everything changed for Sasha and Jayesh after their bonding ceremony. Time didn't seem to matter anymore. It took the completion of her bond with Jayesh for her to understand why she was back in the Chola Valley.

Allie would need her at her best when she returned to the river of time. She didn't need a young girl distracted by the newness of the relationship that would define her and her husband for the rest of their lives. They were individuals with different interests and responsibilities, but they were on the same path now, and would be for the rest of their lives.

Sasha stood along the hillside overlooking the valley below. The sun shined warm on her face. Their time here in the valley was magical. A chance to hit pause on the rest of the world while Sasha prepared for her Proving. Only then would she be ready to return to her duties in the real world. She had to be strong for Allie. And Xera had benefitted from this time as well. She had healed in her time here, no longer afraid of what waited for her at home.

"Xeren!" Sasha called to the small boy playing with his

father and the elephants that called the valley home. They were inspecting Kandula's newest calf. A tiny little female, just the right size for Sasha's son. "Don't let him ride the baby, Jayesh." Sasha darted down the hill with a laugh. "She's not strong enough for riders yet."

Sasha came to a stop beside her elephant friend. "Kandula, I apologize for my small son. He doesn't know any better. His father on the other hand." She darted a glare at her husband.

The big elephant snorted and wrapped his trunk around Sasha's arm. "He says it's okay. The calves are friends and should play together."

"See, I knew it was fine with our big man here." Jayesh stroked the elephant's painted trunk. "I might not speak to animals the way you do, but Kandula and I have been friends for a long time. We know how to communicate."

"Mama, can we go visit the mangroves?" Xeren tugged on her tunic.

Sasha glanced down at her son, marveling at how much he'd grown since his birth. She'd never given much thought to becoming a mother since it happened for most Immortals much later in life through adoption. Yet Xeren had come quickly for them. A natural born Immortal, born within the safety of the Chola Valley Temple grounds. He was a special child. Time managed to touch him here in a way it didn't for adults. He grew strong and healthy. His sun browned skin gleamed in the sunlight, and for a moment, Sasha couldn't breathe as she thought about his future and how he might grow into a young man with a little of herself and his father all wrapped up in a son who was everything to her. Happiness swelled within her as she took Xeren's small hand in hers.

"We'll have to ask your dad if he's up for it." She sank

down beside Xeren. "You know he's old and cranky when he's tired."

"But it's early, Daddy." He looked up at his father in adoration. "Do you need a nap?"

Jayesh crouched down to their son's level. "Your mother thinks she is funny." He swept Xeren up in his strong arms; the boy giggled and squealed as Jayesh settled him on his shoulders. "We will go to the mangrove forest this afternoon." He glanced up to the top of the grassy hill near the temple gatehouse. "But I think your mother might be busy." He turned to Sasha with a worried frown.

"How are you feeling?" He took her hand.

Sasha tilted her head in question. "Happier than I've ever been." She smiled up at her son. She missed her family. Her mother especially when Xeren was born. And there was an ache deep in her soul where Quinn's heart beat in time with hers. She would see her Syntrophos again someday. She just wasn't ready to leave the valley yet. Maybe when Xeren was a little older. Her life waited for her exactly where she'd left it. They could return anytime.

Jayesh pointed to the top of the hill where Mother Raghavan stood, the morning sun blazing behind her as she leaned on her cane.

Fear lanced through Sasha's heart at the sight. She shared a frantic look with her husband before she dropped his hand. "Take Xeren to the mangroves and spend the night camping and fishing." She exhaled a shaky breath as she turned away from her small family.

It was time.

Sasha made her way up the hillside, keeping her eyes on the mother. She was terrified of what her Proving would bring, but deep inside she knew she was ready for it. Had been for quite some time.

She walked silently with the Mother to the other side of the valley where the jungle grew dense with lush green foliage, and wild rocky terrain rose up to meet the mountains in the distance. The wilderness was her domain, so it only made sense that would be where her Proving would take place.

They reached the end of the path where the ancient cobblestones of the temple grounds gave way to vines and green things. Mother Raghavan pointed into the forest, taking up her place as Sasha's mentor to watch over her.

"I'm scared." Sasha hesitated.

"You should be," the Mother replied. "But you are ready, child." Mother Raghavan's gnarled old hand reached up to cup her face in a rare gesture of fondness. "I will be here to guide you."

Sasha took a few tentative steps into the dark jungle, refusing to look back over her shoulder. She'd prepared her whole life for this moment. With a deep breath, she moved forward, her head held high and her steps confident.

She was about to face her every shortcoming. Her greatest fears and all the things she didn't even know about herself yet.

But as the fog rolled in, pulling her up to a powerful plain of existence that wasn't quite reality, but not fully within her mind, she opened herself to the process. She was ready.

And once she was Proven, she and her family would have to return to the river of time.

CHAPTER 40

Aidan | Salt Lake City, Utah | June

Aidan nearly slipped in the blood pooled on the marble floor of the mansion perched high in the mountains overlooking Salt Lake City. The slaughter hadn't been reported yet and already the crime scene was contaminated.

She'd led them on a race across two states in as many days before they finally caught up with her. But they had her now, thanks to Darius. Even in his current state, he'd outsmarted her.

Stefana writhed on the floor, covered in blood and gore. She either didn't speak English or she refused to speak to them in anything but her ancient tongue as she hissed and spit, hurling garbled obscenities at them. At least Aidan assumed her words were curses, judging by the tone of her voice and the wild look in her eyes.

Pilar had the murderer restrained in magnetized cuffs and a collar. They just needed to find a place to take her so she couldn't hurt anyone else.

"We have to get out of here, Aidan." Pilar cast a worried glance at the front door. "This one isn't going to go unnoticed for long. The victim was a state Senator. It's only a matter of time before someone realizes her entire security detail has been murdered. We don't want to be here when that happens."

"Let's put her in the trunk." Aidan lifted the blood covered woman from the floor. The fight hadn't gone out of her yet despite being cut off from her power. Stefana kicked and thrashed as Aidan hefted her over his shoulder.

"What are we going to do about this mess?" Naomi stepped into the foyer from the living room where the victim's remains were. The Senator was having a quiet night alone when Stefana showed up to cross another name off her list. Aidan was almost certain the Senator would have been someone to stand in Marcus' way so he'd had her eliminated. Like all the other politician's who'd come in contact with Stefana, though the U.S. Senator was the highest profile politician yet.

"Leave it. We don't have a choice. Where's Darius?"

"Outside. He wasn't feeling well." Pilar took one last look around the room and headed out to join Darius.

For the last two days Darius had suffered with bouts of sickness, headaches, and panic attacks. There was only one reason for his symptoms. Allie was Proving and it was lasting a long time.

Aidan left the house, crossing the lawn with Stefana still kicking and trying to bite him through the duct tape they'd finally placed over her mouth. He dumped her into the back of the SUV and secured her hands behind her with zip ties and then bound her hands to her feet to make sure she couldn't move. "I'd say I'm sorry, but I'm not." He slammed the hatch closed and went to check on his brother.

"What's wrong now?" Aidan moved to the driver's side to find Pilar and Naomi crouched over Darius slumped on the ground.

"He passed out." Naomi looked up at him, worry on her

face. "She's not doing well if he's still this messed up over it. Allie needs to pull it together or she's going to fail and I don't know what that will do to Darius."

"Allie wouldn't be Allie if she didn't make things harder on herself." He crouched down to lift his brother into his arms. "She will pull through and Darius will be okay." He moved around Pilar as she opened the back door of the SUV so Aidan could settle Darius inside. "She's a lot stronger than she knows, but any Proving at her age is bound to be difficult."

"What are we going to do with that?" Naomi asked, staring at the Immortal in the back window. In the few minutes he'd left her unattended, Stefana had managed to get on her knees, her hands and feet still bound together. She glared at them with hate-filled eyes, banging her head against the window.

"I'll call Liam for instructions. Who knows, maybe she'll do us all a favor and knock herself out." Aidan slipped into the driver's seat, his chest tight with worry for Allie. He had every faith in her that she could pass her Proving, but that he wasn't there to stand vigil for her broke something inside him. He missed her terribly, though the time apart was good for them.

You can do this, Allie. He sent the thought out through their shared connection but an empty, echoing reply was all he got in return.

Chapter 41

Allie | Sterling Tower | June

Tears streaked down Allie's face to mingle with sweat and blood. Half healed scabs covered her arms and legs and most of her face from her fight with her power.

"That's what this is all about." Allie sniffed back her tears and wiped the flaking dried blood from her hands. A Proving was about one thing and one thing only. Mastering her power and defeating her own ego. However, the tasks manifested for her were nothing more than bells and whistles meant to distract her from her purpose.

"I just want a sandwich." Fresh tears blurred her eyes as her empty stomach gnawed at her middle. "And maybe a french fry." She lifted her foot, taking the next step up the mountain with monumental effort. Her legs weighed her down, and each step sent excruciating pain up her spine.

The first thousand steps had come easily, if not a little precariously. She'd almost fallen a dozen times or more, but she was careful to keep her weight shifted toward the mountain.

All those years of training on balance beams came in handy with this particular challenge. Not that she would ever admit it to Gregg or Jin Jing.

As the stairway to nowhere turned around the mountain, she came to a stop.

"Oh, come on," she yelled at the sky. "What am I supposed to do with this?" She leaned against the cliff, aching to sit down and cry, but there was barely enough room to stand, much less sit.

Just jump.

She wasn't sure whose voice echoed in her mind this time. Only that it wasn't hers.

"I am *not* jumping." She stared at the huge gap between the step she stood on and the next one several feet away and far above her head. At least three or four steps had crumbled and fallen into the abyss below.

Salty wind blew her hair back, not giving her any relief as the breeze stung her already chapped skin. Her lips were cracked and bleeding, and she'd give just about anything for an ice-cold glass of water.

"Can't I just quit?" She sagged against the wall, her feet throbbing in time with her pulse. "A visit from Fei Long wouldn't go unappreciated right now," she shouted into the wind, her voice as cracked and dry as the rest of her.

"Come on, Allie. Don't be so helpless." Aidan's voice called to her from above, and he didn't sound at all like her Aidan.

"Oh, crap." She looked up into the cold, dark eyes of the Aidan she only vaguely remembered from her Awakening. "You again?" She stomped her foot and yelped as she stumbled back down a step.

"For crying out loud, that was just rude." She watched as the step she just stood on crumbled away and bounced down the side of the mountain. The gap between her and scary Aidan had just increased by one more step.

"You haven't changed a bit." Aidan stared down at her, his tone saying that wasn't a good thing.

"Did you expect anything different?" She glared at him. She'd been so afraid of this monstrous Aidan of her Awakening she'd run from him. She didn't have the energy for that this time.

"Can you give a girl a hand?" Allie reached out, testing the distance between them.

The dark Aidan arched a brow at her. "You really want to trust me?"

"No." She scowled at him, dropping her hand. "That would be too easy, I suppose."

"You do like to take the easy route." He smirked down at her.

"What's that supposed to mean?" She searched for a way across the expanse so she could be on her way and leave this jerk behind.

"It means exactly what it sounds like." He tossed her a thick vine, creeping from a crevice in the wall.

Allie caught it, giving it a rather dubious look, wondering if it could hold her weight long enough to get her across Tarzan-style.

"Which is?" She sighed, waiting for whatever lesson she was supposed to glean from this encounter.

Aidan shook his head, scowling at her. "You're supposed to be the child of Prophecy, yet you can't navigate the simplest of tasks without asking for help."

"So?"

"It's weak, Allie." He looked at her as though he hated her for taking the role that should have gone to him. For so long, Gregg had thought Aidan was the fulfillment of prophecy. Even Marcus had thought so, seeing in Aidan a rival worthy of his attention.

But the role had fallen to Allie. It had always been hers, and she did the best she could.

"You're pathetic." His words struck her hard, hitting at the hidden insecurities she'd felt all her life.

"Everyone knows I'm not equal to the task," she yelled. "You want it so bad, you take it."

"It's not mine to take. It's yours to screw up." Aidan shook his head, his eyes full of venom and his words biting deep.

"Then how would you handle this?" She gestured at the obstacle in her path.

"I wouldn't have taken this route." He pointed up the cliff face, the most direct route to the top of the mountain, still as distant as it was when she'd taken her first step up the stairs to nowhere.

"Maybe that's your path. This one is mine. Now, give me a hand up so I can get off this stupid mountain." Allie didn't wait for him to respond before she gripped the vine and leapt toward the other side.

Closing her eyes, she reached out, gasping with relief when Aidan's cool and steady hand wrapped around hers. She stared into his cruel eyes, ignoring the satisfied smirk that lit his face as he pulled her onto the ledge to safety.

"Taking the easy way again, Lex?"

"No." She shook her head. "It takes more guts to ask for help when you know you need it."

"Go ahead, climb your way to the top on the backs of others." He stepped around her, gesturing her to move forward.

"Asking for help isn't weak." She took another step up toward her goal. "It's the only way forward in this world. We help each other along, lifting each other up as we go. Refusing help is the best way to fail." She turned her back on the phantom of Aidan, continuing on her way.

"How long will you refuse to see the truth staring you in the face, Alexis Carmichael?"

Allie turned back toward him when she heard a note of sadness in his voice. This time, he looked a little more like her Aidan, yet the monstrous version of him lurked in the shadows in his eyes. "For as long as I need to. My truth is mine alone. You said it yourself." She pointed straight up to the top of the mountain. "Your path is different than mine, and that's okay. We'll both get there in the end." She left him behind as the stairs turned, twisting up the side of the mountain.

She moved faster now. More confident in her steps as the power continued to grow inside her, threatening to burn her alive.

Her legs ached from the incline, but she kept moving. Power buzzed inside her, sliding along her skin, pushing the limitations of her control. But she kept moving, one step at a time, one moment at a time. One breath.

Blood trickled from her nose and leaked from her eyes from the pressure of her mounting power. She would not let it control her, yet she had to give it free reign for the moment.

"You're as bad as you were when you were sixteen and clueless."

Allie barely heard her, so focused on her upward movement. She moved to take another step up, but there were no more steps.

Clouds rushed past her as the wind kicked up, clear and cool at the top of the mountain. The storm clouds still rolled angrily overhead, but the climax of the storm had yet to come.

Allie stumbled from the stairway toward the rocky center of the wide, flat peak of the mountain. She'd made it to the top. Clear of the edge, she sank to the ground in a weary heap. The air was thin up here, but she was grateful for a chance to rest.

"Still oblivious as ever." A shadow fell over her, and Allie didn't want to look up. She knew exactly who this was by the dead, flat tone of her voice, and she didn't have it in her to fight with her gift. She'd have to, of course, that was why she was here after all, but she needed just one more minute to rest.

"Weak and useless."

"You too?" Allie cracked her eyes open and scrambled back against a boulder. This wasn't the Gift-Allie who had accompanied her through the orchard the night Ming Lao died and Quinn was returned to his family.

"You've changed." Allie's voice squeaked in fear.

"And you haven't. While I've grown powerful, you have remained as you were." Gift-Allie's scarlet-red hair billowed in the wind. The streaks of gold and subtle shades of violet in her hair vibrated with energy. This version of Allie was glorious in her power.

The green light of her power sparked just under pale skin, adorned with a multitude of scars and tattoos. Dressed in faded leather from head to toe, this Allie reeked of strength and confidence. She was a terrifying warrior.

Tapping her booted foot, Gift-Allie folded her arms over her chest. She was taller and more muscular. If it weren't for the eyes and distinct features, Allie wouldn't recognize this girl as a version of herself.

Your power is you. Emma's voice echoed in her mind, reminding her again of the fundamental lesson she'd failed to get time and again. Lifting her chin, Allie met her gift's judgmental gaze. *I have nothing to fear from myself.* Allie rose to her feet, standing before the embodiment of her power.

"I am not weak." Allie studied her gift. Scarlet hands stained with blood gripped the sai blades at her hips. The golden green light of her power blazed from her eyes, sizing Allie up and finding her lacking.

With a tremble of fear snaking down her spine, Allie wished she had her weapons with her. She was no match against her gift. Not like this.

As she'd seen countless times in the dreamworld, her thoughts manifested into reality as she placed her hand on her hip, finding her blades sheathed at her sides. She looked down at the weapons that had passed from mother to daughter for generations. They were once her mother's and before that, they belonged to Alísun, her grandmother. Each woman who held them added her strength to the blades.

"I need your strength this day," she whispered to the women of her family as she gripped her sai, pulling them from their sheathes with a musical sound they only made for her.

"Pathetic." Gift-Allie crouched low, ready for a fight to the death because that was exactly what this would be. "There's no one here to fight your battle for you now."

"That's okay." Allie took her stance, settling her feet firmly beneath her. "I'm ready."

"Are you?" Gift-Allie scoffed. "The little girl who didn't even know what she was? You think a handful of years have prepared you for this battle?"

Allie looked back over the last eight years that had passed in the blink of an eye. Was it enough time? Had she learned enough, or was she doomed to fail? Could eight years possibly be enough time to learn all she needed to know, when others of her kind got a century or more to prepare for their Proving?

"I guess we'll have to see." Allie twirled her blades over the backs of her hands, finding a rhythm with the music they sang to her.

Crystalline blades clashed as Allie rushed forward in an offensive strike, testing the waters with the manifestation of her gift. Gift-Allie was a fierce warrior. The product of all her years of training. No matter what she said, nor how hard she fought for supremacy, this version of Allie was nothing more than the core of her being. The very essence of herself.

That she came at her with hatred and taunts of her weakness said more about Allie herself than her gift.

When did I turn against myself? She caught Gift-Allie's lead weapon with her own. She knew what her opponent would do before she did it, yet she struggled to keep up with her.

Stumbling back, Allie nearly went down. She used her own momentum to retaliate, sweeping out with a kick that Gift-Allie evaded, but only by a hair.

Gift-Allie came at her with a blow to the head and a kick to her middle, sending her sprawling to the ground, skidding across the rocky terrain, tearing her skin open in a rush of blood and a spray of gravel.

"That the best you can do?" Her voice fell flat and lifeless. "Do you even know how to fight?"

Allie grappled for her weapons and managed to get her feet under her before her gift came after her again.

Pain erupted from the center of Allie's face as cartilage snapped, and blood spurted from her broken nose. She hadn't even seen her gift move before a foot slammed into her face. Allie staggered back, her vision clouded with blood.

"You're nothing." Gift-Allie kneed her in the chest, flipping her on the ground, her back striking sharp rocks. "You call yourself First Princess, but you're an imposter, posing as a pathetic figurehead who pales in comparison to the women who came before you."

Her words hurt more than her fists, but Allie rolled away from her opponent, coiled in a ball to protect herself. Gift-Allie was relentless.

"Wait!" Allie pleaded, throwing her hand out to stop the steel-toed boot from connecting with her gut.

"You think Marcus will wait?" Gift-Allie snatched her hair, tugging hard as Allie tried to get to her feet again. If she stayed down much longer, this maniac would kill her.

Allie elbowed her gift, using the blunt end of her weapon to send her staggering back. Sucking in a breath, Allie stood on shaky legs, gripping her sai blades tight in her hands. "Enough." Allie spit a mouthful of blood onto the ground.

"Giving up already?" Gift-Allie taunted as she danced around Allie in a circle.

"Never." Allie panted, holding her weapons up to shield her most vulnerable parts. "I may not be as fierce as you'd like me to be, but I do the best I can, and I never give up." Allie met her next strikes blow for blow, the crystal of their weapons singing the same song.

"You're not good enough, and you never will be." Gift-Allie's dead voice carried too much weight. Allie could feel the truth to her words because they were her own. So many times, she felt inferior and lacking the skill to do what everyone expected of her.

"Probably not. We have pretty high standards for

ourselves." Allie winced as the sharp crystal bit into her arm, drawing blood that trickled down to her hand to soak the grip she had on her sai.

"We?" Gift-Allie sneered.

"Yes, we." Allie ducked to avoid a round house kick and fell into a sweeping kick of her own, dumping her opponent on the ground for the first time. "We are the same, you and me. There's really nothing you can say to me that I haven't thought myself. That's where you're getting all this anyway."

"Liar." Gift-Allie charged her, landing a kick to her hip and a blow to her head. Blood poured down Allie's face, and she was certain this newest cut went right down to the bone. "You'll never be good enough to face Marcus."

"No, but that's where our equals will come in handy. Even the prophecy says we won't be alone when we face the darkness."

"Stop saying *we*!" Gift-Allie snarled, aiming a wild kick Allie managed to avoid. "You're the failure. You're the one that will never be good enough to fulfill the prophecy, and you sure as hell will never be enough for Aidan. One day soon, he will find his Complement, and you'll lose him, just as you always feared."

Allie trembled as her gift raged against her, kicking and biting in her quest to destroy her.

Maybe she was right. Allie quailed under her fury, backing away from her strikes until nothing was behind her but the long drop down the side of the mountain.

"He loves you, and you're going to ruin it, just like you ruin everything." Gift-Allie slapped her hard, raking her sharp nails down Allie's face. "In the end, you will fail and everyone you love will die, and anyone who is left will leave you."

Allie braced for the shove that would send her sailing over the side of the mountain, but it never came. Gift-Allie stumbled away from her, her eyes glowing with hate and the fire of her power.

"Of course, he's going to leave me some day," Allie whispered softly. "He has a Complement waiting for him. And so do we." Allie took a step toward her gift, lowering her weapons as she approached. "We resist that inevitable moment with everything we have, yet that won't stop it from coming."

"He'll be better off without you." Gift-Allie sank to the ground, all the fight going out of her.

"Maybe he will." Allie sighed. "And maybe it's time we acknowledge that someday everything is going to change again. Inexplicably, there is someone out there we'll love more than we ever loved Aidan. More than we can even comprehend."

"It isn't possible," Gift-Allie said stubbornly.

Allie watched her, seeing in her gift all the power and strength she possessed, as well as her stubbornness and her refusal to accept the immortal life that was hers.

"You really are a stubborn shit, you know that?" Allie moved to sit beside her.

"I hate you." Gift-Allie's voice shook with the first shred of real emotion.

"Back at ya." Allie pressed a hand over her head wound. It was already healing, but the flap of skin left bone exposed. That was going to hurt for a while.

"You get what we're supposed to do, right?"

"What?" Gift-Allie stared at her blankly.

"We're supposed to kiss and make up. I need your power and strength, but I think you need my empathy and a bit of my mortal brain."

"Your mortal brain is our biggest weakness."

Allie nudged her playfully. "You said 'our.'"

"I can still flay the skin right off your hide." Gift-Allie glowered at her.

"Fine. But say what you like, our mortal brain—the way we see the world from both sides—isn't a weakness like everyone thinks. It's a strength."

"Maybe." Gift-Allie sighed. "But that doesn't mean I have to like you."

"Oh, I still don't like you very much. You're seriously mean, and you could use some major help in the personality department.

"Who gets to take charge?"

"I think that's what we have to figure out, freak-show." Allie took in her gift's blazing green eyes and blood-red hair. A multitude of scars marred her face and arms. She was super scary.

"You're going to say we have to share the responsibility, aren't you?" Her gift sneered at her.

"Yes." Allie pulled her knees up, resting her arms against them. "If we're going to survive facing Marcus, living up to our destiny, and losing Aidan ... and being First Princess, and eventually Queen of Indriell, not to mention leading Soma and figuring out what to do with the Senate, we're going to need each other."

"I suppose you're right." Gift-Allie took her hand. Allie placed her hand, sparking with the green light of her power, over hers and waited for her Proving to end.

But it didn't. Blood still trickled from their wounds, and they still sat at the top of the mountain, staring at each other.

"Man, I thought that was going to be it." Allie groaned.

"You always expect things to be too easy." Her gift glowered at her.

"Don't start that again. You're too hard on us."

"Just be quiet for once in your life. Listen for what comes next."

"Fine." Allie sat with her gift, their hands clutched together in the closest they would ever come to solidarity, and waited.

The wind swept through her hair, cooling her face and chasing the heat of her power away. It still sparked along her skin and raged within her core, but the struggle was gone. She'd never held more power within her than she did in this moment, but her hands didn't shake, and her nose didn't bleed. This was the calm within the storm. She'd mastered her power.

Slowly, the sun began to set, and Allie's power continued to grow and spiral within her. It was such a new sensation she reveled in it, wondering what she would be capable of once she'd passed through the final moments of her Proving.

"What do you think comes next?" Allie turned to her gift and gasped. Her fierce gift had grown translucent as she started to fade. Her wild hair blended with the long shadows of the late afternoon.

"Don't go," Allie begged. She didn't want to be alone here.

"I'll be right here with you," her gift whispered before she leaned into Allie, the wisps of shadows moving into her and settling deep within her core. "Together, we are enough."

Allie let out a sob as the sun dipped behind the horizon, and she was alone once again.

Silence echoed around her in the fading twilight. The

solitude weighed heavily on her, worse than the stairs. Worse than fighting her gift. Allie had always enjoyed her alone time, but this empty silence was more than she could bear. She'd rather start over from the beginning than endure another moment alone.

"Emma!" she sobbed into the silence, but only her echo responded.

Green lightning flickered in the sky as the dark clouds rolled in and thunder rumbled overhead. The storm had drifted closer and closer as the day wore on, and now it was here.

"Emma? Please!" Allie cried. "I need you," she sobbed as the rain came in a torrential downpour.

Tilting her head to the sky, she let the rain wash the blood from her face, wondering how long she would be subjected to this intense loneliness. She ached for Darius. Her Syntrophos was out there somewhere, experiencing this crushing silence all on his own. They'd never spent this much time apart. She needed him desperately, but even separated, he was there in her soul.

Allie closed her eyes and listened to her heartbeat.

Thump-thud-thump. Thump-thud-thump. The extra beat was soft and subtle, but it was there. She'd grown used to it over the years since she'd bonded with Darius. The short beat between the longer beats was his heart, moving in sync with hers. She let that small reminder of him give her comfort now.

How could she ever love or need anyone more than she needed her Syntrophos? Sure, it was a different kind of love. Not romantic or even like the love she had for her family. It resided somewhere between all the other types of love. Would her Complement, whoever he was, ever understand her connection with Darius?

Did she even want that kind of complication in her life?

Allie watched as the stars came out to shine, wishing she had someone to share it with. As she let her vision shift and the night sky came alive with stars and planets at her fingertips, Allie knew she needed the love of a Complement in her life. For so long, she'd resisted the idea of bonding with someone that wasn't her choice.

If she had a choice, she would choose Aidan every day for the rest of her life, but maybe there was someone different out there. Someone she couldn't yet comprehend. It would never happen for her as long as she resisted the idea of anyone other than Aidan. But what was that doing to him?

Aidan had regular glimpses of his Complement. He could see into her life. He saw small things about her that would eventually draw them together. If Allie truly loved him with all her heart, why would she hold him back from the one thing he wanted more than anything?

Tears spilled down her face, shining under the light of the full moon. A cry of anguish ripped from her soul as she realized what she had to do now. She had to let him go. It was time to give him the freedom to find what was next for him. Keeping him for herself would only make this harder for both of them.

"No." Allie no longer had the strength to hold herself up. She slid from the boulder where she'd sat since the weight of loneliness had overwhelmed her. Crashing into the ground, Allie sobbed, her heart shattering into so many pieces she wasn't sure she'd ever find them all to put it back together.

"Come, my darling girl." A cool hand swept the blood crusted strands of hair from Allie's face. "It's time to fight."

"No." Allie shoved the hand away, content to wallow in

her heartbreak. She had no desire to end her Proving. Not if it meant she would have to end things with Aidan. She'd rather stay here and suffer.

"You're stronger than this, Allie-girl." The unfamiliar voice tugged at long forgotten memories.

You must stay with Lily and Carson, my darling, Allie-girl. The ghost of the memory brought fresh tears to her eyes. A sense of abandonment washed over her, sending her back to that little girl chasing after her parents along the beach.

"No." Allie sobbed. She threw her arms over her head, not wanting to remember.

"We had to protect you, sweetheart." The cool hand returned. "And I would protect you still, if I could."

Allie peered through her arms at the woman sitting beside her in the grass. The evening shadows hid her face from view, but her red hair shone bright in the moonlight.

For a moment, Allie thought she was seeing some future version of herself. But the features weren't quite right.

With a start, she sat up. "Kassandre?" She nearly choked on her mother's name.

"I missed all the important moments of your life. I didn't want to miss this one too." She took Allie's hand in hers. Her fingers were long and slender with short, manicured nails.

"How are you here?" Tears splashed on the hands that held hers. She wasn't sure if they were hers or Kassandre's.

"Where do you think we are, darling?"

"In the warehouse at Soma." She sniffed, tilting her head back to get a good look at her mother.

"Not quite." Kassandre smiled. "You've frequented this place." She cast a glance around the grassy slope of the mountain peak. "Your father has taught you well."

"The dreamworld?" Allie thought back over the course of events that had led her to the mountain peak. It made sense that this plain wasn't all that it appeared to be.

"More or less." Kassandre wiped the tears from her own eyes.

"You're dead," Allie blurted.

"I suppose I am." She smiled. "Death is a strange phenomenon for us. It's the end of everything we've ever known, but it's also the beginning of something more."

"Can you come back?" Allie's heart leapt at the idea. Marcus had said there was a way. She suddenly understood Chloe's willingness to leave with him. Allie would go to the ends of the earth and back again if it would give her a chance to know the woman who had given her life.

Lily was and would always be her mom. But she desperately wanted to know Kassandre.

"No, Allie-Girl. I can't. It is best if I stay here and await your father."

"He misses you." Allie feared to blink, scared her mother would disappear and leave her to the crushing loneliness.

"I miss him so." Kassandre sighed. "And my girls too."

"I'm sorry you had to die."

"I'm not." Kassandre wrapped her arms around Allie, pulling her close. "I would do it all over again for the chance to watch you become the young woman you are right now. I regret we had to make certain choices that led Livia down a difficult path, but it was necessary to bring you both together. To this life where you're on the same side, working toward the same goals. A life where you'll each know happiness and heartache."

"She's an amazing woman, my sister." Allie leaned into

her mother, wishing Livia could be here for this. "She's my rock. I couldn't do any of this without her."

"And that is worth all the sacrifices we made."

"What do I do now? How am I supposed the fulfill the prophecy and save the world from whatever Marcus is trying to do?"

"You do the best you can. That's all you can ever do."

"Will I succeed?"

"The future isn't written yet. You know that as well as any seer. The future is fluid, constantly in motion, morphing and changing as we make choices."

"That's a non-answer if I ever heard one," Allie muttered.

"If you succeed, wonderful. If you don't, you and yours will pick up the pieces and march on the way we always have. It won't be the end of everything, this darkness. Don't be afraid of what you can't see, darling."

"If I don't stop him, he's going to change everything," Allie whispered. "I can't see it yet, but I can feel it in my bones."

"Then do what you must. Face him head on with your family at your side and know that no matter how lonely you might feel at times, you are never truly alone. Marcus' biggest weakness is his inability to see the strength in love and the power that love gives us to fight against overwhelming odds and come out the victor. He only sees power."

"I will face him soon, won't I?" Allie asked.

Kassandre nodded. "I must leave you here. Your fight isn't over yet, but it will be soon." She stood, pulling Allie up with her. "Be true to who you are." Kassandre's cool gray eyes locked with Allie's. "You really are the best of us both, but it's your unique experiences that have prepared you for what is to come. Never forget who you are at your core."

"I wish I'd had the chance to know you," Allie whispered.

"Ahh, that is a wish I have made a thousand times. Two beautiful, powerful daughters and I never got to know either of you." A tear slid down Kassandre's face as she pulled Allie into a warm embrace.

"Don't go," Allie begged as Kassandre stepped away.

"Find your way back, Allie. Your fight is nearly over."

Kassandre drifted away with the wind, leaving Allie alone and desperate to follow her.

The stairs vanished. No green light of power showed the way. Darkness fell and the storm raged. Wind whipped Allie's hair from her face. Rain and hail beat down on her as the sky flickered in various shades of red.

"I'd like to go home now!" Allie shouted, her temper rising as she'd had about all she could take of this test.

Alone on the mountaintop, Allie peered over the edge to the swirling mass of waves and rocks below.

"Climb down or jump," Allie murmured to herself, wondering just how far the drop was. "Well, we know I won't die, no matter which way I go." She studied the steep slope of the mountain. There were plenty of hand and footholds, though it could take her hours and hours to make her way down to the jungle and back to Emma.

Allie chewed on her bottom lip, studying the possibilities from every angle. She sensed her gift rising within her. The braver side of herself she'd never acknowledged before this night. In mastering her power, she'd embraced the warrior within as much as she'd always embraced the mortal life that had shaped who she was now.

"All right." She took a deep breath. "The fast way it is."

She paced back to the center of the mountain, hoping she could give herself enough momentum to land in the water and not splatter herself across the rocks.

"I'm not above asking for a little help, Hal," Allie called to the wind. "This island is your creation, so if you want to make this a little easier, I won't stop you."

The gale force wind was her only answer. Maybe that would be enough to help her avoid the rocks. "Maybe make it not so high?" Allie sent a last plea out to the old hermit. She would have to do something nice for him once this was all over.

"Let's do this." Allie charged toward the cliff edge, running as fast as she could before she hurled herself over, her arms and legs flailing out as she started to fall.

It was over quickly. The dark depths of the ocean rose to embrace her.

Chapter 42

Allie | Sterling Tower | June

Warm briny water tickled Allie's face, rushing around her like a soothing balm.

Sand crusted her lips, which cracked and oozed blood. The sting of the brine brought her back to consciousness and she groaned.

She'd never been so exhausted in all her life. Everything hurt.

The early morning sunlight warmed her as she tried to open her eyes. Her vision blurred, and she reached to wipe the sand from her eyelids. She felt like something that had been chewed up and spit out. An apt analogy for what she'd just gone through.

"Emma?" She rolled over, the waves lapping at her feet as the tide moved out. Allie didn't remember anything after she hit the water. But she was here. Alive and well ... well, she was breathing at any rate.

She tried to sit up, but her head throbbed.

"Take it easy." Emma's shadow fell over her as she sat up, her back resisting the movement. "How do you feel?"

"You don't want to know." Allie winced, taking her mentor's hand to pull herself up. The world tilted on its axis for a moment before everything righted again. She bent over and spit out a mouth full of bloody sand, wiping her mouth clean and brushing the sand from her face and hands. "I suppose this means I made it?" Her voice rattled like gravel in her throat.

"I knew you would." Emma lifted Allie's chin to meet her gaze.

Shame filled her, and she refused to meet her mentor's eyes. Knowing Emma had witnessed everything that had passed in the night, she wasn't ready to face her.

"I'll have none of that, Alexis Carmichael. You fought hard, and you came through the other side whole."

"Did I?" Allie mumbled. She didn't feel whole. She felt more like she was full of holes, and everything she was had leaked out onto the sand before them. She couldn't quite hold what was left of her together.

"It's natural, what you're feeling right now." Emma smoothed a hand over her cheek.

"I don't know about that." Allie still stared down at the sand, uncertain how she would ever face anyone again now that she knew who she truly was.

"You faced your true self, and it wasn't a pretty sight." Emma wrapped an arm around her, guiding her toward the beach where a shady cabana waited for them. "Welcome to the club, sweetheart."

Allie stared across the white sandy beach in the warm sunshine of a new day. "How can one person change so much in one night?" Her voice trembled, and her eyes burned with the threat of tears.

"You were up on that mountain for nearly four days, Allie," Emma said gently.

"No wonder I'm so tired I can hardly see straight."

"You just need a little time to come to terms with the

person you are now. Rest and recover your physical self, and the rest of you will follow in time."

Allie nodded. She knew very well that she wasn't the first person to emerge from her Proving profoundly altered. Just last year when Darius had experienced his Proving, he hadn't wanted to see her right away. She understood that impulse now. She wasn't ready to face him yet either.

"There is food. A shower and clean clothes." Emma guided her into the cabana. "I can stay here with you, or I can leave you alone if you need time."

"Don't go." Allie reached for her, fearing the oppressive solitude she'd experienced up on the mountain. "I'd like a shower, I think."

"Then food and some rest?" Emma asked.

"Yes. I'll feel better after some rest." But Allie wasn't so sure she knew how to go back to her life as if nothing had happened.

Graham | Savannah, Georgia | July

Graham and his team of spies spent their days at luncheons and various old-world activities at Alderman Abernathy's estate. An endless parade of afternoon barbecues on the sweeping lawns shaded by ancient oaks, and evenings filled with balls and concerts, singing and even nights dedicated to theatrical performances. Each as dull as Graham could ever have imagined. The absence of technology in his daily life began to take a toll on his mood as pent-up energy threatened to spill out of him at any moment.

Weeks of idle nonsense passed in a blur, and they weren't any closer to discovering Abernathy's role in Marcus' plans than when they'd first arrived.

"We've explored every corner of the great hall." Ezra paced the training room like a caged panther dying to be allowed its freedom to run. "It's time we branch out and leave that blasted tree behind."

"Ouch, two puns with one stone." Graham winced, as eager as his young husband was to get back home so they could help Allie end this game they were playing with Marcus and get on with the rest of their lives.

"I hate that stupid great hall." Ezra flopped down onto

the sofa under the wide picture window overlooking the river. Spanish moss hung from Cyprus trees in the late afternoon sunlight. They would need to leave soon for the evening's festivities, and Graham still had a lot of data to review from the information his gift had collected from the previous night. He was much faster at scanning the data now, but it was still a time-consuming chore.

"I have a good feeling about tonight." Graham typed a line of code into his laptop. He'd built a powerful algorithm to search his uploaded data he'd gathered from the legion of small drones he'd launched into the Alderman's home. Most anyone who stumbled upon the dragonflies or mechanical bees would never stop to consider there might be more to them than the toys they appeared to be.

The Immortals in residence at the estate were so far removed from the modern world they often couldn't wrap their minds around simple concepts like electrical lights or indoor plumbing. They had stubbornly refused to move within the mortal world and had very little knowledge of the technological strides mortals had made in the last few centuries.

"You say that every night." Ezra sighed, running his hands through his perfectly styled hair.

"That's a cute look." Graham grinned at his adorable husband, reaching to mess his hair up even more. He never got tired of thinking of Ezra as his Complement. It still amazed him that they'd been so lucky to have found each other at such a young age.

"Do not touch the hair, my love. I will hurt you if I have to start completely over before we dress for the evening."

"What does it matter when you'll be wearing your mask —you know the one that covers your beautiful hair?"

"Oh, it matters." Ezra scoffed, carefully rearranging his silky soft curls.

Graham caught a whiff of the coconut shampoo his husband used, and he wished for the thousandth time they could have had time for a proper honeymoon. But the world couldn't wait when Marcus was on the brink of destroying everything they held dear.

"Wait!" Ezra sat up straight, staring at the computer screen. "Go back a few frames."

Graham paused the program he had running. They were currently reviewing all the images and video data his drones had gathered. It was upwards of five hundred hours of footage from the last week, and they didn't have the time they needed to review it manually. Hence the new algorithm he'd developed to search for viable clues.

That was easier said than done, considering Graham still didn't know what they were looking for.

"There." Ezra pointed at the screen. "Where is that room? I've never seen it before, and I've been all over that house." He leaned in close to peer at the still frame.

In the next instant, the twin orbs of his gift exploded from his chest, zooming around Ezra and the screen in their excitement to do something productive for him.

"*Has our dude found something useful?*" the girls asked in their creepy, emotionless voices.

Ezra snorted, throwing his head back and laughing. "What did they just call you?" Tears leaked from the corners of his eyes.

"It's better than master." Graham chuckled, pulling his computer onto his lap. "We settled on dude the other day, so we'll see how long that lasts." The girls tended to adopt a worshipful attitude toward Graham, which was strange since most of the time they clearly thought he was an idiot.

"Search for the video Ezra found and bring it up to its most heightened detail." The girls sighed at the easy task, whirling into a cyclone of blue light until the room filled with a three-dimensional view of the video, making it so he and Ezra could interact with the room in question.

"Show off," Ezra muttered under his breath, yet he wore a pleased expression at the display of his husband's power.

"Play all the video we have of this location, girls." Graham set his computer aside, standing up to walk through the three-dimensional space that had filled the training room.

"I've never seen this floor before." Ezra stood up to join him. "Is it part of the great hall?"

"Girls, can you answer Ezra's question?" Graham asked.

"*This location is not on the map our dude has developed,*" the girls replied.

"Is it inside the estate?" Graham rolled his eyes, hating how literal the girls needed him to be. It wasn't their fault. They were a manifestation of his gift, and his gift was all about cataloguing and compartmentalizing literal data.

"*It is.*" The girls blinked at him, their blue light pulsing with curiosity.

"If it were on the map, where would it be?" Graham waited patiently for the girls to pull up the map he had created based on all the areas of the estate his team had searched. The girls zoomed around the map that hung in the air before him, pulsing in the familiar blue light of his gift.

They filled in a small square outside the frame of the map to represent the room.

"Great, now how do we find it?" Ezra crossed his arms

over his narrow chest. "Don't tell me it's like the room of requirement, or I'm going to scream."

Graham gave him a questioning look.

"The dude's husband refers to a room described in the Harry Potter *books,"* the girls replied.

"You've been around Allie too long." Graham laughed, returning to the map in question. "Let's retrace the steps in the video data and see if we can fill in the rest of the map to get us to that room." He turned back to look around the room in question. "It's round, like a tower."

"I don't remember seeing a tower along the exterior," Ezra muttered. "I know that doesn't mean anything, though. That's the problem with this stupid house. It's like a circus fun house, minus the fun."

Graham and Ezra studied the video as the girls played what they had collected from various resources. The room in question didn't appear to be anything significant. It was a small library of sorts with bookshelves and a comfortable looking leather chair in front of a fireplace. There were no stairs leading up to it. No windows. A secret room if he'd ever seen one, and in a house where massive spaces hid inside smaller ones, someone went to an awful lot of trouble to conceal this one.

"Is that ...?" Ezra trailed off as he crossed the room to study the location the girls were showing them now. It wasn't the small library. It looked like the upstairs landing in the wing that belonged to the Alderman and his closest family. "This door is slightly open," Ezra said. "Can we get a look at what's in there?" He tried peeking through the crack in the door, but unless a drone managed to get inside that room or if it flew close enough to look inside, they wouldn't know until they tried to sneak into the room later.

"Girls, can you show Ezra anything?" Graham perched on the arm of the sofa, letting Ezra follow his hunch.

It took them a moment, but as the lights faded around them, another view of the space came into focus.

"Perfect." Ezra peeked into the room. They didn't have access to the interior, but the girls had found a single frame where a drone had flown close enough for a glimpse.

"It's a bedroom." Ezra's eyes took in everything he could see. "One I've not seen, and I've been on this landing a dozen times." He stepped back, studying the door. "I need to get up here tonight." He paced back to the couch. "That door isn't there. There's nothing there at all. Just really ugly wallpaper."

"Show us the landing from other footage we have?" Graham asked.

The girls bobbed eagerly and moved to do his bidding. The upstairs landing came into view a moment later.

"There!" Ezra cried. "See that wide expanse of wall there." He pointed to a space between doors. "All the doors on the landing are spaced at perfect intervals. There should be a door there, based on the layout of the rest of the hall, but it's just a blank canvas."

"Then if a door *is* hiding there, how do we access it?" Graham had a bad feeling it was going to require a power source they didn't have access to. The Alderman liked to create various functions with displays of power that weren't necessarily his. Like his cold fireplaces that acted like air conditioners. Or the way his butler used his elemental gift with water to create showers and running water for his guests to enjoy. Who needed plain old indoor plumbing when you had Immortal powers?

"Girls, can we go back to the last frame?" Ezra asked.

Graham sighed irritably when they didn't answer. "Do I really have to ask you to answer his questions every time?"

"*Yes, our dude,*" the girls replied. "*Confirmation is important.*"

"Then show us the last frame, please."

The girls complied, and a view of the Alderman's bedroom door came back into focus.

"There it is." Ezra marched across the room, pointing to the wall sconce hanging on the wall by the door. It was turned slightly to the right. "That sconce is always pointing straight up, and it's never lit, even when I walk past it."

The Alderman refused to use electrical lights or even gas lights. Yet there were sconces and candelabras throughout the estate. They glowed with power whenever an Immortal was near. Except for this one, apparently.

"It's there for show." Graham moved to stand beside his brilliant husband. "You did it, Ez!" Graham squeezed his shoulders. "The sconce is the key to the room."

"Unless it somehow knows to only work for the Alderman." Ezra frowned.

"Abernathy isn't that advanced." Graham knew it wouldn't be that complicated. "He doesn't expect anyone would ever find out how to enter his secret domain."

"We just need to get into that room when he's not there. The entrance to that tower has to be in this room." Ezra gave him a worried look. "Unless it's also hidden."

"Care to make a wager on it?" Graham grinned.

"What do you know?" Ezra arced a perfectly sculpted brow at him.

"Just a hunch, but I bet you fifty bucks there's a secret passageway through a bookcase in that room."

Ezra snorted. "He can't be that big of an idiot, can he?"

Graham rolled his eyes at his husband.

"Never mind, I'm not taking that bet. That man is dumber than dirt. Of course, it's a bookcase." He shook his head. "His only reference for such things is Sherlock Holmes."

"Exactly." Graham pulled Ezra into his arms, giving him a playful squeeze. "And my brilliant husband just outsmarted him. That was a great catch, Ez. I couldn't do this without you."

"Well, you never have to worry about that." Ezra hugged him back, laying his head on Graham's shoulder. "I have to go put that creepy costume on again, don't I?"

"'Fraid so." Graham laughed. "It's better than mine, though."

"I despise seeing you play your role. It's insulting."

"I don't mind it."

"It's insulting that anyone would think a husband of mine would be such an imbecile."

"Well, let's hope after tonight, we can be well on our way out of here."

"Let's go get ready. For the first time ever, I'm anxious to get to the most boring ball there ever was."

CHAPTER 44

Allie | Sterling Tower | June

Allie rolled over, forcing her eyes shut to block out the afternoon sunlight. Someone had stolen the remote to the fancy blackout shades for her windows, and they were going to have to die now.

Reaching for the half-melted ice cream on her nightstand, she scraped the bottom for all the leftover chocolate bits she hadn't hunted down when she'd retrieved the pint from the freezer for breakfast.

"Naeemah and her *clean* diet can suck it," she muttered, shoveling the full fat ice cream into her mouth. She'd stolen it from the downstairs neighbors when they weren't at home. She was getting most of her junk food that way these days.

Eventually, she'd replace it all, but at the moment, she didn't care about being neighborly.

The ice cream was gone too soon, and Allie thought about taking a shower, but it didn't appeal to her. Running a hand through her tangled, dirty hair she stumbled onto a Cheeto from yesterday's snacks.

"Well, I've reached a whole new level of disgusting." She pulled the comforter over her head and burrowed into the darkness. One more loser trait to add to the growing list of her worst qualities.

She missed Darius, though she didn't want him to see her like this. And she was grateful he and Aidan were still off hunting rogue Immortals with his Syntrophos army.

Allie had worked so hard over the last year to prepare for her Proving. She just hadn't known what to expect of the aftermath. She'd never before experienced depression like this. The self-loathing had hit her hard.

Tears burned behind her eyelids, but she forced them back. She couldn't cry anymore, yet no matter what she did, she couldn't shake the dark mood that had engulfed her since she left the island behind.

She was worthless. A beacon of hope for her generation. The child of prophecy and the savior of the world. Yet all she did was hide in her tower, sending others out to do the hard work while she did nothing.

Leave. They'll be better off without you. Her thoughts whispered to her constantly, telling her hard truths. That her life was some kind of cosmic joke. But she couldn't even leave the tower. Not without the help of a dream walker and she really doubted Briggs would be willing to help her again.

"All right. That's enough." Someone barged into her room, turning on all the lights and ripping the blankets off the bed.

"Mom!" Allie snatched at the sheets, trying to burrow into them.

"Where's your phone?" Carson grabbed the pillows off her head.

Allie ducked under her arm, curling into a ball on her bed.

"Why aren't you answering your phone?" Lily demanded.

Allie refused to look at them, pointing to the pile of broken bits on her nightstand. "I got tired of it ringing." Truthfully, she couldn't bring herself to read the texts from Darius and Aidan. They would know she'd Proven by now. Darius had likely suffered right along with her the way she had with his.

"You remember when you were a kid and you refused to get out of bed when you didn't want to go to school?" Carson sat on the corner of her bed.

"Ugh." Allie sat up. "You dragged me out of bed by my *foot*." She groaned, her head swimming with the movement. She hadn't spent much time vertical in the last week.

"Then don't make me do it now because I will." Carson handed her a comb. "Fix your hair—it looks like squirrels have been nesting in it."

Allie scowled at her dad, snatching the comb from him. "You know, most people around here know when to give me a little space."

"Well, we're not most people." Lily threw an empty trash bag at her. "We're your parents, and for the first time in your life, you're acting like a spoiled princess. We raised you better than that, so get off your butt and clean this room."

"And no more junk food." Carson gathered up the half empty boxes of snack cakes and potato chips. "You're going to eat a real meal tonight, at the dining table with us, and you're going to shower and change into some real clothes."

"And tomorrow, you're going back to work, like an adult."

"They don't need me." Allie ran the comb through her hair, wincing at the tangles. She'd have to put off that shower until she finished combing it out. This was going to be an afternoon job involving detangled spray and patience.

"You know very well that's not true." Lily took the comb from Allie's hand and went to work, attacking her hair like she had when Allie was small.

Carson took the trash bag and started gathering up the remnants of Allie's junk food feast. "We can't ever know what you went through up on that mountain, but you've got to put your boss girl pants on and get back to work."

"I know." Allie sighed, covering her eyes as Lily sprayed her hair with detangler spray.

"Oh, for heaven's sake." Lilly plucked a pretzel stick from Allie's hair and tossed it at Carson. "No more of this wallowing, Allie-girl. We're here if you need to talk things through. But this stops, now."

"Yes ma'am," Allie muttered, hanging her head.

"Stop doing that," her mom snapped. "Hold your head high and be confident in who you are. Remember the confident girl we taught you to be?" She pulled Allie's head back, peering into her eyes. "Find that girl again."

"I will." Allie sat up straighter. "I know my wallowing isn't healthy."

"Wallowing is fine," Carson said. "I've done my fair share of it over the years. It's human nature to retreat into yourself to lick your wounds when life gets hard."

"But you can't stay in bed forever." Allie kicked off her sheets, trying to find the will to show her face again.

"Sweetheart," Lily said. "The only people who know what you faced are you and your mentor. To everyone else, it's just another Tuesday afternoon."

"I know." Allie took a deep breath. "I'm ready for a shower. I stink."

"Yes, you do, but we're only halfway through combing

out this mess, and I'm pretty sure there are more pretzel sticks in here. Did you fall asleep with your head in the bag?"

"Probably." Allie shrugged, grabbing a brush to help.

First a shower and then a meal and maybe she'd feel more like herself again.

CHAPTER 45

Allie | Sterling Tower | June

Allie sat with her mother at the kitchen counter, making cinnamon rolls. The kind in the can with the cream cheese icing. She still wasn't ready to venture out of her apartment, but her hair was brushed, washed, dried, and up in a neat ponytail. She was clean and her pajamas were fresh from the laundry. After a good meal and time with her parents, and a waking night to herself, she was feeling a lot better.

But she was afraid to go back to work. She didn't know how to be the First Princess, the child of prophecy, and the leader of Soma. Not when she still felt like an imposter.

"Remember when you were thirteen and you tried to make these homemade?" Lily pulled the first batch from the oven, piping hot and ready for frosting. Allie had warned her she'd likely eat a whole can on her own.

"Those were awful." Carson lifted three plates from the cabinet, quick to load his plate with the fresh rolls.

"Hey, those are mine." Allie reached for a plate, but Carson backed away.

"Half now, half later when the second batch is done." He withheld the plates until she agreed.

"And in my defense, I was only thirteen, and I had no idea how baking powder worked."

"Do you know how baking powder works now?" Lily snorted.

"No. That's why I have the ready-made ones in my fridge and no baking powder in my pantry." Allie laughed, sinking her teeth into the gooey warm roll. It was the first time she'd laughed in days, and it felt strange.

"I miss the days when you were little." Lily moved to sit at the barstool beside her.

Allie laid her head on her mother's shoulder. "Well, if it's any consolation, I still need you guys. You're the only ones who treat me like a normal person."

"We will always be here to remind you who you are right here." Carson's eyes twinkled as he tapped his chest over his heart. "Even when we're gone, you'll have memories like this one to keep you grounded."

"Well, you'd better plan on living a very long time, because I'm not grown up enough yet. I still need parenting."

"Love you, Allie-girl." Lily pressed a kiss to her temple just as someone banged on the door.

"Duty calls." Allie wiped her sticky hands on a paper towel and went to check the peep hole. She was better, but depending on who was on the other side of that door, she might not be ready to open it.

"It's Grandma and Grandpa." She opened the door with a shy smile. "Hi."

Grandpa Alex pulled her into a hug. "Your grandma tells me you're feeling better."

"I am." She ushered them into the kitchen. "We were just having some breakfast."

"Come join us." Lily smiled, reaching for more plates while Carson started a fresh pot of coffee.

"Thank you." Alísun moved to sit at the dining table and Allie transferred their things to the larger table, and helped her mom put the new batch of cinnamon rolls into a basket.

"It's no problem, we fixed enough for an army, or for one hungry Allie." Lily put the basket on the table, and Allie grabbed more coffee mugs from the cabinet.

"I meant for what you two have done for Allie." Alísun sat perched on the dining chair, her hands in her lap like she was uncertain how to act in such a domestic environment. "It's clear she needed her parents."

"That's what we're here for." Carson poured coffee all around, and they sat down together as a family.

It was just what Allie needed. A chance to have the different sides of her family mesh into one. Lily and Carson had always been close with Navid, but they knew little of her grandparents. Both sides went to great effort to ignore the issues of age and royal titles that might have otherwise stood between them. For this one afternoon, they were just family.

"Tell me, Allie, why haven't you been answering your phone?" Grandpa Alex pinned her with a grave look.

"She broke it into a thousand little pieces," Carson said. "Like it's that easy to ignore your responsibilities."

"Well, it worked for a few days." Allie licked the last of the cream cheese frosting from her fork. She'd eaten far too many cinnamon rolls, but she was feeling so much better now. She'd get back to her bland, clean—well, mostly clean —diet tomorrow. "I'll order a new one tomorrow."

"And we can expect you to return to work then too?" Grandma Alísun gave her one of her queenly looks that used to scare her. "You aren't the head of Soma right now, but we still need you."

"Yeah." Allie hung her head. "I know I can't avoid it forever."

"No one ever said being First Princess was easy, and being queen is even harder, but you do it well, darling." Alísun reached across the table for her hand.

"I'm not queen yet." Allie held on to her grandmother's hand. "Thank goodness for that."

"Oh, Allie, you've already stepped into the role. I am queen in name only."

"Ugh, Grandma, is this another one of those times when you're about to blindside me with a promotion?"

"She's only just Proven," Lily said, a concerned look on her face. "Give her a little more time."

"She's ready." Confidence filled Alísun's voice. "She's been ready."

Allie shook her head. "Maybe I'm ready to take on the responsibility but not the title."

"It's just a word, Allie-girl," Grandpa Alex said. "You give it too much power."

Allie pointed her fork at her grandfather. "Don't throw my own words back at me." She'd just told her younger self that same thing, and here she was, once again, not learning the lesson.

"Then take your own advice."

"Why can't Grandma be queen forever, and I'll just be the First Princess?"

"It doesn't work that way." Alísun gave her a rueful smile. "When a First Princess is ready to rule, a subtle shift in the mantle of power begins. You've been taking on that mantle more and more of late. And now that you're Proven, it's only a matter of time before the shift is complete.

Whether you want it or not, up here." She tapped Allie's forehead. "In here." She pressed a palm against Allie's heart. "You're ready. You only need your head to catch up to your heart."

"But how can I be the next Queen of Indriell when all I do is sit here telling other people what needs to be done? How can I continue to hide in my tower and not do the real work myself?"

"Darling, that is the hardest lesson a young queen has to learn. You will carry the mantle of power until your own child or grandchild is ready to take that burden from you. It is your duty to serve the Immortal population of this world. It is what you were born to do. Maybe you'll be like me, and they won't always need you as much as they do now."

Allie sighed. "I really wish this job came with an opt out clause in the contract."

"I've wished for that many times." Alísun chuckled. "It won't always be so hard. Your involvement will come and go throughout the years based on when and how you are needed. But the very hardest part will always be the need to rely on others to do the hard work while you do nothing. The queens of our family are much beloved, and our supporters will always want to keep us protected. That is why the prophecy said you would gather your equals. They will come to you with the information you need to make your choices as we move forward into a time we know little about. That time is upon us."

"It's just so frustrating to have my hands tied while the people I love put themselves and those they love on the line for me."

"They aren't doing it for you, Allie," Lily said, surprising everyone at the table with her words. "They're doing it for themselves. For the people they love and all the people of your world who can't fight for themselves. Your equals ... Aidan, Darius, Sasha, Chloe, Graham, and Quinn ... they're all out there fighting for the same reasons you do."

"Your mother is right," Carson said. "It doesn't matter if you're mortal or Immortal." He pinned her with his stare. "We're all human, and we fight for what is right. We fight for justice and for a world where we can all live in peace, with respect for each other. There will always be those who will thirst for power they haven't earned, but that is unfortunately the darker side of human nature. A perfect world doesn't exist and never will. We just do the best we can with what we've got, and when we're faced with challenges, we work together to fix them."

"Couldn't have said it better myself," Grandpa Alex said. "Sometimes, I wonder if we do the mortal world an injustice by keeping our world separate."

"No." Carson laughed. "You don't. Most of us couldn't handle knowing the things you can do."

"But we'd likely do things a lot better if we listened to you now and again," Alísun added.

"It's about balance I guess, this job, I mean," Allie said. "The whole world, really. Dad's right, we can only do the best we can. I should be grateful I have so many wonderful people to help me serve our people."

"And that is the one thing I want you to always remember." Alísun leaned toward Allie. "Our family and any who come after us are meant to serve. We may be treated as royals. We may have access to resources others don't, but we are servants to our people. We are responsible *for* them, and at the end of the day, we have to answer *to* them as well."

"Do I have to take on the role today?" Allie asked, fearing her grandmother's response.

"No, darling. The full mantle of power is a heavy load

to bear. It begins when you are named First Princess and continues to shift over time. You are ready for it, but it isn't a matter of crowning you and calling it a day. It takes time."

Allie nodded. "Okay then." She let out a breath. "Then I'll keep taking it one day at a time."

"Speaking of taking it little by little," Alexander said, pulling a handful of messages from his pocket. "You have some phone calls to return."

"I'll sort through them tomorrow unless there's anything urgent."

"Well, I thought this one could wait, but when he couldn't get through to you on the phone, he showed up here demanding to see you."

"Who?" Allie frowned at the message her grandfather handed her. "It's from Vince." She studied the neat scrawl of her assistant recording the number of times he'd called, but she hadn't made a note of what he needed. "Is he here?"

"He's staying in a hotel nearby. He won't talk to anyone but you. I have his number." Alexander slid his phone across the table to her.

Without a thought, she hit send and waited for him to answer.

"Allie?" His voice grated in her ear. He was stressed, and it showed in his tone that he was in a panic.

"What's wrong?" Allie moved to the living room, staring out the windows at the beautiful sunny afternoon.

"It's Kayla. She's missing. They took her right from our apartment."

"Who took her?" Allie headed for her room to find clothes.

"I don't know. They were yours, not mine. She's not the only one to go missing. It's been bad here since your kind tried to take out ours."

"Can you come here?" She shoved her legs into a pair of jeans and bent to look for shoes at the bottom of her closet. "We need to talk in person. I'm so sorry I wasn't there for you, but I'm here now."

"Thank you, Allie. I didn't know who else to call."

"We'll find her. Just get over here as soon as possible. I'll be waiting for you."

Allie groaned when the elevator doors opened, and she realized Raina was the walker on duty today.

"Hiya, your Princess-ship." Raina skipped across the lobby, her wild blond hair a mess of dreads and her worn leather gear looking a little worse for the wear. Allie had offered her new clothes and a trip to the Soma salon, but she refused, claiming she didn't like other people touching her hair, and her clothes were just fine.

"Hey Raina." Allie braced herself, trying to remember to be patient with the girl. She'd been through a lot.

"I'm not supposed to let you out." Raina crossed her arms over her chest.

"I'm not a prisoner." Allie adopted her pose. "I'm just here to meet a friend. Can you please escort me through the barrier?"

"Nope. No can do, Princess-lady." Raina let her arms swing at her sides. "Your grandpa himself called down and told me I'm to go get your fella and bring him inside."

"Fine." Allie sighed. "Then please go get him. This is important. A friend of mine is missing."

"Missing?" Raina's face fell, and for a moment she looked close to tears. "That's real bad luck. I'll be right back." She turned toward the glass doors, and Allie could see Vince pacing along the sidewalk in front of the building. She wanted to race out there and ask him a thousand questions, but she wasn't allowed to set a toe outside the tower. It was infuriating.

"Hey there, your Majesty, you know this guy's a mortal, right?" Raina hesitated at the door. The trip through the barrier could take a while, despite the short distance between the entrance and the sidewalk.

"Yes, Raina. I know. He's an old friend from school. A very important friend whose wife has just gone missing." Allie flexed her hands at her sides, resisting the urge to wrap them around the girl's neck. But Raina couldn't help her quirks. She'd spent far too long in the dreamworld as a prisoner, and she was still recovering. Allie wasn't sure she'd ever fully recover.

"Wife, huh?" Raina glanced back outside. "He's super yummy."

"He is married, Raina. Hands off and please don't freak him out." Raina had a tendency to flirt with unavailable men. It was her way of protecting herself with a little harmless flirtation that would never come to anything.

"Fine." Raina sighed, shoving through the double doors. "Be right back."

Allie waited not so patiently as Raina faded into the barrier, and after several moments, she emerged onto the sidewalk, completely freaking Vince out before they headed back through the barrier.

Finally, he was in the lobby, and Allie was shocked by his appearance. He had lost weight, and his eyes were hollow with dark circles underneath.

"What's going on?" Allie wrapped her arms around him, and he lowered his head to her shoulder, his back shaking with sobs. "They came into our home when I was at work. She didn't have class, so she was home working on her thesis."

"Who?"

Vince shook his head, glancing back at Raina uncertainly.

"Come, let's get you upstairs."

"Is it wise?" Raina asked, dropping her gaze to the floor. "I'm sorry, Pr—er, Allie. "There are already two too many of his kind here."

Allie drew her shoulders back and sucked in a furious breath.

"No, ma'am, I mean no disrespect," Raina rushed to speak. "It's just ... not safe. For them."

"Thank you for your concern for my family, Raina," Allie spoke gently. "But as long as my parents and Vince, and any other mortal resides here in Sterling Tower, they are under my protection."

Raina gasped at her use of the word mortal in the presence of one who wasn't supposed to know anything about the Immortal world.

"Say nothing of Vince's arrival." Allie guided him to the elevator waiting for them. Allie reached for her key in the lock, holding the elevator in place. "I'm trusting you, Raina. Potentially with my friend's life. You understand that, I hope."

Raina bobbed her head and then crossed her heart, mimed zipping her lips and throwing away the key.

"You're a good soldier, Raina."

"Thank you." Raina bowed as the doors closed, and they shot up toward the penthouse floor.

"She's kind of scary," Vince said, his voice still gruff from emotions that were clearly still on the surface.

"She is, but she's harmless. Mostly," Allie added,

turning to him. "We're going to do everything we can to help find Kayla, but I need you to tell me everything."

They waited until they were ensconced in Allie's study with her parents. Vince had asked them to join them.

Vince sat in the white leather chair across from her desk. It wasn't really hers. It was still Livia's furniture since she hadn't had time to redecorate, and Allie still thought of the apartment as her sister's.

"When I came home, the whole place was trashed." Vince scrubbed a hand over the stubble on his chin. "They tried to make it look like a robbery, but they didn't take anything of value." He snorted a laugh. "We don't have anything anyone would want. The only thing missing was my wife. My pregnant wife."

"Oh no, Vince. I'm so sorry." Allie choked on her words, knowing they were never enough to ease his pain.

"You know this is our only chance to have a daughter. That's the way it works for us. She's a Banished Daughter who gave birth to an Immortal child. That means she will only be able to have one other child, and if she loses this one, we won't get another chance."

"We *will* find her, Vince. I promise."

"Things have been hard since the attack on the Coalition." He refused to meet her eyes, not wanting to hold her to her promise.

Lily nodded from her perch on the edge of the sofa, the whole of Atlanta on display behind her through the wall of windows.

"We've heard the stories," Carson added. "It's been that way everywhere with our people."

"What stories?" Allie asked, glancing at her parents.

"Your warning helped," Vince said. "We were able to

help dozens of families avoid the attack and word spread quickly. Some trusted us, many others didn't."

"I know Marcus killed hundreds of the Coalition." Allie sat back in her seat. She'd heard the reports of what came after her warnings. Even her grandfather and Quinn had ventured into the Cleveland Coalition to tell them who their beloved leader was. None other than the Immortal, Marcus Servius. He'd infiltrated the Coalition and ultimately became the current Marches Marius Von Essen, leader of the Margrave who was poised to execute them all now that he'd decided he no longer needed them to carry out his bidding.

"Thousands," Vince corrected her. "Thousands have died or gone missing." His voice was rough, and Allie wondered when he'd last slept. "There are barely enough members of the Coalition left to regroup and rebuild. Not that they should." He shook his head. "Too many lives have been lost because they failed to go into hiding."

"Are you saying the Coalition are now being hunted the way they have done the hunting for centuries?" Carson asked.

Vince looked up into her father's eyes. "That is exactly what I'm saying. But what do they want with my wife?" His eyes were haunted and so full of a pain Allie couldn't even fathom.

"You've been fighting for our people, haven't you?" Carson asked.

Vince nodded. "We've been working with the Banished Daughters, helping refugees find safe places to relocate and disappear. I just don't know what they want with us. That's why I came to you, Allie. I need your help."

"Vince, you and Kayla have always been there for me. It's not even a question. I'm here." She reached across her sister's desk to take his hand. "We're going to find her, and we're going to find out what's happening to all your people." She sat back, releasing his hand.

"We cannot allow the Coalition to reform, but we can and we will make sure those who were once involved are safe from anything Marcus might have planned for them."

Allie had no idea how she was going to make good on her promises. Especially when she couldn't even leave her tower to actually do anything worthwhile. But she refused to let anything happen to Kayla or her unborn child. Not after everything they'd done for her.

Through the years, Vince and Kayla had a way of showing up just when she needed them most. Now, they needed her. And if that meant breaking out of Sterling Tower and hunting down Marcus Servius once and for all, then that was exactly what she was going to do.

Chapter 46

Sasha | India | June

Sasha buckled her seatbelt, settling back for the flight to Atlanta. She kept a protective hand on Xeren, his eyes nearly bugging out of his head as he took in all the sights of the planes taking off on the runway. In his dark jeans and t-shirt, he almost didn't look like her little boy.

"When will we see Grandma and Grandpa and Uncle Aidan?" Xeren tugged on her shirt.

"We have a long flight first." She lowered the shade over the window, not sure Xeren was ready to see the earth drift away as they took off. She and Jayesh had always taught Xeren about the world they would eventually return to. In the same way they'd prepared his namesake, Xera, to reenter society, she was confident her son would make the transition easily.

"And Aunt Allie and Uncle Quinn, too?" Xeren chattered beside her.

"Take a breath, Sasha." Xera reached over to pat her arm. "All will be well."

Sasha exhaled, nodding. Coming out of the Chola Valley was never an easy transition. They'd left their quiet, peaceful life behind to reenter the hustle and bustle of a world that hadn't changed at all.

It was disorienting to think she'd only arrived in India a few months ago. Yet she was returning Proven, with a young son and a husband. She wasn't even certain how old Xeren was. Time was such an unessential thing in the valley. She guessed he was about four now, but that didn't mean they were only in the valley for four or five years. It could have been ten or more. They'd stopped marking the days a long time ago.

When the Mother released them from the valley, Sasha found out Quinn and Santi had left a few years ago along with many of Xera's ancient friends. The rest of them were traveling with Sasha and Jayesh today. It would be interesting to see how long the others had been back in the river of time. She couldn't wait to see her Syntrophos after all this time.

She relaxed when Jayesh returned from the cockpit, taking his seat beside Xera opposite her and Xeren. "We'll be taking off next." He leaned over to offer his son a fist bump.

Xeren tapped his little fist against his father's with a grin that reminded her of Aidan's. There was a lot of her brother's spirit in her child, and she couldn't wait for them to meet. Her heart squeezed at the thought. Aidan and Quinn would be the best uncles a kid ever had and Allie was going to spoil him rotten.

The small private jet began to move, and Xera gasped, letting out a little chuckle as she gripped the armrests.

"It's okay, Auntie Zee." Xeren leaned forward to look out the opposite window. "We're just rolling toward the runaway. Mama said it doesn't get scary until we go faster. Then I'm supposed to squeeze her hand and shut my eyes until my tummy drops, and then we'll be flying! You can hold Daddy's hand."

Xera nodded, smiling. "Thank you for being my eyes, dear one. I think I will be okay now."

And she was. She was as excited as Xeren when they soared high above the clouds, and the little boy described everything he could see so she could see it too.

"We're going home." Jayesh smiled with a shake of his head. "I'm completely shook, but that kid of ours is on cloud nine."

"That's the only reason I'm not crying into my rum and coke." Sasha took a sip of her drink, feeling the first stirrings of excitement thrumming in her veins. In a few short hours, she would see her family again.

The moment the plane touched down, Sasha reached for her phone to text Quinn. She wanted to surprise everyone else, but she needed to be able to find him immediately—and they needed a way through the barrier. The Syntrophos bond buzzed beneath her skin and she couldn't sit still.

"We're almost there." Jayesh squeezed her hand. They'd hired a couple of drivers to take them all to Sterling Tower. Xera rode with Leandro and the other former prisoners in a large van that followed them.

"What's wrong with Mama?" Xeren tugged on his father's arm.

"She's just anxious to see all her family again."

"*Our* family," Sasha corrected him with a smile. "They're your family now too."

"I've never known a true family. Not until you and our son." He returned her smile, his eyes bright with happiness.

"Well get ready for a host of brothers, uncles and sisters because my family is huge." She scooted to the edge of her seat as the driver pulled up to the curb at Sterling Tower.

"Sasha!" Quinn was already there, pacing along the sidewalk in front of the building.

She leapt out of the car and crashed into him, her arms winding around his neck as her heart shuddered, finding its rhythm with his.

"How long?" He pressed his forehead against hers, breathing her in.

"Years," she whispered. "You?"

"Almost three. We just got back a week ago." He pulled away, holding her at arm's length. "It's been far longer for you. You're Proven." He nodded.

"You too." She could sense it in his presence. He had mastered his power while they were separated. She sensed something else too. "You're the anchor."

Quinn looked over her shoulder at Jayesh approaching with Xeren in his arms.

"Oh Sasha. You have been gone for a long, long time," Quinn whispered, his eyes glued to Xeren's face. "Congratulations." He took her hand in his. "Now introduce me to your son and your Complement. We can talk of other things later."

Chapter 47

Allie | Sterling Tower | July

"Do we need to send another team out to help Aidan and Darius?" Allie folded the newspaper with the heinous headlines and set it on the side table in Liam's office. It was getting worse every day. With the escaped Immortals roving the country, killing innocents, and terrorizing cities with storms and unnatural phenomenon, the mortal population was on the verge of discovering the Immortals living among them. It was exactly what Marcus wanted and the one thig they could not allow to happen.

"With Quinn and Santi back, we have another Syntrophos pair who could lead a group," she suggested. "I could go with them." Since her Proving, they hadn't made the switch in authority yet. Liam was doing a great job leading Soma and she was assisting him. She would take the reins from him eventually, but for the moment, she liked their arrangement.

"I don't want to take them away from the work they're doing," Liam said, pushing his chair away from his desk. "The facility they are building will be an asset in the months to come. And I can't afford to lose you."

"Then what can we do to get a handle on these rogue Immortals? How many of them are still at large?"

"The last report I had from Aidan, he and Naomi were tracking one of the most vicious ancients. Once they get her behind bars, there is only one more that needs to be apprehended. The others are dangerous, and we will round them up as soon as possible, but once Elona and Rhaegal are off the streets, we should see a significant decrease in these reports."

"And the Coalition prisons?" Allie rubbed a hand over her brow. There was so much at stake, with the Coalition failing the prisons could crumble into an all out disaster if they didn't get control of them as soon as possible.

"A work in progress." Liam stood to cross the room where a map of the Coalition prisons were clearly marked in color coordinated push pins. "All the green ones are under our control, but we're running out of people to man them. The prisoners need to be released and rehabilitated. If we just let them go we're going to have bigger problems than we already have."

"And the red ones?" Allie studied the map where there were more green pins than red and purple ones.

"Still under Coalition control."

"And purple?" There were more of those than the red.

"Under Coalition control but cooperating with the Senate."

"Really?" Allie was surprised to hear that.

"Some of the Coalition wardens have been reasonable. They know they've lost too many of their numbers and they can't fully man all the prisons. And they don't want to release these prisoners on the world. The Senate still doesn't trust you and they don't believe Marcus is a problem."

"They think I'm the problem," Allie muttered.

"But they are on top of the Coalition situation—in terms of the prisons they know about. All the green locations are ours because the Senate doesn't know they exist.

"Let's try to keep it that way."

The old intercom on Liam's desk buzzed. "Ms. Carmichael? Are you in there?"

"Yes, Mrs. Mitchell!" Allie shouted, not bothering to hit the button.

"For heaven's sake, girl, use the speaker," her assistant shouted back.

"Fine," Allie muttered, shuffling behind Liam's desk, trying not to knock over the piles of documents to hit the intercom button. There had to be an updated version of this archaic system. "Yes, Martha, what can I do for you, Martha?" Allie tried to keep the mocking tone from her voice, she really did.

"Someone is here to see you and Mr. Liam. Several someones, they're spilling out of my office into the hall."

Allie hit the button on the speaker. "Give me an idea of who we're talking about." She rolled her eyes. It was like pulling teeth to get information out of her assistant.

"Wait, Miss, you can't just barge in there!"

"It's Mrs.," Sasha snapped over her shoulder, "and you know very well who I am and how important it is for me to see Allie." She charged into the room, Quinn and Jayesh following behind her.

"Sasha?" Allie leapt from behind the desk to reach her friend. She looked the same. Mostly. Except her hair was longer, swept back from her face in long braids that fell well past her shoulders. She saw the mark of time in her friend's eyes. And the little boy on Quinn's shoulders. Had she said she was a Mrs. now? "How long?" Her throat grew tight with emotion and she pulled Sasha into a hug.

Sasha sighed, holding her tight. "A long time." Her voice broke and she clutched Allie tightly. "I missed you, sister."

"I missed you too, so much." Tears leaked out of the corners of her eyes. "But it was only three months for me."

"We have a lot to discuss, but first, there's someone I want you to meet." Sasha guided the boy forward, and Allie crouched down to his level, holding her hand out to him. He looked an awful lot like Sasha with a hint of Jayesh about his warm brown eyes.

"I'm Allie, what's your name?"

"You're my Auntie Allie?" He glanced up at Sasha who nodded through her tears. "She's the one I've been telling you about."

"Hi." He thrust his hand out with a smile Allie knew so well. It was the same one she saw when Aidan's true smile peeked through. The one she missed with an ache she could hardly bear sometimes. "I'm Xeren. Your nephew."

"Well." Allie's voice trembled as her eyes burned with happy tears. "I am happy to meet you, Xeren. We're going to be such good friends."

The little boy wrapped his arms around her neck, and just like that, he had her heart. She pulled him close and let the family bond engulf them in its warmth. "I will always have snacks," she promised her nephew.

Sasha crouched down beside them, running a hand over her son's hair.

"I love him already." Allie sniffed, not ready to let him go.

"He has a way about him." Sasha smiled, the years reflecting in her eyes. "Hey, buddy." She ran a thumb over

Xeren's cheek. "Can you go hang out with Mrs. Mitchel and Auntie Zee's friends for a little bit while Daddy and I talk to Allie and Liam?"

Xeren nodded, turning to Allie with a serious face. "You said something about snacks?"

Allie laughed and went to dig through her purse in search of a gooey chocolate snack cake she'd been saving for herself.

"He's never going to forget you said that," Jayesh said, opening the door to let another woman join them. Allie nearly dropped the cake as the woman's ancient lifeline swept over her, but she'd spent enough time with her grandparents to push past the surprise.

"Please make yourselves comfortable," Liam said, making sure they had enough seats for everyone.

Allie took Xeren's hand and led him into Mrs. Mitchell's office with his snack cake. "Mrs. Mitchell will take good care of you while I catch up with your parents and Uncle Quinn."

Allie was hesitant to let him go with her assistant. She wanted very much to take her new nephew down to the warehouse and spend the day playing with him, but there was so much to do, and never enough time to do it. Maybe when this was all over, she needed to take a trip to the Chola Valley Temple for a little R&R—just not for a lifetime.

As she closed the door behind her, Allie turned to one of her dearest friends. "A lot has changed for you in a very short time. Well, short for me." She moved to sit on the sofa beside Sasha, turning to the woman with the opaque eyes. "I'm Allie. It's lovely to meet you."

The woman bowed her head. "An honor to meet you, First Princess, my name is Xera."

"My nephew's namesake?" She shifted in her seat so she could get a good look at Sasha. She couldn't take her eyes off her friend. Quinn had only just returned himself, but he and Santi hadn't been gone for nearly as long as Sasha. They'd had a lot to discuss about the place he was constructing in the dreamworld. It would be an oasis, much like the Chola Valley Temple, without the sacrifice of so much time. If they were going to have untold numbers of freed Coalition prisoners on their hands, they would need somewhere to send them.

"The valley sets us apart from others, leaving us with only those the Mother deems vital to our individual journeys. Xera and I spent many years together, preparing her to return to the modern world."

"And you come home Proven and with a family too? Congratulations, niece." Liam pulled his desk chair around to sit with them around the coffee table.

Allie couldn't stop smiling. For a moment, she could feel the years that stood between them, but it was so good to see her friend find the completion she'd wanted so badly.

"Thank you." Sasha nodded. "But we have news."

"I'm sure you do, or you wouldn't be here." If Allie could go somewhere and hit pause on her life, she might never come back.

"Marcus," Xera began and hesitated for a moment. "I know him as Lord Teigan."

Allie nodded. "Please go on."

"I have a hard time understanding how he's become the vicious man Sasha tells me he is. He was always a hard man, but he was one who would fight for what he believed in, though he was never cruel."

"It's been a very long time," Allie said. "People change."

Xera nodded, her blind eyes staring a hole through

Allie. "The man you know as Marcus Servius is my Syntrophos. He believes I am dead, and everything he's done, everything he has become, was born in the grief he bore for me and my Complement. We were his family and he was our anchor, and without us, he's fallen prey to his baser instincts."

Dread filled Allie's mind and soul as her baser instincts responded to this information. She'd just been handed her biggest weapon against Marcus.

"Have you found your Complement, Lady Xera?" Liam asked, showing a little more concern for the lady while Allie plotted how best to use her.

"I haven't seen Vitor in thousands of years, but I hope to rejoin him someday. This world is so big." She shook her head. "I don't know if it's possible for two souls to find each other in all this ... noise.

"We will help you find him. For one so old, I wonder if he is in a Coalition prison?" Liam mused out loud. "I'll check the manifests and see what I can find on him."

"That would be wonderful, thank you, sir," Xera said.

Allie turned to Sasha, her mind still reeling in a thousand directions at once. "What are we going to do?"

"The best we can." Sasha said softly. "That's all we can do."

"I realize you all need me to get to Marcus. I only ask that you offer protection and a safe haven for my people," Xera continued.

"Of course," Allie said, finding her compassion. "You are all welcome here for as long as you wish to stay. We have plenty of room for you and your people here in Sterling Tower. We will do everything we can to help you in your transition from the valley into the modern world."

Xera nodded. "In return for your kindness, I will do

what I must to help you defeat Marcus. I know how his mind works, and I can help you thwart him. Though, I would beg you not to kill him and his Complement for the atrocities he's committed."

"Marcus has never completed the bond with his Complement," Allie explained. "He believes such bonds weaken the Immortal race. He clings to the old ways when Indriell nobility scorned the bond as beneath them, choosing the most powerful as their companions to produce the strongest children."

"That was before the Great War changed everything." Xera shook her head. "What must he be thinking?"

"He refuses the bond because without it, he cannot be killed and that is the thing he fears the most."

"Who is this poor soul he's tormented?" Xera asked.

"Her name is Porcia, a powerful woman who has worked tirelessly to help us defeat him."

Xera nodded. "As will I. Please hold my identity close to you, your Majesty. Keep it for the moment when you need it the most. When I reveal myself to him and he understands that I know all he has done, his shame will be his undoing."

Allie wasn't so sure the man had any shame within him, but as long as his Syntrophos chose to fight on her side, she had a trump card he would never see coming.

Allie leaned over the coffee table toward Xera, and the woman locked eyes with her. "I thank you for your aid, and as I said, you and your people are welcome under our roof, but we will not hold you here. You have all spent too much time behind the walls of prisons."

"Thank you, Princess. You are a testament to the women who came before you. They would be proud."

CHAPTER 48

Graham | Savannah, Georgia | July

For once, it wasn't a ball.

Graham wished it was a ball. He could disappear so easily among the dancing couples too consumed in their own little world to notice the Lady Gray's favorite pet.

At first, the lords and ladies of the local society found Graham an exciting addition to their mundane lives. But they quickly grew bored of him and the amusing trinkets he made for them. Thanks to the mask he and his brother had created, he now faded into the shadows. It had taken them weeks to get the power of his mask just right, but it worked perfectly.

Once they were accepted into his inner circle, Abernathy and his minions saw Graham as the exotic pet the Gray Lady presented him as, but over time, the power of the mask worked its charms, and they paid less and less attention to him. Thanks to Quinn's ability, their eyes now slid right past him. They saw him, but he was never their focus. And if they happened to look for him, crouched beside his mistress at the end of his leash, they quickly forgot what they were looking for. More often than not, the end of the Lady Gray's leash held an empty collar no one ever noticed.

For weeks, he had searched the estate with Ezra and Wes while Brooks, Porcia, and Graham's aunt and uncle kept the Alderman's attention. Tonight shouldn't have been any different, except it wasn't a frivolous ball or tiring dinner party. Tonight was an initiation night. And the Alderman's people were in high spirits.

"Stay close to me until it starts," Porcia advised her entourage as they left the barge at sunset. "I don't know what this initiation will entail, but you can bet it won't be an easy one."

"How many initiates do they have?" Gabrielle asked. "For such an oddball community, I would think they wouldn't have much interest."

"That's what I thought too," Porcia said, "but it seems Abernathy and his socialites have been busy recruiting those who prefer the past to the present. I'm told there are more than a dozen new initiates preparing to join the Alderman's ranks here.

"Can't we just slip away like we usually do?" Wes asked, adjusting his crocodile mask in place. He and Ezra were the Lady's footmen. Their tasks were to see to her comforts to and from the estate, but otherwise, they weren't needed every minute of her time with the Alderman.

"Possibly. But we'll be expected to participate." Porcia sounded nervous—and she was never nervous. "The League lives for these nights. The powerful will be more apt to notice if someone is missing—even with our masks. Wait until they are fully distracted by the challenge and then get inside that tower room. That must be his private lair where he keeps his most sensitive information. Find out what Marcus is planning for his Aldermen so we can get out of this place. I'd really like to get back to my children." Porcia marched up the front steps where the Phoenix awaited their arrival.

Dressed in their finest costumes, Porcia, Brooks, Aunt Gabrielle, and Uncle Lou joined the others gathering in the great hall. Based on the elaborate costumes on display, this would be the event of the year.

"Just when I was thinking this place couldn't get any weirder." Ezra sighed. "Extra creepy bizarro-land kicks it up a notch."

Graham followed his husband's gaze to the center of the great room where at least a dozen men and women stood in their birthday suits behind red velvet ropes. Each wore a mask of a woodland creature. Except these weren't jewel encrusted masks with porcelain smiles and plumed feathers. These were cheap Halloween masks made of plastic with elastic bands to hold them in place. Graham saw several bunnies, foxes, and deer milling about the dais where they were on display for the evening's festivities. There were at least thirty initiates.

Graham vividly remembered his own initiation into the League of Ancients where he and handful of others had to run naked through a gauntlet while the league members beat them and attacked with their powers. As a technologically gifted Immortal, the League normally looked down on Immortals like him, yet he had performed well that night and was accepted, despite his lack of flashy abilities they respected. He wondered how many of those waiting to be humiliated and abused tonight would even make it through the initiation. Less than half, he expected.

"What's the challenge?" Brooks asked, hovering around Porcia as her official escort. The ladies of the League thought he was Porcia's young lover, and they swooned over him every chance they got.

"I'm not sure yet, but I have a bad feeling it's going to be ugly." If Porcia was feeling uncertain about the evening's events, she hid it behind a mask made of more than mere metal and jewels.

Chapter 49

Graham | Savannah, Georgia | July

"Ladies and gentlemen!" Alderman Abernathy called to get the crowd's attention. "Welcome to my humble abode." The short little man waded through a crowd that stood head and shoulders above him, yet he strutted like a peacock in his elaborate costume.

The Alderman almost always wore his baroque style pirate mask completed with a variety of pirate themed costumes. Tonight, he wore a painted leather mask of reds and golds in the form of a hound. His red costume matched perfectly, including a leather tail and a golden bugle he wore at his hip.

"Oh, surely not," Porcia whispered as excited murmuring spread across the crowded hall. There were more than a hundred members present tonight. More than at any other event they'd attended since their arrival in the Savannah river country.

"What is it, Mistress?" Graham mumbled, his eyes cast down at his hands and his back hunched as he worked on his latest creation. It was a hunk of wire and cogs no one would give a second glance, but it held a very important device he hoped he would need tonight if his hunch was correct. For now, it served as a prop in case anyone paid him more attention than expected.

"What do you think the challenge will be, my pet?" She tugged on his leash, allowing him a moment to look up. She gestured at the initiates in their absurd masks. A young man wearing a faded and chipped fox mask that looked like someone had retrieved it from the gutter.

"Fox and hound?" Porcia's voice took on a cold edge of anger.

"Surely not?" Gabrielle whispered, moving to stand beside her mistress. "The initiations are nothing less than barbaric, but this is ..."

"Disturbing," Graham finished for her. It would be an old-fashioned hunt. Complete with horses, likely real hounds, and a host of *creatures* to hunt.

"We are in for a real treat tonight, my loyal subjects." Abernathy moved to stand on the stage at the center of the room, a less than subtle attempt to make him taller and more important. "The days of the hunt have long past in this dreadfully modern world, but we shall revive the old traditions for this one night."

Excitement crashed like a wave across the room as the members of the League erupted in conversation.

The Alderman held up his hand to waylay their discussions of what to wear and which of the Abernathy's horses would be most desirable for the hunt. "First we dine, and then, at midnight, we hunt." He lifted a golden goblet carved with the imagery of a traditional fox hunt and guided his guests into the banquet hall for dinner.

"When we get settled with the first course, slip away and find that room," Porcia said in a hushed whisper so low even Graham almost didn't hear her.

"Yes, Mistress." He shuffled behind her, eager to be on

with it.

"You should be free for a couple of hours but watch your back. Not everyone will be at the banquet."

Graham nodded and crouched on the floor beside Porcia as she took her seat at the Alderman's right hand at the head of a long U-shaped table. There were other tables where lesser guests would dine, but the Alderman's table was the desirable place to be tonight.

"My Lady Gray." Abernathy reached to pour her a glass of wine from his personal carafe. "You and your guests shall accompany me on the hunt. I have horses prepared for you."

"A gracious host, as ever, Mr. Abernathy." Porcia gave him a nod and sipped the wine from her goblet. "Delicious."

Graham waited patiently as the Alderman's mortal servants marched in to serve the first course of ox tail soup. The servants at the estate always got Graham's blood boiling. Emaciated and mute, they went about their work like mindless sleepwalkers, unaware of what happened around them. The house steward, Mrs. Jessop controlled them, sending them out to clean and serve until they dropped from exhaustion and lack of sleep.

Graham wasn't sure if the Alderman just refused to feed them, or they lacked even the basic instincts to feed themselves. Either way, most didn't last long under Mrs. Jessop's control.

Porcia laughed at something the Alderman said as she buttered a small piece of bread she dipped into her soup bowl and fed to Graham. She waited to see if anyone would acknowledge her actions, but no one even glanced at Graham.

That was his cue to slip his leash. Taking a small key from his pocket, he worked the gears that locked his collar in place, breathing a sigh of relief when it was off.

No one even looked at him, too caught up in discussing which *creatures* they were eager to hunt. The initiates had joined them in the banquet hall, standing in small groups on raised platforms for the Alderman's guests to taunt and torture.

Several initiates were wearing more than their fair share of the first course. By the time this dinner was over, the banquet hall would look like the aftermath of a high school cafeteria after an epic food fight.

These people were disgusting.

Graham couldn't call attention to himself, so he waited for the footmen to serve the wine for the next course. Already, a host of footmen waited in the wings to serve the second course of raw oysters. Graham had at least seven more courses before he would need to return. Plenty of time to meet Ezra and Wes upstairs in the Alderman's private wing.

While the diners were busy finishing their soup and wine, Graham stooped low and scurried to the nearest door, eager to escape another endless dining experience with the League.

Creeping through the now empty great hall, Graham shrugged off the shuffling gait of his persona and made his way toward the grand staircase at the front of the house.

"How much time do we have?" Ezra called from the shadows of the second-floor gallery.

"They're about to serve the second course." Graham reached for his husband's hand.

"So that gives us a few hours, then," Wes said. "Seven or eight more courses?"

"At least. They'll be at it for hours."

"Wasn't this supposed to be an initiation night?" Ezra asked.

"The hunt begins at midnight."

"Hunt?" Wes frowned.

"Foxes and hounds and all that nonsense." Graham shook his head.

"So these bloody ... idiots are going to hunt people?" Ezra wrinkled his nose in disgust.

"Seriously?" Wes's eyes widened with surprise. "What happens if they catch you?" His voice came out a bit higher than normal.

"Nothing good." Graham and Ezra moved down the hall toward the Alderman's wing.

"Crazy rich people." Wes followed, still muttering about idiots with too much time and money and not nearly enough sense.

"Quick, in here." Ezra pulled Graham into a room across the hall from where they needed to be. Wes ducked in behind them. "Someone's coming."

They moved deeper into the room. A study meant to look like its master had just left, but after a second look, Graham realized it was a decoy. A place where Abernathy probably met with members of his League, but no real work happened here.

"Come, my little duckies." A deceptively sweet voice echoed down the hall. "The Alderman will expect you all to be ready to serve soon."

Graham knew that voice. Mrs. Jessop, the house steward. A woman with little power, other than her single ability that made her useful to a man like Abernathy. She was the only Immortal on the estate who did not wear a disguise.

They crept toward the door to get a look into the hallway. Mrs. Jessop had already passed the study, but a long line of mortals wandered after her.

Graham gripped the doorknob, his knuckles turning

white with the effort to keep himself from ripping it open to save those poor people.

"Well, that's heartbreaking," Ezra whispered behind him.

"Eat up, my babies." Mrs. Jessop clucked at them like they were chickens in the yard. She scattered bits of bread down the hallway. Starving, the mortals silently wrestled for the tiny scraps of food.

"We have to do something," Wes said. "Allie won't stand for this."

"She will burn this place to the ground before she lets them do that to anyone else," Graham agreed. "But for now, we have to do what we came for so we can get out of here and get these people the help they need."

"What's he want with mindless, half-starved servants anyway?" Ezra asked.

"It's a power trip," Wes said. "People like Abernathy are always trying to make themselves appear powerful when they really aren't.

"Where is my darling little mama?" Mrs. Jessop wandered back through the crowd of her minions, offering bits of stale bread from her pail. "There she is." She wrapped her arm around a young woman with long, thick blond hair. "Can't have you wasting away now. Not in your condition." She gave the woman a hunk of fresh bread slathered in butter. "I saved this just for you, dearie." The steward ran a hand over the woman's hair, smoothing out the tangles and tucking a lock behind her ear. "And there's more where that came from, but just for you. Don't tell the others." She giggled, the sound a bit mad as it echoed down the hall. "We have to take care of that little Immortal bun in the oven. He'll fetch a high price for the Master."

"No." Graham sucked in a breath as he saw the pregnant woman's face. "That's Kayla." He lunged toward the door but Ezra and Wes held him back.

"If you know her, my love, we will help her, but not like this," Ezra whispered.

Graham gripped the door frame, willing himself to let her go. "She's our friend from school. I don't know how she got tangled up in the Alderman's snare, but we have to get her out of here."

"She's safe enough for now." Wes said, nodding toward the end of the hall where Mrs. Jessop gave Kayla a small carton of milk and a cold chicken leg from her pail. "They're feeding her more. It's obvious they want the baby to be healthy and she's just starting to show. As long as she's pregnant, she'll be okay. That gives us time to figure out a way to free them all. Not just her."

"I know, you're right." He let out a frustrated groan, pacing back inside the gallery where priceless paintings hung in the shadows.

When the hall grew quiet again, Graham led them back out to the empty expanse of ugly wallpaper where there should be a door. He had to remain focused on their task and worry about Kayla another time. But he couldn't even detect where the door might be hidden.

"Is there a trick to this?" Wes asked, staring up at the wall sconce that was the key to entering the Alderman's bedroom.

"Let's hope not." Ezra reached up to turn the sconce to the right.

They waited only a moment before the entire wall moved aside, leaving another one just like it behind. This one had a door.

"Clever." Graham reached for the door, holding his

breath. “It’s locked.” His shoulders fell, and he wanted to punch something. They had to get in that room.

“Wait.” Wes reached for the wall sconce, searching inside the frosted glass sphere. “Got it.” He withdrew an old key made of iron.

“This guy should really think about updating his security system.” Graham shoved the key in the lock, and they were inside the Alderman’s private chambers.

“Should we shut the door and panel?” Wes asked, uncertain. “What if that triggers some kind of alarm?”

“I’m not so sure the Alderman would bother with an alarm system,” Ezra said, already searching the room for clues.

“Shut it.” Graham made the call. “If it has an alarm, we’ll deal with it later.”

“Good thing I didn’t take that bet.” Ezra stared up at a wall of bookshelves. “I’m pretty sure you’re right about the entrance to the tower.”

“The man’s a colossal idiot.” Wes shook his head. “How do we find the trigger?” Wes tried pulling a few books from the shelves at random, and Ezra searched the shelves for lock or handle.

“There.” Graham pointed to the floor in front of the middle shelf. “See how the scratches in the wood arc out like something’s scraped it a thousand times.”

“It swings out, then.” Ezra tried pulling the shelf toward him, but it didn’t budge.

“What’s that at the top?” Wes pointed at the back corner of the top shelf.

Ezra was the tallest and easily stuck his hand back there, feeling around until a mischievous smile spread across his face. “Got it.”

He gave it a yank, and something clicked, and the bookshelf popped out a few inches.

"Nice!" Graham slapped him on the back, and together they pulled the hidden door open. Behind the bookshelf, spiral stone steps curved up in the darkness. As they entered, closing the door behind them, faint lights hummed to life in the glass spheres set into the wall. Just like in the rest of the house, the lights were triggered by movement and powered by the Phoenix's gift.

The stairs led to the room they'd seen from the drone footage. A small circular room with five floor-to-ceiling bookshelves spaced at even intervals like the doors in the house. Each shelf housed first editions of classical literature and the Alderman's personal journals among other leather-bound books so old the print on the spines had worn away.

Graham reached for his power, letting it fill him as the girls materialized in front of him. "Search the journals here for data to review later. We don't have much time so start with the most recent and work your way back."

"Yes, master." They dissolved into a thousand smaller spheres and went about their task. Graham didn't bother correcting them. They were going to call him master whether he liked it or not.

"Is this it?" Wes frowned as he took in the simple room of cold gray brick and the soft flickering light that followed them wherever they went.

"Can't be." Ezra started looking for more hidden doors.

Graham studied the fireplace and the leather chair that didn't look like anyone had sat in it in a very long time. "This isn't right." He shook his head, turning toward the shelves. "These are all doors." He moved to the shelf closest to him.

It took Ezra and Wes another minute or two before they had them all open.

"Perfect." Graham had to put his shoulder into it to get the first one opened all the way. It was a tunnel that led deep underground. "We'll do this one if we have time."

The second door led to an armory, housing all manner of weapons and armor from ages past. There was even a full suit of armor that looked to be just the right size for the small Alderman.

"Jackpot," Ezra grunted as he shoved the next door open.

"This is it." Graham stepped inside the chamber. The plaster walls were covered in maps and pictures of key places. "The war room." He sent the girls in to collect data and launched one of his pocket drones to collect video and pictures of everything.

"Let's check the last two rooms." Graham backed out of the war room.

"You gotta come see this." Wes ducked out of the next room.

Graham gasped as he entered the cold room where the unmistakable humming of computers called to his gift. "Hates technology, does he?" Graham searched his pockets for the hunk of metal he was just working on. Turned out he was right about needing it.

"What's that?" Ezra peered over his shoulder.

"A twelve-terabyte hard drive." Graham slid the hidden USB port from the twist of wires and cogs and went to work on transferring everything he could get from the wall of computers. It was an older desktop system with three monitors, and nothing sophisticated or complicated to hack. Graham was into the main drive within seconds, and all of the Alderman's data was his for the taking. He'd have to study it later in greater detail when he had the luxury of time.

"What's in the last room?" he called over his shoulder.

"The study," Ezra called back. "The real one."

Graham left the computer to finish downloading to the drive and ducked out to the main chamber.

"*Master, we have catalogued the Alderman's war room and his journals from the last century.*" The girls whirred around his head like hyperactive clouds.

"We need everything you can find in the study." Graham ducked into the last room where the Alderman's study had the air of a place he used often. Green light glowed from a Tiffany lamp plugged into an outlet under the desk. An old typewriter sat in a place of honor right beside a gramophone with a vintage record of *Bach's Cello suites.*

"Kind of a mix bag of technology." Wes looked around the room while the girls did their work.

"Yeah, something tells me he'll upgrade to a smartphone in a few hundred years when the rest of us are flying around in our spaceships and vacationing on Mars for the summers." Ezra picked up a leather-bound volume on the desk.

"What in the world is this?" He flipped through the book with a frown.

"I don't know, but there's a shelf full of them over here." Wes picked up another volume with the letter "A" on the spine.

Graham grinned. "I think that's old-world Google." He took the book from Ezra. "It's an encyclopedia."

"Ohhh." The other two bobbed their heads. "That's what old people used before the internet." Ezra set the book back where he'd found it. "Wait, look at the page it was open to." Ezra waved them toward the desk. "It's like a Wikipedia page—oh wait, I just got that! It's all about the ways plantation masters built their slave quarters, so there was no hope of escape. The shanties were built right at the center of the plantation, guarded on all sides by endless fields, a maze of fences, and the quartermasters who guarded them day and night."

"What's Abernathy want with that kind of information?" Wes's voice took on an angry note as he looked at the images of young men and boys, slaves to their white masters. They didn't look any different from him.

"Look at this, you guys." Graham moved to a map of the estate hanging on the wall opposite the desk. There were new additions sketched on scraps of paper and taped to the wall beside the map.

The drawings were done to scale with architectural details, perfectly straight lines and angles, with clearly noted dimensions for the overall layout. The bottom dropped out of Graham's stomach when he realized what he was looking at.

He reached for another drone in his pocket. He'd kept this one for exactly this kind of moment. He needed all the information he could gather from this room. The map was something he couldn't afford not to get a record of.

The drone was a small beetle, no bigger than his thumbnail, but it contained a powerful camera with a Bluetooth connection that would immediately transfer images to his online storage and then delete them once they were uploaded. He could leave it behind without the need to retrieve it. It was his last one.

He'd just set it loose when a voice called out from the Alderman's room below.

"Time to go." Graham took one last look at the map and

grabbed Ezra's hand, all but dragging him back to the tower room behind him.

"Who's up there?" Footsteps sounded on the steps. "The Alderman will have your head for invading his space!"

It was Mrs. Jessop. They'd all seen enough of her treatment of the mortals she commanded to know they couldn't risk landing in her clutches.

"The tunnel." Graham shut the bookcase concealing the study behind him, and Wes darted across the room to close the others.

The girls zoomed out of the war room and flew into the dark tunnel. Ezra closed the bookcase behind them, and they were cast into total darkness. No magical spheres of light waited to light their way. At least not the ones that adorned every other room in the house. But Graham's girls glowed with the light of his power, illuminating the dreary tunnel in their blue light.

"Go," Graham whispered, shoving Ezra and Wes ahead of him.

"Don't think I won't find you." The bookcase groaned and scraped against the floor as she tried to open it.

"Stay close to me." Graham moved behind Ezra and Wes, hoping for a miracle to get them out of this. The three of them could easily take the woman on her own, but they could not risk blowing their cover.

Mrs. Jessop was right behind them now, and there was nowhere to hide. As they spiraled down under ground, the pathway widened into a corridor that split in two directions. Graham grabbed Ezra and Wes and threw them against the wall, crouching in front of them among the shadows. The girls faded into mist, and he willed the power of his mask to protect them for at least a few moments.

The thin layer of steel against his face grew hot as his power churned inside him.

"What are we doing?" Ezra hissed in his ear.

"Hiding." Graham kept them pinned behind him. "I could use your help, Ez." Immediately, Ezra's hands grew warm where they gripped his arm. Ezra had a way of suppressing his Immortal presence. It allowed him to sneak up on even the most powerful Immortals before they were aware he was close. Between Graham's mask and Ezra's talent, they had a chance of fooling her.

"I may not be powerful, but I can still hear you." Mrs. Jessop came lumbering into view, wielding a smoldering torch in front of her. The smell of burning pitch filled the small space, but she waved the torch into every corner, her eyes sliding right over them where they stood pressed against the wall.

Graham held his breath, hoping she would fall for it and move on quickly. The mask would only shield them from view for so long and then it wouldn't matter how well Ezra could suppress their Immortal presence.

"Keep running, I'll find you one way or another." Her face pinched into a frown of indecision before she chose a tunnel and left them in darkness.

"What just happened?" Wes asked.

"My brother helped me create this mask." Graham sucked in a deep breath, lifting the hot mask from his face for a moment. "He loaned the use of his power to give my mask a bit of his gift for invisibility. We were hoping it would be something I could use in a dire emergency. I think we just used it up."

"God bless your brother and these bloody awful masks." Ezra's voice trembled in the darkness. "Not that they aren't beautiful." He laid a shaking hand on Graham's shoulder.

"Don't worry, if I never have to make or wear another mask, it will be too soon."

"Maybe you should take up needlepoint as a creative outlet," Wes suggested.

"Someone's been in the Alderman's quarters!" An angry voice echoed behind them. "Search the rooms."

"Crap, what now?" Ezra gripped his hand tight.

"Run." Graham pulled his husband along with him into the tunnel Mrs. Jessop hadn't taken. He just hoped it led to an exit, or they were going to be in real trouble. He didn't think his mask would save them a second time tonight.

The voices behind them grew faint as they ran along the dark tunnel that continued to twist around and downward. Eventually, the tunnel straightened until they were running at a slight incline. Judging by the enormous tree roots growing through the walls and up from the floor, they were running right along the edge of the river through the old pecan orchard the Alderman was so proud of.

"Where do you think this leads?" Ezra asked, running just ahead of him.

"Hopefully out and not a dead end," Wes responded.

But a dead end was what they got.

"Dammit!" Graham punched the dirt wall at the end of the tunnel.

"Language, honey," Ezra reproached. "Wouldn't want anyone thinking you're a neanderthal."

Graham cracked a smile, but despite Ezra's jokes, there was only so long before the people behind them caught up. They had to get out of here now.

"We don't have time for your jokes, Ez." Wes paced the tunnel, searching for a way out that didn't exist.

"Calm down, people." Ezra sighed. "How many blasted fake doors have we gone through tonight?"

"Good point." Graham ran a hand over the crumbling stone walls.

"The question we should ask ourselves," Ezra said, bending over and studying the bricks along the bottom of the tunnel. "Is what would Indiana Jones do?"

"Okay, you're spending way too much time with Allie and her Netflix obsession."

"It's amazing. You're watching them with me when we get home."

"Got it." Wes grunted as he shifted something, and the crumbling bricks moved aside to reveal a moonlit path into the woods.

"Brilliant." Ezra crawled through the narrow opening.

"Thanks." Wes followed him.

"For what? It was my brilliant idea. You were just pacing around waiting for a miracle." Ezra elbowed him, and Wes rolled his eyes.

"Enough bickering, you two." Graham hefted the broken stone pillar that acted as a switch to close the tunnel, sealing them off from their pursuers. "We have to find our way back to the barge and hope Porcia will meet us there soon."

Something rustled in the forest, an echo of heavy breathing and hurried footsteps crashing through the undergrowth. All three of them crouched low among the bushes as something lumbered from the trees and ran down the path, the sound of a bugle not far behind.

"Was that a ... naked man in a fox mask?" Wes asked.

"I think he was bleeding." Ezra started to stand, but Graham pulled him back down.

"Wait." Graham shushed them. A moment later, six riders came barreling over the crumbling wall of the tunnel, hounds barking and horns blaring.

"What the bloody hell?" Ezra looked to Graham for answers. "That wasn't a..."

"A fox hunt? Yeah. That'll be the evening's entertainment." Graham climbed up the wall to peek over the edge. "The house is back this way. And it's not close." He climbed up, turning to offer a hand up for Ezra and Wes.

"These people are completely crackers." Ezra turned to where the riders disappeared down toward the river.

"Rich, old, bored Immortals." Wes shrugged. "But I blame the idiot in the fox mask for signing up for this."

"I'd really like to go home now." Ezra started for the house, but as they crested the hill, a sprawling town spread out before them. Nestled in a valley among the rolling hills of the estate, with the river on one side and the forest on the other, the little town was closed in on all sides.

"What is this place?" Ezra stopped to study the small buildings below. The construction was new and nearly completed.

The arrangement of buildings seemed oddly familiar to Graham.

"Is it some kind of camp?" Wes asked.

Without a word, Graham called on his gift, sending the girls into the seemingly deserted town to gather images and data. "It's the slave quarters for his mortal servants," Graham spoke through gritted teeth. If he could get his hands on Abernathy right this moment, he thought he might rip him apart with his bare hands.

"What is he playing at?" Wes's voice grew thick with anger.

"I don't know." Graham shook his head. "But I think after tonight, it's time we take what we've learned back to Allie, so we can do something to help these poor people. We can't leave Kayla here a minute longer than we have to."

CHAPTER 50

Aidan | Death Valley, California | August

Aidan wiped sweat from his brow as he prepared to land the chopper along the dusty, barren desert below.

"We need a break this time," Naomi shouted into the headset so he could hear over the noise of the helicopter. "A real one. With soft beds and a nice big steak dinner."

Aidan grinned, nodding his agreement. "Not sure we'll get that out here."

"Then let's fly this thing to Vegas and get a suite."

"Sure. Right after we drop off our cargo." It wouldn't happen. They both knew that, but it was fun to dream.

After tracking and hunting down the murdering Immortal, Stefana, Aidan and his fellow team members worked with Liam to find a place to detain her. They'd found it in the Coalition prison located in Death Valley California. The only such prison in the United States. It was a small facility that suited their needs perfectly.

Now, Stefana was behind bars within a highly magnetized cell where she would never see the light of day again, and the prison belonged to them. With the Coalition failing, only a handful of mortals had manned the prison upon their arrival. Having negotiated a surrender with Liam, it was a smooth transition.

Aidan had dismissed the mortal guards, giving them each provisions of water and food, a compass, and a map. It was up to them to find their way out of the desert heat. He didn't feel bad about it either. The condition of the prisoners was atrocious. Only a few dozen prisoners called Death Valley home, and they were half starved, dehydrated, and near death. He imagined they each had succumbed to death many times over the course of their imprisonment here.

Now, under Pilar's direction, they were thriving and stronger. It would take time and a lot of red tape to determine which prisoners should be released and which needed rehabilitation, or a more humane prison cell. Those decisions would come later. After the war with Marcus was settled.

"How many others do you think are still out there?" Naomi asked, staring at the endless expanse of mountains outside her window.

"At least a dozen. Maybe more. One less for sure." Aidan gestured at the cargo hold behind them. They had only managed to bring in a few of the worst ones so far. But today they had a real gem in their possession. She was a nasty piece of work that had taken them weeks to entrap.

A storm of dust swirled around them as Aidan landed the military chopper they'd acquired from the prison tucked away in a barren sea of sand among the Sierra Nevada mountains. Far into the desert and outside Death Valley national park, the small circle of buildings blended with the dreary landscape.

Gemma and Ruthie came out to greet them. The oddest paring of all the Milan Initiative, Gemma was much older than Ruthie. Aidan's cousin Erin was with them too. Newly bonded with Gemma, the Complements didn't want to be apart. The three of them made an excellent team with Gemma at the center as their anchor.

"Who do you have?" Gemma called over the roar of the chopper blades.

"Her name is Elora, and she's mean as a snake." Aidan shut down the chopper, moving to the rear of the helicopter. "We had to cage her." He lowered the cargo door, and they all stood back while the steel cage with a high-powered magnetic field was lowered down onto the transport cart. They'd quickly learned how to use the equipment here. Even though it left him feeling guilty to use such force against one of his own, these Immortals deserved it.

"We found her in Phoenix, Arizona after she blew up seven city blocks with her power." Naomi gave the report. "Mortals claimed it was a massive gas leak, but Elora has some kind of explosive power that even rivals Neela and Ivy's collective power."

Ruthie gasped, taking another step back. She was still young, not yet twenty, and her progress was much slower than Aidan's had been at that age. These things still took her by surprise.

"Is she still dangerous?" Ruthie cast her gaze at Naomi. "In there?" She pointed to the cage where the petite brunette lay curled up in a ball, trembling in rage.

"It's best we get her in a cell quickly," Naomi replied, moving to roll the transport cart inside the main building. Ruthie followed, carrying a wand the prison guards used to keep the Immortals in line. It delivered a shock and a bolt of magnetic energy like a taser, enough to drop the most powerful of their kind in an instant. It turned Aidan's stomach to use it, but they had no other choice.

"It's hotter than the seventh level of hell out here," Gemma said. "Let's get back inside where it's almost cool."

Aidan followed her, wishing Elora was the last of the escaped prisoners, and he could go home to Allie. The time apart had been good for them, but he missed her and was ready to go home. He'd spoken to her several times since her Proving and she was doing fine, but busy as ever. And so was he. As long as there were Immortals like Elora and Stefana on the loose, he couldn't justify abandoning his responsibility to hunt them down and bring them in.

But like always, thoughts of Allie had him wondering if he did go home now, would it be any different than when he'd left? Or would they end up right back where they were?

Chapter 51

Graham | Savannah, Georgia | August

"What's he doing?" Wes asked in hushed tones Graham ignored as he flicked through images and spreadsheets of data the girls had compiled for him.

It wasn't that they magically did the work for him. They were just a physical manifestation of his ability to sort, compartmentalize, and digest an enormous amount of data in very little time.

"He's sorting through all the data we've collected since initiation night," Ezra explained.

"And those little blue balls of light just show him the important stuff?" Wes hadn't taken his eyes off the way the girls morphed into lines of code one moment and detailed maps and crystal-clear images the next. He'd always seen the girls in their usual form, so this was his first time getting a look at how they worked.

"Not really," Ezra replied. "They're just the tools he uses to make sense of everything in a tangible way. He's basically a walking, talking, handsome computer with a brain I can't even comprehend."

Graham snorted at his husband's apt description of his

gift, but he had little reason to laugh after everything he'd spent the last two weeks studying.

"He hasn't slept in days, and he has to be starving," Ezra whispered, a note of worry in his voice. "He's been at this all night and most of the day without a break. I don't even think he's stopped to pee much less get a decent look at his handsome hubby."

"If you order me a pizza or two, I'll take a break." Graham flicked a finger, and the map he was exploring from Abernathy's study zoomed in to give him a better view. He was looking for dates and handwritten notes that might tell him more about the things he'd discovered from the Alderman's war room.

"Way ahead of you, love," Ezra said. "Pizza arrived about a half hour ago."

Graham nodded. After everything he'd seen, he wasn't really hungry. The thought of food turned his stomach, but if he was going to keep going, he needed food. Already, the girls were growing dim and sluggish.

Flicking back to the video footage of the war room, Graham played through the frames in slow motion, studying the details again to make sure he was absolutely certain he had the dates correct. Finally, he stepped back with a weary sigh, letting the girls fade into him.

"What did you find?" Wes asked, and Graham shook his head as he sat down between Wes and Ezra on the soft leather sofa in the training room.

"It's bad." He ran a hand through his hair. "We have to leave today if we can. No later than tomorrow. As soon as Porcia can say our goodbyes, we need to get back to Soma. We don't have much time left to stop Marcus from ruining our world."

CHAPTER 52

Aidan | Death Valley, California | August

"You look like crap." Pilar sank down into the pleather recliner beside Aidan in the prison break room.

"Thanks." Aidan leaned back into his own recliner, hoping sleep would take him. He preferred sleeping during the day whenever he could. It was easier to avoid the pull of Allie's dreamscape if they never slept at the same times. He loved their visits in the dreamworld, but leaving her again and again just got harder each time. He needed to see her for real, but at the same time, he dreaded it. Dreaded seeing the same old look in her eye. The one that said she loved and adored him but didn't truly see him.

"Good job with Elora. She looks like a little pixie, but she packs a mean punch."

"She's a nightmare. Make sure you hold onto that one. I don't ever want to have to hunt her again."

"I've got another one for you two."

"Come on, Pilar. We just came in a few hours ago. At least give us a night to recover."

"You can have tonight, but you're leaving at first light."

Aidan sighed. "So much for that steak dinner," he muttered.

"Steak dinner?" Pilar's eyebrows shot up in question. "That's not going to happen, but we've got barbecue chicken and ribs out back if you're that hungry."

"You should have led with that." Aidan sat up, his stomach growling at the thought of real food that didn't come from a drive thru window.

"That can wait a few more minutes." Pilar rested a hand over his. "This one's going to be hard."

"You've said that about literally every single Immortal we've had to track."

"I mean it this time." Pilar folded her hands in her lap. "This guy's a big fish."

"Tell me what you know." Aidan kicked his footrest down and swiveled to face her.

"His name is Rhaegal," she began.

Aidan's brow creased. "That sounds familiar."

"You probably studied him in your Immortal history lessons. He was second only to Tomás during the Great War."

"Tomás was the one that started it all," Aidan said.

"And Rhaegal was his first student. He is power hungry and eager to start up his old games again."

"History said he attacked and stole hundreds of gifts from Immortals of the time."

Pilar nodded. "Probably even more and it drove him mad. He is doing it again. While the others are laying low, getting their bearings about them in this modern world, Rhaegal is attacking Immortals across the country. The mortal government officials are calling him a terrorist."

"Where is he now?" Aidan asked.

"Oklahoma City."

"I was hoping this one would be a little closer to Georgia." Aidan sighed. "Just for a quick visit."

"You can take a break after you bring Rhaegal in. Consider that your reward." Pilar promised.

"What's his deal?"

"He's ripping the city apart with storms. They won't survive it much longer."

"So he's the storm guy? I've read about the record-breaking weather going on there."

"He's responsible for massive tornados and electrical storms. The city is desperate for relief. So far no one has openly suggested the storms are unnatural, but it's only a matter of time."

"But isn't this Rhaegal guy hunting Immortals?"

"Yes, but there seems to be someone in Oklahoma City he desperately wants. You need to get to him before he attacks again. If he gets any more powerful and erratic, he'll be impossible to catch."

"All right. We'll leave as soon as we've rested." Aidan stood up to go find food and Naomi. If he had to guess, he'd say she probably already found the food.

"Aidan," Pilar called after him. "Be careful. This one is dangerous. You should be ready for anything."

Aidan nodded, his mind already turning with thoughts of how to capture Rhaegal, Master of Storms.

Chapter 53

Graham | Sterling Tower | August

"Wait! Graham, it's late and she's sleeping." Briggs raced after him toward the elevators. "Do you know how cranky she gets if you wake her up on a sleeping night?"

"Yes, actually, I do." Graham stepped onto the elevator, holding the doors open for his entourage. "I grew up with her, remember?"

"And if she comes out swinging when you knock on her door, it's not my fault." Briggs stepped back, shaking his head. "I'm just the walker on duty. I'm not a security guard."

"Dude, that's exactly what you are." Ezra snorted as the doors closed, and they shot up to the top floor.

"She's not that bad, is she?" Wes asked nervously.

"She might snarl a bit at first, but she wouldn't want to wait when she finds out what we've come to tell her."

"Which is what?" Porcia demanded. "You've been vague and evasive since you dragged us out of Savannah."

"I don't want to explain this twice." Graham's stomach churned with the stress of having so much knowledge and no idea how to act on it. He felt ready to explode with all the information he'd absorbed in the last two weeks. Even now, he was still trying to process it all.

As soon as the elevator doors opened again, Graham marched down the hall and banged on Allie's door, hitting the doorbell for good measure since she was such a sound sleeper.

"Hurry up, Allie!" He banged on the door again. "Get your butt out here."

"Yeah, that's not going to piss her off," Wes muttered.

"We don't have time for this." Graham's hands clenched at his sides. He and Porcia had made the last minute decision to leave Aunt Gabrielle, Uncle Lou, and Brooks behind. They needed a way back in once they were ready to act, and since this all started as a ruse for his aunt and uncle to join the Alderman's community, it placated Abernathy when Porcia made their excuses for leaving, promising to return soon.

"Do you have a death wish?" Allie snarled as she snatched the door open, her hair a wild bird's nest on top of her head.

"It's important or I wouldn't have risked your wrath," Graham said dryly as he shouldered his way into the living room, stopping in his tracks when his eyes landed on the three mortals standing in their pajamas, looking irritated. "Oh, sorry Mr. and Mrs. Carmichael, Vince. Didn't mean to wake you."

"Well, you woke the whole house, so let's hear it." Allie shuffled into the kitchen, grasping for the coffeepot.

"It's good to see you, Graham, honey." Lily Carmichael followed her daughter, wresting the bag of coffee from her fumbling hands and sending her back toward the living room.

"You too." He wanted to say more to the woman who

was sort of his biological grandmother, but he didn't know how to have that conversation, and now wasn't the time. One of these days, he wanted to meet Allie's mortal sister, Josceline, the woman who was his surrogate mother.

Allie rubbed her bleary eyes and shuffled toward him. She wrapped her arms around him. "Glad you're home safe. Didn't mean to snarl."

"She's going to need some caffeine in her before she's coherent," Carson said. "All of you come in and have a seat. Our daughter has manners during normal waking hours. Not so much when she hasn't slept in four days."

"Sorry about that." Graham and Ezra moved to sit on the sofa beside Vince, and Wes took a seat on the ottoman beside Ezra. Graham turned toward his old high school football friend. He had a very good idea why Vince was here. "She's fine."

Vince rubbed a weary hand over his face. "Who's fine?" His voice was gruff, and he didn't look as though he'd slept much in recent weeks.

"Kayla. I've seen her. She's okay."

All the air seemed to rush out of Vince's lungs as he reached for Graham's arm. "How? Where? You *left* her?"

"It's a long story and I will tell you everything. But for now, focus on the fact that she and your unborn child are healthy and safe and we will bring her home just as soon as we can."

"What's happening?" Allie snorted as she lurched from her seat on the leather chair across the room, her eyes wide and blinking. "Oh, right. I'm up. Promise."

"Okay, Allie, I'm going to need you to shake it off and pay attention," Graham said. "We've got work to do.

Allie yawned and stretched her arms up over her head. "Wait did you say something about Kayla?"

"Let's start with the missing mortals," Graham said. "I imagine you've heard about more than just Kayla going missing?"

"Yes. Hundreds of Coalition men and women have gone missing since the attack." Vince sat with his hands clenched in fists in his lap.

Graham studied Vince for a moment before he continued. "Is it going to freak anyone out if I show you some stuff?" he asked Allie. "You know, in my special way."

"Probably, but I think we're well past the need for secrecy. Go for it."

Graham called on his power, letting it manifest into the twin orbs of his gift. He got a few gasps of surprise, but that was all. "Show Allie the map of the Alderman's slave quarters."

"*Yes, master.*" The girls bobbed and morphed into the images they'd collected from Abernathy's study.

"Slave quarters?" Allie sat up straighter, taking the mug of coffee her mother offered her.

"Abernathy keeps mortal slaves to run his household." He went on to explain their mindless activity, but when he mentioned their emaciated forms, Allie reacted as though she'd seen it before.

"It's Marcus." She shook her head. "What does he want with human slaves?"

"Besides the obvious?" Porcia interjected. "Marcus hates the mortal population. He views them as cockroaches who have stolen a world that never belonged to them. He will kill as many as he can and enslave the rest."

"True, but the *Master* learned something important about them when his attack on the Coalition failed," Graham continued. "He now knows how to ... manufacture Immortal children."

"Oh God," Vince choked. "That's what he wants with Kayla? But our child won't be Immortal. Not this time."

"He doesn't know that. And it's best for Kayla that everyone involved believes the child she carries is Immortal."

"Are they starving her?" Vince's voice shook with anger.

"No. She's being treated well. I can't imagine she's very happy with her circumstances, but she's healthy. You need to focus on that."

Vince nodded. But the look on his face said he was eager to get his hands on the people who had taken his wife from him.

"Hundreds of others just like her are in danger of much worse treatment. We have to save Kayla, but we need to save every single mortal under his control as well."

"Which means we can't go in there guns blazing." Allie set her coffee mug on the table beside her. "We have to be smart about this." She turned back to Graham. "Is this the only ... farm?"

"I'm certain of it." Graham nodded. "I have the intel on what went into building this first farm. It's a recent endeavor, still in the early stages of development. They won't move forward on a larger scale until he has every Banished Daughter and Coalition Son in his possession. But there are other plans he will put into action very soon. Plans we have to intercept."

"They are *farming* humans," Vince fumed. "And you want to wait?"

"Vince, you know what this man is capable of." Allie cringed. "She is my friend, I want to leave right now and go in there and fix this, but I have thousands of others to think of too."

"I don't care about your Immortal friends." Vince

picked up a white porcelain vase and threw it at the wall over Allie's head. "They won't die at his hands so easily as my wife and child will!"

Graham leapt from his seat, putting himself between Vince and Allie, his arms raised in surrender. "He's going to destroy the world as you know it. And it's going to happen within the month if we don't stop it now. Let us take the head off the beast, and we will bring Kayla home. I will go get her myself."

Carson moved behind Vince, laying a steadying hand on his shoulder. "Sit down, son. Let's work this out so as few lives as possible are affected by this madman."

Vince nodded, letting Carson guide him back to his seat.

"Tell me everything," Allie said once Vince was settled and calm once more.

"The aldermen are future kings, hand selected by Marcus and poised to seize control of North and South America, as well as Europe and Asia and the rest of the world." Graham pulled up the images from the war room, and the girls put them on display. "Each alderman has planted his political henchmen within the state and federal governments across the world. He's had quite a few low level politicians across the country eliminated to pave the way here in the U.S."

"We know about those murders." Allie hung her head, like the weight of the world rested on her shoulders alone.

"Hey," Graham said softly until she looked up. "We've got this. I promise."

She nodded for him to continue.

"In a few weeks, when Marcus gives the order, each of the aldermen will seize control of the state and federal governments all at once, collapsing the United States and every other country on the planet. Then the aldermen will step in to set up their kingdoms."

Allie shot out of her seat and paced to the windows overlooking the city. "Less than a month?" The blood drained from her face. "We'll never be ready." She pressed her head against the cool glass window.

"Yes we will. I have their entire plan, play by play. We can cut them off before they can act." Graham crossed the room to her side.

"Abernathy has set himself up to be the King of Savannah, which will include all of Mississippi, Alabama, Georgia, and South Carolina. The man pretends to be an eccentric buffoon, but he is the military strategist behind the whole plan, and he has all of his pieces on the board, ready to strike. Once the dust settles, King Abernathy will control the slave trade, funneling mindless mortals to the other kingdoms where they will be little more than cattle to the lords they serve.

"And people like Vince and Kayla will have it far worse as they're forced to produce as many Immortals and Banished Daughters as they possibly can. Then Marcus will control who gets to be parents of these children. He'll ensure they are taught what he wants them to believe. He'll have an entire world loyal to him within a generation."

"The armies of the world won't let this happen so easily," Carson said. "Unless this Abernathy man has the generals under his thumb too."

"He does." Graham nodded to the girls to show them the dossiers he had gathered from the Alderman's computers. He had the details of every single politician, alderman, and general in Marcus' pocket, along with their official orders.

"He has negotiated a takeover with key government officials—greedy mortals—who have agreed to support him."

"Why would they do that?" Allie returned to her seat and fumbled for her coffee mug on the table. "Why would he even bother negotiating with mortals?"

"You're not going to believe this," Graham said.

"I can hazard a guess," Porcia said. "He's promised to make them Immortal, hasn't he?"

"Yes. How did you know?"

"Same old man, same games," she sighed. "During the Roman Empire when I first met Marcus, he played the same power games. That little trick is one of his best. Promise a greedy, power hungry man Immortality and they are putty in your hand."

"Wait." Allie choked on a laugh. "That's not even possible." She glanced around the room. "Right?"

"No, but they don't know that." Graham went on. "Once the aldermen seize control, the mortal world won't know what hit them, and anyone Marcus has made ludicrous promises to won't be in a position to do anything about it."

"He has an army, doesn't he?" Carson said. "That's the only way he'll be able to control the mortal population from fighting back. We'll be at war, and who knows how long that could last."

"He doesn't have an army per se," Graham said. "But he has control of the Coalition prisons."

"No he doesn't." Allie said. "He may think he does, but the Coalition is falling apart. He left the prisons manned by skeleton crews. They're giving up left and right. We have control of more than half of the prisons across the world and the Senate has seized a few as well. Others are under Coalition control but they are cooperating with the Senate."

"Perfect." Graham grinned. "One less thing for us to do.

Marcus believes he will release the prisoners into the world the way he did with the Bermuda prison. Except this time he intended to send them out like a plague of locusts to destroy the mortal population with a chaotic war they couldn't hope to win. But now that he doesn't have that option... I think we can fool him."

"Even if he doesn't have the prisons, he's still going to slaughter any mortal who stands in his way," Allie said, her voice full of defeat. "With the Banished Daughters and Coalition Sons under his protection on this *farm*, Marcus means to enslave and annihilate whatever is left of the mortal population. Sure, we'll have a slump in the birth rate, but he'll make sure we recover over time. And when it's all said and done, we'll live in a world none of us can even recognize." Allie collapsed back in her chair. "No wonder the prophets of old couldn't see past this."

"He's ready to act. He has all his ducks in a row. All he has to do is give the orders." Graham's hands shook with the need to act.

Allie sat up straighter. "You say you have every part of his plan?"

"We do."

"Well, what if when it comes time for him to give the orders, we make sure there's no one there to take those orders?"

"My thoughts exactly." Graham shuffled through the file he'd brought for Allie with everything outlined in detail. "Study this." He placed it on the coffee table.

"The Senate knows nothing of this," Porcia said, her face blank of emotion. "He's had them busy chasing his phantom and turning their focus on Allie and Soma. He's made her the enemy."

"They are broken and blind to what's happening right

under their noses." Allie flipped through the file, studying every component of Abernathy's war room for herself.

Porcia moved to stand beside her. "We can't count on them to do anything to stop this. They act too slowly, and before they even know what's happening, Marcus will set himself up as the supreme ruler of the world. He will return us to the days of Indriell, but rather than our benevolent queens who have always ruled justly and for a finite period of time, we will be subjected to just one king with a host of puppet kings at his beck and call. And he will never be satisfied, no matter how much power he seizes for himself."

"We need a plan." Graham moved to join them. "We have to be ten steps ahead of him every step of the way, or we're going to lose everything."

"In the end we're going to need the Senate to see him for what he is." Allie tapped a finger against her empty coffee mug. "We have to lay a trap for Marcus and the Senate and we need them both to walk right into it."

"We're going to need a war room of our own," Graham said.

"If we play this just right, we can fix this," Allie said.

"You have to kill him, Allie." Porcia turned to her, tears shining in her eyes. "That is the only way this will ever end. I love him. I always will." She closed her eyes, wrapping her arms around her middle like she needed to hold herself together. "He wasn't always this way. He was a strong and firm man, but he could be kind. And he knew how to love." She stepped away from Allie, turning her back. "But this isn't the man I loved. That man is dead, and in his place is a monster who cannot be allowed to live. I've known it would come to this someday." She choked on a sob.

"I think today is some day, Allie," Graham said. "And you're the only one who has the power to kill him."

CHAPTER 54

Aidan | Oklahoma City | August

"This place is wrecked." Naomi craned her neck as they entered Oklahoma City in a rented SUV. Miles of destruction stretched out in every direction from the city center.

Even now, dark clouds loomed heavy overhead, churning like a whirlpool in the green tinged sky. Rain sheeted down on them in a torrential downpour.

"We better get settled somewhere quick." Aidan hit the gas as they neared Bricktown where they were staying. Most of the neighborhood around Bricktown was still intact, but judging by the state of the clouds and the rush of rain, they might be in for a rough night.

Which likely meant their prey was close.

"That cloud is freaking me out." Naomi kept her eyes on the sky as they gathered their few belongings and headed into the hotel.

"Just in time," the frazzled clerk at the front desk said as they entered. "Looks like you're going to get a front row seat to a classic Oklahoma City tornado."

"Looks that way." Aidan cast a nervous glance through the glass doors where hail the size of ice cubes had started to rain down.

"You can check in after the storm clears, I was just about to close up and head to the parking garage with everyone else. Come with me." The man spoke in a rush, keeping a forced smile plastered on his face.

"Sounds like fun." Naomi moved to search the streets for signs of their Immortal friend. He'd have to be nearby if the storm was raging right over their heads.

Most of the hotel staff were going about their business like it was just another day, but that churning cloud they'd seen hovering over the city when they drove in was looking decidedly cone shaped.

"We need to get out there if we're going to find this guy," Naomi murmured as the clerk gathered their bags and led them into the garage where all the hotel guests waited, wearing various shades of worried expressions.

One group of women in formal dresses shrieked when a geyser of storm water gushed up from the drains and spread across the garage floor, leaving ankle deep water in its wake. There was a bridezilla somewhere either freaking out or getting drunk.

"Time to get out of here." Aidan shrugged his backpack on his shoulders, checking that his weapons were easily accessible in case he needed them. The pair of daggers would do in a pinch.

Naomi already had her pack on her shoulder. "There's an exit over here." She kicked the bags with their clothes against the wall behind a truck. A moment later, they were on the street, and between the wind and rain, they weren't going to make much headway.

Aidan called on his power, wrapping them in a cool oasis where the rain and wind couldn't touch them.

"That's better." Naomi sighed, and they picked up their

pace. The streets were empty of people, but the floodwaters rushed between buildings like a torrential river. A flicker of orange lightning streaked across the sky, crashing into a streetlight a few blocks over.

"Good a place as any to start." Aidan led the way, keeping them dry and their view as clear as he could. Around the corner, they got a good look at the open sky and the wide maw of a cyclone churning above them. It hadn't touched down, and he hoped it wouldn't if they could get to the source of it quickly.

"There!" Naomi pointed down the street where several figures stood in the rain, waiting for them.

It was a trap.

"Is that ... Fei Long?" Naomi peered into the unnatural darkness of the late afternoon, but it was obviously a dragon they were seeing. And they only knew one person who had a dragon.

"What's Chloe doing here?" Aidan turned to Naomi in question.

A car floated past them as the storm runoff continued to gather in the streets. Its driver managed to climb through the sunroof to escape. Cursing and throwing a punch in the air, the mortal, soaked through to the bone, watched his car drift away. And then he turned and walked into the nearest hotel. Aidan saw him make a beeline for the bar, relieved he wouldn't need to be rescued.

Chloe however ... Aidan took a step forward, pulling his weapons from his pack. "Get ready. I'm not sure what to expect here."

"Well, we can't leave her, even if she does have a dragon." Naomi fell in step beside him as they made their way up the incline of the deserted street.

"I had a feeling they would send you. Though it's a dreadful night for a reunion," a familiar voice called to them in the darkness.

Aidan gripped his daggers as a spike of fear shot through him. "Marcus." He was proud to hear his steady voice because inside he was trembling with the memories of all the agony this man had put him through.

"I'm with you, Aidan," Naomi murmured, sticking to his side, her own weapons drawn at the ready.

"This is the boy you brought us here for, master?" A reed thin man stood behind Marcus, hissing in his ear. "He is weak."

"Enough Rhaegal." Marcus held up a hand.

Aidan studied the other figures in the darkness. He knew them well. "Selena, always a pleasure." Aidan offered the dangerous ancient woman a smirk. That she was here with Marcus meant Aidan was out of time. He might not walk away from this encounter unscathed.

"He's after you?" Naomi whispered as she came to the same realization. Pilar had said there was someone in the city Rhaegal was hunting. It turned out that was all a ruse to get Aidan here.

But Aidan wasn't so much worried about himself. He turned to the other woman standing beside Marcus, her eyes smoldering with the light of her power. "Chloe, what are you doing here?"

"Isn't she magnificent?" Marcus stepped into the light cast by a lamp post, gazing up at the towering Fei Long. She was a lot toothier than Aidan remembered, and she didn't look like she was happy to see him or Naomi.

"Chloe has always been a treasure." Aidan stepped into the light with Marcus, Naomi dogging his steps. "But I'd like to hear from her." He turned back to his lifelong friend, but Chloe's expression gave nothing away.

"I am fine, Aidan." She stood with her bo staff angled in front of her, like she thought he might attack at any moment.

"Whatever it is, Chloe, come with me now, and I'll get you home."

"I am home." Chloe dropped her chin, refusing to meet his gaze. Fei Long roared and hissed at him.

"Yes, our dear Chloe has recently joined us, of her own accord." Marcus moved to stroke the scarlet scales of Fei Long's hide.

It didn't make any sense. The Chloe he knew would never willingly go with Marcus. Not unless she was there to spy on him for Allie. But Allie would never have put Chloe in such a position.

"Why are we here, Marcus?" Naomi's voice echoed with the rolling thunder. "I am out of patience, and I don't care for the rain show your skeleton man is putting on. This city has been through enough storms since your arrival."

"Naomi. Always the shrill one." Marcus shook his head. "You know, Aidan." Marcus stood with his hands behind his back, oblivious of the rain that had soaked them all through to the skin. "It is possible for a man to rise to power without his Syntrophos at his side. I've seen it done." He cocked his head with a smile. "I believe your father is a good example of that."

"Get to the point, old man." Aidan studied their positions, trying to see if he had a chance to get between Chloe and Selena. Knowing Selena could syphon a gift away from her victims in an instant—and considering the condition was permanent—he didn't want to risk it. Not unless he had no other choice.

He met Chloe's gaze for a moment, and she gave a subtle shake of her head, warning him not to take that path. He couldn't fathom how she'd come to be with Marcus, but she wasn't so far gone that she didn't care how this ended for Aidan and Naomi.

"You owe me, boy." Marcus dropped the chipper tone he usually adopted in these situations. He sounded more like the man Aidan knew all too well.

"I owe you nothing." Aidan gripped his blades in white knuckled fists, itching to see them slice through Marcus' throat.

"I wasted far too much time training you." Marcus' eyes burned with anger, and Aidan reached for his power, letting it churn within him, filling him to the brink of pain, just the way Marcus had taught him. "I won't waste another moment. You're mine. Come with me now or face Selena. She will drain you dry before you draw first blood."

Aidan shook his head. "What's option number three?" He sank into a crouch. "We both know I'm not yet Proven. You don't want my power before it is fully matured."

"There is no third option. You overestimate your importance, young Aidan," Marcus said with a chuckle. "You fooled me into believing you were the child of prophecy. You did it to shield your little redheaded girlfriend from me. She's the one I seek. Did you know Allie is Proven now? And ripe for the picking. I just need a little carrot to dangle, and she'll come running from her tower."

"She won't fall for it." Aidan and Naomi moved as a unit, keeping their eyes on their surroundings.

Marcus threw his head back and laughed, the maniacal sound echoing along with the roll of thunder. "She's already fallen for it once. She's predictable, your girl. The prophecy was right about one thing. Her heart guides her. And it will be her ruin."

The rail-thin Immortal continued to let the storm rage over the city, the enormous funnel cloud sending strong winds sweeping through the streets, ripping signs apart, uprooting trees, and blasting out windows. Lighting struck at regular intervals all around them, taking out the city's power and casting them into total darkness except for the light of the full moon.

The wind was so strong Naomi staggered back a step, her hair whipping in the wind.

Aidan looked up as the cyclone roared overhead. He caught a glimpse of the full moon high above them, just as the maw of the tornado began to dip toward the ground.

He found himself wishing his sister was here. Sasha could fight this Immortal and his storm while Aidan could only push the temperature up or down by a few degrees. If he could make it cold enough, it might lessen the intensity of the storm or at least keep the tornado from touching down.

Aidan's core burned hot as his arms and hands grew ice cold, letting the chill leave his body. The temperature around him began to drop, but it wasn't enough.

Fei Long roared, sending a jet of liquid hot fire into the sky, negating anything Aidan might have done to break the storm apart.

"I've got this. Just keep them busy," Naomi said, her voice tight with the strain of pushing her power to the brink.

Selena came for him, her eyes red and swirling, mesmerizing. Aidan tore his gaze away from her, lifting his lead dagger to block her sword. He could fight her and hold her off. And he could make a good show of it while Naomi did whatever she was trying to do. He trusted her when she said she had it under control. Aidan fell into the zone, letting his body take over the fight, anticipating Selena's next move before she made it, but he refused to meet her venomous gaze. That was how she took her prey. She didn't need fancy swordsmanship to overpower an opponent. Once they fell into her eyes, they were hers.

"Give it up, Aidan." Selena's sword crashed into his crossed daggers, and he nearly disarmed her. "The Master always wins. It's foolish to resist him."

Aidan ignored her, pushing her back toward the master she served, though he knew how much she despised him. He also knew she didn't care enough about herself or anyone else to leave him now.

"Where is he?" she demanded, her eyes cooling as she reined in her power.

"Who?" Aidan pulled himself back from his battle trance.

Selena lashed out with a series of blows that drove Aidan into the street, putting distance between their fight and Marcus. "Michael."

It took Aidan a moment to remember who she was talking about. Michael was the man who had attacked him years ago at the orchard battle. The night Aidan had realized Allie was his Complement, and he almost paid for his distraction with his healing gift. Michael was the man who had tortured Quinn and Santi with his psychological gift that warped their memories and stole years from them.

And he meant a great deal to this woman.

Michael was also the man Allie had turned her Judgment gift on. She'd stripped him of his Immortality. Even now, he was somewhere in a cell deep in the underground because Greggory McBrien didn't know what else to do with him. No one could know what Allie could do, and Michael was living proof of her ability.

"You know where he is, don't you?" Selena pushed him, her sword raining down on him, ripping into his flesh with a dozen cuts meant to make him panic so he would make a mistake.

"No," Aidan lied. "I don't." He couldn't risk Allie's secret. Even if he could use it to buy Selena's loyalty for a few moments to help him escape Marcus' grasp.

"Tell me he is alive," she begged. "I can't feel him anymore, but if I live, he cannot be dead. Unless Livia has turned on us."

"I wish I could help you." Aidan hated himself for it, but he took advantage of her hesitation to drive her back across the street. With a whirl, he landed his dagger in her side. He scraped against bone as his blade found its mark in her kidney. As he pulled the dagger out, blood spurted, and she crumpled to the ground in a heap. She would likely bleed out before she could heal and it would take her longer to regenerate from such a wound.

"Lecia!" Marcus shrieked, as though he cared she was hurt.

A wave of power crashed into Aidan, digging into his skull like an icepick.

You are nothing, Aidan McBrien. Yet, you dare strike my most loyal servant? The words echoed in his mind as Marcus put himself between Aidan and Selena—the woman he now called Lecia. "Rhaegal, see to her wounds!"

Aidan fought to push Marcus from his mind. He'd had years of practice guarding his thoughts, though it took everything he had to do it now.

Is that girl worth everything she's put you through? Everything her family has done? It's time they pay for their sins! Marcus wasn't just projecting his thoughts into Aidan's mind, he was filling it with lies. Visions of Allie with other men. False memories of her manipulating Aidan to get what she wanted. Of her entire line bringing atrocities to the world.

"No!" Aidan roared, shoving Marcus from his mind.

"Your queens have taken everything," Marcus shrieked, spittle flying from his mouth. "They have turned this world into a perversion of what it was. And they will pay for it with their lives. Starting with your princess. None of her line will survive what's coming." He pointed a shaking finger at Aidan. "No queen will ever lay a hand on Lecia or anyone else I treasure, ever again." His eyes blazed with fury and insanity. "No queen will be left to stand against me and the world I will build on the ashes of this one."

"What about Livia?" Aidan moved to circle Marcus, putting himself within reach of Selena, though Chloe and Fei Long guarded her while Rhaegal tended her wound, trying to keep her from bleeding out long enough for her to heal. "You raised her as your own, yet she is of Allie's line. She serves as the First Princess's most trusted ally."

"Livia was always meant to be collateral damage." Marcus shrugged.

"Collateral damage like Justice?" Aidan threw his son in his face.

"What do you know of that useless boy?" Marcus seemed truly shocked at the mention of the son he'd abandoned years ago.

"That he's not so useless." Aidan chanced a look at Chloe, hoping to remind her of what waited for her at home. He knew how much she hurt, standing by while Justice didn't see her. He knew that pain firsthand. Was that what drove her to Marcus?

"No one matters to me anymore." Marcus forced a confident tone. One Aidan didn't buy. Whatever Selena was to him, he cared about her. Cared for her more than anyone else in the world. Even his own Complement.

"Bring him with us," Marcus called the order to his companions as he moved to gather Selena's limp form in his arms. Blood seeped from wounds she would recover from. "He is mine now. The princess will drop everything to come to his aid. And then we will take their power." He gazed down at Selena, his eyes crazed.

"That's our cue to get out of here," Naomi whispered from behind.

Aidan moved faster than Rhaegal's lightning, lurching into the shadows as the ground where he just stood cracked into a thousand pieces.

Fei Long roared, hissing a stream of fire in his direction, only narrowly missing.

Aidan called on his fire gift, praying it worked with dragon fire. Power shot up his arm as he pulled the white-hot dragon fire into his hands, grappling with it for a moment before it began to gather and grow. He couldn't hold onto it any longer.

Flinging up a wall of fire to protect them from Marcus and Rhaegal, Aidan rushed to Naomi. It was the only advantage he could give them, and it wouldn't last long with Rhaegal's storm chasing them.

"Let's go." Naomi took his hand.

It gutted him to leave Chloe behind, but she was an adult, free to make her own choices. And she had a dragon. She could leave whenever she wanted. If she was with Marcus, she had a good reason for it, and he had to trust her.

"The storm." Aidan followed Naomi, not sure if their

escape would work. "He'll chase us down and kill a thousand people with that thing." Aidan pointed up to the sky.

"What thing? Haven't you been paying attention?" Naomi gripped his arm and dragged him around the corner.

The wind was a gale force, trying to push them back the way they came. "I was a little busy." Aidan looked up to see the funnel cloud falling apart.

"How did you do that?" He broke into a run beside his Syntrophos as they darted through the streets of Oklahoma City, dodging storm debris and broken glass.

"It's a full moon," Naomi panted beside him, her eyes swirling like pools of aquamarine with the light of her lunar power.

Abandoning their luggage, they made it back to their rental and were speeding away from the city into the flat farmlands of the Midwest before Naomi explained.

"It's a full moon, which means I'm at my strongest, and it also means atmospheric pressure is at its highest. More pressure in the atmosphere equals tranquil weather. I just put everything I had into driving up the air pressure to dispel Mr. Skeleton's tornado."

Aidan grinned, shaking his head at his Syntrophos. "I do not know why that man continues to underestimate you, but you just saved our butts back there."

"Now, we just need to figure out why Chloe's with him, what's with him calling Selena, 'Lecia,' and why he seems to actually care about her."

"I think it's time we go home," Aidan said as he took the turn to get on the highway that would take them back to the Tulsa airport where they'd flown in. They needed to get as far away from Oklahoma City as quickly as possible.

Naomi nodded, glancing over her shoulder to watch their rear. "Something weird just happened back there, and

I think Allie needs to know about it. He might not have gotten his hands on you tonight, but that doesn't mean he won't use someone else she loves to lure her into a trap."

"Let's get a flight for Atlanta." Aidan's heart kicked up at the thought of finally seeing Allie again.

CHAPTER 55

Allie | Sterling Tower | August

"Aidan?" Allie's voice sounded strange to her own ears as she looked up from the visions she was studying along the beach. Aidan walked toward her, his raven dark hair blowing in the breeze, the late afternoon sunlight glinting against the natural highlights that almost seemed blue. She wasn't certain he was real or if he was a vision.

"You're so pretty." A silly smile lit her from the inside out. He wasn't dressed for the beach. He was dressed for battle, in full gear and well-worn leathers that hugged his muscles. "I missed you, I wish you were really here." Allie's mouth went dry at the sight of him. Her pulse pounded in her ears, and she wasn't even sure what she was saying. Or if she was even speaking at all.

"I missed you too." His eyes shot right through her. He could see everything she was, with all her flaws laid bare, and yet he was still standing there, loving her.

"Wait, you're really here?" she blurted, her eyes widening in surprise as she scrambled from her lounge. "You're mine." The words fell from her mouth before she realized what she'd said. Alarm bells went off in her head but she couldn't seem to put the pieces of the puzzle together in her mind.

"I am." He took a step toward her.

But Allie wasn't ready for this. She wasn't ready to give a name to what she was feeling. She took a step back into the shade of the cabana, averting her eyes and putting a clamp on her feelings.

"You like my island? It was a terrible place during my Proving." She dragged Xera's lounge chair to sit beside hers, fussing with a beach towel. "But it's my oasis now. You can sit here, beside me." She tried brushing the sand from the chair, but she might as well have tried to brush the sand off the beach. Nothing had escaped Xeren's sandcastle activity.

"You met your nephew. Isn't he amazing?" She turned to the table beside her chair. "Want some lemonade?" Her hands shook as she lifted the pitcher. "It's fresh squeezed, or so they tell me."

"Allie." Aidan's breath brushed the back of her neck as his shadow loomed over her. His hand pressed against hers, forcing her to set the pitcher down before she dumped it everywhere. "Look at me."

"No." She shook her head. "I don't think I can."

"Please?" His hand fell to her hip, and she shuddered at his touch. Closing her eyes, she leaned back against him. He tugged the hat from her head, tossing it to the ground where it drifted on the wind toward the jungle.

"My hat!" Allie lurched after it, chasing it, but unable to catch it. She glanced up at the mountain she'd only recently climbed. She'd do it all over again to avoid what was happening right now.

"Alexis Ann, come back here and face me." His voice held a hint of amusement, but her feet were rooted in the tall grass growing along the edge of the jungle.

She shook her head like a stubborn child. She could not look him in the eye, knowing he could see everything she'd seen about herself during her Proving. It was too much. She could not look at him and see the love in his eyes. He'd probably always seen her flaws and loved her still.

"What are you afraid of, Lex?" Aidan's shadow fell over her again, and she could feel his warmth, yet she couldn't make herself turn around.

"I'm not ready," she whispered.

"Of course, you are. Otherwise, this wouldn't be happening."

Allie hung her head, scared out of her mind to let herself believe it might be true. She couldn't even think the word, she was too afraid it was just some cosmic joke ... that he'd been hers all along and her efforts to resist the inevitable had wasted too many years.

"Alexis Ann Maree Carmichael, I know you know. Now, please turn around. I've been waiting a very long time."

"No. I'm Jon Snow. I know nothing." She tried to run away, but he wouldn't let her.

"Fine, Jon Snow." Aidan hauled her back against him. "At least look at me."

"Nope." She tilted her head up to the sky, searching for strength. "How long?" she finally whispered, tears burning her eyes.

"Since the orchard."

Allie's shoulders fell and the tears came. It explained so much. She sank to her knees, sorrow and anger warring within her for dominance. Her shoulders shook, and she wasn't sure she'd ever be able to look him in the eye without shame for all she'd put him through.

"Allie." He knelt behind her. "I'm so sorry."

"*You're* sorry?" She choked on her tears. "What do you have to be sorry about?"

"For ... circumstances that have taken the choice from you. What we are ... it's taken so much from you. Robbed you of the life you always wanted."

"And it's given me more than I could have ever dreamed. You're too good, Aidan." Even now, he thought her reactions were his fault, that she was mad ... at *him*.

"I don't understand." He sighed. "You're angry. I can feel it." His voice was raw, and he knelt behind her like an open wound she could heap more hurt and sorrow upon, like so much salt. "I can go if you want. Just ... give me a minute to work up the courage."

"No!" Allie scrambled on her knees to turn around, reaching for him, but still not able to look up. "I am angry. So angry ... at *me*." She slammed a fist over her heart. "At my stubborn stupidity that has brought you nothing but heartache." Her vision blurred as she stared at the grass. "Since the moment I met you, I've brought you pain." She tried to beat her chest again, but Aidan caught her hands.

"That's not true." His voice shook with emotion. "You've brought me so much joy, Allie."

"How can you say that when you can see..." She broke off with a sob.

"See what?" he demanded.

Allie finally looked up, her gaze locking with his. "When you can see me. As I truly am? The inept girl with the mortal brain. The Clairvoyant who can see the future, and somehow still never knows what's coming."

Aidan's hands slid up her arms, gripping her shoulders. "That's not what I see." He dipped his head to press his forehead against hers. "You don't get to tell me what I see when I look at you. You don't get to claim responsibility for any of my actions since the orchard. None of that matters now. It's in the past, and we have our future to look forward to." His voice grew tight, like he couldn't contain his emotions. Couldn't contain the love he felt for her. "And Allie, it's going to be a good one, babe." His hands moved to cup her face.

Allie shook her head; she couldn't do this. She didn't have the strength. Tears ran down her face as she looked into his eyes shining with tears of his own.

"So help me, Alexis Ann. I need you to say it. I need to hear the words fall from your lips so I can kiss them."

"I'm scared," she whispered, clinging to his shoulders.

"Of what?" He brushed her tears away with his thumb. "Tell me what's going on in that head of yours. I've never once gotten it right, even when I let my walls down and we share thoughts, I never know what you're thinking or how you arrive at the conclusions you make. It's one of the most infuriating things I love about you. So just say it, tell me what you're afraid of."

"Losing you." Her hands slid up from his shoulders to brush her fingertips across her face. "That's been my greatest fear since the beginning."

"You aren't going to lose me, Lex. I'm right here. I'm yours forever, and no one is going to take me away from you. Ever."

Allie sniffed back her tears, pulling away from him. "You left." She sat back on her heels, looking at him with the pain of his absence in her eyes. "To escape this, you left, and it brought you *years* of torture."

"I had to. It was too new, and I didn't know how to keep it from you. I needed a little time apart. It wasn't supposed to be years. You had Darius. And then Naomi happened, and I thought a little more time wouldn't hurt."

"And then the Milan Initiative happened," Allie said, shaking with rage she had no outlet for except herself.

"But nothing like that will ever come between us again." He was almost frantic in his need to convince her all would be well now.

"I knew." She tilted her head, studying his face. A face she'd seen so many times in her dreams and visions. Glimpses of his life she hadn't realized she was seeing. "That's why I pulled away from you in the very beginning. I knew if I loved you, you would leave me, and I couldn't bear it, so I tried to stop it from happening so I could keep you. Even if that meant we could only be friends."

"What are you saying?"

"I'm saying I *knew* I would lose you. That's where all my fears came from. Don't you see, Aidan?" She took his hands in hers. "My clairvoyance told me even before my Awakening that if I loved you, I would lose you. And I did. For a while. But I didn't lose you to someone else like I always feared."

"And now?" His eyes searched hers for clues to what she was thinking.

"And now, we are sitting here on the ground between a jungle and a beach that shouldn't even exist, and all of that's in the past. I don't have to be afraid of something that's already happened. I lost you because you needed time. We both did. And now we're here, a complete hot mess, but we're whole. Whole individuals who have had separate experiences that have shaped us into the adults we've become."

"Say it, Allie," he whispered, closing his eyes as a tear rolled down his cheek.

"And now I know you're my Complement," she whispered. "And you and I get to love each other forever." Fresh tears fell from her eyes. "And it's more than I can bear to think about because it's so much more than I deserve."

Aidan pulled her into his arms, crushing her against him as his lips found hers. Nothing else mattered. Not the world on the cusp of falling apart around them. Not the million things they had to do to hold it together with nothing more than duct tape and hope, and the thousand working parts that had to go right at every step they took from here. For a single moment, all that mattered was they finally had their forever. She would get to keep him, always.

And just like always, he pulled away just when it was getting good.

"Wait." Allie held him tight. "Is this why you always pull away?" She searched his face.

"Yes." He let out a breath. "Letting things go too far could have pushed it on you when you weren't ready. When I kiss you, and you make it clear you want more than just kissing, the bond starts to well up within me, and I couldn't—wouldn't—do that to you." He moved to stand, pulling her up with him so he could wrap his arms around her and hold her close.

"Okay, but why didn't you just tell me?" She tilted her head back, staring up at him. "It would have made everything so much easier if we were on the same page."

Aidan threw his head back with a laugh as his hands slid up her arms to wrap around her throat, humor dancing in his eyes. "I knew you were going to say that, you infuriating woman." He let his hands fall away. "You really are the most exasperating woman I've ever met."

"Well, it would have saved us a lot of heartache if you'd just told me what was happening."

"And what would you have done if when you were seventeen years old, still in high school, and I told you I knew we were Complements and would be together forever?"

"I'd have freaked out. But I would have been okay with it. Eventually."

"Sure." He snorted a laugh. "That's the calm, cool-headed girl I remember."

"Okay, so there might have been an Allie-shaped hole in the wall after I ran away in hysterics." They turned to walk back to the beach where the sun was just beginning to set, their arms around each other.

"Coming to the realization on your own was vital. For me to push it on you by allowing the bond to form, or by telling you, it just isn't done."

Allie shrugged. "It would have been hard, but I would have dealt with it. Traditions are meant to be broken."

"It's not tradition. To Immortals, such a thing is equal to rape, Allie. Telling you was an option I would never have considered." They came to a stop near the waves, and Aidan turned to her, tucking an errant curl behind her ear. "I would have waited a thousand years or more for you to come to me in your own time."

"I feel awful for making you wait." She ducked her head, biting her lip.

"Well, the waiting is over, and like you said, it's in the past. Now, we have our bonding ceremony to look forward to."

"Oh." Allie pulled away, nerves churning within her stomach at the thought of a wedding. She was only twenty-three. And she had a prophecy hanging over her head to deal with.

"Oh? What does this 'oh' mean?" He scowled at her, tugging her back to his side.

Allie laid her head against his chest, wrapping her arms

around his waist. "Can't we just enjoy being together for a little while before we make the leap into marriage?"

Aidan growled, holding her tight to his chest. "Alexis Ann Maree Carmichael, you're going to be the death of me."

"I hope not," she murmured. "For now, can we just enjoy the sunset?"

"You should know by now that anything you want, if it's within my power to give it, is yours. Even if that's just a beautiful sunset and a peaceful moment to enjoy it together."

CHAPTER 56

Allie | Sterling Tower | August

"You've missed a lot." Allie stared up at the stars twinkling in the sky over the island, for once not trying to analyze how Hal did the things he did in the warehouse. However he did it, he deserved a raise. Not that he let her pay him. Any time she brought it up, he snarled at her, so she just brought him tasty food she promised she didn't cook.

"I'll catch up." Aidan hugged her closer, and she burrowed into his side in the lounge they'd dragged onto the beach to share like old times. A driftwood fire crackled beside them, and if she closed her eyes, the last years melted away and they were just kids again. Stressed out kids who hadn't a clue what lay ahead of them.

Allie snorted at the thought.

"What?" Aidan glanced down at her.

"I was just thinking about nights like this when we were kids. We didn't know what stress was back then."

Aidan laughed. "We were young and so stupid, and it's extra scary to realize those days weren't all that long ago."

"Right?" She laughed at the happy memories of a time she'd never see again outside her own memories.

"So, this Xera lady that came home with Sasha. You were saying she's been a big help?" He urged her to go on.

They'd spent most of the night catching each other up on the things they'd missed while they were apart. And getting distracted by the newness of their growing bond. It wouldn't fully form until the ceremony, but it already hummed deep within her, warming her from the inside out. She hoped that feeling never faded.

Allie sat propped up on her elbow so she could see him in the firelight. "You're not going to believe this, but Xera is his Syntrophos."

"Who? Marcus?" His voice grated over the name they both despised.

"Yes. All this time, we never knew it. He believes she and her Complement died in the Great War. And when the time comes, I think she's going to be vital to defeating him."

"He's completely unhinged now." Aidan ran an absent hand through her hair.

"You've seen him recently?"

"Yeah, that's what brought me back. I fought with him in Oklahoma City a few days ago. Chloe was with him."

"Is she okay? Tell me everything." Allie turned toward him.

"She seems okay, but how did that happen?"

"She was with me when he tried to use my parents against me. When he saw Fei Long." Allie shook her head. "He wanted her."

"What made her go with him?"

"He said her mother's soul didn't go far when she died. That when Chloe created Fei Long as a tribute, she gave Ming's soul a place to go so she could watch over her daughter."

"So Fei Long is...?"

"Ming Lao." Allie nodded. "At least she's somewhere in there."

"And he promised to bring her back." Aidan sighed. "She knows better than that."

"I thought so too, but she went to him instantly. He has a way for getting inside your head, making you believe things that aren't true."

"He tried to twist up my thoughts too." Aidan ran his hand along her arm.

"I couldn't sway her," Allie said. "Something he said to her mind made her go. And she hasn't responded to any of our attempts to reach her."

"We might not see it, but she knows what she's doing."

"That's what Justice says, and I want to believe it, but you guys didn't see her. It was like a switch flipped inside her. Like she went all in with him the moment he promised she could have her mother back."

"No. Chloe is stronger than that. She's still with us."

"I hope so. How was she when you saw her?"

"Rigid. Distant," Aidan began. "Marcus was with her, treating her like a prized pet. But he also brought one of the ancients we've been chasing. A powerful Immortal who can create storms. I guess Marcus figured Pilar would send me and Naomi to fight this Rhaegal guy."

"Rhaegal?" Allie's jaw dropped.

"You've heard of him?"

"Sasha told me about a memory Xera showed her. She and Marcus fought against him during the Great War. He's the one who supposedly killed Xera and her Complement, Vitor, and now he's working with him?"

"I think that's what must have changed him. Losing his Syntrophos, though he should have sensed she was still alive."

"When she recovered from her wounds, she was in a prison behind a magnetic field that cut her off from her power. It masked their bond, so he truly thought he'd lost her. She's been in the Chola Valley, so I imagine he still doesn't sense her. After thousands of years, that bond won't return quickly."

"Choose the right moment to reveal her and he may crumble."

"I doubt that." Allie snorted. "He doesn't care about anyone enough to let them distract him from his goals."

"No, that's just it, Allie." Aidan moved to sit up. "You should have seen him when I fought Selena. She was vicious, and I knew we were done for if she got her hands on us. I went for the kidney shot, and she was bleeding out on the sidewalk in the middle of a tornado. Marcus went berserk, like she was the most precious thing in the world to him, and he thought I'd actually killed her. He called her by a different name. Something like ... Leesha."

"Lecia?" Allie gasped, grabbing his face between her palms. "Are you absolutely certain that's what he called her?"

"Yes, why do you look like I just handed you the sun?"

"Because you have." Allie lunged to her feet, dragging a hand through her hair. "Sasha said the day Xera died on the battlefield, her Complement couldn't get to her. Rhaegal had caused an earthquake and opened a canyon to separate them. Vitor was fighting for his life on one side, and Xera was on the other, bleeding out from a thousand wounds Rhaegal had inflicted on her. Marcus—Lord Teigan at the time—tried to help her, but she made him promise to protect Lecia. Her daughter. *Selena* is Xera's daughter. That's why he reacted like a madman when you hurt her."

"Oh my God, Allie. I think I could have actually killed her." Aidan moved to stand beside her.

"How?" Allie asked.

"Because her Complement is mortal, Allie." Aidan gripped her arms. "You used your power against him the night I realized you were my Complement. When Michael attacked me and tried to take my healing gift, I was gone. I was so caught up in the realization that you were mine—that I would never lose you—he got the best of me. *You* saved me that night."

"But I gave him a death sentence," Allie whispered.

"And we still don't know what it would mean for Jin Jing or Navid's immortality if they were mortally wounded. Neither has a Complement bond that roots them to this world any longer. And now, neither does Selena."

"So in that moment, Marcus thought you had taken his last link to Xera from him."

"He had Rhaegal treat her wounds right there in the middle of our fight. She's healed by now, but it was close."

"But how would he know about Michael? He wouldn't have any reason to believe she could actually die."

"Selena can't sense Michael, they know something is wrong with their bond. I imagine Marcus has guessed what you did that night in the orchard."

Allie clenched her fists as a smile erupted across her face. "Do you know what this means?"

"Xera and Selena are the key." Aidan returned her smile. "Marcus needs Selena to take your gift and give it to him. That's her power and your gift has a better chance of surviving if she's the one to do it."

"And if we show Selena—Lecia—her mother is still alive then we can probably bet that she won't be so eager to serve the man who imprisoned her mother for seven thousand years." Allie's heart raced in her chest as so many things slipped into place. The prophecy was right. She'd gathered her equals and one by one they'd gone out into the world and brought back the information she needed to defeat Marcus.

"You've brought me the final piece of the puzzle." She took Aidan's hand and started running for the bridge.

"Where are we going?"

"We have a lot to do. I'll catch you up to speed on the way."

"On the way where?"

"Barcelona. I've got two birds to kill with one stone."

CHAPTER 57

Allie | Barcelona | September

Allie sat behind her parents' old desk in the empty Senate chamber.

Today was the day the world was supposed to end, and she still didn't know if they'd done enough to stop it. Her equals had been busy these last few days.

As usual, she was nothing more than the figurehead they rallied around. And she was okay with that. She was just a useful tool, and her moment was coming where she'd get to add her two cents. She hoped it was enough.

"You're ready." Alísun stepped into the chamber, glancing up at the oculus in the ceiling, open to the afternoon sky. It was a beautiful day to end a war before it had a chance to take root.

"I hope so." Allie sighed, her nerves on edge, and she expected to be sick at any minute.

"I don't mean for today." Her grandmother stepped up onto the dais at the highest point in the room. She ran a hand over the aged wooden surface of the highest office in their world. "She sat here for a few years and ruled our people in her own way."

"I'm trying to channel a bit of her strength from this

chair. I need all the help I can get for this." Allie's thoughts were with Kassandre today, wondering if her mother's sacrifices would finally pay off.

Alísun hopped up onto the desk, crossing her legs like she sat a throne. "She ruled here with you father, yet she never took the mantle of power. Kassandre was my named heir for a time, but our world never needed her the way it has needed you."

"Are you messing with me, Grandma? Please tell me you aren't picking the worst possible moment ever to do what I think you're about to do?"

"It's time, Allie-Girl." She leaned forward. "And it's not my decision. You've already taken the role, darling. Now it's just a formality."

"Does it have to be today? Now?"

"Yes, my darling. The mantle of power doesn't belong to me anymore, and it weakens me to hold it for you. I am so very, very tired." She sighed. Alísun seemed to age right before Allie's eyes. Not in a literal sense, but in the way a parent or grandparent finally lays down the role of responsibility for a child who is no longer a child.

"How does it happen?" Allie resigned herself to the responsibility she was born to.

"Give me your hands." Alísun held her hands out.

Allie grasped hold of the queen's slim, cool hands that began to warm the moment their skin touched. Alísun closed her eyes, and they sat there silently for a moment.

A terrible burden settled on Allie's shoulders, weighing her down until it felt as if her spine might buckle from the heavy load she would have to bear for the rest of her life—or until she named her own heir many, many years from now.

"How do you do it, Grandma?" Allie whispered, hardly able to draw a breath.

"It gets easier with time, as you become accustomed to the weight of responsibility. I'm afraid I don't have a pretty crown to place on your head, my darling. Just the love I bear for you and our people."

Allie's shoulders fell, and her back bent as she tried to draw the mantle of power around her. It felt as though she carried every single Immortal of the world on her back. She supposed that was the gist of it. They were her people. Her responsibility now. She would have to find a way to shoulder the burden on her own.

Except she wasn't on her own.

"Is it possible to share the role?"

"How do you mean?"

"Let's say I love a certain man, and he's a really good one I intend to keep forever."

"And you wish to share your role with him?"

"I do. If he's willing. And once we're bonded." She still wasn't sure she was ready for that yet. It was just really nice to know she'd get to love Aidan forever. How she got so lucky, she'd never understand.

"That could be arranged, in time, if your council and all parties are willing."

"Good to know. Let's stick a pin in that for now, we have bigger fish to fry today."

"You are Queen Alexis Ann Maree Carmichael now. Seventh Queen of Indriell," her grandmother whispered in a solemn voice.

A rush of power welled within Allie, bolstering her strength and stamina. Suddenly, the enormous load she carried felt a little lighter. She sat up straighter.

"What just happened?"

"I named you, darling. I've passed your heritage on to you so that every woman who came before us has given you her strength so you may bear the burden of their legacy a little easier."

"Why couldn't we have led with that?" Allie took a breath, and her shoulders quit trembling.

"A little trick my mother played on me." She winked. "Just don't ever forget how heavy the load you carry is when you try to do it all on your own. Everyone needs help now and again."

"I won't be forgetting that." Allie wiped a bead of sweat from her brow. "Is that it? Is it done?"

"It's done."

"And people will see me the way they see you?"

"They will. Just remember to guard who you are in here." She laid a hand over her heart. "That Allie is for you to treasure. She's for your family and closest friends. Queen Alexis is for the people."

"Thank you, Grandma. You have been the very best role model and teacher a queen in training could ask for. And the best grandma any girl ever had."

"Now, you're ready." Alísun winked, slipping off the edge of the desk. "Give 'em hell for me, will you? These fools need someone young and strong to shake things up."

"You've got it." Allie winked, watching as her grandmother made her way out of the chamber, her step a little lighter and her eyes sparkling with a youthful glow Allie had never seen in her before.

"All right." Allie relaxed back in the chair her mother once sat upon. "Let the games begin."

"Not without me, you don't."

"Darius!" Allie flew out of her chair and down the steps to the Senate floor, slamming into her Syntrophos. "I wasn't sure you were going to make it in time."

"Not a chance. I missed you too much." Darius

wrapped his arms around her, their bond humming between them.

"Let's not do this whole separation thing again." Allie clung to him, and with Aidan nearby, she felt the first stirrings of what it might be like for them when they were a fully bonded Syntrophos.

"Agreed. Next time, you're coming with me."

"Let's hope there isn't a next time after we're done here today." Allie didn't want to let him out of her sight.

"I see we have a whole new source of drama to look forward to. You finally put my brother out of his misery?"

"You knew?" She gasped in surprise.

"It was so obvious, but I'm glad you got the happy ending you tried to resist. But please, tell me you're our anchor and not him?"

"We both are. So that should be super fun." With a fully bonded Syntrophos the anchor sat in the middle of the bond as the leader and most powerful of the three.

"Well, you are equals. So I guess we won't be finding that balance that will make this relationship easier until Naomi settles on a Complement?"

"And you too."

"Oh, I'm settled." Darius' face flushed pink with pleasure.

"Shut up!" She hugged him tight. "Oh wait, who is it? Please tell me it's Pilar and not some psychotic Enlightened maniac you picked up on the road."

"It's Pilar." A stupid-happy grin spread across his face. "It was a slow realization for both of us."

"I call dibs on double wedding!" Allie clapped her hands.

"Bonding Ceremony," Darius corrected her.

"Nope. We're doing the full on mortal wedding with a few Immortal traditions sprinkled in."

"You have fun trying to get Pilar into a frilly white wedding gown."

"Ew. No. No white dress for me either. I'm so excited! This is going to be amazing. You'll be my best man, of course."

"Uh, don't we have a madman to capture this afternoon?"

"Yes." Allie heaved a sigh.

"Then catch me up to speed and we'll talk wedding plans after."

"Deal. We don't have much time, so pay attention."

Chapter 58

Allie | Barcelona | September

"Start with the Senate Chamber and work your way through the building."

Allie leaned back in her mother's seat, adopting a relaxed manner when she was anything but. She knew that voice all too well. She'd heard it reverberating through her mind on an endless repeat. *Did you think it would be easy? To face me all on your own?*

No, it hadn't been easy. Nothing about their journey to this moment had been easy. It wasn't her journey to claim because so many people had been involved. From the sacrifices Kassandre and Navid had made for their daughters, to Lily and Carson dedicating their lives to raising Allie, to each and every one of her teachers, mentors, and equals. It had taken a village to get her to this moment. She just hoped she could make them all proud.

"Are you ready for this, Liv?" Allie glanced at the seat beside her where her sister sat in their father's chair.

"I've been ready for this moment my whole life."

"Well, I'm not." Darius dragged a chair up from the lower dais to sit between them. "Okay, now I am."

The Chamber doors burst open and Selena—whom

Allie now knew to be Lecia—entered first, her weapons drawn and ready for a battle that wouldn't happen. At least Allie really hoped it wouldn't. Guards fanned out around her, startled looks on their faces when they found the Senate floor empty, except for Allie, Darius, and Livia.

She waited, hardly able to breathe until Marcus stepped into the room, Rhaegal at his side.

Darius sat between Allie and Livia, his hand resting on the sword at his hip, twitching like he wanted to use it now before they even got started.

Allie's heart shattered into a million pieces when Chloe stepped into the room behind Marcus, her face revealing nothing.

Marcus' face was also a bland mask, refusing to reveal his surprise at finding them here, sitting in the seats that had once belonged to their parents.

The doors slammed shut behind the most dangerous man the world had ever known, and Allie let out a relieved sigh. The trap was a success, and he'd walked right into it. Samantha and Bennett stood guard outside the Chamber doors. No one would come in or out without Allie's permission, and they were prepared to take lethal action should anyone try escaping. Even Marcus himself couldn't escape the vaporous poison they would generate if it became necessary. It was funny. Thanks to Marcus, they had learned that little trick at the Milan Initiative.

"Ms. Carmichael." Marcus halted at the top of the stairs leading down to the Chamber floor. "It seems we meet again." He refused to even acknowledge Livia or Darius.

"I suppose you weren't expecting us." Allie put on her best poker face, waiting for him to ask the real questions.

"I was expecting the Senate to be in session on such an auspicious day." Marcus continued down the stairs until they were on a level with each other. Chloe followed closely behind him.

"It is an auspicious day, isn't it?" Allie let a smile play around the corners of her mouth, careful not to let her nerves show.

Some of the color drained from Marcus' plain symmetrical face, and he took a step back, nearly toppling over Chloe standing behind him. "I see your grandmother has passed the torch. I suppose she thought you'd need all the help you could get."

"Probably." Allie shrugged. "But I'm not above accepting help when it is offered. That's the real difference between you and me." Allie pulled the mantle of power around her, letting it strengthen her voice.

An intrusive force pressed against her mind, searching for a way in. Yet, the sharp pain of Marcus' gift never came.

"He is nothing against you, sister." Livia sneered at the man she'd once called father.

"Aren't we above such things, Marcus?" Allie sighed, running her fingertips over the gavel her mother might have once used. It looked as though it had seen the hands of many Chief Justices. "I am stronger now. You said it yourself last time we met, I wasn't ready." She leaned forward. "I'm ready now."

"Where is the Senate? What's happening?" Selena spoke up for the first time.

"The Senate will convene shortly," Darius explained.

"We have a few matters to discuss first. Matters that involve you, Selena. I would strongly urge you to make better choices when certain things come to light in the next few moments."

"What do you think is happening here, Alexis, my

dear?" Marcus smiled. "I don't have time for your games, girl."

"You may call her your Majesty or Queen Alexis." Livia slammed a fist against the desk where she sat. "Either way, I suggest you find a tone of respect."

Allie cocked her head to the side. "The real question, Marcus, is what do *you* think is happening today?"

"I have business with the Senate."

"No, you don't. Your days of scheming are at an end, old man." Darius ran his fingertips over the sharp blade of his sword, letting a trickle of blood coat its shiny surface.

"Guards, will you please remove Ms. Carmichael, this boy, and her *sister* from this Chamber? They are wasting precious time."

Marcus' guards began to approach the dais, and Allie stood, embracing her power, letting the rage of her Judgment gift fill her. Her eyes pulsed with the light of her power, and she raised a hand, a spark of green light flickering between her fingertips. "I wouldn't recommend it unless you'd like to face my wrath."

The guards hesitated, their weapons raised, waiting for further instruction.

"Do not test me." The power of all the ancient Queens of Indriell filled her voice, and every single soldier lowered their weapons at once.

In the same instant, Fei Long exploded from Chloe in a cloud of golden vapor. She filled the room, towering above Marcus and his remaining loyal minions, wrapping her wings protectively around them.

It was going to be like that, then.

"You won't be meeting with the Senate today, Marcus." Allie ignored Chloe's dragon and the ache that sank like a stone in her chest at the sight of her friend on the wrong side. "You came here today believing you would take over the Senate and dissolve our government. But it's over. It's all over. I believe you're familiar with my good friend, Graham Loukas, also known as the Grim, as well as the Tinker within your League of Ancients." A door opened behind her, and Graham came to join them on the dais.

"So we have met." A flash of anger lit Marcus' eyes for a moment before he schooled his features. "How could it possibly matter what a child with a handful of tech gifts brings to the table?"

"Oh, it matters." Allie reached out to meet Graham's fist bump. "The prophecy said I would gather my equals. Graham is one of many you have underestimated."

"I don't think so." Marcus motioned for Selena to follow him as he turned to leave, Fei Long hissing a stream of fire at the dais.

"Going so soon?" Darius called after him. "But we've only just begun."

Marcus halted as an indigo cloud of noxious gas rolled under the door.

"You might not want to breathe that in," Allie said. "You remember the Milan Initiative, right? A pair of your best trained Syntrophos are ready to melt your face off with the toxic fumes your minions forced out of them through your brand of brutal training. I imagine it will work on the dragon as well."

Selena and Chloe were the first to back away. Marcus turned, and with a nod of his head, Rhaegal flew into action, calling down a bolt of lightning from the oculus above. Wind raced in through the opening in the domed ceiling, whirling around the chamber into a cyclone of power.

Allie had to grab onto the desk to keep her feet under her.

"Enough!" Sasha and Quinn made their appearance as the mask of Quinn's invisibility fell away, and the Syntrophos pair stood on the galley level above the exit.

Sasha embraced her power as she leaped from the galley, landing between Marcus and the exit.

"I guess it comes down to you and me, Rhaegal, Master of Storms." Sasha's eyes blazed with the golden light of her power as she called down her own storm. Sasha was a fierce Immortal and master of her power. She'd learned much during her time in the Chola Valley—and it seemed Mother Raghavan was right, Sasha needed her full power to go head to head with Rhaegal.

The wind bit at Allie's face, and everyone on the dais had to duck down below the desk.

"Is anyone watching Marcus?" Graham shouted. "We can't let him get away."

"I'll go." Livia pulled a blade from her boot, preparing to dive into the raging storms as the two Immortals fought on the Senate floor.

"He's not going anywhere, Livia. No one can get out of this room without going through Samantha and Bennett first, and even if he did manage to get past them, he'd still have to get out of the building, and we have it surrounded with dream walkers."

The building trembled and lightning crashed above them, striking the domed ceiling. Shards of glass and chunks of plaster rained down on their heads.

"And then there's Sasha." Darius peeked over the desk, and a block of stone almost took his head off before he ducked back down. "No one is getting past her."

Since her Proving, Sasha's gift for controlling the wind had amplified. She was more powerful than ever and not only through her natural talent, but in the completion of her

Complement and Syntrophos bonds as well. She was an anchor, and anchors were some of the most powerful Immortals in the world.

Where she once had an affinity for controlling the wind and temperatures, she now mastered it. Lightning crashed and wind roared, but as the Chamber grew cold, Rhaegal's storm fell apart.

"Have you all forgotten he has a dragon and now a new exit?" Livia shot across the room, prepared to slit throats if she had to.

Allie and Darius climbed out of their hiding spot to find the room completely wrecked and the powerful Rhaegal on his knees at Sasha's feet, a magnetic collar around his throat.

"Well, that just happened." Darius shook his head, impressed.

Allie exhaled in relief. After the short battle, Sasha had taken out Marcus' best chance at defeating them. Depending on which way Chloe would lean, this might be over already.

Quinn stood above in the gallery, his arms crossed over his chest, just waiting for the moment he would get to do the thing he and Allie had talked about at great length before leaving for Barcelona.

Selena kicked at the chamber door, trying to break through the ancient wood. Within seconds, the inky poison began to drift under the door again. This time, it sought out Marcus, Rhaegal, and Selena, pooling around their feet and avoiding Chloe and Fei Long altogether.

Rhaegal reached for a weapon tucked in his boot, but Sasha kicked it out of his hand before he could get a firm grip on it.

"I wouldn't try that again," Allie's voice rang out like a command. "My girl, Sasha, is a Chola Assassin, packing loadstone bullets and itching for a reason to use them. I would suggest you not give her one, unless you'd like to be unconscious for your trial."

"Trial?" Marcus sounded incredulous.

"Yes, haven't you figured that out yet, Marcus?" Allie dusted off her seat and sat down. "I thought you were all knowing. Where were we?" She glanced at Graham sitting beside her. Livia and Darius had taken up their weapons, standing guard at the foot of the dais.

"The League," Graham reminded her.

"The League of Ancients." Allie shook her head. "Never has a group of people needed therapy as badly as that crowd."

"Might want to speed this along, Allie," Graham murmured.

"Right. So, thanks to my equal here—the kid with a handful of tech gifts as you put it—we have your aldermen. All of them. We have every single pawn you've put in place within the mortal governments. You will not be staging a coup. Not today, or any other day. Your aldermen are already in prison, awaiting their own trials. My people saw to that early this morning."

"You expect me to believe you managed to pull that off right under my nose?" Marcus' eyes filled with fury, and his face darkened to a shade of red that couldn't be healthy for his blood pressure.

"I infiltrated Alderman Albert Abernathy's estate," Graham explained, leaning on the desk. "It really is a shame the League disdains mortal technology as much as they do, especially Abernathy. It took a while, but I found his little war room filled with hard copies of all the evidence I needed. From there, it was fairly easy for Allie to take them out before they could do any real harm."

"Same for the generals and politicians you bribed," Allie continued. "Boy, were they mad when I told them you couldn't make good on your promises since it's impossible to give someone immortality they weren't born with. Those guys have seen one too many vampire movies."

"And they're being charged with treason as we speak," Graham added. "It was easy enough to plant evidence of their crimes with my cute little technology gifts."

"And as for your disgusting Immortal *farm.*" Allie leaned over the desk, rage tugging at her power, itching for release. "You will pay dearly for what you've done to those mortals—the ones who have given us the life in our veins. Yet first you try to destroy them, then when you realized how important they actually are to our very survival, you treat them like cattle to breed for your own gains!" Allie slammed a fist on the desk, her heart pounding in her ears. "No more. As we speak, those precious mortals are being liberated from Abernathy's estate.

"Rein it in, Allie," Sasha called from where she still held Rhaegal on his knees. "You'll get your vengeance, but not before he understands what he's done. Not until he stands here alone, stripped of everything."

"I've had enough of this." Marcus seemed to flicker before her eye as he moved away from Sasha and Rhaegal.

"Where are you going, Mr. Servius?" Allie said in a mocking tone. "There is no crowd for you to melt into with your gift for evasion. I'm afraid you're going to have to hear me out." Her voice rasped in her throat as she sat down. "I could march each of my equals out here and tell you how they've thwarted you. How *they* have stopped you from destroying their world, but even that wouldn't get through to you. But I have a weapon that will destroy you right where you stand."

"I'd love to see this weapon of yours, but I think we'll be leaving now." Marcus turned to Chloe, his aura burning with the intensity of his telepathic power.

"No!" Chloe's voice echoed across the silent Chamber.

Marcus grabbed her throat, squeezing tight as he lifted her until her feet barely touched the floor. "Your dragon will fly us out of this building, right now."

But Chloe resisted him, her eyes swirling with her own power. Fei Long roared in fury, breathing a stream of fire in Marcus' face.

He released her, and she dropped to the floor amid Marcus' shrieks of pain as he clutched his face.

"Chloe! Are you all right?" Allie shot out of her seat to see if she was hurt.

"Yes." She rose to her feet, a stream of dragon fire exploded from her mouth, and she drove Marcus back down to the Senate floor where Darius and Livia stood ready to restrain Marcus. "You're a fool," Chloe spat. "And you deserve everything coming to you."

"You disobey me now?" Marcus snarled. "Now when you believe all is lost?"

"I was never with you!" she hissed. "You think I came with you because of a few empty promises to bring my mother back?" Chloe's voice deepened, resonating with the power of her dragon. She raised her hands as if she would claw his throat out with the black talons that tipped her fingers. "She's been with me every day since she died at the hands of that woman you once called daughter." She pointed to Livia.

"How many lives do you think you can ruin before it comes back to haunt you? You taught her to hate." Chloe lashed out at Marcus with her talons. Blood spurted from his charred face, and he backed away. "You filled her mind with your garbage and sent her out into the world, destroying a piece of her soul and everything she touched. My mother is dead. Not because of Livia, but because of *you*, and you think you have my loyalty?"

"I knew she didn't betray us," Allie cried, pumping a fist in the air.

"I don't need you to drag my mother back from her grave." Chloe's voice returned to her own, and the fire died in her eyes. "She's right here." She clapped a fist over her heart. "And I carry a piece of her with me inside Fei Long. The only reason I went with you that day was so I could be right here, right now, on the day you get what you deserve."

"I'd have brought you with me, Chlo," Allie whispered.

"I know." Chloe didn't take her eyes off Marcus. "I chose this path so he would bring me and not another of his minions that would have provided a more likely chance of escape. I let him believe he had my loyalty so I could do my part as one of Allie's equals."

"You've done your part and then some, Chloe Long." Allie's eyes burned with the threat of tears.

"I didn't turn my back on you, Allie." Chloe sounded close to tears herself. "I need you to know that."

"I believe you. You've always had my trust, Chlo."

"It was the only path open to me." She glanced up at Allie, her eyes full of pain and sadness. "Everywhere I looked, my choices led me down the wrong path. For nearly a year, I've been searching for a solution. And then I went to Cleveland with you and a new path opened for me. One that wouldn't end with me on the wrong side of that painting. I had to go with him."

"Just as you had to leave Kelleys Island to find your own way all those years ago. Your path has always been a tough one, but you brought me the Scholars and Prophets last year. The ones who have seen beyond the darkness to what lies ahead for us now. You and Graham figured out what was happening with the Bermuda prison. And *that* is where Sasha found her," Allie said.

Chloe's eyes snapped up to the dais where Allie sat. "The weapon you mentioned?"

"The very one, and the real clincher here is Marcus gave up a bit of the story himself. Isn't that right, Lecia?" Allie glanced up to where Selena stood by the Chamber doors. "You should come down here for this. I promise it will be worth your time."

"Finish him, Allie." Chloe shoved Marcus toward the dais.

"Aidan, can you come out here, please?" Allie called over her shoulder.

"Whatever you think you have, this isn't over, girl," Marcus snarled.

"You want my Judgment gift, right?" Allie stood, taking the few steps down to the Senate floor. She would end this face to face with him.

"Ready when you are, babe." Aidan stood with one foot up on the dais, looking like a one-man arsenal with every possible weapon strapped to his chest. Naomi and Darius stood with him, looking just as intimidating.

"We're ready." Allie nodded.

"You won't get away with this." Marcus stepped back, searching for a way out. "Lecia, be ready. We're leaving."

"I think you've lost this fight." Lecia made her way slowly down the steps to the Chamber floor. "At least for the moment." She turned toward Allie. "He won't ever stop until he takes our vengeance."

"Hold that thought." Allie studied the woman for a moment. She was like Livia had been once upon a time.

Empty eyes stared back at her. "He needs you. You're the one with the ability and the strength to take my Judgment gift and give it to him."

Lecia stared a hole through her, not blinking.

"He can't do it without you, can he?"

"Of course, I can," Marcus snapped.

"Anyone could do it," Lecia explained. "But it's a traumatic experience for everyone involved—the gift might not survive it. Or it might not manifest in just the same way. Unless you're me, and you have a more delicate hand for the art." She sneered at Allie. "Someday soon, I'll rip your gift right from your chest, and you won't be able to stop me."

"Lecia?"

Aidan and Naomi stepped aside as Porcia escorted Xera into the Chamber.

"Mother?" Lecia backed away from Allie, glancing from Xera to Marcus. "What is this? A trick?"

Marcus sank to his knees, all the color draining from his face. "It can't be."

"Lecia." Xera rushed forward, taking her daughter into her arms. "I'm so sorry, darling. I'm so sorry I wasn't there for you."

"No. No, you died. You and Father both. That's what he told me." Shock and disbelief filled Lecia's face.

"The bond." Marcus shook his head. "I felt it die, right here in my chest. I felt it the moment you died, taking a piece of my soul with you."

"Is that why you could never complete the Complement bond?" Porcia demanded, linking her arm with Xera's. "Was the pain so great when you thought you lost Xera, you decided you would never bond your soul with another, not even me?"

"Losing Xera destroyed me. I couldn't bear it." Marcus

bowed his head, unable to look at either his Syntrophos or his Complement.

"But you didn't lose me." Xera stepped forward, grasping her daughter's hand. "Vitor and I didn't die that day on the battlefield. Not permanently. With what I thought was my last breath, I begged you to take care of Lecia. You knew how we wanted her raised." Xera stepped in front of Marcus, her voice grating with power and the force of her immense lifeline. "You knew we had to be so careful of her gifts because others would want to use her. Exactly as you have. You taught my child to hate! Taught her to use her remarkable gifts as weapons. Look at her. Do you see the empty, soulless look in her eyes? You put that there." With a resounding crack that echoed across the chamber, Xera slapped him.

"I sought vengeance for you. For Vitor. They took you from me, Xera." Marcus groveled at her feet. "The queens are everything that is wrong with this world."

"No, Teigan. You are what's wrong."

"I won't do it." Lecia turned to him. "Not anymore. You told me they were dead," she hissed at him through gritted teeth before she dropped to her knees at her mother's feet. "Forgive me, Mother. I let him manipulate my mind for far too long. I let him drive all feeling from me until I am nothing but an empty shell. Had I known you lived I would have searched the ends of the earth to find you."

"All is forgiven, my child." Xera ran a hand over her daughter's hair. "You were young and your father and I left you in his care. It's not your fault."

"Where is father?" Lecia asked as Xera pulled her back to her feet.

"We are searching the prisons for him. We believe he

was taken by the Coalition at some point in the distant past. We're going to find him and we'll be a family again."

"I swear, Xera," Marcus said. "I thought you were dead. The bond was gone. There was no other reason for it to vanish." Marcus finally looked up at his Syntrophos. "Where have you been, my rock? My soul. Where have you been all this time?"

"Exactly where you left me." Xera's blind eyes filled with tears. "On that awful island prison."

"Sasha and Jayesh found her and her people just after you brought down the magnetic barrier surrounding the Coalition prison in Bermuda," Allie explained. "The torture was on your order, wasn't it?" she pressed. "You wanted them pushed to their breaking point over and over so when you set them free, they would descend on the world like beasts, consuming everything in their path."

"You see how they blinded me," Xera whispered. "Do you know how many times they burned my eyes until my sight failed to return?"

Allie glanced up at the galley where Quinn stood watch. This was almost over. "You managed to release the ancients from the Bermuda prison, yet most followed Xera. They were weak and afraid and wholly unprepared for the modern world. Sasha and her team found them holed up in a hotel on San Salvador Island, just trying to put the pieces of their lives back together. The others found their way onto the mainland, murdering and setting the world on fire just as you planned."

"It will still happen," Marcus shouted, a manic gleam in his eyes. "You can't stop it. It's been set in motion already. Every single Coalition prison across the world is under my control." He let out a laugh that chilled Allie's blood. "They're already free, and they're hungry enough to kill them all." He cackled like the insane madman he was. "Every worthless mortal cockroach on this earth will die as they should have thousands of years ago. This world belongs to the Immortals!"

"No, it doesn't. Not anymore," Aidan said, stepping up beside Allie. "And you don't have the prisons, Marcus. We do. When you tried to annihilate the Coalition, when you decided you no longer needed them, you left the prisons without enough guards to hold them."

"With the help of the Senate, we have quietly seized control of the prisons in recent weeks. Allie looked down on the man who had ruled her nightmares for far too long. He wasn't so scary anymore. "You've lost everything, Marcus. And I'm afraid it's time to pay for your crimes."

"The Senate despises you, you'll never get them to buy your story." Marcus tried to scramble to his feet but Darius pushed him back down.

"We're ready for you, Quinn," Allie called up to the galley.

Quinn took a step forward, dropping Santi's hand. With a familiar flicker of light, the seats filled, and Allie got a glimpse of the entire Senate body holding hands, creating a circuit for Quinn's cloaking power.

"They've been up there the whole time." Allie watched as Porcia made her way up to the galley to take her seat among them. It had been a very long time since she sat with them, but she was still an elected official.

"What happens now?" Xera asked.

"Now, I give you a chance to make your peace with him." Allie stepped back.

Xera studied Marcus for a moment. "There is nothing of the man I once loved in this creature. My Syntrophos died a long time ago."

"Xera, please forgive me." Marcus clutched at her hand. "I did it for you. It was all for you." He sobbed and pleaded with her for forgiveness.

"Don't you dare associate *my* name with what you have done." She clutched a fist over her heart in some sort of symbolic gesture. "You did this for you. Had it gone the other way and I was the one who thought you had died, I would have laid you to rest and found my peace with it. I would have found a way to live without you."

"No, Xera, please." Marcus pressed his head on her feet.

Xera beat her fist against her heart, again and again. With each beat, Marcus sobbed harder. "You are forsworn, Teigan. From this day and every day that comes after it, I will never speak your name again." She beat her chest harder. "I will not think of you. I will not acknowledge I ever knew you."

"Collar him." Allie wrapped her arms around Xera as Aidan and Naomi stepped forward.

Allie thought she would feel victorious the moment Aidan snapped a magnetic collar around Marcus' throat. That watching Naomi handcuff his arms behind his back with magnetized shackles, she would feel some profound moment of relief as the prophecy was fulfilled and her duty was complete.

It was the moment she won her life back. Yet, she felt nothing but a deep sorrow for all the people this one man had destroyed. She felt no victory. She couldn't even find the rage within her to do the thing she was supposed to do.

"Your Majesty?" the acting Chief Justice Edward Thomas called from the galley above. "There is still the matter of his sentencing."

"Of course." Allie sighed, not sure she was ready for this next part.

Chapter 59

Allie | Barcelona | September

"Ladies and gentlemen of the court." Allie stood on the lower dais, looking up at the Senate seated in the gallery. "I think we can all agree that Marcus Servius deserves a swift and brutal punishment for his actions."

Murmurs of approval drifted across the chamber.

"An ancient prophecy said I would defeat the darkness that threatened our world. That darkness is this man. The prophecy also states that I will—"

"I'd like to address the Senate if I may, your Majesty?" The voice came from the shadows of the destroyed Chamber.

"Dad?" Allie hissed. "What are you doing here?" Navid —Ashar—was supposed to be dead, and she wasn't sure what the Senate would do to him if they discovered he'd faked his death, or what they might do to Livia if they found out she was the assassin who'd killed Kassandre.

Navid stepped carefully across the rubble of the chamber, coming to stand on the dais beside her. "Trust me?" He took her hand, and Allie nodded.

"Is that ... Ashar?" Whispers swept through the Senate body.

"It is." Navid smiled. "Though I have not gone by that name in quite some time. You may call me Navid. Father of your queen."

"What of Kassandre?" Chief Thomas asked. "Do you mean to return to your seat of power?"

"No." Navid shook his head. "My Kassandre died many years ago, as you all know. Due to extenuating circumstances I am not at liberty to discuss, I survived the death of my Complement. Kassandre orchestrated everything that has happened in the years since her death. Including her death. Together, we manipulated every moment of our daughter's lives. And it has all come to fruition today."

"You've both done well." Navid gazed from Livia to Allie. "Your mother would be so proud." He turned his attention to the Senate, searching faces for what, Allie couldn't fathom. "Yet, there is one more hurdle to jump." He sounded so weary. Like he'd carried the weight of the world on his shoulders for the last twenty years, and he did it alone.

"Dad?" Allie whispered, but he just squeezed her hand.

"Right now, some of you are wondering how best to punish Marcus Servius for his crimes. You've seen it all with your own eyes. This man can't deny anything he's done in his attempt to bring our world to its knees. And my daughters can't deny all that they have done to prevent that from happening."

"We are grateful for their assistance," Chief Thomas said. "Though the days of Indriell are long past, we cannot ignore the mantle of power that has passed down through the generations to your daughter."

"What is that supposed to mean?" Fear shot through Allie like an arrow. They'd gone down this road before, arriving at the conclusion that she had no authority in the modern world.

"It means we owe you an apology, your Majesty." Chief Thomas bowed his head. "You demanded we hold an election and we ignored you, choosing to believe you were nothing more than a figurehead of a long-forgotten world. We stood in your way when we could have helped. For that, you have our ... *my* deepest apologies."

"There is still the matter of sentencing." Porcia stood, addressing the court. "Perhaps former Chief Justice Ashar could provide his services one last time."

Services? Allie's mind reeled. She'd always anticipated she would be the one to meet out her Judgment against Marcus. That was what the prophecy claimed. But Navid was once known as Judge, Jury, and Executioner. He had his own brand of punishment that had enhanced the ability she'd inherited through her mother's line. An ability that cost him dearly every time he used it.

"It would be my honor to serve." Navid gave a nod of respect to Chief Thomas. "I would ask for the assistance of Quinn Loukas, Commander of the dreamworld."

"It would be my honor to assist," Quinn said from where he stood with Santi in the galley.

"Dad, what are you doing?" This wasn't the way this was supposed to go.

Hush, Allie. Aidan pulled her back, pinning her between himself and Darius. *Your father is still trying to protect you. Let him do it.*

Darius nodded, slipping his hand into hers. "Let him do this."

"Not like this." Tears ran down her cheeks as she realized what her father was protecting her from. She was supposed to punish Marcus. That was what the Prophecy said. But if she did, then the Senate would know the full extent of her power.

He has used his gift many times for this court. Marcus needs a swift and brutal punishment, but it doesn't have to be yours. Aidan held her tight, his eyes boring into hers.

I can do it, she insisted. *Marcus deserves my brand of Judgment.*

And the Senate, who already fears you have too much power, will never let you walk away a free woman.

And if Dad does this now, he will have to enter the dreamworld to do it. It will push him far past his threshold and put him right back where he was when Brecken imprisoned him. That almost killed him! He doesn't have a Complement to tie him to this world. We can't let him risk it. Using his Judgment gift is what made him lose control time and again in the past. I don't want to put him through that again.

Quinn will help him. Please, Allie, let this happen.

Let me give you your life back, daughter. Navid's voice joined Aidan's in her mind. *It's the last thing your mother asked of me, and I mean to do it.*

"Aye."

"Aye."

"Aye." The Senators cast their votes, all in favor of Navid and Quinn stepping forward to punish Marcus.

"Bring the condemned before the Senate," Acting Chief Thomas commanded.

Aidan gave Allie a last look before he and Naomi dragged Marcus to the center of the Chamber to hear his sentencing, leaving Allie with Darius.

"You will never hold me." Marcus said calmly, his eyes still wet with tears. "I will rise again and thwart you all." His words were firm, but they lacked some of the fire can confidence Allie had come to expect from him.

Acting Chief Thomas ignored him. "Marcus Servius, also known as the ancient, Lord Teigan, the Senator, Robert Sinclair, as well as the Marches, Marius Von Essen, leader of the Coalition. The Immortal Senate hereby sentences you to a lifetime of imprisonment, assisted by the Immortal, Ashar, former Chief Justice, also known as the Judge, Jury, and Executioner, and modernly as the Immortal Navid. Also assisting is the Immortal Quinnton Loukas, Commander of the Dreamworld.

"No prison will hold me." Marcus snarled. "I have loyal subjects who will come to my aid."

"You will submit to Navid's Judgment gift where he will send you into a coma-like state for one decade," Chief Thomas paused and looked down on Marcus. "I'm told it will hurt a great deal for every single moment of those ten years, and I hope it is a kind of pain none of us could possibly imagine. During that time, Navid and Quinnton will work together to construct your prison cell, which as it has just been explained to me, will not exist in the dreamworld proper. Mr. Loukas has recently returned from the Chola Valley Temple where he has learned from Mother Raghavan herself how to construct a world that straddles a plain of existence that is neither in the dreamworld, nor the waking world, but somewhere in between. There, you will stay for an eternity, sealed off from thc world you have tried to destroy. Let your madness consume you there, and know that after today, no one will think of you again."

Marcus jerked his head toward Allie, his eyes insane with anger. "This isn't over, girl."

"I think it is," Allie said wearily. "You lost."

Chief Justice Emily Thomas joined her Complement.

"Marcus Servius, you will be escorted from this room to the place where the Immortal Navid will immediately send you into the coma that will hold you for ten years. May you die a thousand deaths and never atone for the heinous crimes you have committed." Like the sound of a death knell, she banged a gavel on the galley railing, calling a host of bailiffs forward to escort Marcus from the Chamber along with Navid and Quinn.

After Marcus was gone, the Senate sentenced Rhaegal to a lifetime in prison—the regular kind of prison where he would never hurt anyone ever again. .

Allie walked over to the dais where her parents once served. Picking up the gavel resting on the Chairman's desk, she banged it to get their attention.

"Ladies and gentlemen of the Senate, I believe we have an election to discuss."

CHAPTER 60

Allie | Sterling Tower | October 31

The election was set for the following month—right on schedule twenty-five years after the last election that put Allie's mother and father in the most powerful position of the modern Immortal world.

When the Senate had discovered Allie and Aidan were Complements, not yet bonded, they asked them to run for the top office.

Allie laughed. She might have even said "not it."

Aidan had flat out refused. They had no political aspirations. In that, they were on the same page.

Edward and Emily Thomas were currently campaigning for the office they had held for the past several years; they were expected to win in a landslide vote. Many other Complements vied for the second seat. Among them were Allie's nomination.

Naeemah and Gregg would likely win the office, and Allie couldn't think of anyone she trusted more for the job.

Allie still didn't know what her formal role would be in the modern world. Whether she would even have a role wouldn't be decided until after the election.

Currently, she didn't have much of an opinion on what

that role should be. The mantle of power belonged to her. She dearly hoped she'd never need it again, but it wasn't something she could just give up. Already, it was too much a part of her.

"You're wearing a green dress?" Livia rolled her eyes. "Allie, I thought you wanted this to be a traditional mortal wedding.

"Well, mostly I do." Allie turned on the platform, studying the simple Grecian dress that hugged her body without a lot of fuss. Though it still managed to be one of the most beautiful dresses she'd ever seen, thanks to Chloe's expertise. "Aidan likes it when I wear green, and it's my favorite color. And I'm having a Halloween, birthday, beach double wedding so it's not like it's super traditional anyway."

"Hold still," Chloe muttered around a mouthful of pins. It was so good to see her getting back to her creative roots. She'd changed a lot over the years, from the sweet, mild tempered girl of her youth to the strong, fierce woman she was today. Allie wasn't sure she'd ever share what she went through during her time with Marcus, but she was more settled now than she had been before. She was finally on the right path.

"I still can't believe you've waited this long to complete your bond," Sasha said. "When I finally saw Jayesh, I couldn't wait a moment longer than necessary."

"We've had a little bit of crazy on our plate," Allie said. "And excuse me and my mortal brain but I'm twenty-three. Practically a teen bride here."

"Leave her alone, girls." Lily dabbed at her eyes. "She's allowed to move at her own pace. And she's doing this whole, sort-of-mortal-wedding thing for me and her father."

"For me, too," Allie said. "I grew up thinking this is the kind of wedding I wanted, so that's what we're doing."

"Knock-knock? Can I come in?" Aidan stuck his head into the room, and Allie grabbed her purse from the table beside her and threw it at him.

"No," Lily shrieked, pushing Aidan's face back through the door and into the hall. "It's bad luck for the groom to see the bride in her wedding dress before she walks down the aisle."

"Okay," Aidan said from the hall. "But you guys know I can still see her in the telepathic sort of way. Love the green, babe."

"Right." Allie stepped down from the platform, admiring her own mental picture of Aidan in his smoky gray tuxedo. "It's kind of hard to surprise the groom when he lives rent free in my head."

"Aww." Sasha sighed. "I'm so excited we're finally going to be sisters."

"Sash, we've always been sisters." Allie smoothed a hand over her dress. She'd thought she would be nervous on her wedding day, but she couldn't wait for the ceremony.

"You can come in now, Aidan." Lily opened the door. "Sorry for the silly mortal traditions."

"It's not silly, Mama Lily." Aidan bent to kiss her cheek. "It's sweet. Can I borrow my wife-to-be for a quick moment?"

"Did you bring me coffee?" Allie shoved her feet into her slippers. She'd won the argument with Sasha about the sky-high heels she'd wanted her to wear. Allie didn't know how long she was going to have to stand waiting for the bond to begin. She wanted to be comfortable in case they were at it for hours and hours.

"Is the sky blue?" Aidan waved Darius into the room,

carrying a truckload of iced coffees and chocolates for the ladies—like the perfect best man/nervous groom.

"I love that you know me so well." Allie leaned in for a quick kiss from her Syntrophos and her Complement, one on each cheek. "Now, are you two here bringing me problems or presents?"

"We are in a problem free zone for the next several weeks, so it's presents." Darius handed her an iced coffee and a white chocolate Oreo truffle. "I brought the snacks, he's got something ridiculous up his sleeve. Oh! And I've got your something blue." He ducked back into the hallway for a moment and when he returned, he was sporting a peacock blue tuxedo jacket. "Tada!" He held his arms out wide and Allie laughed.

"You're my something blue!" She threw her arms around him, still laughing. "I love it."

"I'll see you up there." He dropped a kiss on her forehead and headed out, slapping Aidan on the back as he went. "Sorry about that, I know it's a tough act to follow."

Shaking his head, Aidan knelt down, taking a knee as he presented Allie with a tiny black velvet box.

"Oh. I need my camera." Lily sniffed, digging through her purse.

"What are you doing down there, big guy?" Allie scowled at the box. She wanted some traditions, but this dated one wasn't for her.

"*Not* asking you to marry me. We already made that decision together."

"Okay, that's a point in your favor. What's this box thing you've got there?"

"I thought you might like the tradition of the ring." He opened the box and Allie laughed.

"Do I get extra points for creativity?"

"Yes, now stand up and tell me what the deal is here. Is that a thumb ring?"

"It is." Aidan removed the thick platinum band set with emeralds. "This is a symbol just for us." He took her hand and slipped it onto her left thumb. "A bit of tradition in the circle that never ends." He ran his fingertip around the band. "And a little something that shows I will always try to understand you. Though I can read your mind, half the time I still don't know what you're thinking or feeling. And I don't see that ever changing. But I do know you. I know your heart, Allie Carmichael. I know and love every single quirky thing about you, and I will spend the rest of my Immortal life as your partner, the love of your life, and your best friend."

"Sorry, that was really sweet, brother, but I'm the best friend," Darius interjected.

"You're her ride or die guy. You're the one who's going to take her skydiving or whatever insanity you think she needs when things get too serious. You're the one who's going to help her bury the bodies or hide the shopping bags when she spends too much money on shoes."

"True." Darius crossed his arms over his chest. "And that makes me the BFF."

"Sorry, but that's me. I'm the one who's going to watch every episode of *Friends* with her a thousand times. I'm the one who's going to make sure she never tries to cook anything and remind her that she's a brilliant artist who needs to spend more time creating and less time worrying over spreadsheets."

"Okay, we're both her BFFs," Darius relented. "But I'm still her ride or die guy too. And I have a date with a special girl, so I have to run." He turned to leave.

"I think it's time." Carson danced around Darius and stepped into the room. "You ready, honey?"

"See you at the altar." Allie kissed Aidan's cheek and looped her arm through her father's. Together, they headed toward the warehouse where she would bond her life with Aidan's with her closest family and friends watching over them.

"How are you feeling?" Navid asked as he joined them. Taking her other arm, they crossed the grassy slope to the edge of the lake.

"Good." Allie looked from Carson to Navid, smiling and her heart full of love. "Feeling like the luckiest girl in the world to have two wonderful fathers on the best day of my life. How are *you* feeling?" A shadow of worry filled her as she studied his face. He looked tired, but otherwise healthy.

"I'm fine, sweetheart." He'd served his Judgment more than a month ago and Marcus was in a deep, nightmare-filled sleep, confined to a cell in a former Coalition prison somewhere in Europe. "Quinn was able to help me maintain control of my power and though I had to stay in the dreamworld longer than I should to complete the judgment, I'm recovering quickly."

"Good. I need you to take care of yourself. Both of you." She turned to Carson. "I'd like to have both my dad's around for a very long time to come."

"We'll do our best, sweetheart." Carson smiled.

They made their way across the bridge to her island where all the people she loved sat in chairs arranged around two platforms on the beach. It was tradition that the bonding take place with only those closest to the groom and bride, but Allie couldn't choose just a few people.

And it was a double ceremony with Darius and Pilar who were already taking their place on the second platform.

"Good luck, Dare!" Allie whispered shouted to the amusement of their friends and family.

Carson and Navid escorted her down the aisle with Lily leading the way. There she waited for Aidan to join her. He walked with his parents and Naomi.

A smile lit Allie's face as he approached. She could hardly wait to start their life together. Their—mostly—normal life.

Allie stepped up onto the dais with Aidan, taking his hands in hers.

"I don't know how to do this," she whispered.

"We're not supposed to." Aidan beamed down at her. Gone was the broody young man who had been through so much heartache and too many trials. Here was her Aidan, the strong and capable warrior with an army of Syntrophos, and a little bit of the mischievous boy she hadn't seen in a long time. Now that there were no more secrets between them everything had changed.

As they faced each other, the world disappeared and it was just them.

Hi. His thoughts brushed at hers.

Hi. She stared up at him.

For the longest time I've withheld my thoughts from you. I think I'm done with that. A wall shifted in her mind and he was there in a way he hadn't been since he'd left for Germany so many years ago.

I missed this. She let her thoughts mingle with his, their bond humming between them, content that they were finally together.

Aidan flooded her with memories and thoughts of all the things he'd wanted to say while they were apart. He shared every moment he'd thought of her, every song that had reminded him of her.

As the bond expanded within Allie, she gave him her thoughts and experiences. Every moment when something happened that she'd wanted to share with him. Every lonely night she listened to his music and thought of him. They were open, their souls bared to each other. They saw all the flaws and imperfections in each other and they still chose to be here.

"It's always been you, Aidan," she whispered, reaching out to touch his face. "Even when I tried so hard to resist it, we were always meant to be right here together."

EPILOGUE

Allie | Chicago | One Year Later

"After this one, let's go home." Allie clasped the magnetic collar around the Immortal's throat, trying to ignore his stench. "We've been on the road too long, and I miss my bed. Being Aurors isn't as glamorous when you're cranky, tired, and hangry."

"There's no such thing as Aurors. We're bounty hunters." Darius finished lashing the Immortal's feet together with zip ties.

"I'm not sure we can be bounty hunters when we aren't collecting bounties." Allie held a hand over her nose.

"I think we might be able to go home for a nice long visit," Pilar said. "This is the last of the Enlightened." She wrinkled her nose at the filthy Immortal. "We seemed to have saved the most pungent for last."

Aidan and Naomi moved through the crowd of sick mortals in the park along Lake Michigan. Most were delirious from the illness the Immortal spread to every mortal he came in contact with. Aidan's eyes burned with the heat of his power as he did what he could to heal them, and Naomi did what she could to keep them warm and comfortable. They would be sick for a while, but they would recover.

The media was calling it the super flu, and thousands were in packed hospitals across the country. As soon as people came in contact with Ronan, the illness took them where they stood, which was why they were currently freezing their butts off in the park well after sunset.

Aidan and their team had been tracking Ronan for months and they finally caught up with him, which was quite a feat since even Immortals were affected by Ronan's brand of pestilence. But they had Aidan on their side, and he kept them safe from the disease.

"Let's get this guy on a plane to Death Valley." Darius waved a hand under his nose. "I can't take the smell anymore.

"Ivy and Neela are meeting us at the airport." Naomi came to join them, supporting Aidan who was looking like he was ready to drop from using his power all day.

"They'll deliver Ronan to the prison for us." He slumped against Allie's side.

"And someone needs a decent meal." She took him by the arm and helped him into the SUV. "And some decent rest."

"Roger that." Aidan relaxed back into the seat, closing his eyes. "Let's go home."

Allie watched the sunset as they flew toward Sterling Tower in the helicopter, anxious to see her parents and friends after so many weeks away.

After the election, which was a landslide victory for

Edward and Emily Thomas as well as Gregg and Naeemah, Allie had been invited to meet with the Senate to discuss her position. They'd asked what she wanted and readily agreed with her desires.

Allie and Aidan now shared the mantle of power between them, making it a much easier burden to bear. She'd struggled to ask him, unable to find the right words, but he'd seen it in her thoughts and said yes without hesitating.

It wasn't the power he craved. He'd only wanted to share the burden with her.

Legally, they were the Queen and King of Indriell with the power to weigh in on the big issues their world faced. If they wanted, they had a voice within the Senate. A voice Allie intended to use to advocate for the youngest generations. With their newly elected Chiefs of Justice, things in their world were quickly changing for the better.

Maybe one day she and Aidan would run for Senate or maybe even the top job, but that was the distant future. For now, she was happy chasing down the bad guys and bringing them to justice. The prison sort of justice. She still hadn't used her Judgment gift and she hoped she'd never have to.

She and Liam were trading off Soma responsibilities, so it was never too much for either of them. They made a good team. Pretty soon it would be her turn to take the lead for a while and she was ready for it.

Aidan set the helicopter down on the roof of Sterling tower. The dreamworld barrier was gone, but they were still using Dahlia's security system to ensure the safety of those inside the building. With Dahlia's gift, Sterling Tower had taken on a personality of her own.

"The old girl is happy to see us." Darius hopped down from the helicopter and reached to help Pilar and Naomi down.

As soon as her feet hit the ground, Naomi ran to meet Briggs, waiting for her by the door. They were perfectly content with their relationship as it was, but Allie was almost certain they would be Complements if either of them could ever face the idea of settling down with just one person.

"The whole family is waiting for you." Briggs held the doors open for them and Allie flew down the stairs, eager to see her sister and Sasha with Xeren and all the people she loved.

As she opened the door to her penthouse, the green light of her power lit the way.

"Guess who's back." Allie and Aidan stepped into the foyer and Xeren came running for them. Aidan swept him up into his arms and the little boy giggled as they joined the rest of the family waiting for them.

"About time you two got here." Lily called from the kitchen where she was cooking with Allie's grandmother. "We've got all your favorites for dinner."

Allie made a beeline for her mom and grandma, hugging each of them tight. "Is that mac and cheese with ham?" She bounced eagerly.

"Yep, about a hundred pounds of it." Lily pulled a huge bubbling cheesy mass from the oven. "It's tough work feeding this family."

"It's good to have you home." Alísun gave her an extra hug. "We've missed you so much."

Darius and Pilar came in behind them greeting Sasha and Jayesh.

"Allie!" Chloe darted into the kitchen. "It happened. Can you believe it? Justice finally got his head out of his rear end." Her eyes were shining with happiness.

"Finally?" She searched out Justice, sitting in the corner with Graham and Ezra. Everyone was here and it was wonderful.

"Hey, it's about time, Justice," Darius shouted over the din. "I thought we were going to have to shake it out of you."

"Oh, Chloe." Allie pulled her into a hug. "I'm so happy for you."

Fei Long lumbered across the room, shoving people out of her way in her eagerness to get to Allie.

"Who's my favorite dragon?" Allie crouched down to give her head scratches. A part of Ming Lao was somewhere inside of the beautiful creature. Even though she was no longer with them in body, she was still watching over all of them in spirit.

Allie moved to sit on a stool in the crowded living room watching her family with happy tears in her eyes. Aidan and Darius played on the floor with Xeren, and Lily and Carson chatted with Liam and Livia. Kahlynn sat on the floor playing a video game with Grandpa Alex. Her family had grown over the years. She was a lucky girl.

She met Aidan's gaze and the green light of her power intensified. She'd seen this moment before. Both during her Awakening and her Proving. It changed each time she saw it, but this was no vision. It was reality. There were more happy smiles in this real-life version than there had been in her visions—and a few faces were missing. Her mortal sister for one. And the two children she'd seen playing with Aidan in her visions. It was always a boy and a girl. She'd seen them at different ages. She still didn't know them, but the potential for them to join the family someday was still there. And that was enough for Allie. She wasn't ready for kids just yet.

THE END

A NOTE FROM MELISSA

We made it, you and I.

It's been a long journey with Allie and Aidan and I want to thank you for your endless patience and excitement for each new book. You have no idea just how much you all mean to me. With every email, Facebook comment and private message, you've touched my heart with your love for the Immortals of Indriell, and you've been with me in spirit every step of the way.

I started writing Emerge in 2009 on a whim. Now it's thirteen years and seven books later and the story I set out to tell is finally complete.

It's been one heck of a ride and I hope you'll follow me on to the next adventure.

Melissa

WHAT'S NEXT?

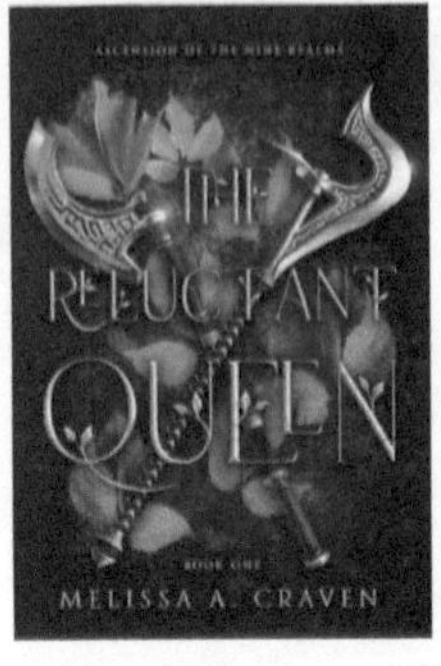

Heir to the Valkyrie throne, Alithea belives she is better suited to the battlefield than the throne room.

On the eve of her betrothal ceremony where she will finally meet the young man the queen's council has chosen for her--the man raised to serve her every need--Alithea makes a desperate decision that will change her life forever. Rejecting her birthright, she flees across the broken bridge to the human realm where she must hide her true Valkyrie nature.

When the queen's Berserker bounty hunter finally catches up with her, Druan gives her no choice but to return to a war-torn world where her mother and all those she loves are trapped, powerless to resist the vicious usurper queen. To save her people, Alithea will have to do the one thing she swore she would never do. Ascend to the Valkyrie throne and take her seat as the High Queen of the Nine Realms, all while keeping a dangerous secret that could destroy everything.

The Reluctant Queen is the first book in a brand new series by Melissa A. Craven. Get ready to dive into this reimagining of Asgard in a post-Ragnarok world where the gods are all gone and the Valkyries rule in their place.

Keep reading for a preview of Thea's story

THE RELUCTANT QUEEN PREVIEW

The dead guy was hot.

Not that he was actually dead yet. But he would be in a few hours.

I kept my head down as I pulled a draft beer for one of my customers. Angling the frosted mug to reduce the foam, I suppressed the urge to meet his gaze. That would only freak him out and I didn't need a bar full of panicked people.

"Come on, beautiful." He leaned over the counter. "My friends are losers. I could use some intelligent conversation. What time are you off?"

"It's been a long shift already." I slid the frosted mug to one of the many customers vying for my attention. "Can I get you a drink?" I tried steering the conversation back to bartending.

"I'm DD for the night." He nodded toward his group of idiot friends raising a ruckus at the pool tables.

"Poor you." I smiled, pouring a row of tequila shots for a table of giggling sorority types.

Next place can't be a college town. I moved to the end of the bar to wait on a few new arrivals. College kids wouldn't know what a decent tip was if it hit them in the face.

I arrived in the sleepy little Carolina beach town just a few weeks ago, but I was already scouting my next move farther up the coast and away from Wilmington. I was always on the move, never settling down in one place for long. It was the way it had to be. I liked the smaller coastal towns, especially in the off-season. A person could disappear in the outer banks of the Carolinas.

"How about a drink after work?" The hot-dead-guy was back again and I wanted nothing more than to lose myself in his friendly banter. But his death called to me, begging me to meet his gaze.

I closed my eyes, absently pinching the bridge of my nose to quell the tension brought on by his arrival. "Like I said, it's been a long shift tonight. I'm diving face first into my bed for some serious sleep as soon as I leave here." I tried to give him a friendly smile, while keeping my eyes cast down at the sink full of dishes I should be washing before Kelly arrived for her shift.

"How about tomorrow? Or your next day off?" He persisted, attempting to capture my gaze. It was only natural he was drawn to me in his last hours.

I winced. He wouldn't have a tomorrow, and the last thing he needed to be doing right now was wasting what little time he had left with a total stranger. A stranger who didn't have the power to save him. No one could. When your number was up, you were out of time.

I cast a wary glance around me as the tension from resisting my natural impulses threatened to overwhelm me. My throat tightened and my palms itched. Sweat pooled at my back. I wouldn't be able to hold it off much longer.

"Why don't you go back to your friends and try to enjoy the rest of your evening?" My mesmerizing voice came out in a low, grating rasp.

He nodded slowly, blinking. "Good idea."

The boy gave me one last glassy-eyed stare and then turned toward his friends. The tension in my shoulders immediately subsided. He would obey the one who had seen his death. The one who would guide his soul to the afterlife in Andlang. A place I could never enter. There was a time when my ancestors could come and go from the beyond as they pleased, but that was before the last age. The afterlife was different now.

"What's up, Thea?" my coworker, Kelly, asked as she tied on an apron. "You don't look so good, girl. You got some wicked dark circles under your eyes. When's the last time you slept?"

I swiped a palm across my face, schooling my features. It wouldn't do for Kelly to see too much. "Thank God you're here. Would you mind if I duck out early? I have a raging headache."

A headache I wouldn't be able to shake until the boy met his end. I had a job to do and now that I'd seen his violent death looming on the horizon, I wouldn't be able to rest easy until my work was done.

"Sure, get some sleep, girl," Kelly said. "I've got this."

"Thanks." I cast a last glance over my shoulder at the dead man walking. He was laughing with his frat-boy friends. He still had time, but I was already running on borrowed time. I rushed to the back of the bar to the alley exit.

The rows of historic southern downtown buildings were punctuated with creepy dark alleys lined with shady back doors and leaky dumpsters. I darted toward the alley entrance, hoping I could make it down the block to the public parking lot, but the familiar cramping of my shoulders and the tightening of my eyes told me I would have to risk doing this here.

I glanced behind me at the rusted old fire escape and headed straight for it at a run. With a carefully aimed jump, I latched onto the ladder to pull it down, but it didn't budge. *Even better.* No one could follow me now. I pulled myself up and quickly scaled the ladder to the rooftop above. I scouted this rooftop when I first took the job at Harkers Tavern. It was the tallest structure around and it would do in a pinch.

I headed for the shadows at the back of the building, kicking off my shoes and shedding my black t-shirt along the way, grateful for the human invention of racer back sports bras. They were perfect for nights like this. I flung my hair clip to the ground, letting my long dark hair cascade down my back. I suppressed a shriek as the white-hot pain of transformation cleaved my skull in two. I collapsed, hunching over as my body buckled and my skin split from shoulder to waist.

I gasped as bones cracked and reformed and my hands and feet bent in an unnatural way. Blunt fingernails curved into talons. My legs ached as the bones lengthened and hollowed, making me taller, lighter, and more agile. Feathers sprouted from the gashes in my back, unfurling and stretching like limbs seldom used. As my wings expanded, so did my shoulders and ribcage lighting my body on fire, raging with the heat of my natural form. Every inch of me hurt as my heart throbbed in my chest and my breath came in great ragged gasps. It had been far too long this time.

I lay on the blacktop roof, spent, but I felt more alive

than I had in months. Climbing to my feet, I trembled with the suddenness of my change. Valkyries took on their natural forms only when they had a duty to perform. Since coming to the human realm I'd had little need for my Valkyrie.

Rotating my head from side to side, my vision began to clear. Avian vision. It was always an adjustment. Rubbing the palm of a taloned hand over my face, I could feel the sharp angles of my cheekbones in my otherwise human face. I took a step forward on bare feet, my curved toenails clicking on the surface of the roof. The enormous weight of my wings tugged at my shoulders as I walked. Raven black and silver feathers dragged behind me like a cloak, my arms resting at my sides.

The momentary fatigue passed as the strength of my Valkyrie flooded my system. I flexed my wings, all six of them. My primary wings arched high over my head, unfurling with black and pewter feathers. Secondary wings moved in perfect sync with my primaries. Silver and pewter feathers stretched wide to a span of double my height. My tertiary wings pointed to the ground, falling behind me with feathers of silver and white. Retracting my massive wings, I stepped up to the edge of the building, away from the lights of the nearby boardwalk.

My dark hair fell nearly to my waist, threaded with fine black and silver feathers blending with the fall of my wings down my back. Among the shadows, one might think I was a human girl with incredibly long hair, so fine were my feathers. But I was not human. I was Valkyrie. And death walked in my shadow.

His soul called to me as I ran from rooftop to rooftop, barely pausing to jump across the gaps between buildings. I could fly, of course, but I couldn't risk being seen in this world. Humans no longer believed in the old gods or the creatures they created to outlive them.

I was close. I could hear the steady thump of his heart and the bass beat of the music from his car down on the street. He waited at a deserted intersection for the light to turn green; his drunken buddies in the backseat still acting like idiots.

After a lifetime of this, I still felt the urge to intervene. The intense desire to save him from the violent death awaiting him once he crossed into the intersection. But I also knew from experience that death would have his due. Even now I could feel him breathing down my neck from the shadows.

"Patience," I murmured into the void. If I intervened, death would get more creative and the next time it would be far worse than a quick end by car accident.

I stood at the edge of an old brick building, the talons of my bare feet gripping the red brick facade. I could see the other car speeding toward the intersection, not paying attention to the light changing from green to yellow. That driver was drunk, having neglected the responsibility to elect a designated driver the way my charge and his friends had. Yet the sober driver would pay the ultimate price for the other man's hubris.

My breath caught in my throat as one light turned red and another green. The gods were cruel when they created the first Valkyries to collect the fallen from battle, sentencing me and my kind to a lifetime of service to death. Like carrion birds on a battlefield, my ancestors once had the honor of selecting the bravest of the fallen to send to the afterlife where only the greatest warriors were taken. But that was before the gods nearly destroyed my world. More than a thousand years later, the Valkyries ruled in place of the gods, yet we were still chained to death. Only now our charges weren't limited to heroes of war, but victims of violence and cruel ends as well.

The blare of horns and the crunch of metal and shattered glass brought me back to the present. I wouldn't leave the boy to die alone. His friends would live, but only I could help him now.

Just as I was about to swoop down, I heard the unmistakable sound of a pair of massive wings spreading in the darkness. My blood ran cold and my spine went rigid. I didn't pause long enough to see the other Valkyrie. I turned and ran back the way I'd come, leaving the boy's soul for the other to claim.

My heart hammered in my chest as I flew out over Harkers Sound toward Gloucester and the mainland. There was only one way off of Harkers Island by car and I couldn't risk it. I flew high enough so that anyone who spotted me would think I was a bird of prey out for a late-night hunt. I couldn't go home. There was only one course of action now that Mother's bounty hunters had caught up to me ... again.

I had to leave. Tonight.

I couldn't fathom how they'd found me so fast this time. I should have had a few more weeks at Harkers Island before there was any danger of discovery. But they were getting more daring. More vicious as they pursued me.

I flew until the cool ocean breeze calmed me and cleared my mind. *Mother's bounty hunters will never drag me home before I'm ready.* My life belonged to me. Not my mother or my people. I would return to Valsgard one day. On my own terms.

I circled the barn, searching for any sign of followers before I landed. The forest around me went silent, acknowledging the predator in its midst. I originally chose this spot for its privacy and location far from the main roads. Any chance of discovery here was slim.

My wings dragged over the uneven ground as I opened the huge barn door. Mounds of dry hay bales stood unmoved along the back wall where I stacked them a few weeks ago when I first arrived on Harkers Island. I went to work, moving them to the other side of the barn, slowly revealing the car carefully concealed beneath a heavy gray tarp. She was my pride and joy. I smiled as I pulled the tarp free, eager to get behind the wheel again.

The classic black convertible was the only luxury I allowed myself to keep from one place to the next. I drove a cheap beater car to work—one I could afford to lose if I had to abandon it on nights like this one.

I kept the trunk stocked with everything I would need to start over. Clothes, money, my perfectly legal-looking identification documents I'd paid a fortune for, even a supply of food, water, and camping gear.

I wiped at the sweat beading my brow. I needed to get moving. I could sense the boy's soul was at peace now, but I was still too anxious to change back to my human form. I needed to calm down. I caught sight of myself in the driver's side mirror, my dark wide eyes in a panic. Tonight was a close call. Too close.

"Get a grip, girl." I took a deep breath, running my fingers through the fine feathers cascading down my back, plucking bits of hay from my wings. For nearly three years, I had avoided my Valkyrie form as much as possible. I couldn't risk the chance someone might see me and I'd end up on some supermarket tabloid. While I enjoyed my simple human life, I missed my Valkyrie.

I stared into the mirror, concentrating on steadying my breath—in and out—slowing my heart rate. With my mind focused, I watched my reflection as the black void around my eyes began to recede and my cheeks returned to their fullness. The swirling darkness of my eyes faded back into their natural green, sparkling in the moonlight. I arched my back as my wings faded and my shoulders returned to their normal state.

Now I needed to get moving. Fast.

I threw my telltale feathered hair back into a messy bun and pulled a fresh t-shirt over my head before I slammed the trunk closed and slipped into the front seat. Easing out of the barn, I headed for the dirt road that would lead me along the back coastal roads that crisscrossed up the east coast. Following the plan I'd mapped out weeks ago, I'd have to drive most of the night, but it was safer than the highways. I would head north to Cedar Island and find a new hideout for the next time. I'd make a new life along the islands of Pamlico Sound. I could disappear there for at least a year, moving slowly up the coastline all the way to Virginia Beach.

"Mother's bounty hunters will not catch me. Not this time."

With the top down and the wind in my hair, I began to relax, driving carefully along the rural roads—not too fast and not too slow. Nothing to attract unwanted attention.

At almost two a.m., I was the only one on the road. I wouldn't be getting any sleep tonight or the next. I had to move quickly and with stealth. Maybe even find a little island among the nature reserves where I could make camp until the bounty hunters lost my trail.

I slammed on the brakes just as something ran out in front of me. The unmistakable jet-black wings had me hitting the gas a second later, racing around the woman in the road. Checking my rearview mirror, I looked for signs of the others. There were always four. And they were vicious. The price on my head was a fortune few bounty hunters could resist.

"Wait!" I heard a desperate cry over my own frantic gasps.

I felt the flutter of wingtips as they passed over my head to land on the hood of the car. Dark wings framed his fine features, pale skin, and short dark hair.

He was a Valkyrie. The kind that shouldn't exist. I hit the brakes again as I met his gaze, certain I was about to die.

Panicking, I bolted from the car and ran down the deserted road, my boots pounding against the pavement as I searched for a way out. I cursed myself for transforming back to my human form. I wouldn't be able to manage the change again for at least a day and I could use my wings right about now.

"Stop, please?" The male Valkyrie begged as he circled above me. "I won't hurt you."

It was silly, the way I ran. I could never outrun a Valkyrie in flight, but I also couldn't seem to make my body respond to that bit of knowledge.

He landed in front of me and I skidded to a halt. His black as night wings lowered behind him as he took a tentative step toward me, his hand outstretched as if to gentle a scared pet.

"I just wanted to meet you," he said.

My eyes darted all around, my mind a chaos of panic. I

was going to die right here and I'd never get to see my sister again. I always thought I would return once things at home had settled down. It never occurred to me that I'd never see them again—never get a chance to make things right with Mother.

"I've never met another angel before. I'm sorry if I scared you." He raised his hands to show me he was unarmed.

Angel? I turned to face him, and my eyes widened in shock. In the darkness and the midst of my freak out, I hadn't realized he carried three sets of wings, just like mine. He had first generation Valkyrie blood. The mark of high royalty.

"You're a seraph, right?" He took another hesitant step forward. "Like me."

"What?" I shook my head in confusion, trying to figure out where this male, *royal* Valkyrie had come from. And why he didn't seem to have a clue what he was.

He's faking it.

"Seraph?" He wasn't making any sense. My heart hammered in my chest as he approached.

"An angel of death. I'm sorry if I stole your thunder back there. I couldn't let him die alone like that, and I didn't realize he was yours. I didn't know there were others like me." He gave a nervous laugh. "I'm Ben." He lifted his hand toward me like he wanted us to shake hands and be friends.

"Ben?" I said softly. "Is this some kind of joke? Some pathetic attempt of my mother's to get close to me?"

"Joke? No," Ben said, frowning. "You have a mother?"

"Are you for real?" I finally took a breath.

He shrugged. "I thought I was alone."

"You are. You shouldn't exist," I said flatly. "Your kind aren't permitted to live. You should know that, and if you had any sense at all, you would leave right now and forget you ever saw me."

"Permitted to live? Angels would kill their own kind?" His face twisted in disgust.

I let an incredulous smile curve my lips. "You really expect me to believe you don't know what you are? Does my mother think I'm that stupid?"

"Listen, I don't know who your mother is, and honestly, I don't know much of anything else either. I've lived my whole life on instinct alone and only know what I've been able to find out through a lot of research and assumptions."

"You think you're an angel?" I felt a pang of sympathy for the guy. If he really didn't know what he was... Had some distant royal dumped him here in the human realm because she couldn't face her duty?

Ben rubbed the back of his head in frustration. "What other creature has the wings of a seraph? What creature guides dead souls to heaven?"

"Heaven? You've been researching the wrong stories," I said with a frown.

Maybe this guy was for real and he truly didn't know what he was, but that was a risk I couldn't afford to take. All male Valkyries were born grounded in their human form except for a rare few scattered throughout history who were born with a female Valkyrie's ability to transform. Those unfortunate children grew into terrible men who could not contain the power of the Valkyrie form. My ancestors decided ages ago that a true Valkyrie male could not be allowed to live—particularly a royal who could serve as a vessel of the gods. Ben should have been executed at birth. Except Ben's mother had obviously tried to save him, secreting her son away in the human realm to give him a chance at life. She would die for that betrayal.

"What can you tell me?" Ben asked. "You're the first I've ever met like me. Whatever that means, I need to know."

"You are Valkyrie," I whispered. "A dangerous one."

"Valkyrie?" Ben tested the word. "I never even considered it."

"Well, now you know." I turned back toward my car.

"Wait." Ben followed. "I have a million questions."

"I bet you do," I said, picking up my pace. "But I'm not the one to answer them. Sorry. I travel alone." I reached for the door handle.

"At least tell me your name?" Ben pleaded.

"Jessica Jones," I said without missing a beat. "Have a good life."

I sank back into the driver's seat and buckled my seatbelt. I had a long night of driving ahead of me. As I pulled away, I glanced back at Ben standing in the center of the road, watching me leave. A weird urge to protect him came over me. Or maybe it was just guilt. If I left him without a warning, bounty hunters would find him and execute him on sight. It was my duty to let that happen.

I gripped the steering wheel, fighting with the instincts that told me to leave him as a distraction to throw my pursuers off my trail. But as I watched him in the rearview mirror, I felt like I'd just abandoned a puppy on the side of the road. A puppy who could tear my world apart if given the opportunity. Still...

I hit the brakes with a deep sigh of regret.

CONNECT WITH MELISSA

Can't get enough of Aidan and Allie? Did you know there's a Prequel Novella all about them leading up to the months before they met?

Make sure you're on my email list so you can stay in the know about all my new releases, download exclusive free books, bonus chapters, and other great giveaways you won't want to miss. (Especially if you love cute dog pictures!)

Sign up here and get a FREE copy of Edge: An Immortals of Indriell Novella

About Melissa A. Craven

Melissa A. Craven (the "A" stands for Ann—in case you were wondering) writes Young Adult Fantasy with crossover appeal to other genres and audiences of all ages. She believes in stories that make you think and she loves twisty plots, and playing with foreshadowing, leaving clues and hints for the careful reader. She draws inspiration from her background in architecture and interior design to help her with the small details in world building and scene settings. Melissa is also the indie manager and a staff reviewer at YABooksCentral.com. You can follow her reviews and her contributions to the YABC blog at the link below. And if you love Sweet Romance and Contemporary Fiction, you can find Melissa's books in those genres under her pen name, Ann Maree Craven.

Join Melissa's Facebook Group, Fantasy Book Warriors

Follow Melissa at Melissaacraven.com

facebook.com/MelissaACravenAuthor

instagram.com/melissaacraven

bookbub.com/authors/melissa-a-craven

amazon.com/Melissa-A-Craven/e/B00VSPF86W

Also by Melissa A. Craven

Check out all of Melissa's books at Books2Read.com

or at your favorite retailer

Immortals of Indriell Series:

Emerge (Book 1) | **Catalyst** (Short Story) | **Edge** (Book 0) | **Judgment** (Book 2) | **Scholar** (Illustrated Character Journal) | **Volunteer** (Short Story) | **Captive** (Book 3) | **Assignment**: Novella | **Heir** (Book 4) | **Betrayal** (Book 5) | **Runaway** (Book 6) | **Proving** (Book 7)

Queens of the Fae Series

Fae's Deception (Book 1) | Fae's Defiance (Book 2) | Fae's Destruction (Book 3) | Fae's Prisoner (Book 4) | Fae's Power (Book 5) | Fae's Promise (Book 6) | Fae's Rebellion (Book 7) | Fae's Refuge (Book 8) | Fae's Return (Book 9)

Ascension of the Nine Reams Series:

The Reluctant Queen (Book 1)

The Rejected Queen (Book 2)

The Rebel Queen (Book 3)

www.ingramcontent.com/pod-product-compliance
Lightning Source LLC
Chambersburg PA
CBHW030523310726
48979CB00010B/1784/J

* 9 7 8 1 9 7 0 0 5 2 2 2 0 *